CRAIG MARTELLE

STARSHIP LOST

aethonbooks.com

STARSHIP LOST
©2023 CRAIG MARTELLE

This book is protected under the copyright laws of the United States of America. No part of this publication may be reproduced, stored in a retrieval system, or transmitted, in any form or by any means, without the prior permission in writing of the publisher, nor be otherwise circulated in any form of binding or cover other than that in which it is published and without a similar condition including this condition being imposed on the subsequent purchaser. Any reproduction or unauthorized use of the material or artwork contained herein is prohibited without the express written permission of the authors.

Aethon Books supports the right to free expression and the value of copyright. The purpose of copyright is to encourage writers and artists to produce the creative works that enrich our culture.

The scanning, uploading, and distribution of this book without permission is a theft of the author's intellectual property. If you would like to use material from the book (other than for review purposes), please contact editor@aethonbooks.com. Thank you for your support of the author's rights.

Aethon Books
www.aethonbooks.com

Print and eBook formatting by Steve Beaulieu. Artwork provided by Vivid Covers.

Published by Aethon Books LLC.

Aethon Books is not responsible for websites (or their content) that are not owned by the publisher.

This book is a work of fiction. Names, characters, places, and incidents are the product of the author's imagination or are used fictitiously. Any resemblance to actual events, locales, or persons, living or dead is coincidental.

All rights reserved.

ALSO IN STARSHIP LOST

Starship Lost

The Return

Primacy

Engagement

Devolution

Delivery

Arrival

SOCIAL MEDIA

Craig Martelle Social
Website & Newsletter:
https://www.craigmartelle.com

**Facebook:
https://www.facebook.com/
AuthorCraigMartelle/**

Always to my wife, who loves me even though I work every day writing stories.

Starship Lost team Includes

BETA READERS AND PROOFREADERS
WITH MY DEEPEST GRATITUDE!

James Caplan
Kelly O'Donnell
John Ashmore
Brian Roberts

Get ***The Human Experiment*** for free when you join my newsletter. There's a zoo but the humans are the ones being studied...
https://craigmartelle.com

CHAPTER 1

Humanity spread to the stars, and then they fought the only enemy they've ever known — themselves.

"Engines are down. Offensive weapons are offline. Defensive weapons are down. Missile tubes are locked out. Ship is on a ballistic trajectory out of the system," Helm reported.

The captain hung his head. "All hands to damage control. Pri one is life support – we need air."

"Ship's on fire, Captain," the deputy said softly.

"Deploy the foam. Sensors, where are the Malibor?"

"Sensors are down. We're flying blind."

To punctuate the sensor report, a staccato of high-speed electromagnetic accelerated projectiles ripped into *Chrysalis*. The damage to the ship was so extensive, the new impacts added little to the ongoing cascade of failures.

"The ship is dying," the deputy offered. "Septimus is lost."

Septimus. The Borwyn home planet.

"Not on my watch. All hands, damage control. Abandon the bridge, all but you, comm. Listen for emergency calls and log who's still out there," the captain ordered. "We'll return for them as soon as the ship is able to fly. She's the toughest bird in the fleet, and we will be back!"

The command crew raced off the bridge and into the acrid air choking the corridor. They scattered to their designated damage control stations.

The captain ran as quickly as he could keeping his magnetic boots attached to the deck. He didn't dare fly through zero-gee when he couldn't see what was in front of him. Cracks and groans followed a long sigh.

As much as he didn't want to listen, it was the sound of the ship dying and taking the crew with it. There were no lifeboats, no escape pods. There was only riding the ship until it perished.

But the captain wasn't ready to die. He dove into the central shaft and pulled himself to the primary ventilation system. A railgun round had ripped through a primary control unit. He dug the wires out to bypass the controls and turn it on at one hundred percent. The ventilation system kicked in, using the ship's stored energy to drive air through surviving ducts. The air started to clear once it passed through the filtration system.

The crew threw themselves into the fight to save the ship. It barreled away from Septimus and Armanor and toward deep space. Nothing could slow it down except a planet's gravity or the engines.

They were blind, but the final course hadn't been taking the ship anywhere near a planetary body. Next stop – interstellar space.

When the captain finally collapsed from exhaustion, he didn't remember the last time E-mag rounds had impacted the hull. It had been hours, maybe even days. He took a deep breath. The air had cleared while the lights continued to flicker in their dismay at the damage done to the ship's electrical grid.

He roused enough to know that this was no time to rest. They needed to get the engines repaired to generate power to survive, to generate propulsion, no matter how limited, to stop the ship from disappearing into the void.

The darkness called to them, but the captain wasn't ready to answer. He had a ship to save. And Septiman willing, he had to get back in the fight. The Malibor had been weakened. Now was the time to finish them.

CHRYSALIS WOULD RETURN, BUT NOT FOR FIVE DECADES, AND NONE OF THE LEADERSHIP TEAM WOULD SURVIVE TO SEE IT.

―――

"Now is the time of pain. It is the time when, once more, our survival is at stake. It is the threshold to take us into the future, *or* it is the cataclysm," Captain Jaquay "Jaq" Hunter delivered the speech she had thought about her entire life. And now was the time to say the words during the final leg of bringing *Chrysalis* home. "Fifty years ago, our forefathers saved a battered and beaten ship. They survived and gave us purpose. It is our duty to carry on their legacy. It is our duty to liberate Septimus."

The ship smelled of polished steel like it was new, a far cry from the truth of having been underway for decades but less than a year on their trip from the far reaches of the Armanor star system where they'd had to live.

"Are we a go?" the second in command, the deputy asked. Commander Crip Castle stood at his station to the left of the captain's chair.

The captain winked at him.

Crip declared, "*Chrysalis* is ready."

The Borwyn had lost the fight but never conceded the war.

That had been more than a generation ago. Now they were headed home to reclaim their planet and reunite with those left behind.

Ultimately to Septimus. The Armanor star system had twenty-four planets in twelve orbits, balanced and competing. Septimus was opposite Sairvor in the fifth orbit. Until a year ago, Chrysalis and the survivors had been in the ninth orbit, far from home.

Jaq held up her hand. She had more to say. She scanned the bridge to make eye contact with her crew.

Toward the rear of the bridge, an oldster sat with one of the younger generation on either side, helping her stay upright. She was the lone survivor of those who had left Septimus decades earlier on a broken and dying ship.

She was stooped with age, and what remaining hair she had had turned white long ago. The oldster's eyes were closed and her mouth open while her head hung to the side. She was taking one of the many naps she would take during the day.

The moment of the Borwyn's triumphant return wouldn't be witnessed by the only remaining crew member who had stepped foot on Septimus. The original crew was down to one.

The rest of the crew had been born and raised on *Chrysalis*, a much different ship than the one that had fled the final battle.

"We have trained our whole lives for this." All eyes were fixed on the captain. "The Malibor fleet is aged and broken. We have restored our home to greater glory. Made it better than it was, better than our enemy's ships." Although she was young, her sharp eyes missed nothing. Her mind was constantly addressing the problems of the ship and the best ways to engage the enemy.

The greatest upgrades to their combat power came from the ion drive and the crew's interaction with the ship, working faster and better until the will of the captain was the will of the ship.

That necessity had developed from the minds of the next generation, the ones born on and to the ship.

The captain finished her speech. "It's time. Bring us to course vector three-six-two, star angle minus five. First stop, Farslor."

Farslor was one of two planets in the sixth orbit around Armanor. *Chrysalis* would use it to slingshot toward Septimus.

"Your turn, Shepherd. Wish us well."

Silence settled over the command deck. The crew's spiritual leader stepped away from the oldster. He was much younger than the senior command crew, but his role was every bit as significant. The morale of the crew depended on being in good stead with the god their home planet was named after, Septiman.

The man spoke softly. "The winds blow inexorably toward the future. We follow the stream as we follow life itself. There is perpetual day in the darkness among the stars. There is enlightenment for those who seek the light. May the blessings of Septiman embrace this crew and help guide their hands to victory and the glory of the reunification. Until then, the battle is joined."

The crew replied as one, "The battle is joined."

Commander Castle said, "That's it, people. Everything we've been waiting for. Any Malibor ships in orbit around Farslor or nearby are targets. Treat them appropriately. Battle stations. Battle Commander Risor, offensive weapons online. Defensive weapons on standby."

"Offensive Weapons, report." The battle commander pointed at the officer to the left of his station.

Tram Stamper nodded while inputting commands. "Offensive weapons coming online. E-mag systems are twelve for twelve, with obdurium projectiles immediately available. Four missiles in the tubes and at the ready."

The electromagnetic launcher accelerated heavy metal projectiles to one-tenth the speed of light and hurled them into the void of space. The E-mag system could send ten projectiles every second at a target hundreds of thousands of kilometers away, and they had a dozen individually targetable E-mags to send a hundred and twenty penetrators per second toward unwitting targets.

Twelve for twelve. Twelve E-mag launchers ready to fire. Tons of projectiles banked and prepared to enter the breaches.

The battle commander looked to his right. "Defensive Weapons?"

"On warm standby," Gil Dizmar confirmed. "Eyes on the radar, ready to activate automated systems."

Untested automated systems. Only one person had been alive the last time the system had been fired in combat.

A lifetime ago. They had tested as best they could. Chain guns would fill the vacuum of space with projectiles to interdict inbound smart weapons. That was their purpose. Would they respond like they did in the old days?

The battle commander reported, "All systems are go as per your orders, Captain."

Jaq strolled around the bridge with her hands clasped behind her back. She gazed at consoles and ventilation outlets, foam dispensers for damage control—all of it. The ship was as ready as they could make it. The crew had trained hard.

All eyes were on her.

"Ready?" She rested her hand on a youthful crew member's shoulder. To survive, the first-generation crew had children. Those children were now having their own. The second generation filled positions from key leadership to manual labor billets. The captain's parents had tended the hydroponics bay. Every job was of equal import to keep the crew alive and prepared to fulfill their mission.

The youngest of the third generation were together at a central point of the ship, with secured bulkheads surrounding them. They'd emerge when it was safe and someone let them out. The oldest worked as members of the crew.

Little more than a child, the crew member smiled weakly, her face pale under the red bridge lights. Her seat gel was unstressed from her forty-kilo mass. Only thirteen years old but a prodigy, like many of the children of the gifted Borwyn who had crewed the ship when it had first launched.

"We're all afraid, Ensign." Jaq used the crew member's rank to take the emotion out of her statement. "We're afraid of what we might find on Septimus. We're afraid there won't be anything left, but we're not afraid of the Malibor. While we've prepared for war, they haven't had an enemy to face. They think they've won. They don't know we're coming, and most of all, they won't know what hit them."

The two shared a moment before the ensign returned to her monitor. She was one of four systems operators. Active radar, passive sensors, and other technical operations fell within the responsibility of the Sensors section. The ensign was the most junior officer on the bridge. The captain would keep an eye on her.

Jaq continued her tour. Each officer settled into their gel-packed acceleration chairs. Soon they'd hit the burners, and with the help of Farslor's gravity, they'd run up to three gees to arrive with a flair and at a speed that would make them hard to hit.

"Vectoring thrusters?" the captain asked when she reached the thrust control station.

"Five by five, Captain," the thrust control operator replied. He added a thumbs-up framed by a dark smile. "The faster, the better."

A ventilator droned for a few moments. Recycling the air

kept the oxygen at a consistent twenty percent. Fan bearings had been a challenge to replace. The ship had mostly upgraded itself with frictionless bearings, but a few of the fans had been kept for nostalgia. The equipment proclaimed its age with a hum and a howl, then settled into a rhythm, ending with a final thump as the duct closed.

The old system reminded the crew of where they'd come from. They waited for the series of sounds to stop before continuing their conversations.

Ozone drifted through the air—another relic of past technology.

"When we come around Farslor for a hard burn toward Septimus, remember what Number Two said. All Malibor ships are targets. They won't know what hit them. Let justice be ours."

The crew responded as they'd been taught for years, repeating, "The battle is joined."

"Victory is ours!" Jaq pumped her fist and climbed into her seat.

The oldster's voice crackled during the pause in activity. "Vengeance shall be ours."

Jaq winced. She didn't think vengeance was a winning strategy since the god Septiman spoke of peace first. However, their history had taught them differently. Reaching out an open hand to the Malibor delivered only pain and suffering. Justice for the rejection of peace, but not vengeance.

"Accelerating through one gee," the thrust control officer reported.

The gel firmed around the crew to keep their blood from pooling in their limbs. It prevented injuries during unexpected turbulence if they skipped through a gravity well or crossed a solar wind. They were heavily shielded against radiation, and growing up in space gave them some natural resistance.

Adapt or die.

There was far more turbulence than one would expect in the vacuum of space.

The engines couldn't be heard on the bridge, being half a ship away from the power plants that energized the ion-propulsion system. Micro-ion thrusters lined the outside of the ship for attitude control. Conduits traveled along the secondary hull, and a backup system ran down the central axis.

Energy and life support were critical for keeping the crew alive. Four officers ran the sensor systems. Two were on environmental controls, and both were experienced engineers. They wouldn't be on the bridge otherwise.

They were there because they knew the systems inside and out from working on them over the years. They knew where to send the repair crews and how to restore atmosphere no matter the circumstances, even if the cause was a hull breach. They knew how to close off the section with minimal loss of life so a patch could be placed by automated systems.

Everyone had a role to play. There was no engineer on the bridge for the energy systems. The chief engineer stayed with his engines and power plants. His team was bigger than any of the others. Power was life.

"No ships. Unpowered systems in orbit, probable relay satellites," the sensor station reported.

The main screen showed a visual representation of the area in front of the ship, with an overlay of tactical information. The absence of icons could have been either good or bad, a shortcoming within the system. Given the report, there was no question that the sensors were operational.

It began as a subtle vibration, barely enough to tickle the senses through the gel of the seats. It was more a feeling, an itch at the back of the neck. The first jerk came without warning. The ship responded with a groan and a creak like an oldster walking down the corridor after a power nap, showing her age with finesse and flair.

The ship accelerated through two gees. Lieutenant Ferd Alpinist, Thrust Control officer reduced the thrust from the main engines, letting Farslor's gravity do the work.

The outer hull heated up. The vibration increased to a hum and then a howl as *Chrysalis* plunged toward the upper atmosphere. The ship's friction slowed its forward momentum.

"Back us out of the atmosphere. We're probably leaving a fire trail!" the captain shouted over the roar.

Nav tapped the controls, then tapped more furiously. The nose of the warship rose, and the buffeting returned to a subliminal vibration. Thrust Control continued to add energy to bring up the speed lost during the maneuver.

"Sorry, Captain. Misjudged the thermosphere. It shouldn't have extended that far from the planet." The navigator couldn't turn around to see the disappointment on the captain's face.

The crew's eyes were forward, faces held by the gel, which only allowed them to look at their own screens.

The roaring throughout the ship stopped, and silence returned. "It's my fault. I won't let it happen again."

"Log the data for reference should we ever need to reuse Farslor for a slingshot maneuver. Sensors, make the adjustments necessary to provide the data Nav needs. No matter which planet or moon we fly past, we can't be frying the outer hull. *Chrysalis* isn't made for that."

Jaq had let more anger creep into her voice than she'd intended. She knew it was operator error, but getting her pound of flesh wouldn't change anything that had happened. No one knew better than Mary Minshaw what mistakes not to make a second time. They didn't need a too-steep angle of incidence.

The ship would have a hard time if people kept making mistakes. The warship couldn't fight since miscues would compound. Doubts crept into the captain's mind, dark, destructive thoughts that would tear the crew apart.

"Nice recovery, Ferd," the captain said in as calm a voice as she could muster under two gees of acceleration. "You too, Mary. We're on course. We'll have a clear view of Septimus momentarily, something I've waited for my whole life."

Redirect the crew's thoughts away from failure toward success.

"Steady on course vector three-six-two, star angle minus five," Crip said into the silence.

The screens showed clear...until they didn't.

"Weapons platform," the sensor chief announced. "Offset angle negative thirteen, down five, range ten thousand."

"Light 'em up," the battle commander ordered.

Offensive Weapons growled and snapped his teeth. "E-mags five through eight, firing." It was clear after two seconds that the rounds would miss. "Recalibrating." The pause seemed to last for infinity, but it was only three heartbeats. "Firing."

"There you go, Tram. Nice adjustment," Crip said when a flash showed where the weapons platform had been.

The red icon on the screen blinked three times, then disappeared.

"Updating the software to account for gravitic pull," Tram stated. "It'll take a while. We'll use a little eyeball one-oh-one and blanket the target next time."

The captain had to fight not to clear her throat, which would have shown her dismay. The crew was raising her anxiety to a level at which she felt like ordering them to continue around the planet and head away from Septimus until they could get it together.

"Gunship!" Dolly shouted in a high-pitched voice.

Just like that, their opportunity for a second chance was gone.

"Confirmed." The battle commander used his eye controls to center the Malibor ship in his targeting array. "Take out that ship, Mister Stamper."

"Match vectors. Firing Pattern Two Baseline, all guns shoot."

"Targeting. Firing Pattern Two Baseline, twelve of twelve E-mags. Fire."

From the command deck, they couldn't tell that the electromagnetic guns were firing, but an overlay on the main screen showed the outbound streams as a single green line. One hundred and twenty obdurium penetrators per second raced into the void.

"I'm showing no power on the Malibor gunship. Target is cold. I say again, target is cold." The young sensor operator had calmed. She gave the new report in an even voice.

"Confirmed," the sensor chief added.

The gunship did not attempt to maneuver. It stayed where it was as the barrage of penetrators enveloped it, hammering it until the ship broke apart. There was no venting of atmosphere or reactor going critical. The Malibor gunship was destroyed by the eager Borwyn crew, though the vessel was already dead.

CHAPTER 2

Peace is never an option since the ideas of surrender and submission are abhorrent.

"Captain?" the second asked.

This wasn't what they'd expected. It wasn't even close.

"Ferd, slow us down so Mary can bring us around the planet for a better look. Abandon the slingshot maneuver. What in the holy Balzano is going on?"

"Planet's surface shows minimal power output," the chief reported.

"How can that be? There should be a Malibor colony and outpost." The captain wanted to walk around to clear her mind for possibilities she had never considered. She needed to reframe her understanding of the war and the expected battles. However, the gee forces were still too extreme.

The ship bucked and jerked as it reentered the upper atmosphere. The anticipated friction made the droning less intense and the rough ride smoother. No one spoke. The crew was left to their thoughts while *Chrysalis* slowed. Each went about their duties. Confusion roiled across the command deck like a coolant leak.

In an instant, the premise of the last fifty years had changed.

Chrysalis stopped bumping across the thermosphere and assumed a standard orbit, racing at twenty-five thousand kilometers an hour around Farslor.

"Weapons platform, offset angle plus four, up one, range seventeen thousand," Sensor Chief Slade Ping announced.

The target was on nearly the same plane as *Chrysalis*, but not quite. It was one degree above their current course and orientation, the relative position in space at which the ship would aim. There were no fixed positions, so the Borwyn had abandoned those guidelines long ago. As a fleet of one ship, they'd never had to consider coordinating their fire.

It made engagements easier but harder, too. They were a single target for the enemy.

They assumed the Malibor were still the enemy. They had yet to see anything that countered that attitude.

The air handling system kicked on as the ship stopped accelerating, relieving all feeling of gee forces. The captain was first to release herself from her gel chair and float free. She pulled her retractable line off her shoulder harness and hooked it to the rail that lined the overheads, then activated her magnetic boots, which clunked to the deck. They rarely tethered, but Jaq was taking extra precautions while they operated within enemy space until she knew whether it was necessary or not.

When the fans shut down, the captain spoke. "We need to find out what happened. Since we've been in Farslor's shadow for our entire approach from out-system and have never left orbit, what are the chances we've been seen from Septimus?"

"None," the sensor chief replied. "Response time from Septimus is a week at full burn because we're in the pass.

Farslor is closer to Septimus this year over the three lull years."

"Did you see anything between us and them?" the captain pressed.

"Nothing," came the confident reply.

"Number Two, what can we do with a week's time?" The captain knew the answer, but she liked getting Crip's input. He saw things from a different angle.

"We can take a landing ship down there and snoop around. Maybe they have answers we're not going to find from orbit." He pulled himself from his seat and clipped to the overhead, not bothering to activate his boots. He flew across the bridge to the sensor chief's pod.

Jaq had heard all she needed to hear. "My thoughts exactly. Determine an optimal landing site where there is power but a minimal amount. Collect data on this orbit, confirm on the next, and launch the landing team on the third. Crip, you're in charge of the ground crew."

"The battle is joined!" He took one last look at the sensor screens before propelling himself toward the corridor, swimming gracefully above the heads of the crew in their chairs on the command deck. The captain waved as he slipped by. He twisted in the air to unhook his line without interrupting his momentum.

The captain returned to her station but stayed out of her chair. She tapped her screen to activate the ship-wide comm. "Combat Team."

The appropriate channel opened.

"Combat," came the eager baritone.

"Prepare to go dirtside. Commander Castle is on his way down to give you further instruction."

"Oorah, Captain. Dirtside it is." Sergeant Max Tremayne closed the connection.

"One week, people," the captain told the crew on the command deck. "Make the most of it for your teams." She eased to the navigator. "Mary, how are you going to occupy yourself?"

"I'm going to practice not diving us into the atmosphere by easing our orbit from seventy to ninety thousand kilometers. As soon as I have the launch coordinates, I'll take us close. Save the combat team from some of the rough ride."

"Don't burn too hard. We only have a few years on that reactor. Don't want to cut us short." Jaq winked at her.

"I'll avoid the frivolity of it all." Lieutenant Minshaw smiled while waving, ending with a finger snap. She returned her attention to the screen and used eye movements to control the ship. "Let the vertical slalom begin."

The planet climbed the screen until it half-filled it, then steadied. The ship accelerated slightly, but not enough to entice the captain to unhook her tether. Jaq moved slowly around the command deck.

The ship's vibrations radiated through her magnetic boots. The view of the planet changed to show a quarter of it before the image settled anew.

"Commander Risor, if you would be so kind, recalibrate those E-mags. Seems to me there are targets of opportunity surrounding this planet that aren't disposed to return fire."

The icons of two more weapons platforms appeared on the screen, but they showed cold like the others.

Slade shook his head. He had no answer as to why the sensors only now discovered the platforms.

The battle commander freed himself from his seat to join the offensive weapons officer. "Tram, let's see what we need to do. One shot, one kill. It'll save us a lot of grief when we find the Malibor."

"You think they're out there?"

"Compared to Farslor, Septimus is a paradise. They had

fifty years to move their people to our planet. They're out here, all right, and they're not going to be happy that we're back. They might even call *us* the invaders."

―――――

"Sergeant," Commander Castle said by way of a greeting, offering a quick handshake.

The two men clamped their boots to the deck while the short-lived contest of strength took place. It was a rite of passage to enter the combat team's spaces. The commander gave as much as he received. They let go with a mutual approving nod.

The sergeant quickly returned to the business at hand. "Commander, what's the loadout?"

"Pulse rifles and stunners. Chest protection. Helmets. Cold weather gear in the lander, just in case."

"Gloves and hats, then. Roger." Max turned to his people. "You heard the commander! Gear up and line up."

The team had been magged to the deck, awaiting their orders. Once received, they galvanized into action. Two soldiers released their boots to float above their comrades, hooting as they passed. A hand reached up to snag a boot that drooped too low and yanked the man back, swung him in a circle, and sent him flying in the wrong direction.

The sergeant shouted, "Order!" an instant prior to catching a faceful of the wayward private. He dragged the soldier to the deck. "As you were."

A sheepish grin suggested he wasn't put out by his miscue or realignment at the hands of his fellows. He clumped toward the locker bay from which the team had started to draw their gear.

The sergeant and the commander shuffled after them at the end of the line.

"I'll brief the team when we're in the lander," the

commander said, gesturing. "The Malibor appear to have abandoned Farslor. Our job is to find out why."

The sergeant leaned close. "That'll take us about fifteen minutes." He laughed. "Or we might never learn why. They're completely gone?"

"There's the rub, Max. There are power signatures down there, faint but real. We could run into a little resistance."

"You know what they say, Commander. Resistance makes the heart grow fonder."

"Absence." Crip looked askance at the combat team leader when he realized he was being messed with. "You snack-cracker."

"Thank you. I do my best."

They moved forward. Gear distribution was well-practiced. "I assume we want prisoners. Stunners first, big guns second unless they try to kill us first. Then big guns from the outset."

The commander nodded, then slipped on his chest protector and snugged it tight. He placed his harness over the top and packed it with four spare power modules. The pulse rifles ate through power, delivering only twenty to twenty-five shots per module. Standard procedure was to swap out power at twenty shots and keep the old module in case of an emergency to eke out another shot or five.

When Crip looked up, the sergeant was ready to go. "You don't spend enough time down here, Commander."

It was the sergeant's job to prepare, like the sergeants who'd preceded him. Max Tremayne was the lucky one, born at the right time for the return to Septimus.

It had taken the engineers a long time to perfect the ion drive and the smelting processes in a Lindor moon's extreme cold, but it had had the minerals they needed and the raw materials required to save *Chrysalis* and upgrade her. Life had been harsh for the survivors and their progeny.

In the minds of those left behind on Septimus, the starship had been lost.

Max would lead the first combat team to take the fight to the Malibor. His attitude was upbeat. It could be nothing else.

"I don't know what I'd do without my daily comeuppance. It's like a warm blanket after life support breaks down. It's warm because it's peed on, but hey, take what you can get," Crip joked.

"To the lander!" the sergeant ordered.

The team moved quickly, using the measured pace necessary when walking in boots with the magnetic clamps engaged. Single file, they followed in each other's footsteps down the corridor.

A body appeared at the top of the loading chute. The shepherd.

"Give us our happy sendoff, Shepherd!" The sergeant didn't care about the blessing, but his people did, and the ship's leadership did, including Crip Castle.

The shepherd drew the circle of life before him, the symbol of Septiman. "A river flows, scarring the ground beneath until the beauty of life is revealed. There is strength in victory. There is beauty in strength but also ugliness. Bring the word of Septiman to the people of this planet." He mumbled the closing prayer.

Max stared with his mouth open, then shook off the team's blessing and pumped his fist.

They continued to a vertical tube, stepped over the opening, and with a gentle push on the overhead, dropped toward the ship's keel, which was where the landing ships were stored. Six total in six launch tubes. The landers would use as little energy as possible to descend since they needed their fuel for the launch from the planet and acceleration to achieve breakaway speed to return to orbit.

A small nuclear power plant drove an oxygen collector to top off the liquid oxygen tanks. The goal was to return to the ship with half a tank, enough for the next landing. There they'd collect more, turn it into LOX, and repeat.

That was the plan. This was the first real test of a landing module. The elements to turn oxygen into fuel had been found in significant quantities on an asteroid. Hydrocarbons mixed with oxygen to produce the required thrust. *Chrysalis* had enough hydrocarbons to send ten landers on a hundred trips, as long as they could keep extracting oxygen from a planet's atmosphere.

They hoped it worked. If it didn't, they'd arrive empty and be down one landing ship until they could obtain more liquid oxygen. That wasn't an easy proposition in space.

The team moved into the lander and settled into their seats.

"You know," the commander started as he stepped out of the access tube, "we have a couple hours before we go."

"You left that part out," the sergeant replied. He leaned past the commander. "Everyone out. Regroup in the team room. T minus two hours and counting."

"Roger," came the collective reply without a hint of disappointment.

They'd practiced boarding and dismounting every day they'd been soldiers. What was once more?

The team was largely from the second generation and ranged from thirty to forty years old, but space hadn't aged them like they would have aged if they lived on a planet. Life on the ship had emotionally matured them more quickly while retarding their physical development at the same time.

The team had specialists of all kinds. A crew member couldn't join the combat team unless they'd successfully served in one of the other sections on the ship. From engineers to physicists to astronomers to doctors, the team could handle almost any situation they encountered.

That was the intent, anyway.

While they were filing back into the team room, the shepherd looked like he had more to say.

"Say it, Shepherd. Give us some words of wisdom to send us into the enemy's maw." Crip asked.

"The enemy is only a friend who turned his back on you. He may once again show you his hand."

"Amen, Shepherd. I'll probably slap that hand of his, although I hope that's not the case. I've never killed anyone." The commander surveyed the group. "None of us have, but we've trained for it. Still, I think I would prefer not to, especially since you can't get answers from the dead. Not easy ones anyway."

"We have our stunners. We'll take 'em alive. They'll only die if they fight back, and then they'll just die with the knowledge that they weren't good enough, not this time." The sergeant made a fist. His face turned hard, and the smile lines radiating from his eyes creased and deepened.

"Train hard, fight hard," Crip said, nodding at the sergeant.

He didn't speak further. The two men were the same age but had been challenged by different career paths. Both had wanted to be in the combat team, but Crip Castle had seen he could do both. He had quickly gotten bored with the training since he picked up the information faster than anyone else. Still, on the ground, the sergeant was in charge.

"Do we have more details on the environment? Anything beyond open scrub?" Max wondered.

"You have all the info I have. Windswept scrub, but how high is it? I hope it's not higher than the lander's stilts." Crip shrugged and stared into the distance, recalling the landing site details he'd pulled on his way to the team room.

"It would stop being fun if branches punched through the bottom deck." Max chewed the inside of his cheek. "No fun at all." He held his hand up, and the room instantly quieted. "One last hydration check, then a protein bar, and get on the ship. We'll study the ground survey in there."

"I like your plan, Max," Crip replied. "I'll join you shortly."

Without another word, Crip unclamped his boots and pushed off the wall to fly down the corridor. The sergeant wasn't responsible for him, so he didn't bother to watch. Max headed for the water cooler to get a drink.

Crip grabbed the rail to slow down, then pulled toward a side corridor. He reached a vertical access tube and drew himself up two decks. He eased into a thruster control engineering station where two crew worked.

"Can I get a moment?" he asked.

Two lieutenants worked side by side. One nudged the other. "I have it. Don't go far in case we hit more turbulence," the male engineer said.

Lieutenant Taurus Lindman nodded. The dark-haired and willowy woman, who was the same age as the commander, moved into the corridor. She braced herself with a foot on a lower rail and a hand on an upper. The commander moved close and spoke softly. "I'm going to Farslor with the combat team. I wanted you to know."

"I figured. Shouldn't you be in the lander?" She looked over her shoulder at the ship's position relative to the planet.

"Sometimes we need to take a moment to appreciate why we do what we do."

She smiled. "Return to Septimus. We're going home."

Crip frowned. "This ship is the only home we've known. There's more out there, but I believe we live for each other."

"Is this another proposal?" she asked, tilting her head.

"Perseverance could eventually pay off," Crip countered. He leaned in for a quick kiss.

She responded warmly.

"Eventually I'll say yes, but not today. I hope that gives you enough incentive to get yourself back to the ship. I won't say yes to a corpse, or more likely, a popsicle if you get stuck down there. Go on, Mister Starry-Eyed. Don't get yourself demoted to bilge cleaning."

"That sucked last time." He laughed and backstroked his way down the corridor, waving at Taurus.

She returned his wave and watched him crash into the end wall of the corridor. The commander straightened, did a flip, and kicked off the overhead to propel himself down the tube.

He accelerated through the corridors to the team room, which was now empty. He recovered his weapons and bolted into the lander.

"Ten seconds," Sergeant Tremayne stated. "Did she say yes?"

"Not yet," Crip said.

The team chuckled.

"We're laughing *with* you, not *at* you, Commander."

"I feel the love," Crip replied.

The lander's pilot, who operated the vessel from a station in the keel, counted down to one, after which the lander was ejected. The remote pilot took over.

"Prepare for a rough ride," the remote pilot announced.

The ship started bucking in the upper atmosphere. The pilot slightly adjusted its trajectory, which reduced the violence for a moment before it started afresh, driving the straps into the combat team's shoulders. Better strap bruises than flying around within the lander, beating themselves and each other up.

"How many drops?" the commander shouted over the din of the turbulence from the friction of atmospheric entry.

Max replied by holding up one finger. They'd made a test landing two decades earlier on a moon farther out in the system. There had been no atmosphere, so it had been a smooth landing and return to the ship. They had done it during a shakedown cruise that had proved *Chrysalis's* ion drive was not yet ready. It had taken twenty more years to perfect it for intrastellar travel.

Max spoke. "No one has dealt with this before. That makes us the pros!"

Crip snorted. "Keep your heads down and your eyes open. We have no idea what to expect down there. Minimal power doesn't mean harmless."

CHAPTER 3

The brightest stars in the sky aren't stars at all.

The command deck was silent as the lander dropped away from the ship. It took a few moments until the heat of reentry flamed around the carbon-fiber heat shield.

"May Septiman guide you to a soft landing," Jaq muttered.

The main engines briefly engaged to propel *Chrysalis* into a higher orbit.

"Status," the captain requested. She was holding onto the rail between bouts of inertia and weightlessness.

"Defense weapons hot," the battle commander reported.

"Sky is clear. Passive scans are showing no active comm channels."

The sensor operators remained embedded in the gel of their seats in case they had to make tactical maneuvers. The captain stood on the command deck more than anyone else. The second would have been up too if he'd been there, but he was winging his way toward the planet's surface.

"Any other intel on the planet? A power source? I have my idea of what that means, but what's it mean to you?"

The acceleration ended, and the ship returned to zero-gee. The captain pulled herself to the sensor pod. The operators were wrapped around the central station.

Slade Ping extricated himself from the gel and floated free. "It's energy generation. We focused our scanners on that area when we were in the upper atmosphere but couldn't see any distribution networks. It's like a turbine spinning freely, generating a current that is then diffused without powering anything. Infrared showed no heat sources. This isn't even pre-industrial level. Maybe they died out, and the last person didn't lock out the water wheel."

"'Water wheel?'" The captain was confused. She pulled herself closer to the chief to make sure she'd heard correctly. All she knew was the technology on the *Chrysalis*. She hadn't contemplated sources of power beyond the ones the ship used. She didn't have the time.

"Just an example. A stream of water turned a wheel, like using kinetic energy to pass an electrical conductor like tightly coiled wire through a magnetic field at a high rate of speed. It's called electromagnetic induction." The chief failed to keep the smug look off his face.

"As you were, Chief." Jaq stared blankly while working the information through her mind.

"We can see that because the emissions aren't natural."

"It isn't shielded." It was a statement, not a question. "We shall soon see what it is. When will the combat team touch down?"

The navigator repeated the information from the main screen. "Touchdown in five. Lander is tracking true, five by five."

"No weapons acquisition radars. No enemy fire. Lander is green," Ping added.

The lander cleared the upper atmosphere and transitioned with a bump to smooth air. The combat team squinted at each other across the round inner module, in which they sat in seats lining the outer wall.

"Max, couldn't you have put together a better-looking team? Or is your intent to frighten the enemy into submission?"

"Commander! It wouldn't do to kick you off the team. I'm not sure who I'd go to for that request since you're next in the chain of command. We'll have to scare the enemy. My apologies."

"You are an a-hole of all a-holes."

They checked the time in unison and nodded once.

Sergeant Tremayne delivered the order. "Odd numbers, face left!"

The soldiers stood, turned left, and paired off. They raised their hands and pounded their shoulders hard twice, followed by a palm strike to the chest to ensure their body armor fit properly. Then the even numbers pounded and punched. Max leaned into his strike on the commander, who grunted at the impact.

"Like I said. A-hole." The commander made a fist and held it before his chest. Power.

"Seats!" the sergeant called, and the soldiers sat. The lander touched down so gently they could barely feel it. Max gestured at the commander, and the group hopped to their feet. "You have the honor to be first off."

"The honor is yours, Sergeant Tremayne. You've earned it." Crip nodded once and gave the thumbs-up.

Max shook his head. There was insufficient room to change the order. "It's all you, Commander."

Crip gave the order. "Follow me out, form a perimeter, and observe."

The sensors checked the air beyond the outer hull. "Oxygen, nitrogen. Five degrees C. A little cooler than you're used to, but at least it's not freezing," Max reported. "Cleared to open."

The outer hatch cycled. Crip pumped his fist, and the hatch opened outward. He pushed it open the rest of the way and vaulted over the few steps to land in the scrub they'd expected. He hit hard and rolled, body feeling like it weighed five times more than normal. His legs collapsed beneath him as if he'd been in a losing fight.

He pointed behind him without taking his eyes off the landscape and shouted over his shoulder, "Use the stairs."

The sergeant ushered the group out, waiting to go last. He didn't need the honor of being the first Borwyn to step foot on Farslor. Recognition was for the soldiers and the combat team. They were on the first mission of the return home, a return that had started before any of them were born except one.

Max hurried down the lander's steps. Well, he went down as fast as he could, considering he weighed more than he ever had in his life. He opened a panel and placed his palm on the pad behind it. The steps started to retract, and the hatch closed.

The team was deployed in a wide circle around the lander.

Crouching, Crip searched for the sergeant. Max had gone prone and was aiming his pulse rifle away from the lander. He moved the barrel slowly back and forth.

Crip kneeled next to him. "Status?"

"I don't see anything. Lander's external cameras didn't show anything. I think we're out here by ourselves, but just in case we're not, you should probably get down."

"Roger," the commander replied. Before he could drop to the ground, an arrow whistled through the air and thudded against his body armor. Crip watched it fall to the ground, unsure of what had just happened.

"Get down!" Max shouted.

Crip dove through a rugged bush. His bare forearms bore the brunt of the damage. He rolled sideways and scrubbed his bleeding arms on his midsection. "It burns. There's a toxin on these plants."

"I know," Max replied. He held up a forearm to show reddening scratches. "But I wasn't crying about it. I thought it went without saying not to tear up your body."

"A-hole." Crip pointed. "I see one!"

Everyone saw the individual since he was running away from the encounter. Max aimed and fired, and the enemy disappeared into the brush. The sergeant was up and after him as fast as his tortured legs would carry him.

"What if it's a trap?" Crip yelled after him.

Max halted, then crouched and took a knee. "I see him ahead. He's down." He kept his eyes on the target. "Combat V."

The soldiers moved forward slowly, peering over the barrels of their pulse rifles. After the attack, taking a prisoner was the second priority. Another arrow appeared out of the low bushes, flew with unerring accuracy to hit the V's extreme left flank, and embedded in Andreeson's arm.

He grunted from the injury and recoiled, snap-firing with one hand to spray the scrub from which the arrow had originated. He then took a knee and scanned the area to his left.

Private Binfall moved to Andreeson's side to render first aid. Bandages had always been a standard part of their kit, but none of them had never used them before. but here on Farslor, two minutes into their first real operation, they already had multiple injuries and only they were there to treat them.

"It's a clown show," Max muttered. "Clear the brush. Rapid fire on one. One!"

The unit methodically sprayed the brush surrounding its position. An eerie silence descended, a silence Crip realized had not existed before.

"Spread out two by two." Max pointed with his working hand down the vectors he wanted them to go, hatcheting once for each pair.

They separated into six groups of two and tactically maneuvered farther into the scrub, spreading out as they went. Max found that it was getting easier to walk since his body was accepting the planet's gravity.

"Got a corpse over here." Andreeson moved his arm gingerly while keeping his weapon trained on the body.

Crip was sure the enemy was dead, but he wasn't sure enough to stop staring. It was his first time seeing the dead body of someone who hadn't died of old age.

"Another here," Danzig reported.

"Consolidate our position ten meters beyond the bodies." Max held his fist in the air and flashed five fingers twice.

Max passed the first Malibor victim.

Crip stopped to examine the man. Max continued ten more meters before kneeling in a combat-ready firing position.

"One shot." The first thing the commander noticed was the smell. It was as if the individual had never washed. His matted hair and dirty skin suggested he was little better than a caveman. Furs covered his body, and the rudimentary bow was a pliable sapling with a woven bark string. "There must be large animals around here. He's wearing a hide."

"It's embarrassing to shoot them, but they could have yielded to our superior firepower," Max remarked.

"Maybe they have no idea what superior firepower is," Crip offered. "Close with the next ones and take them in hand-to-hand. Then use the stunners. We might get a scratch or two, but we can take them without killing them. These aren't the enemy we came here to fight."

"Sounds like a plan, Commander." Max used the hand and arm signal for switching weapons—the finger gun.

The soldiers slung their rifles and drew their stun pistols. Max hesitated. The pause had given him too much time to think. The smell would never leave him. It was as the commander had said. The first kill was hard, even though it had been easy to raise his weapon and fire. It had been simple mechanics.

Dead-simple.

Something penetrated the edge of his consciousness. Someone was calling his name, but his voice sounded far away. He jumped when a hand gripped his shoulder.

"Max?"

"Don't sneak up on people like that, Crip."

The vacant look left Max's eyes.

Crip had studied the effect of combat on people. He didn't know if it was an urban myth or much ado about nothing, so he hadn't bothered the others by bringing it up. He now realized he should have. It was real.

"Bring the team in for a quick confab," Crip requested. "Now, please."

Focused tasks. Direct orders. Get the team back on track.

The soldiers rallied to where Crip now stood, making himself a target. It was important for the leader not to show fear. Although Max was supposed to be in charge on the ground, Crip was the ship's deputy, the second in charge. He'd already been shot once. He had been too fired up to realize how little threat these people posed. He knew better now, so he stepped up and instantly changed the standard operating procedure.

Half the soldiers oriented outboard with their weapons pointed at the open scrub while the others, facing a soldier called Bony and Max in the middle, pointed their weapons at the ground. None of them put their stunners away.

Crip gestured in the direction of the power source. "Our mission is to find out what's generating the energy signature we saw from the ship while assessing the combat power of the Malibor. We already have a good idea that the Malibor were set back hundreds of years while the Borwyn continued to move forward. It was slower than we wanted because of our limited resources, but we still moved forward. Look at our weapons compared to theirs."

The commander palmed his stunner and turned it over in his hand, appreciating the clean lines and the simplicity of its function. He hooked the Malibor bow with his toe and lifted it to his free hand, then held it in front of him. It had been stripped of its bark and smoothed, but beyond that, it was little more than a stick with a string bending it. It was the next evolutionary step above spears. Or maybe they hadn't retrograded as far as spears.

A light breeze touched his face, and Crip took a deep breath. The air was crisp but clean.

"Max, leave two soldiers here to watch over the bodies and protect the ship. If we're outnumbered, deadly force is authorized. If they only snipe you with arrows, scare them away or stun them. We'll stay in touch."

He tapped the comm unit on his chest. Crip studied the horizon while Sergeant Tremayne arranged the soldiers. He left the dead Malibor, plus Andreeson and the soldier who'd helped him, Binfall. The others formed into a column of twos. Max moved up front. He gestured for Crip to bring up the rear.

The rallying cry for the team hadn't been repeated since the first contact. and Max knew it was time to bring it back.

"The battle is joined!" he yelled.

CHAPTER 4

Take care in your wishes upon a falling star.

"Fire!" Captain Hunter ordered. Two of the twelve E-mags barked into the silence of the void, sending a stream of penetrators into the latest unpowered weapons platform. It was their fourth on this orbit. "Secure weapons."

The platform deteriorated into shattered debris.

"Collect some of that debris, Battle Commander." The captain was floating free. She kept her arms crossed, seemingly oblivious to spinning sideways to the command deck's orientation.

"Deploying a recovery drone," Alby Risor noted. "We'll collect it on the next pass."

The battle commander released himself from his chair and floated free. The mid-level rail was smooth beneath his fingers, polished by decades of use. It was plain metal, unpainted, as were most surfaces inside the ship.

Alby pulled up next to the captain and gave up trying to match her rotation after his initial failed attempt. He clung to the rail until he could engage his magnetic boots. "I'd like to bring one on board the ship."

Jaq studied him as she continued to rotate.

He smiled weakly. "Intact."

She snorted. "An intact Malibor weapons platform on the *Chrysalis*." She said it like she'd just eaten an unsavory serving of mushy peas on licorice bread.

"None of them have blown up. They've simply come apart. I'd like to see what made them tick, but more importantly, I want to know why they died."

"What if they're *not* dead? They could still be loaded with ammunition. Maybe their power sources died, and the Malibor lost interest in protecting this planet from a nonexistent threat. We knew we had survived, but they did not. The last they saw of *Chrysalis* was when it was venting atmosphere and spinning out of control toward deep space. Both the battle and the war were over."

Alby gripped the captain's shoulder to stop her from spinning. "As far as they knew. It wasn't over for us, and now we're back. Won't they be surprised?"

Jaq locked her boots to the deck. "How can you guarantee you won't blow up the ship?"

The battle commander knew what he needed to do. "We clear Cargo Hold Seven and add three layers of blast deflectors, and we only work on the device with the outer hatch open. The force of any explosion will be redirected into space. We might sustain minor damage, but we'll be able to quickly repair it, and we only bring it aboard after conducting an initial evaluation during a spacewalk with the platform and our engineers tethered to the outer hull."

"I prefer the no-risk approach. What can you do to get the risk down to zero?" The captain's eyes unfocused as she calculated the risks and rewards. Studying fifty-year-old technology held no allure for her, but finding out why it was still there had value.

Had the Borwyn and the Malibor fought to a draw? Had both sides been damaged nearly beyond their ability to recover? The records from the final battle were scarce since most systems were in dire condition, and the crew had fought to save their lives, not collect data. The story of the final battle and escape had been told by the survivors. There were few sensor records to support the tale.

"We could deploy a team to study it from afar and *not* bring it aboard. We'll have to stop the ship and match its position in orbit, though."

The captain dipped her head and slowly turned toward the thrust control station. "Reactor status." The displays at each station contained the information dashboard for the ship's systems, but when the crew was out of their seats, they had to count on what was displayed on the main screen. Jaq spent less time in her seat than the rest of the crew on the command deck. She counted on them to inform her of changes.

"Ninety-seven percent and recharging."

"Estimate usage and recharge time in bringing the ship to a complete halt at the zero gravity point between the planet and the moon, next pass, using friction to slow us down as much as possible."

Ferdinand Alpinist focused on his interface and used eye control to augment his fingertips' data input. After twenty seconds, he had the answer. "Estimate ninety-one percent, with a recharge time of four hours."

"Then getting us back up to speed?"

Acceleration took more energy than anything else. Discharging the capacitors into the ion drives helped create thrust, and recharging the capacitors let them do it again. Being below fifty percent energy output added significantly to the recharge time. Fifty percent was the hard deck the captain dared not go beyond.

"Seventy-four percent, followed by eight to ten hours recharge, depending on systems' load beyond acceleration."

Systems load. Like weapons usage. If they had to accelerate due to enemy activity, their energy levels would drop precipitously toward the barrier, forcing them to disengage and run for their lives while they had sufficient power to do so. They had not solved the problem of unlimited power to stay and fight a drawn-out space battle. The best they could do was hit and run. While delivering a powerful punch, they couldn't return for more than a second pass.

"Next orbit, drag us to full ahead slow, then use thrusters to full stop. We'll stay dormant below the weapons platforms' orbits and make like a hole in the sky until we've recharged to one hundred percent. Use thrusters for station-keeping. Battle Commander, you have four hours to learn everything you can from that platform."

Alby tapped his nose. "You know I'm going out there."

The captain fixed her cold, gray eyes on the battle commander. "Then let me add another parameter to your orders. Don't get anyone killed. That means you, too."

He half-smiled and tossed his head. "You've got a big old crush on me. I knew it."

"Get out of here before I change my mind." Jaq dismissively waved a hand over her shoulder without looking at him. She adjusted her stance until she faced the board. They'd already destroyed four weapons platforms and identified two more. Navigation had selected the one they would approach next, based on an optimal flight plan.

The captain accessed the ship-wide comm. "Engineering. Is there any way we can use the heat from atmospheric braking to recharge our systems?"

The engineer replied from the other end, "We never contemplated that. I won't have any people to look into it until after this ill-advised spacewalk the battle commander is going on with some of my best people. It's absolute rubbish!"

"What if they learn something you can use?" The captain smiled. The chief engineer always had more stress than he could handle if someone asked him or simply listened to his constant barrage of complaints. He was exactly where he wanted to be, doing what he loved.

"Doubt it," the chief engineer snapped.

"Heat recharge. Add it to this month's long-term plan." The captain started to close the link, but the engineer kept talking.

"We don't have extra parts or any research materials left. Adding it to the list doesn't get it done."

"You should probably stop taking stims and get some sleep, Bec. What if the weapons platform has some of the raw materials you need?"

"Doubt it."

"You're off the clock, effective immediately. Go to your quarters. See you in twelve hours." Jaq stabbed a finger at the exit.

The chief engineer had pushed until the captain had had enough.

"Who's going to run Engineering while most of my people are gone?" His voice had lost its acerbic edge.

"I will. That way, I can make sure you're not there. Get some sleep and come back when you're ready to carry on a conversation like an adult."

She closed the channel. The captain wasn't angry. Most

conversations with the chief engineer went that way. Jaq had only to plant the seed. Bec Draper would think about it when he was trying not to, then offer a solution. He didn't have to add it to any list. By virtue of the captain mentioning something, it was on one, planted like the mighty hardwood trees of Septimus, forever rooted in the ground while reaching for the sky.

Some people required gentler handling than others. That was what the captain had been trained for. Others required a firm hand. In all cases, the mission was paramount. Did everything they were doing align with their goal?

Return home to Septimus. That had been the captains' guiding light for the past fifty years. From one to the next, they had prepared the ship to go home.

That goal was in sight. Jaq just wanted to go, but they had other work to do. Conditions were significantly different from what they had expected. She needed to figure out why before they continued.

She headed off the bridge. "Chief, don't break the ship. I'll be in Engineering." She waved at Ping on her way out.

The group lumbered through the corridor in space suits on their way to the cargo bay. That space was being reconfigured in case they determined the weapons platform to be safe enough to bring aboard.

All Alby Risor had to do was convince the captain it would be fine, even though she had already said no. Half the battle was getting the first "no" out of the way. The next fight would come after they examined the platform.

In the cargo bay, they found their space mobility packs, small frames they strapped into and flew through space. Ten suits and five packs. They would double up, one person flying and the other hanging on as if their life depended on it since it did.

They'd also use tethers, but no one wanted to rely solely on the hope that the line would hold up under the rigors of space flight. Although they had been tested extensively, many legacy systems were ancient and not getting better with age.

The battle commander detailed who would fly and who would ride. The bigger of the pair drove the frame, and the smaller would cling on. They'd found that method worked best.

Alby strapped in and cycled the controls. The pneumatic thrusters were at one hundred percent and operational. A short burst from each confirmed tight releases through the small multidirectional nozzles. Those provided enough thrust to get them going in the right direction and keep them going, followed by enough juice to slow them down when the time came.

The others wearing mobility packs conducted their own checks.

Ten strong, they walked toward the cargo bay door. *Chrysalis* skipped off the atmosphere, and nine of the ten were launched toward the overhead. Alby was the only one who'd engaged his magnetic clamps. His tethered companion jerked over his head until the line caught, then twisted feet-first toward the overhead. Alby looped the tether over his arm and yanked his flying partner back down. The young man crashed into the top of Alby's suit.

"Yes, sir. I'll clamp myself down. Sorry about that," he mumbled.

The crew was uncomfortable driving their spacesuits in zero-gee. The magnetic clamps activated differently from the ankle-bump they were used to in their ship's jumpsuit.

Alby gestured at those milling about the overhead. "Get down here!"

He couldn't be angry with them. The entirety of the crew's

efforts over the past fifty years had been getting the ship ready to get back into the fight. That meant raising a new crew from birth to handle the challenges of operating in space. They were indifferent to being tossed about. They took it in stride, just like Alby. He wasn't much older than the others on the boarding team. They'd all been born and raised on the ship. They knew no other environment.

They swam effortlessly to where Alby waited and, one by one, clamped themselves to the deck.

All had been outside the ship in a spacesuit. Alby had made sure of that. It was standard practice for engineers working their way up through the ranks to start with low-level maintenance duties, even though they were some of the most dangerous tasks on the ship. They had to be done, and everyone survived that rite of passage to move into the engineering spaces, where life was a lot easier.

Until Alby had called for volunteers by name, which defeated the purpose of asking. He wanted who he wanted, which was the privilege of rank. There was no one he had to ask besides the captain, and she had given her approval.

The ship bucked and screamed in defiance of the atmosphere scraping its keel. The buffeting lasted three minutes, then four, and when it stopped, zero-gee returned with no hint of artificial gravity.

"We're here," someone said over their suit comms.

The cargo bay door cracked open. The view beyond showed deep space. No planet. No system star. Only the void in its vast emptiness.

When the ship slowed to match the orbit, the weapons platform reflected Armanor's light from the far side of the ship.

"Target is confirmed," Alby reported.

The other four flyers verified the target by pointing in its direction. It was low-tech, but it worked.

"Push off, easy as it goes. No radical maneuvers, no matter how good you are with the mobility pack," Alby warned. He took two magnetized steps and released, then jumped out the door and goosed his controls in a silent whisper to accelerate.

The others raced past, then powered down their thrusters and waited for the battle commander to catch up. He tapped his jets a miniscule amount at a time until he was barely going faster than the others, then coasted up to them and moved in front. The weapons platform looked larger as they approached.

Alby hadn't completely internalized the size. It was much bigger than a lander, at least five times as large. It bristled with weapons but without lights or other demonstrations of active power.

"Invert and decelerate," Alby ordered. He rotated feet-first and touched the controls, then focused on the view between his boots to gauge his rate of deceleration. In open space without other references, he was hard-pressed. He called the ship. "Any way you guys can give us a tactical assist? Am I slowing down too fast?"

"Stand by," the sensor chief replied.

Alby hit the jets with a little more vigor. He'd rather stop dead in space than crash into the weapons platform. The closer he got, the less congenial it appeared.

The dark metal brooded before the incoming party, bristling with protrusions and sharp angles. It menaced space even in its silence.

It was not designed as a respite for weary travelers. It had one purpose – destroy the enemy.

Alby's purpose was to figure out why the weapons platform was no longer fulfilling its reason for existing.

Its enemy had returned, but the platform was no longer ready.

"Any day now, Chief!" Alby barked.

"You're going to stop a hundred meters short." Chief Ping enunciated clearly to avoid misunderstandings.

Alby turned to face the platform. It appeared even more menacing than when he'd been looking between his boots. "We'll stop short and proceed with extreme caution. Do not touch the platform until we are sure it won't become active."

The battle commander's tether partner accessed their private channel. "How are we going to confirm that without touching it?"

"Good point. Let me clarify to the team." Alby switched to his broadcast channel. "We'll touch it after we've examined the exterior. They had to be able to conduct maintenance on this thing or reprogram it. Find those interfaces or access points."

The team acknowledged his order. The sensor chief hadn't been correct. By inverting, Alby hadn't continued reducing his speed by making incremental adjustments to the thrusters. He and his tether partner continued toward the platform. Alby bunched up his legs to turn around, then unfolded them, angled away, and touched his thruster one last time. They came to a stop five meters short of the platform.

The two held their breath while they waited for something egregious to happen. Behind them, *Chrysalis* partially blocked the view of Farslor, a mostly brown planet with shocks of green and blue. The deputy was down there with a combat team. The battle commander was in space, fifteen to thirty minutes from the ship. The captain was in Engineering.

"This seemed like a good idea," Alby mumbled.

"It's nice to get out every once in a while," someone replied over the still-open channel. "Thanks for saving us from our boring existence."

Alby snorted. "Okay, you criminals. Stay where you are for the moment. I'll assess this bad boy first, and then we'll proceed together."

With his tethered companion held tightly, the battle commander used minimum power to drive the two of them around the outside of the weapons platform.

Alby narrated as they passed. "Two rail guns, facing side, length ten meters each. Chain guns and repeaters interspersed for close-in defense every twenty meters. Anti-landing mesh stands out from the framework. That's what gives this platform its shadowy appearance. I can't tell if the mesh is part of an activation protocol, as in, the platform goes live the instant someone touches it. I recommend we put small shaped charges on the weapons before we engage the mesh."

The tour continued as the battle commander completed his trip around the beast. Eight railguns, sixteen missile ports, and dozens of close-in weapons. A prominent feature of the platform was twenty-meter-long projections ending in sharpened points. They could have been aerials or an electrified defense system or something as simple as hardened spearpoints to drive off undesired visitors.

"We will attempt to land on the unit," Alby reported.

"We will?" his tethered companion asked.

"Relax, Godbolt. There's no power, and it's the logical next step." With one last bump to his thruster, Alby rotated away from the platform to land feet-first on a space between spear tips. "Impact."

The touchdown was gentle. The mesh gave a little, then drew back to the solid outer hull of the platform. Alby untethered his companion, who activated his magnetic boots to attach to the metal beneath the mesh. The young man bent down and wrapped his fingers in the netting.

"Metal, wired. At some point, it could have been sensor mesh or an electrocution screen."

Alby gingerly stepped away from Godbolt as if he were walking on eggshells. He wanted to think he was being respectful of the Borwyn's old enemy while silently admitting that he was afraid. The Malibor had been their mortal foe. They were masters at killing. Alby was Borwyn. He wanted to believe his fear was healthy, but he had hoped his scientific curiosity would outweigh his trepidation.

He moved to the nearest projection and discovered that it was a physical construct. He couldn't see an electronic connection or a polished tip for ease of conducting electricity into an unwitting foe. "Watch the bristly stuff," Alby warned. "The mesh needs to be shorted out to be safe."

"Over here, Commander." Godbolt pointed at a box beneath the netting. "Old-school."

Cables ran into a box that was partially open. The heavy copper wire inside suggested it was a transformer and power distribution system.

Alby's eyes lit up. "We can use that wiring. Cut the feed lines."

Four heavy cables entered the box. Godbolt placed a thermite charge on each and stepped back. With a single command, the four devices activated and burned through the cables. That was far easier than hacking through them with a bolt cutter or an axe.

"If you'd be so kind, good people of the engineering and recovery team," Alby started, "join us on the platform. If there are any more distribution boxes, cut the lines going into them. Don't get caught up on the protrusions. That'll ruin your day."

The team eased forward until they impacted the platform. Alby checked the computer strapped to his wrist. Two hours and forty-five minutes before they needed to be back on board *Chrysalis*. He had five pairs of engineers working their way across the Malibor weapons platform, so he hoped it would be enough time.

Progress was slow at first since the engineers were reluctant to move across the mesh too quickly for fear of tripping and spinning off into space.

Alby finally surrendered his space mobility equipment and tied it to two anchor points, one of the spears and the mesh surrounding it. It wasn't much of an encumbrance but enough that he felt freer without it. He moved more quickly and with a purpose, even though there was a greater risk of becoming detached from the platform. It would waste time if someone had to use their pack to retrieve him.

He decided to use the mesh to pull himself hand-over-hand across the platform. It also gave him a better view of what was beneath the screening material.

"The mesh is your handholds. You can thank me later." Alby wasn't smug about it. It had taken him a long time to figure it out. A smarter engineer would have adjusted within the first minute.

The person closest to him gave him the thumbs-up. He gestured back while keeping his fingers wrapped tightly around the netting.

"Contact. We have an access hatch. It's not an airlock," an engineer named Nanticoke reported. "It has a manual access lever."

The battle commander stopped hand-over-handing himself across the platform. "Stand by. Where are you?"

"Opposite side from you. There are no lights or digital interfaces. I'm pulling the lever."

"No!" Alby shouted. He hurried toward the edge on his side of the platform, but it was too late.

The unit vibrated.

Alby froze. "Nobody move!" He waited. "What just happened?"

Fresnor, Nanticoke's tether partner, spoke slowly. "The hatch exploded out of the platform." She didn't continue.

"Nanticoke, report." Alby renewed his movement toward the other side.

"He's gone, sir. The hatch cut him in half and sent him spinning into space." Fresnor gagged, then closed her channel.

CHAPTER 5

The stars are indifferent to the machinations of man.

Sergeant Tremayne approached the outskirts of the rudimentary village. Beyond many thatched-roof- and mud-brick huts stretched the ruins of a modern society.

Gleaming metal and glass and stained concrete. The sergeant gestured for the combat team to stop. They crouched and waited while he worked his way back to Commander Castle.

"Which way do you want to go?"

Crip scrubbed his chin as he studied the ruins. "We have to deal with the locals before we can go exploring, so we had best go into the village. I don't see any tracks into the old city. They probably avoid it. Did we nuke it?"

Max shook his head. "I never heard that we attacked Farslor. Why would we?"

The commander stammered his answer. "I-I don't know. It sure looks like it was destroyed and abandoned at the same time. There had to be a reason. They didn't do this to themselves, did they?"

"Those are a lot of questions, Crip. We don't have any answers, but the power source is somewhere in there. It might be dirty, but we've got rad scanners. Better keep them turned up." He slapped the commander on the shoulder and returned to being the point man.

Max walked effortlessly, now accustomed to the gravity and the burden his body carried because of it. He held up his hand almost immediately, gestured at his eyes, and flashed two fingers, then pointed with his whole arm.

Two people ahead.

He renewed his approach, waved his off-hand at the Malibor, and gripped the stunner tightly in the other. "Hello!" he called in a friendly voice.

An elderly man and a young girl stopped, faced him, and slowly backed away.

"We want to talk with you." Max ignored their fear. He gestured at the ruins beyond the village. "What happened to the city?"

The two glanced at the ruins.

"War. The Borwyn tried to destroy us, but we survived!" The old man spoke with a heavy accent.

Linguists had suggested that the two languages had cross-pollinated enough in ancient times to be understood by both. Max found it comforting that a language barrier wouldn't add to their difficulties.

"The Borwyn didn't do this," Max replied. "I'm Borwyn, and we did not attack Farslor. We defended Septimus until we could defend it no more, then we escaped. We were only now able to return after fifty years." Max stabbed a finger at the ruins. "We did *not* do this."

"Bah!" The old man waved at the combat team. "I was here! The bombs dropped, and the world changed at the hands of the Borwyn. Go away. Go back to the stars and leave us be."

Max was intrigued, as was Crip.

The commander holstered his stunner and walked forward with his hands up. "You're one of the oldsters? We only have one from the before generation left alive, but her time wanes."

"What do I care about that?" The old man made a rude gesture.

The young girl bolted, running as if her life depended on it. The combat team watched her go.

"Secure the perimeter." Max indicated positions on the edge of the village that included two small barriers like fences but none of the huts. He didn't want to encroach.

"You'll be sorry!" The old man got angrier with each passing moment.

"The war is over," Crip tried. "We're just like you, trying to get on with our lives."

A minor commotion drew their attention to the huts at the far end. The villagers were assembling. Shouts signaled that they did not welcome the combat team.

Max leaned close to Crip. "At least we made contact. I don't think this is going to go how we want it to."

"I have to agree. We can't kill them, though. We need to hold the moral high ground."

"We already killed three of them. When they figure that out, they'll probably be less kind than they are now. Is it time to go yet?"

Crip shook his head. "Did we figure out the power source? Since the answer to that question is no, we'll continue with our mission until we get our answer. That means we need to deal with the villagers, our secondary mission. Don't kill any more of them, please."

The sergeant stood. "Non-lethal only. If our position is overrun, we'll rally at the rocky outcropping at our five o'clock." Max pointed at a series of boulders about a hundred meters away that were left over from a past ice age. "Make sure they don't overrun us. Rough count is," he looked at the mob coming their way, "thirty."

The team consisted of eight soldiers, but their weapons were superior to the farm implements the villagers carried. They approached, shouting for the Borwyn to leave. Ten meters away, Crip fired his pulse rifle into the air. The *crack* of the discharge stopped the villagers in mid-step.

"We're not here to fight, but if you want a fight, we'll give it to you." Crip fired once more, then slung his weapon, leaving his hands free. "We didn't attack your planet. Not fifty years ago, and not now. Farslor is yours, a Malibor colony. We only want to know what happened and what the power source emanating from the ruins is."

The old man was in front of the group. "There's no power left. Don't you think we'd be using it if we could? Borwyn are dumb."

"If you *could*..." Crip enunciated slowly. "We think it's buried. A generation system that survived the blast. We only want to be sure it's safe."

"Bah!" The old man made a rude gesture.

Too many villagers mirrored it.

"That's nice." Crip wanted to be rude back but didn't have it in him. He felt sorry for the survivors. "Is this all? No one else survived?"

The old man's eyes darted around in panic. He settled down when he decided what to say. "Thousands survived. Tens of thousands!"

"I'm not looking for secrets. This isn't an invasion, so whether it was dozens or tens of thousands makes no difference to us. I'll let you in on a secret. We're going home to Septimus. Do you know what we'll find there?"

In a calm voice behind a smile, the old man replied, "Pain. You'll find that returning will not be as easy as leaving."

Crip glanced at Max. "How do you know anything that's happening elsewhere in the system?"

The old man tapped his nose, tipped his chin at the sky, and gave them the finger again.

"Would you stop that? We're trying to talk like adults." Crip stared him down.

The crowd quieted.

Crip raised his hands. "We are Borwyn, but we aren't the ones you went to war with. We're only trying to get home."

Commander Castle was pleading for a conversation. This was the first chance anyone had had to talk to the Malibor. He saw lives hanging in the balance of a new war. He saw salvation in a few kind words. Winning without fighting. He'd read that too while studying the deeper meaning of leadership.

The villagers grumbled and eased forward.

"That's far enough," Crip told them.

Without a word being spoken, the villagers all rushed them at once. Four stun pistols crackled, then the combat team fired again and again. Crip stumbled backward, drawing his stun pistol. He tripped and fell, grunting when he hit the ground.

They were coming. He had no time to get to his feet, so he fired while lying on his back. The combat team cleared their lines of fire until all eight soldiers were dropping villagers. One of the Malibor jumped over a stunned victim and slashed down with a rake. The impact on the soldier's helmet cracked the aged wood, but the soldier was driven to his knees. He shoved his pistol between the villager's legs and pulled the trigger. The man sprang into the air and crumpled to the ground a full meter away.

"Cease fire!" Max shouted. "Cease fire." He hurried from body to unconscious body.

Those who hadn't engaged with the soldiers backed away, fear on their features.

"No one is dead, thankfully."

The team separated the villagers and laid them out comfortably while the conscious group watched.

"Mission continues. This way." Max strode through the village into the ruins. He followed the small sensor he carried, turning it left and right to manually zero in on the power source. After a hundred meters of wading through the overgrowth that was attempting to reclaim the city, he was on top of the source. "We need to go down." He stared at the ground, which was a mix of rubble, scrub, and dirt.

The soldiers scattered to scour the vicinity for a stairway or access shaft but came up short after fifteen minutes.

"Does that thing tell you anything else?" Crip asked, but he knew the answer. It only registered the strength of the power source, nothing else. It was a passive device, not an active scanner. They needed the ship's systems for that. "Set up a relay. I want to talk with *Chrysalis*."

The team had one soldier who carried the equipment, but each could do what needed to be done. No one specialized since they didn't know what to expect or who they might lose in a firefight.

"Nothing," Danzig reported while walking toward Max and Crip. When he reached them, he stopped and raised one eyebrow.

"It's buried." Crip stomped his foot. It felt like solid ground. The breeze was long gone, but a scent drifted through the area, a combination of an earthy aura and shipboard ozone.

"The villagers are up." Max drew his stunner. "And they don't look happy."

Crip held his hands over his head and shouted, "We don't want to hurt any of you."

"The battle is joined," Max whispered out the side of his mouth. It wasn't what Crip wanted to hear, but it was true.

"Get 'em!" the old man yelled, and the villagers ran toward them.

The sizzle and pop of the stunners filled the dead space between the shouts of the villagers. The first to near the team tumbled to the ground, but unlike last time when they were tentative, they kept charging, unperturbed by the stunners. Some dropped, but the others reached the closest soldiers and overwhelmed them.

Two soldiers disappeared under the onslaught. The arc and buzz of the stunners fell silent under the writhing mass of bodies.

"Time to fight like adults," Max growled. He unslung his rifle and fired into the air, then blasted a villager away from one of his soldiers, then another and another. "Back up, or we'll kill you all."

Three Malibor bled into the dirt of the ruins. The trauma on their bodies from the point-blank shots left no doubt that they were dead.

The pulse rifle's launch system roared with more noise than the villagers were used to. Max fired into the ground in front of them to back them up. The three dead got the attention of the rest. They were horrified by the violence in their village, from the Borwyn and from themselves.

Two soldiers waded into the villagers and pushed them away from their team members. The soldiers staggered out, faces swelling from the beatings, noses and cracked lips bleeding.

One soldier raised his rifle.

"Cease fire!" Crip called before the man could exact revenge for the damage done to him. The commander moved between the two groups. "There's been enough killing. Stand down."

The villagers couldn't take their eyes off their dead.

"We only wanted to talk," Crip continued angrily. "How do we get below?" He motioned at the ground with the barrel of his weapon.

"You don't." The young girl who had raised the alarm stuck her head out from behind one of the older members of the group. "This is it. What you see."

The cryptic message left the commander with questions. There was something underground. Was it a buried power plant or a radioactive source that had powered a functioning plant? He wasn't sure he would ever discover the truth.

"There *is* something below the ground, something with power that we could see from orbit. We want to make sure of two things. First, that it's not a threat to us, and second, that it's not a threat to you."

The old man spoke again. "We've been living here for a while now, and no one died until you showed up." He seemed older than before. The stunner had not been kind.

"True." Crip walked away from the bodies so the villagers wouldn't have to see them while he was talking. He shrugged. "Time to go. I'm scrubbing the mission."

He hatcheted a hand to his left, around the villagers, and headed toward the lander.

Max moved close, challenging them to attack as his pulse rifle drew a figure eight in the air between them. The villagers didn't move. The shattered bodies created a barrier the Malibor weren't willing to cross. Six dead on the day the Borwyn arrived.

They hadn't gotten their answers, and they hadn't opened relations. Fifty years couldn't dampen the hatred.

The Borwyn and the Malibor were still at war.

CHAPTER 6

As much as we wish it were otherwise, war remained.

"We lost Engineer Nanticoke," Alby transmitted to the ship. "Killed opening a hatch to the interior. We're continuing our exploration of the platform."

Silence was the reply. He thought about repeating the message but decided against it. He pulled himself toward the opposite side, where the booby-trapped hatch had cost him one of his team members.

The comm crackled. "Jaq here. What happened?"

"Nanticoke tried to access a hatch before anyone could provide a second set of eyes. It's my fault. I didn't set the expectation that no one was to move to Phase Two of the operation until I cleared it."

"It's war, Battle Commander. Even a war from fifty years ago. War is dangerous because it's meant to kill people. An old weapons platform that should have been safe isn't. Big surprise."

"I'm glad we didn't bring it on board. We're continuing our survey for the next ninety minutes. It has materials we want to recover, like precision-machined railgun magnets, bundles of copper, and a mesh I'd like to study more. That's before going inside and seeing what kinds of control panels and circuitry are driving this thing."

"Please take care." Jaq Hunter spoke softly. "There's nothing on that thing that's worth the loss of any more of our people."

"I'll be back in touch when we're finished or time runs out, whichever comes first." Alby closed the channel to the ship and opened the group channel.

"No one touches anything without a second set of eyes confirming it's safe. If there are any questions, call me, and I'll make the decision. I'm responsible, so if there's a risk, it's mine to take. I'm on my way to the access point. Fresnor, stand by."

"Roger," the engineer replied. She hooked her fingers into the mesh and stared at the opening that had cost the team her tether partner. He'd driven the mobility pack. She wasn't sure of her abilities with it. She'd broach that with the battle commander when he arrived.

In another minute, Alby reached the opening. He stopped and stared into the void, trying to locate Nanticoke, but the two halves of the engineer and the hatch were too far from the platform to be seen by the naked eye. He was long gone. His burial in space was complete.

Alby turned his lights and attention to the hatch and the open space within. He produced a small wrench and dragged it along the edge of the opening, looking for other traps that would be triggered by the Borwyn's intrusion. Nothing happened.

"Was it poor luck? An inordinate buildup of pressure behind the hatch?" Alby asked.

"I think so. Bad luck, and he was right in front of it instead of off to the side. Battle Commander, I don't think I can drive the mobility pack."

"We'll take care of it, Fresnor. Don't worry. We'll get you back to the ship. But first, let's go inside. Don't touch anything."

She shook her head and intertwined her hands more tightly with the mesh.

"Godbolt, are you back there?" Alby kicked off the platform while hanging on, which pointed his face away from the hatch. Godbolt was two meters away. "Good. We're going in."

"Nothing would make me happier," Godbolt deadpanned, continuing to move toward the battle commander.

With one gloved hand gripping the frame tightly, Alby entered the open space. He stayed steady to keep his lights focused on the interior of the weapons platform. The passage was just wide enough for him and his suit. Panels lined both sides for the full ten meters of the interior. There were no side passages, only the main transit down the length of the rectangular platform.

"Going in." The commander eased into the passage before activating his magnetic clamps, then held his breath and closed his eyes. When he opened them, he was pleased that he was still alive. He didn't know what he'd been expecting.

He shook off his trepidation and moved to the first panel, then released the manual lock and slowly opened the panel. Inside, he found technology from the old days. It had been cutting edge fifty years prior, but the system had failed. He studied the symbols long enough to understand that the circuits would activate if power was restored. He flipped the switches to open the connections and create a gap that would stymy the flow of energy through the system.

Going from one panel to the next, he shut the system down. At the end, he found the power source—a miniaturized reactor without a core. "What happened to you?"

"Nothing," Godbolt replied.

"I was talking to this little gem. With a small amount of

radioactive material, we could bring it back to life, but why is the core missing? What did the Malibor do with it? Too bad we're out of time. We won't learn why. Not right now, anyway." He switched to the ship's channel and transmitted, "Request to bring the platform on board. All systems have been manually shut down. The weapons platform is safe."

"No one is going anywhere. We have a ship inbound," the captain replied. "Looks like a Malibor gunship."

The captain stood in Engineering, fixated on the sensor data. A ship, inbound from the void between the sixth and fifth planetary orbits. Had it come from Septimus or its twin planet Sairvor? Had it come from Farslor's twin Fristen, the planet where the Malibor originated? Or had it been in orbit around Farslor all along?

Those questions needed answers, and for all she knew, Jaq had the entirety of her race on board. She activated the ship-wide comm. "All hands, we have an inbound Malibor gunship. Assume your battle stations and prepare for combat."

A frightened-looking junior engineer stared at the screen.

The captain snapped her fingers in front of the young woman's eyes until she got her attention. "Despite my best effort to give the chief engineer some time off, we need him. Recall him and have a hot pack of kava waiting when he gets here."

The captain trusted the junior engineer to follow orders. Jaq pushed off and flew down the corridor to the central access shaft. In zero-gee, the elevator was inoperable, so the crew pulled themselves up or down the shaft. It made movement around the ship easier. She went up the shaft and past the primary and secondary communications and power conduits to the mid-ship deck where the bridge was located.

She flew onto the bridge and clamped her boots to the deck so she could stand, then turned to her battle commander. His station was empty. Her second's seat was too.

Jaq laughed. Fifty years in the making and the first combat engagement with the enemy was going to take place without two of the top three. Without three of the top four if the chief engineer couldn't be roused.

"Tram, you're the battle commander." She motioned for him to change positions. There were more systems linked to the commander's console, and he would need to access them all. "Comm, get me Commander Risor."

The channel crackled. "Alby, you guys need to hunker down. I'm taking the ship out. We can't be a stationary target."

"I know, and I'm sorry to miss it. We'll continue to study the weapons platform and try to figure out why they depowered it. Don't forget we're here. We have about nine hours of life support left. Otherwise, we're going to have real problems."

"I know. We'll be back before you run out of air. Just in case, I'm going to drop a lander for you. If nothing else, take it to the surface of Farslor. Gotta run, Alby. Keep your head up."

The channel closed before the battle commander could respond.

The captain had cut it short because she had contact with the combat team on the planet's surface.

"The Malibor are here, but they're like cavemen. No technology. The power source is buried, with no hope of getting to it without major excavations. We don't have that kind of time since the locals are hostile. We tried to talk with them, but they blame us for all their problems. Did we nuke Farslor after the final battle?"

"What? No. We didn't nuke any colonies. We couldn't. The ship was barely alive. By the way, good timing on your contact. A Malibor gunship is inbound. Hold tight on the planet until we give the all-clear and can confirm that we'll be in a stable orbit for your return."

"What if you don't give the all-clear?" Crip wasn't a fan of the inevitable answer.

"Then you better learn to live with the locals." Captain Hunter closed the channel. She didn't have time to talk more. *Chrysalis* needed to get underway to stymy long-range gunfire.

"All hands, this is the captain. We'll be getting underway for our first trial by combat. Into your seats and prepare for high-gee maneuvers. All department heads confirm status. We push in thirty seconds."

The status board showed red across the ship. Then a green light confirmed the mess deck had been shut down and the serving crew was secure. One by one, over the next ten seconds, everything turned green. Only Engineering was red.

The captain settled into her seat and tapped her screen to get a direct channel to Engineering.

"Thought you were going to start this without me?" the chief engineer answered.

The department flashed green.

"Nope. Thanks for trying to get some rest. All things being equal, this should be over quickly. Prepare for full speed."

"When have all things ever been equal?"

The captain closed the channel before the chief engineer could draw her into an extended philosophical debate. Just like with the ground combat team and the engineering team on the platform, she didn't have time to tell him what he knew.

Take care of the mission. Take care of his people. She'd already lost one member of her crew, and she had no intention of losing more. The crew was the hardest thing to replace, the most finite of resources.

"Thrust Control, accelerate all ahead full, three gees max. Nav, begin evasive maneuvers as soon as we pass two hundred meters per second. Bring us to vector zero-niner-seven, star angle plus two. When we have a firing solution, fire as many E-mags as we can bring to bear."

"Targeting, lead and bracketing. Stand by to fire. Defensive systems, be on the lookout for inbound missiles. Sensors, dial up the sensitivity. No surprises!" The stand-in battle commander had slid into his role and demonstrated that no one was indispensable, not even the captain.

She listened and watched. She'd given the orders, and it was time for the crew to do their jobs. Power was at ninety-four percent.

It's only one gunship, she thought. She was afraid to lose the "new" feel of the ship, even though it was far from new. It had been repaired to be better than it was, but maybe not. That concerned her more than anything else. What if they couldn't recover from damage?

Jaq clamped her jaw shut and held on. *Chrysalis* charged to three gees acceleration. The ship twisted when the thrusters changed orientation. The main engines kicked it down the new vectors. *Chrysalis* slid through a series of maneuvers, working its way closer to the captain's designated course.

The second the ship assumed its course, the battle commander reported, "First salvo is on its way. Maintaining a steady rate of fire."

The ship hummed with the launch of sixty penetrator rounds a second from the massive E-mags at the inbound gunship.

The Malibor ship started evasive maneuvers.

Chrysalis clung to the front of the acceleration curve. Navigation tweaked the controls to spiral down the line of approach.

Their thirteen-year-old sensor operator, Dolly Norton, was the first to see incoming ordnance. "E-mag rounds inbound. On-screen." The main screen flashed to show the trajectory. Dolly's voice was loud but still that of a little girl.

The captain didn't care about the ensign's voice. They'd all been thrust into their roles before they were ready since the original crew had died young because of the trials they'd suffered during the escape and survival phases.

"E-mags are holding. Maintaining sustained fire. Bringing four cannons to bear," Tram announced.

"Very well." The captain felt like she needed to say something, though nothing was required. The crew worked as they were supposed to. "Tram, what are your thoughts on this gunship?"

Tram Stamper smacked his lips. "Checking us out. The big question is, from where? If he came from Septimus, he wouldn't be here yet. He wasn't in orbit. The first gunship looked like it was abandoned. If they come at us one at a time, I'm good with that."

The ship hummed with the continued E-mag firing. It provided a level of comfort to the captain to know that the ship was delivering the weapons they'd worked so hard to develop. The air handler kicked in for ten seconds of droning, then powered down.

"Reduce acceleration to two gees. All ahead full, new course vector one-two-eight, star angle plus three. Tram, prepare for a single missile. I don't want to tap-dance with that ship. I want it dead."

"No tap-dancing, roger. Maybe a good game of mumblety-peg." The stand-in battle commander chuckled as he worked his controls against the lessening gee forces while Thrust Control throttled back. "Target is locked. Range twenty thousand kilometers. Waiting for optimal range of ten thousand."

Incoming fire forced Nav to repeatedly adjust their heading, veering off the captain's desired course. Survivability was paramount.

"New course, zero-niner-seven, star angle plus four, Mary. Fast as she'll go, Ferd."

Mary Minshaw, the navigator, tapped quickly, preferring the tactile interface to the visual one. "Coming to course zero-niner-seven, star angle plus four."

Ferd tapped the thruster controls to drive the ship to and along the new course.

The ship groaned with the hard turn. Two gee acceleration across a lateral orientation added to the stress on their bodies. The crew settled into their seats during the maneuver, unable to do much other than breathe while tightening their muscles to keep the blood flowing.

They came out of the maneuver after twenty seconds.

"Target is accelerating away," Dolly shouted against the crush of gees.

The main screen showed the distance between the ships increasing.

"Launch the missile," the captain ordered.

"Pausing E-mags. Fire." Tram mashed the virtual button. The missile was electromagnetically ejected into space. Then the liquid oxygen rocket motor kicked in and accelerated the weapon toward the Malibor gunship.

All eyes watched the maneuver play out while the missile slowly flew toward its target.

Tram maintained a running report. "Resuming E-mag fire."

Shooting down one's own missile would be poor form. It would also cost them one of their precious missiles. Those were another finite resource, not as bad as personnel, but not something to be wasted.

The E-mag rounds narrowed the gunship's escape routes, driving it toward the missile's engagement envelope.

"Brace for impact!" Dolly's voice no longer sounded small. The ominous warning came as a clanging bell echoed throughout the ship.

Jaq had dreaded this moment. She'd heard it called "blooding the crew." Taking their first battle damage. She had no time to ponder the implications. A heavy thud reverberated through the hull, though the gel in her seat kept the impact from shaking her very bones. She tensed harder than was required to tolerate the gee forces.

From the corner of her eye, she saw the single missile veer off-course. Her heart sank into her stomach. Before nausea overwhelmed her, the missile returned to its lethal course and signaled that it had gone terminal, adding kinetic energy to the warhead's yield.

A ping and a thud, then five more E-mag rounds struck for seven total impacts on *Chrysalis*.

"Damage report!" Jaq would have jumped to her feet if they weren't maneuvering.

"Impact!" Tram stated.

"No damage is showing on the board," the environmental control station shouted into the din on the command deck.

Jaq gritted her teeth. The icon on the main screen showed that the gunship was now debris traveling on a slow ballistic trajectory toward Farslor's upper atmosphere.

"Target is destroyed," Tram announced. The battle commander pulled up readouts from the sensor team. "Keep your eyes peeled. No surprises."

The sensor chief replied, "We're on it. Refining our parameters and changing the sweeps. Deep space takes priority over the planet."

Jaq checked the numbers. Available energy had dropped to seventy-eight percent. Environmental Control showed the air at one hundred percent. Despite the impacts, the ship had not lost atmosphere.

"Nav, instigate a flight route around the planet that will slow us down using the least amount of energy and gets us to the weapons platform to pick up our people before they run out of air."

The navigator turned the big ship toward the planet while requesting a short acceleration. "We'll slow on the far side of the planet. Two hours to the platform. Energy cost is three percent."

The captain itched to get out of her seat, but the ship accelerated to two and a half gees before the main engines idled. *Chrysalis* raced toward the upper atmosphere, but thanks to the lessons learned from previous orbits, the ship flew above the turbulence.

"Ninety minutes to braking maneuver," Nav stated. She knew the captain wanted to get out of her seat and pace in the restored zero-gee.

"Get damage control teams to the outer shell and look for holes. I can't believe nothing penetrated. All hands, set Condition Two throughout the ship."

Condition Two was first step toward normalcy from Condition One, battle stations. In Condition Two, the bulkheads were raised and system diagnostics were run to update the ship's status on environmental controls and weapons and everything between except the mess deck. The chow line would be closed until the ship returned to Condition Three, standard readiness when the ship was underway. The mess deck hands were members of damage control teams since they weren't actively engaged with the ship during combat operations.

Teams maneuvered through the corridors quickly under zero-gee. They systematically checked their assigned areas and reported up the chain of command.

The captain floated free around the command deck, sharing

smiles and nods with each of the crew. They'd survived combat, and the only cost they'd had to pay was in power. They'd rebuild their energy stores by spending time. They needed peace for eight hours to return to one hundred percent.

"Nav, calculate the best trajectory for the combat team to meet us in the vicinity of the weapons platform."

"Calculating." Mary Minshaw worked the numbers and sent them to Ferdinand Alpinist at Thrust Control for verification.

He checked the calculations and gave her the thumbs-up. "Flight profile calculated and transmitted to Lander Control."

The captain loomed over her chair and tapped the comm for a direct link to Lander Control. Whenever a lander was off the ship, the policy was that the remote pilot remained in position. That was where she found him.

"I have the flight profile. Entering it now. I'll need the combat team on the ship and ready to take off in fifteen minutes if we're to make this window." The remote pilot didn't waste time with pleasantries. He needed the captain's help.

"I'll contact them directly." Jaq tapped her comm once more. "Commander Castle, please respond."

Silence was her only reply.

CHAPTER 7

Confront, consolidate, and move on. The battle won't favor those who stand still.

Crip jogged on, despite how tired he felt. The entire combat team was dragging, doing little more than throwing one foot in front of the other. Once the decision to retrograde had been made, there was no reason to waste time. What Crip hadn't taken into account was the toll the gravity would take when combined with the trials of multiple engagements.

The only answer they'd gotten was that the Malibor weren't a threat, even on the ground. Farslor was no longer an outpost. The people on the planet had been abandoned like the equipment in orbit.

Sergeant Tremayne's team wouldn't return with in-depth answers, but they would return.

A tendril of smoke from the vicinity of the lander caught Crip's eye. "What's going on up there?" Newfound energy drove his legs, and he raced in front of the rest of the team.

They saw the smoke and followed with equal zeal.

Getting trapped on cold Farslor wasn't in their plan. They had no more than three days' worth of food and water.

The crack of a pulse rifle drifted through the air.

The team lost its cohesion on the wild run toward the ship. Crip was the first to stumble and fall into a dry streambed from a bygone epoch. The soldier behind him landed on top of him. Two cleared the drop but stopped and returned to the others.

Max was the first up, and he scrambled through the scrub up to the level plain. "Keep an eye out," he ordered the two soldiers who'd returned before helping the others across one by one. He designated one soldier and pointed at the others, gesturing them into position. "Inverted V. You're on point."

"Sorry about that," Crip muttered.

Max slapped him on the back. "You act like it's your first time in combat."

The group returned to a slow jog. Max and Crip both realized they weren't as tired as they'd been.

"Business as usual, Max." The commander lowered his voice. "It's not as easy as the training manuals suggest."

"Not in the least. 'Eye-opening' is the phrase you're looking for."

They struggled for deep breaths from their exertions, which ended the conversation. The smoke grew darker as they closed on the lander.

A flurry of arrows greeted the soldier on point. He tried to dodge, but it was too late.

"Stunners!" Crip shouted.

"Stunners only," Max confirmed.

Gilmore went down. Two other soldiers fired their rifles into the ground before rotating the weapons to their backs and pulling their stunners.

"Report!" Max worked his way to the front of the inverted V.

The first soldier he ran across waved his hand in front of his face, the hand signal that he hadn't seen anything.

Max moved forward in a crouch until he reached the fallen soldier. One arrow had hit him in the throat, just above his body armor. The blood had gurgled out through the tear and was still dripping, but the soldier had no pulse. Max fought the urge to rage against the locals.

What if he and his team had to stay here? This wasn't a war he desired since killing them all seemed like the only viable option if he wanted to guarantee his people's safety.

It was a viable but deplorable option. Being on the combat team was a position of honor and one they had aspired to. At that moment, on the planet's surface, looking at his decades-old friend, he realized why the position was held in such high esteem.

It was hard, harder than he'd ever imagined. Close-quarters combat wasn't glorious. It was messy, and people died. It was dirty. He was worn down physically and emotionally. No training could have prepared him for how deep he had to dig within himself. One couldn't exercise what they'd learned in such a short time on Farslor. All they could do was train to be miserable and still fight, but they hadn't done that.

His lip twitched as he summoned the adrenaline he had left. One final fight to clear the way to the lander.

Crip appeared at Max's side. "The battle is joined," he whispered.

"Victory is ours," was the programmed reply, though Max didn't feel like they'd won anything. No one did. "The battle..." His thought trailed off.

The commander rested a hand on his friend's shoulder, then shouted at the scrub in front of them.

"I'm going to stand up. Don't shoot me since we'll shoot

back with everything we've got. We don't want to kill any more Malibor. There's been enough death already."

Crip put his stunner away and slowly stood. He kept one arm in front of his face and neck, limiting access to a killing strike, offering his protected chest as the largest target.

"Parlay! Send someone to talk with me, and I'll meet them halfway."

"You can offer us nothing we didn't have before you arrived," a Malibor voice shouted back.

"We can offer our departure from your planet, but you are standing between us and our ship. The smoke suggests you tried to burn us out, which means you want us to stay. If we stay, we're going to fight you. If we fight you, we will win."

Crip pulled his pulse rifle around to the front. He blasted the ground in front of where he assumed the Malibor were hiding and stitched a line to the left, then to the right of that point.

His pulse rifle sent a small shock into his hand, signaling that the power pack was at its limit. In a well-practiced maneuver, he released the energy module and let it fall to the ground. He slipped one of his four spares into the empty slot until it clicked home. He bent at the knees to dip low enough to pick up the spent power pack and secure it in a pouch.

They didn't have enough spares to leave anything behind.

"Parlay!" Crip repeated. "I won't shoot whoever comes forward." He cracked a few more rounds into the air.

A Malibor hunter rose. He wasn't a soldier like Sergeant Tremayne and his team. He wore heavy furs and carried a bow with a half-full quiver.

Crip slung his rifle and walked slowly forward, glancing down to place his feet where he wouldn't trip. He stopped when the Malibor was three meters away. They looked each other over. The hunter couldn't comprehend the strange trappings of the Borwyn soldier, but he respected what he saw.

He knew he was outclassed and that he would die in a fight. That fear was obvious in his stance and expression. Crip realized the Malibor were like the Borwyn. Had circumstances been different, he wouldn't have been able to tell the hunter from one of the soldiers. He thought that was important to share.

"We're not so different, you and me," the commander started. "We're trying to do right by our people and survive until tomorrow. You live down here while we live up there."

Crip tipped his chin toward the sky. "All we want is to get home. There's no reason for us to kill each other down here. This is your planet. We have no claim on it. We only wanted to see what was generating the power near your village."

The Malibor shook his head. "We don't live there. Bad spirits." He pointed in the opposite direction, past the lander. Black smoke continued to rise and curl around the ship.

"Bad spirits. I can see that." Crip kicked at the dirt. "We only want to get to our ship and leave. We'll take our injured with us."

"He's not injured. He's dead." The Malibor said it matter-of-factly, not as a boast or a challenge.

"I know. Injured in the line of duty. Died on the battlefield. For what it's worth, I'm sorry about the three of yours who got killed."

"That's why we're here. They didn't return. Our people return, or we find them."

"No one left behind. It's a good policy. It makes it easier to wade into battle if you know your body won't be left to rot. Peace of mind."

"Peace of mind." The Malibor glanced around, then

motioned. Two others stood, arrows nocked, but the bowstrings were not drawn back.

"What are the furs you wear? We didn't see any big animals around here. We didn't see *any* animals, not even rodents. No sources of meat." Crip avoided breathing through his nose because of the Malibor's rank smell. It was like they didn't have enough water to bathe.

"They are out here. You make much noise. No wonder you didn't see them. They heard you coming and hid."

"I don't doubt that. We didn't plan on being low profile. We wanted to find the power source we detected and whether the Malibor were still here. You are, but in much smaller numbers than we expected. We didn't drop any bombs on Farslor. That wasn't us."

"Excuse me if I don't believe you." The hunter snorted and sought equal derision from the others.

"It most definitely wasn't us since none of us were alive during the battle for primacy, but I don't think it was our ancestors either. Our ship was heavily damaged at Septimus, and that's a long way from here. We barely survived to make repairs, and it took fifty long years before we could come back. What do you say we start a new trend where we stop hating each other for whatever transgressions were in the past?"

"We have always hated the Borwyn, and here you are again, killing our people. Nothing has changed."

"Everything has changed. You've lost your technology while ours has improved. We're also willing to talk. I'm not going to threaten you. Your bows are no match for our weapons, even though you managed to kill one of ours. He was a good man with a wife and a child. Will that child grow up hating the Malibor?"

"He should. He's *our* enemy."

"*She's* not your enemy." Fatigue threatened to overwhelm

Crip, but he couldn't show how tired he was. The Malibor wouldn't respect weakness. The commander waved his hands. "Stand up, people. We're going to the ship, and we're getting out of here."

"We haven't said you could go."

"The first thing you said was that you didn't want us here, so we'll be leaving. Without further bloodshed, if you don't mind. No one else needs to die."

Crip offered his hand. The Malibor looked like he wanted to hock a spit bomb into it, but the commander stepped closer.

"Go on, take it. Let this be the first of the last. If Private Gilmore is the last to die in this war, let that be his honor and how we will remember him."

The Malibor took Crip's hand and squeezed as hard as he could. His grip was firmer than the commander's, but he didn't let up. The Malibor dug his ragged nails into the back of Crip's hand, but still, the commander didn't let up or compromise his integrity on what should have been a simple handshake.

In war, nothing was simple. Crip finally had enough and pushed the Malibor's hand away. "Nothing personal, but I hope we never meet again. If we do, please, talk first, shoot later."

"No promises, Borwyn."

"I hear you, Malibor. No promises." Crip motioned for the team to pass the three hunters to his left.

One of the team stopped and kneeled next to Gilmore's body. He pulled the dead soldier into a sitting position, then eased him over his shoulder to carry him back to the lander.

The team slipped past, stunners still in their hands. Crip waved and walked away, not looking back at the Malibor. He tensed, still expecting an arrow. Nothing vital was exposed, but he didn't want to take an arrow in the back of his leg or arm. No arrow came.

He'd made enough of an impression that the hunters didn't

attack when his back was turned, or maybe the Malibor respected their superior firepower. Commander Castle wouldn't learn the reason, not this day. He hurried toward the lander when they were out of bowshot.

Max was waiting for him in the burned scrub, the source of the smoke. The torched undergrowth didn't reach the lander. The ship was safe. Andreeson and Binfall peered at him from within the open hatch.

"They came at us," Binfall explained. "We needed better cover."

Andreeson had turned gray and had a slight sheen of sweat on his face, and bags showed deeply under his darkened eyes. Binfall crossed from his side of the hatch to help Andreeson stand.

"He's got a fever. I think the arrow wound is infected," Binfall said in Crip's direction.

"I'm sure there are bugs on this planet we've never been exposed to before. Report any cuts and let's get them cleaned out." Crip glanced at his own arms and those of his teammate, Sergeant Tremayne.

The team made way for the soldier carrying Gilmore to use the ramp first and strap the body into a seat.

Crip tapped the soldier with the comm unit. "Get me the *Chrysalis*."

"Inside the ship. We'll link direct." He hurried up the steps and into the lander. Less than a minute later, he called for the commander. "They tried to call us about thirty minutes ago."

"We weren't in a position to answer." Crip shrugged. There was nothing he could do about the past.

The soldier stepped aside to give the commander access to the comm panel embedded in the bulkhead of the lander.

"This is Commander Crip Castle calling *Chrysalis*. Please respond."

The soldier looked sideways at him as if the crew of *Chrysalis* wouldn't respond when they heard a call from their people.

"Hey, Crip. Jaq here. You missed your return window. You'll need to wait another day before an optimal launch window opens."

The comm crackled, then went silent.

Crip shook his head. "I'm not sure that's going to be possible. We have a fragile but temporary truce with the locals. They won't be so keen on us staying."

"What's your fuel recharge status?"

"We're at eighty-five percent and climbing. System shows another hour to one hundred percent."

"Stand by."

Crip envisioned the captain requesting a new flight profile for the lander with a launch in an hour. A hundred percent would get them into orbit and give them an additional fifty percent to maneuver back to the ship, but that would leave the lander unusable until more oxygen was found to refill its tanks.

When the captain returned, she delivered her best offer. "In eight hours, you'll be able to launch and maintain minimal burn after you reach orbit for one turn around the planet before slowing down and marrying up with *Chrysalis*. Our calculations show you'll have forty percent fuel remaining upon arrival. That is acceptable. Any earlier launch would deplete the fuel to a level we consider unacceptable."

"Eight hours it is. I better go outside and talk with the locals. I'll send my report when I return, but the command summary is that we lost one soldier, Gilmore. Andreeson is injured and requires medical attention because the arrow wound is infected. We ended up killing a number of the locals after they attacked us. The locals have degraded on the evolutionary scale to little more than cavemen. The energy source is buried and inaccessible. End of report."

"That's not the most optimistic report I've ever heard," Jaq replied. "You were the first...the Malibor. It's not a surprise...in a fight...death."

The comm cut in and out, and Crip asked the captain to repeat the last. The ship traveled beyond the horizon. The crackle ended when the signal was lost.

"Well, that wasn't what we wanted to hear. Max, establish a watch of two people on and everyone else resting. Take a better look at Andreeson, and I'll see if I can make contact with the Malibor again to update them."

"You shouldn't go alone." Max pointed at Danzig.

The soldier stepped into the hatch, blocking the way out. When he received the nod from Sergeant Tremayne, he stepped down the stairs.

Crip leaned close. "I'm exhausted, Max. I'll try to talk to him, then come back. Put me on the first shift, two hours. We'll let the others get some sleep first. I'm sure they're worse off than I am."

"Not really, but we only have eight able bodies and that includes you and me. I'll stand watch with you, Crip, before we turn it over to the next shift. Here." He palmed a packet from the lander's storage cabinet, a packet of kava syrup. The drink was condensed to the consistency of toothpaste. The rush of caffeine gave them the taste but not the texture. They were told they could mix it with water, but no one had ever taken the time to try it.

Crip accepted it, unscrewed the top, and squeezed the entire packet into his mouth. He chewed and swallowed, then screwed the lid back on and handed the packet back to the sergeant.

No waste. That was how they were raised and how they'd stayed alive.

"Let's see what there is to see, Danzig."

The commander tapped the man's shoulder, and the soldier led the way off the lander.

Max filled the space behind them, using the hatch's frame to protect most of his body. He held his stunner, and his pulse rifle was within easy reach.

Ten meters from the lander, Crip yelled, "Hey, Malibor! The ship's broken. It'll be about eight hours before we can take off. Don't get mad!"

Crip cupped his hands around his mouth and repeated the message in multiple directions. He continued into the scrub another fifty meters. An arrow whispered through the air, thudded into his chest protector, and fell harmlessly to the ground.

"Come on! Don't be a jag."

The Malibor stood up a mere ten meters away. "You make too much noise, Borwyn."

Crip chuckled. "I probably do. Maybe that's why my love interest won't marry me."

"She has a choice?" The Malibor held his bow loosely while walking forward.

"Of course. Yours don't?" Crip had never had to contemplate cultural differences. Growing up on a ship insulated them from variations of what they understood as normal.

"Women are the only reason we survive. Men get killed too easily. Why aren't you dead?"

Crip rapped his ballistic protection with his knuckles. The thuds were less than impressive. He picked up the arrow and tossed it to the Malibor.

"Eight hours. Then we'll leave."

The Malibor shook his head. "I don't know what eight hours

is. Sounds like it'll be after nightfall, though. You don't want to be out here in the dark if you don't know what you're doing."

Crip checked the sky and how far Armanor's star had traveled across it since their arrival. "It'll be well after dark. It'll get cold, no?"

"Too cold for you. You need furs."

"Are you willing to trade?"

The Malibor pointed at the pulse rifle. "For one of those, I'll give you my fur."

"We can't do that. I signed for this rifle. The supply officer will have my butt if I don't return it."

"Why would someone want your butt?"

Crip wondered if he was being intentionally obtuse, but the Malibor had degraded from what the Borwyn considered to be a civilized society where one could talk in a way that came across as uncivilized. He was taken aback.

It jarred his mind. Who was more civilized?

"No one wants my butt. It's just a stupid saying. I can't trade my pulse rifle. We'll have to button up our ship and ride out the cold until we can launch. You'll see us and hear us, no matter how far away you are. You think I'm noisy? Just wait until our ship shreds the air on its return trip to space. I apologize in advance for the damage it'll do to the calm of a Farslor night."

"Our nights are calm and cold. The stars wink. The crystalline frost settles. Fire streaks mar the sky."

They were standing in the middle of the scorched scrub. Crip couldn't see the Malibor starting the fire. He suspected it had been his people, shooting their pulse rifles at the ghostlike enemy.

"Fire streaks. Meteors? Stones and debris burning up on reentry. We'll try not to add to that. When we reach escape velocity, we'll simply disappear into outer space."

"There are stories that we too lived among the stars. Is it true?"

"Only one star." Crip glanced at the glowing orange ball tracking across the sky. "We both lived on planets, but we worked in space. The Malibor had outposts on multiple planets and moons." He kicked the blackened dirt. The untainted ground beneath covered the char. "I better get back. We'll button up and be out of here tonight."

Crip wanted to disengage. He could stay out there and talk as long as the Malibor hunter was willing, but the commander was bone-tired and barely able to stand. His eyes betrayed him by trying to close and send him to sleep while he was still on his feet. He waved since he wasn't up for another hand-crushing contest and walked away.

Danzig followed, putting his body between the Malibor and the commander. For the second time, they left the engagement without further conflict. The Malibor had known the arrow wouldn't penetrate the body armor. He'd shot it to show what he was capable of.

Maybe he had watched the first three hunters engage the combat team and seen Max cut down the one who had launched the first arrow into Crip's chest and the follow-up fire that had killed the hunting party.

Crip gestured for Danzig to walk beside him. The soldier did so reluctantly, continually glancing over his shoulder at where the hunter had been. The area was empty, with no sign of movement.

"The battle is joined, but it's not the battle we were expecting," Crip remarked.

"Not at all. These guys are no threat to us. Well, we lost Gilmore, but we could have killed all the Malibor without blinking an eye. That's not what I imagined it would be like."

Danzig had been cerebral about the idea of ground combat, but the reality had been a shock.

"More glory, fewer boots on the ground?" Crip suggested with a tired smile.

"I don't care about boots on the ground. Maybe it was the glory. Being elite."

"We are, and we have to continue to be, the elite soldiers *Chrysalis* needs. We're the only ones in our generation with any experience fighting the Malibor. That's a big responsibility. We have to refine our processes for when we meet the next bunch.

"Who knows? They might have pulse rifles. But Farslor? This planet isn't a threat. We may not have found allies here, but someday, they could be our friends."

They reached the hatch.

"Did he shoot you?" Max asked.

"He did, but it was just to show us he was watching from somewhere we couldn't see."

"That ditch we fell into. The dry streambed. They're using it to move since it keeps them below the scrub." Max wasn't guessing.

It had been clear to the sergeant, but Crip was too tired to have seen it for himself.

"Get some rest, people." Crip let Danzig through. "Two hours, then next shift."

As soldiers do, the group sprawled throughout the lander's cabin. Many were asleep in less than a minute.

"I say we close and secure the hatch, set a proximity alarm, and catch some sleep," Max suggested. "We can only see about one-third of what we need to see. They can't get in, although they could make trouble. How confident are you that they'll leave us alone?"

"Even though he shot me, I think the Malibor is a man of his word." Crip nodded tightly. Despite the kava he'd consumed earlier, he was barely able to keep his eyes open. "I don't think I've ever been this tired in my whole life."

"The gravity and the air. We're not used to it, yet we acted like we were invulnerable." Max glanced at the seat Gilmore was strapped into. "Obviously, we're not, but you know what we are?"

Max waited for Crip to shrug one shoulder. The commander didn't know the answer.

"We're the best we've got, and we're only going to get better."

"That's how I see it. Secure the hatch. It's time to declare victory and bag some zees. Tomorrow will be a long day too, but different. I need to find out what *Chrysalis* has been up to. I hope I didn't lose my job while I was down here with the combat team."

CHAPTER 8

Victory will belong to those who are last to commit their power reserves.

Jaq Hunter climbed into her seat to prepare for the braking maneuver.

Nav counted down. When she reached zero, the ship bounced and jerked from grazing the upper atmosphere. The sudden slowing threw the command deck crew against their restraints. *Chrysalis* came out of the turbulence, then dove back in steeper and rougher.

The captain took short, choppy breaths to get through the worst of it. The ship seemed to float out of the last of it as it returned to the calm of space.

"Inverting," Mary called from the navigation console. The ship rotated on its transverse axis until the aft end pointed in the direction of travel.

Thrust Control, Ferdinand Alpinist, reported the next action. "Main engines firing in three, two, one."

The crew wedged into the gel of their chairs as a hundred thousand tons of ship slowed from the main engines burning against the momentum. Two minutes stretched to three before Ferdinand updated the crew.

"Cutting main engines. Thrusters only." The ship slowed until zero-gee returned. "Forward momentum is zero. Position in space is five hundred meters from the weapons platform."

"Well done!" the captain cheered, unhooking herself and pushing free. She floated out of her chair, grabbed a rail with one hand, and tapped her comm unit with the other. "Alby, this is Jaq. How is your team holding up?"

The reply was crystal-clear. "We had to wedge inside the platform and tape ourselves in to preserve heat since the bleed was too great in open space when we are trying to conserve power. Outside of that, it'll be nice to be home."

"If you look outside, we're sitting opposite the access hatch if I read the scans properly." She glanced at the power meter. Sixty-eight percent. They'd used more than estimated. They were going to be idle for a while. "We'll be making like a hole in the sky while we recharge. Bring your people home."

"On our way," Alby replied. "We're also bringing the platform. I'm confident it's safe."

"Cut that garbage out of there and let's go home," Alby told the team.

Only the closest person had access, but she made short work of the tape and the two panels they removed. She passed the panels behind her. The next engineer dutifully reattached them.

The first eased out until she could grab the mesh that surrounded the platform. She headed for her mobility pack. The others followed one by one.

They'd talked about what needed to happen when the ship returned. The only thing left was to execute the plan.

Once outside, it took fifteen minutes for them to recover their packs from where they'd tied them, get them on, and ease to the back of the platform opposite where *Chrysalis* was located. They lined up and waited for the battle commander to give the order.

"Activate thrust, lowest power setting, for a manual count of five seconds." Alby counted to three and ended with, "Now, now, now."

The mobility packs pushed their people into the weapons platform. Alby grunted with the effort to hold himself steady until he reached the five-second count. At his word, everyone cut their power.

The weapons platform moved at a glacial pace, but it didn't go where he wanted it to. He knew who was at the far end in the direction they were traveling. "Fresnor, hit your jets for three seconds."

She dutifully complied. The platform turned in the right direction, but only for a moment, then started to spin. "Angus, fire your jets for two seconds."

The left end complied and stopped the spin. Alby had those in the center and to the left activate their packs to gain momentum in the direction of the cargo bay they had left many hours earlier.

Alby was ready to get out of his suit. This was the longest he'd ever been on a spacewalk. Same for every surviving member of his team. Too many firsts, but the recovered platform would give them refined metals and the materials necessary to build replacements for critical systems aboard *Chrysalis*.

The weapons platform slowly moved forward. After several more minor adjustments, it cruised toward the ship at two meters a second.

"Move to the other side. Our next maneuver will be to slow this pile of space junk and ease it into the cargo bay."

They had five minutes. Alby hurriedly pulled himself hand over hand to the opposite side. Even if he lost his grip, he had his mobility pack and could get back, and with their momentum, all of them would head toward the ship. They only needed to slow down to make the final adjustments to get the platform into the bay.

Godbolt asked the question they were all thinking. The ship was huge, but the cargo bay looked like a tiny doorway to a different world. "Is this thing going to fit?"

"I believe we make our own luck," Alby replied. "*Chrysalis*, this is the battle commander. Can you send us two plasma cutters? We need to trim off the pieces that stick out of this abomination."

Not the railguns but the spikes. Those had been designed to make it too dangerous for a ship to get close.

"Roger. Two plasma cutters and their operators. While you're out there, can you check the dorsal area from Frames Four Fifty to Six Hundred?" the captain requested.

"Say what?" Alby was done being outside the ship, especially when it came to a mundane request that was better delegated to the maintenance and engineering staff. Then again, he had eight engineers with him.

"We engaged a gunship and took a few hits, but we couldn't find where any of them had penetrated. We need to know what happened with those impacts. We counted seven."

"*Chrysalis* got shot up by a Malibor gunship? Where did it come from? What happened to it?"

"Destroyed, Alby. Tram is angling for your seat. He did a great job, but we were unable to avoid some of the incoming. That's why we need you to check since you're already out there."

"Godbolt and I will personally look into it, and Tram can't have my position." Alby checked the orientation and alignment of the weapons platform. It slowly and surely continued toward the ship. "Can he? You're not firing me, are you?"

"Alby, get a grip on yourself. However, you don't leave the ship anymore if we're at risk of getting attacked."

"Since we're in the inner system and constantly at risk, it sounds like I won't get to leave the ship anymore," Alby countered.

The captain didn't mince words. "Exactly." She wasn't happy about the battle commander and her second being gone during the engagement. It wasn't sitting well with her, but she couldn't say that. She was too tactful.

Alby didn't reply. He returned his attention to getting the weapons platform on board *Chrysalis*. Then he'd let the engineers dismantle it. It was the greatest find of the new era.

"We should gather more of these things."

"We haven't even dealt with this one," Godbolt replied.

"I think I'm going to call you 'Dark Cloud, the black hole of joy.'" Alby ordered a series of thrust maneuvers to slow the platform while aligning it with the opening. The platform stopped fifty meters short of the bay's entrance.

Two teams jetted out of the bay, each pushing a plasma cutter between the pair of operators. They expertly flew to the platform and touched down gently so as not to upset the fragile equilibrium of its geostationary orbit.

Alby went over to the first team as they were setting up.

"We'll cut these spines off. What about those things?" A gloved hand pointed at a railgun barrel.

"Leave those intact. We'll want to study their engineering before dismantling them. Just the death spears."

"Is that what we're calling them?"

Alby shrugged inside his suit. It didn't translate to anything the cutting crew could see. "We're open to better options."

The plasma torch came to life, and the operator leaned into it. The spears were made of a heavy material that resisted the cutter's initial efforts. After the metal heated up, it yielded, but the process was slow.

Alby was ready to get back to the ship. "Newton. Take charge of keeping this thing steady while they're cutting on it. Salvage those spikes, too. They seem to be made of a metal we could use."

"Goes without saying, Commander," Newton replied. "Good luck finding the holes in the ship."

Alby chuckled. "You make it sound less than flattering when the last thing this ship needs is holes punched in the hull. We're doing Septiman's work." He invoked the Borwyn's deity, but when it came to the final judgment, his words would probably be considered blasphemous.

It wasn't the worst thing he'd done. His mood darkened. Nanticoke wouldn't be returning to the ship. He'd been killed by the hatch leading into the weapons platform, and whether or not it had been a booby trap, the result had been deadly.

"We'll be back as quick as we can." Alby dropped the tether for Godbolt to strap herself to him. He pushed away from the platform before activating the mobility pack.

The two soared away from the cargo bay, which was located close to the ship's keel, and veered toward the spine on the upper side. Internally, the decks were oriented transversely from the engines to the bow so acceleration gave the impression of gravity, but the ship had been built with a keel and a spine in case it ever had to land on a planet. It was far too heavy to stand on its engines.

If it landed, it would never take off again.

Alby knew the ship's structure as well as anyone, so he

unerringly flew to the aft-most frame and landed. He activated his magnetic boots. Godbolt released herself from the tether and locked her boots to the metal hull.

"We're looking for impact points," the battle commander reiterated. Godbolt was a junior engineer, but she also knew the ship. It was a massive construct but small when it encompassed one's entire existence.

They clumped methodically back and forth across the frame, crouching to rake their beams over the surface. Godbolt found the first impact point and summoned the commander.

The dent was barely noticeable, but the external coating had been stripped off. Ably leaned over it, then lay on the deck to examine it with only the clear screen of his helmet between him and the impact point.

"This couldn't have been traveling very fast," Alby proclaimed. "Let's find the others, but if they were fired by the same cannon, they wouldn't have penetrated either."

After finding the second, the rest followed a line. They had all left a slight dent while blasting off the hull's outer coating.

Alby commed the ship. "We found the impact points from the attack. Started at Frame Five Seventy-two and tracked at an angle to the dorsal spine at Frame Five Sixty. They are small dents only. Zero effect on hull integrity. No further action needed unless you want to slap some paint over them. Were you able to get a look at their cannons? These couldn't have been fired at full power."

"Thanks, Alby," the captain replied. "We tracked other rounds coming in at a usual speed for a railgun attack, but we never saw these coming until the last second."

"After fifty years, why are they thinking about spoofing our sensors? I wouldn't consider that. Rounds on target is all that matters. We're not at that level of sophistication, especially since defeating our systems yielded nothing. Seven rounds impacting with no damage is a complete waste."

"Maybe they didn't know how dense our hull is?" the captain ventured.

"It's the same ship. A ghost from the past. We haven't increased the hull density or thickness in all that time. They used to know how to hurt us."

"Collect the data and return inside. Let's recover the teams. We can debrief once we've returned to full power." Jaq sounded less confident the longer she talked to Alby. He'd made hard observations that challenged her beliefs.

"Where are we with the ship's energy? I've been disconnected out here."

"Not good. We're under seventy percent. I'm sure you won't like that we used one missile to take out the gunship."

"You're right about that. A missile on a gunship? Seems like overkill, but at least with the Malibor platform, we can replace the missile sooner rather than later, maybe. These look kind of small. They might be close-in defensive missiles. Still, better than nothing."

The battle commander signed off. He had a great deal to think about, like conserving power to use for their offensive and defensive weapons as well as improving power generation. Maybe the Malibor platform had answers since he was running low. He needed a shower and time to think.

With Godbolt on the tether, he returned to the platform and saw that the spikes had all been removed.

"We found a weak spot at the attachment point next to the hull," the cutting crew explained.

Alby took his position. With only his mobility pack active, he stayed on the center of balance and activated it to rebuild momentum, then pushed the platform toward the cargo bay door. The team scattered around the derelict, one person sporting a mobility pack at each of the four sides to adjust as they closed. A push here, a pull there, and the final adjustments were made. No one was at the front in case they couldn't stop it. It wouldn't do to crush one of their own.

Alby grabbed the netting in both hands and stood on the frame as it squeaked into the cargo bay. He activated his jet in short bursts until it slowed. The platform crunched into the far bulkhead but stopped moving. "Chain it down! And close the outer doors."

The retractable doors slid through their tracks and clicked together. A second set rolled down from the ceiling. The cargo bay started the long pressurization process, but it wouldn't be heated until the ship's energy stores were restored to full power.

Alby moved past the beast filling their cargo bay. Under the full lights, he saw it for the monster it was, a relic from a long-ago war with a single purpose: to destroy. The same could be said of the *Chrysalis*, but that was wrong. The *Chrysalis* carried and supported life. It could destroy too since it was also a relic of that war.

The battle commander wanted to figure out why the Malibor would shut down their weapons platforms and abandon a gunship while using ineffective weapons.

He needed more information and hoped the combat team on Farslor's surface had found something to help.

CHAPTER 9

A war that lasted generations goes beyond the understanding of why it started to leave the combatants with only a desire to defeat their enemy.

The toe of a boot stabbed into his ribs. Crip's eyes popped wide open, and he stared without blinking as dull images came into focus. Max loomed over him.

"What day is it?"

The sergeant snorted. "It's actually nighttime, but we have about thirty minutes before takeoff. You wanted me to wake you."

Crip fought to get to his feet without stepping on the other soldiers. Max was the only one who was upright until Crip joined him. He used the small urinal in the lander.

"Got any more of those kava packs?"

They both moved stiffly, recovering from lactic acid buildup from the overuse of their muscles to fight the gravity on Farslor.

Max pulled open a panel and fished around inside until he found one. "The last one. For what it's worth, I feel as bad as you look."

"I'm not sure how we could train for heavier gravity." Crip opened the kava pack and squeezed a small amount into his mouth. He let it sit on his tongue to dissolve. "This is better than the stuff from the kitchen."

"It all comes from the kitchen. I think they take greater care with the food that gets packaged for the landers. I'm sure they'll appreciate your kind words once we get back home."

"I'll talk with them. It's nice to be able to eat something because if we had to count on our hunting prowess, we'd be on the starvation diet."

"I hate those." Max nudged a nearby soldier with his toe.

Crip nodded at the hatch. "How cold do you think it is out there?"

"It'll wake everyone in a hurry. It's that cold."

They popped the hatch and cracked it open. A brisk wind blew frigid air across the plain and into the cabin. Crip recoiled. He and Max fought to get the hatch closed.

The soldiers grumbled and stirred, shivering from the burst of extreme cold.

"Rise and shine, moonbeams. It's time to get this tank into the sky. Thirty mikes, and we launch." Max worked his way through the stirring bodies littering the deck in the lander's passenger compartment.

Andreeson had been given the bench seat to lie on. He was pale but still breathing.

"Have some water."

Max produced a flask as Crip watched from the other side of the module. He nodded approvingly. The commander moved from one soldier to the next as they straightened up from where they'd dropped gear.

Sleeping with their equipment was a team standard in case they had to evacuate. Now that the ship was getting ready to launch, everything had to be secured. There could be nothing flying around the cabin to hit the team members or any of the delicate flight or environmental controls.

"Did you see anything out there?" Max asked when Crip made it to him.

"Nothing. It's dark, and I don't see the Malibor using torches. The wind would wreak havoc. I bet they returned to their village and hunkered down. They'll realize we're good for our word when this baby rockets out of here."

"Sergeant Tremayne," a soldier called. He pointed at a gauge on the bulkhead. It showed the liquid oxygen store at five percent.

"That can't be right." Max tapped the screen.

Crip eased in next to him. "Backup is in the overhead."

The commander pointed. The sergeant climbed the inset ladder and pulled himself into a tiny space above the main cabin. He opened an instrument panel and activated the secondary system.

The numbers glared at him. Five percent. He accessed the comm system. "*Chrysalis*, this is Commander Castle. We have a problem."

The captain didn't answer. Tram Stamper replied, "How can we assist?"

"Oxygen did not recharge as it was supposed to. It vented instead or something. We haven't looked into why it failed. We're down to five percent, and I'm afraid we're not going to make our backup window for a return to orbit."

"Let me get Bec for you. The chief engineer will know what to do."

The channel crackled, followed by a brief whistle. "Oxygen tank didn't refill? You're screwed."

"Thanks, Bec. That's a lot of help. Why would it fail?"

"Valve jarred loose during landing. Pump failed. Lots of reasons. The LOX system checklist is in the panel to the left of the main controls. Once you hit zero, you'll need an external feed to begin the recharge process. You'll need to hurry and find where the system is interrupted before you drop to zero."

"That's one thing I understand. I'll be back in touch as soon as we have additional information."

Crip eased out of the space and slid down the ladder. Max was waiting and handed over the checklist. "I heard. First check is a series of valves." He pointed at the space above.

"Your turn, Max. It's a little tight for a big husky man like me." The commander patted his stomach and waved the checklist.

"You gotta lay off those command-deck-sized portions, Crip."

"Let's figure this out and get out of here."

Max quickly scaled the ladder and climbed into the overhead.

Crip read from the checklist. "Panel Four A, lines two and three. Valves should be closed. Line four should be open."

"Two and three are closed. Four is open. Next."

Crip flipped the pages to find forty-seven lines in the checklist, spread across five pages. "Secure the panel and move to Four B..."

The first four pages were inside the ship. They didn't find anything. Dread crept over them when they finished. They had to go outside.

"We're all going," Crip announced. "Half to watch into the darkness and the rest to light up the outside of the lander so you can see what you're doing."

Max took the checklist. "I did the grunt work in the tight space. You can do the great-outdoors climbing."

"If only rank meant something in this Borwyn's army." Crip threw up his hands in surrender. Rank didn't mean much. It was assigned to positions, as it had been in the old days, but it changed as positions changed. Chain of command existed since somebody had to be responsible for making the final decision. They'd grown up together and were all friends and family.

Crip briefed the team. "You four, take the cardinal points of the compass and aim outboard with your pulse rifles. Fire into the air if we take any incoming." He received nods of understanding from the four he'd designated. "You three, point your beams where I'm going so I can see what I need to see."

They buttoned their clothes tightly around them, complete with ballistic vests, and gear. Anything to add a layer. They pulled their helmets down over their ears and their collars up to protect their necks. They weren't covered as well as they needed to be, but even minimal protection would keep them from getting hypothermia in the short time they'd be out in the windy cold.

"Popping the hatch," Max reported. Even though he'd braced himself for it, the cold hit him like a slap in the head. He rushed out, using the steps to keep from falling. The more he moved, the more limber he became. He was sore but still functional.

The others filed out quickly and closed the hatch behind them. Andreeson wasn't in good shape, so he stayed inside. He didn't need to struggle with the cold on top of the poison from an infection.

They activated the small beam lights they carried as part of their standard kit. They were useful aboard a ship as well as on a planet at night. Crip unlocked the footholds on the outside of the ship to climb up to the area where the oxygen collection and processing equipment was located.

"Next up. Intake valves Sixty-Four A and Sixty-Four B. Push them open and examine the inside. The metal should be smooth."

Both were locked shut. "I can't get them open."

"I think we found our problem." Max looked up from his checklist and moved to the side to give Crip a better angle for his light.

The commander leaned close. The wind tore at his eyes, and tears streamed down his face. His eyelashes froze. He struggled to hold on while blocking the wind with the other hand and blinking rapidly to clear his sight. Scorching had melted part of the intake flap, effectively welding it closed. Crip removed his small multi-tool, which they all carried due to its utility in dealing with shipboard problems. They had wondered about bringing them to the planet's surface, but using it now showed that they'd made the right decision by not streamlining too much.

He scraped and scratched to reestablish a line for the gap, then used the tried and true method of hammering on it. He beat it into submission, and it finally broke free. When it opened, the valve inside howled as it took in air.

Crip climbed down. "That sucked." He held his multi-tool out to Max.

Max held his hands up. "Now that you're the expert, no need to relearn the same lessons over and over." He tucked his hands under his arms to stop the burning sensation caused by the cold.

Crip knew Max was right. He blew on his hands to warm them before heading up the ladder to tackle the second intake, then had a thought. "Can you check the system to see if it's working like it's supposed to?"

Max went into the ship, securing the hatch behind him. It was getting colder, and with each access of the lander, it got colder inside, which made it harder on their injured teammate.

The sergeant took longer than Crip thought he should. He wouldn't climb until Max confirmed the system was working. Otherwise, they'd have to continue through the checklist, which they should probably do anyway. He talked himself into it and put his foot in the first ladder hole when the hatch popped.

"It's working. The gauge had gone down to four percent, but it's climbed to five. The system shows green on the display."

"Are you warm enough?" Crip snarked since he wasn't happy. Max didn't look happy either.

"Andreeson's gone."

Crip stepped off the ladder and gripped Max's arm. "The ignominy of being the first to engage the age-old enemy. We brought ten to the planet and will take all ten home. The two we've lost sacrificed for what we had to do—find the Malibor and determine if they're a threat. Funny thing. They aren't a threat, yet we lost two of our people. We can isolate the colony on Farslor by not returning. They will do no more harm to our people."

"Makes me angry that they died for no reason."

"They didn't. They died in the pursuit of answers from the hostile natives. Answers never come easy or cheap."

Max nodded. "Never. With throat guards and antibiotics, everyone would have walked away from here."

"Like I said, answers weren't cheap. We'll get better with each engagement, but all our rules and recommendations will be written in blood, I fear. Until then, all we can do is our best. Let's get this intake fixed and settle in for the inevitable return of the Malibor hunters. Are you sure you don't want to climb up there and clear the flap?"

"I'm sure. Thanks, Crip. Get it fixed so we can calculate how long it'll take to refill the tanks and get a new launch window from *Chrysalis*."

"I'm betting eleven hours. It'll be light again before we can take off." Crip carefully and agonizingly slowly climbed the ladder. The wind bit into him when he rose above the plain. It took more scraping to clear the tiny gap that would free the cover and let the intake valve pull in fresh air from the great outdoors.

Two minutes of scraping were followed by ten furious seconds of pounding, and the flap opened. The valve engaged and threatened to pull Crip's sleeve into it. He recoiled too far and leaned away from the ship, dropped his multi-tool, and frantically scrabbled to retain his grip on the ladder. He spread his legs to paste himself to the side of the ship and hung there for a second.

"Got your tool, Crip. It almost hit me." Max moved to where the commander could see him. "Are you okay up there?"

"Right as rain," he replied. He'd never experienced precipitation falling from the sky, but a water pipe had once burst on *Chrysalis*, and it rained on everyone in that corridor until they were able to close the valve.

Crip eased down the ladder. He glanced into the pitch-darkness surrounding the lander, but his night vision had been ruined by his beam light while he'd worked on the intakes.

The others could see better but not well enough to take on the Malibor. Neither Max nor Crip thought they would be out there, though.

"Back in the lander," Max ordered.

The combat team hurried into the ship. Andreeson was now strapped upright next to Gilmore. Both bodies were cold and getting colder.

The liquid oxygen gauge showed seven percent.

"Two percent in five minutes. I'm good with that. We might be able to get out of here before dawn." Max looked optimistic.

Crip shared his enthusiasm. He was ready to go home.

They all were.

"Better contact the ship," Crip muttered.

He hovered over the comm unit while Max tapped the buttons.

"*Chrysalis.*" Not the captain. It was one of the rare times she was sleeping.

"Commander Castle on the surface of Farslor. We had a problem with the lander that we didn't identify until moments ago. It will take at least four hours before we are able to take off. We're going to miss the current launch window. We need updated flight profiles."

"Roger. Will pass to the captain when next she's on the command deck, which should be well before you need the launch data. If not, we'll wake her."

"We'll stand by and watch the oxygen tanks fill."

"Is that entertaining?" the crew member asked.

The absurdity of the question made Crip chuckle.

Max started to laugh and kept laughing.

Crip keyed the microphone. "As entertaining as watching paint dry. Castle out."

"Can you rig this thing to show a movie?" Max asked out of the blue. He was focused on Larson, a self-described systems hobbyist.

"I've always wondered if it could do that," the soldier replied.

He produced a small toolkit from an inner pocket as if he'd known he would need it. The first thing he did was disconnect the monitor and slide it out of the frame.

"We probably shouldn't watch," Crip said. "Hey," he called over his shoulder after turning his back on Larson. "Don't break anything. We need to fly the lander back to the ship. If you strand us here, there won't be enough clothes to keep you warm while you live out the rest of your days in the frigid scrub of Farslor."

Larson snorted and continued to dig into the wiring behind the monitor. "Is that your idea of motivation? Threats and implications?"

"They won't be able to recognize your rotting corpse," Max whispered.

"Far too cold outside. It would take a long time to deteriorate. A really long time."

"So don't strand us. We'll be over here getting comfortable." Crip motioned with his chin toward the opposite side of the lander.

Once there, Max leaned close. "Do you think that's a good idea?"

"Not at all. It's a horrible idea, but our people could use a distraction. I think the risk is worth it. A secondary system monitor can't take the whole ship down, can it?" The whites of Crip's eyes were visible in his apprehension.

Max's mouth fell open. "You're not sure?"

He moved toward Larson, but Crip stopped him.

"I'm kidding. I know it won't. The worst that'll happen is we lose that monitor showing backup system statuses. The backup to the backup is in the overhead."

The lights in the lander flickered and went out.

"Nothing, nothing. Necessary for the changeover," Larson reported in a calm voice.

"Larson!" Crip growled. "Don't make me chuck you out the hatch."

The lights came back on, along with the primary systems monitor. LOX showed ten percent and climbing.

Max pointed. "There's some good news."

The commander's shoulders settled. "We have a lot of problems, and right now, we can't do more than what we're already doing. So, might as well relax. We'll launch when we can, and if dawn arrives before then, we still won't go outside. There's no reason to talk with the Malibor. They already have to think we're liars. Or incompetent. Neither is very good."

"Avoid them until we fly."

"That's the plan," Crip agreed. "Is that movie ready to play? Come on, Larson! I thought you were good at this stuff."

Max stood. "The shepherd has words for situations like this. We can't forget where we've come from or that Septiman's hands cradle us in our time of need. May our fallen comrades find peace in his arms. May we find our way home using the tools Septiman has given us."

Crip nodded once as Max sat. The team grumbled their amens.

CHAPTER 10

Ingenuity comes from necessity.

"They what?" Jaq Hunter wasn't amused. She wondered why they hadn't noticed that the lander wasn't processing oxygen before the team left to explore the power source, but chewing out the night watch wasn't the answer. He was only reporting the information.

The watch didn't repeat himself. It wasn't that the captain hadn't heard or understood. "They'll get back when they can. At least they rectified the problem. These are firsts for all of us."

The night shift battle commander returned to his position across the command deck when he realized the captain was satisfied with the report and wasn't looking to extract a pound of flesh from the nearest target.

Jaq activated the comm link to the lander. "Commander Castle, this is *Chrysalis* requesting an update." She waited for a minute, then repeated her call. "Are they in range?"

She knew they were, but the communications station confirmed that. "They're directly below us at present. We have a clear line."

"Commander Castle or Sergeant Tremayne, requesting an update."

The comm crackled to life. "Crip here. We had a problem with the air intake valves. Entry welded them closed. I see this as a problem for future lander missions. I'll talk with Engineering when we get back. We're up to forty percent now. It won't be long. We'll fly when we hit eighty since we expect the Malibor to cause mischief if we stay too much longer."

"I thought the locals devolved into little more than cavemen," the captain countered. Her tone was impatient.

"They have, but they're smart. I have talked with them on a couple occasions. I've not earned their trust because we're still here. We haven't done what we said we were going to do. We came here in peace, and the first thing we did was kill three of their hunters. It wasn't the best way to start relations. And before you say it, I know we're at war with the Malibor. We're staying out of their business until we launch."

The captain mulled over the answer and softened. More of her people doing the best they could. "If we have to send another shuttle, let us know. We'll do what we have to to get the team back. Stay sharp, and stay alive. If you must, take the fight to the Malibor and keep the space around the ship clear."

"Thanks, Jaq. We're going to need more upgrades to the landers. Infrared scanning, better heat shields, integrated technology, and better heat within the module. It's cold in here, and we need more than one blanket per person." Crip had nothing else to do as the LOX refilled, so he was happy to give his report over the comm. "We lost two people. Gilmore and Andreeson, but we're bringing their bodies back home."

The captain didn't descend into the darkness of a new war. "Let us know when you'll be able to launch, and we'll provide an updated flight profile. We can move to meet you, so you can leave whenever you're ready without having to wait for a window."

"I like that answer. I guesstimate it'll be about two hours to eighty percent."

"Give us ten minutes, and we'll take care of it. To all members of the combat team, the battle is joined."

"Victory is ours," they replied in unison.

"You've earned the victory and made the sacrifice that helps bring us closer to home. The ultimate goal, returning to Septimus. We must never lose sight of that, no matter the trials between. Hunter out."

Three irreplaceable crew members had been lost on the first day of their return, and they had not yet reached Septimus.

"This was supposed to be an outpost," Jaq lamented. "Nothing more."

"Captain," Alby said from the hatch. He was holding on to stay steady. "If I heard correctly, we destroyed four weapons platforms, captured a fifth, and destroyed two gunships. Plus, the team on the surface of the planet made contact and determined that the enemy we leave in our wake is not a threat. Hard lessons, but worthwhile."

"Alby, good to have you back."

The commander pulled himself across the bridge, deftly gripping the last mid-rail to keep from running into the captain. He angled upright and activated the magnetic clamps in his boots to stay in place. "With a small power source, we can reactivate the weapons platform. No need to build our own. We activate these, reprogram them, and toss them into the mix with the Malibor. Let the platforms force the enemy out of their attack plan. They make mistakes, and we capitalize."

Jaq replied, "I like the idea of shooting the enemy from multiple sources, but I don't like the idea of trusting Malibor technology to do it."

"We spent three hours inside that thing and learned a lot about it. I think we can reprogram it by replacing its computer core. We analyze and reprogram while it has no access to its systems, then we reinstall. When we complete one, we can clone it and subvert any others we find." Alby waggled his eyebrows while nodding.

"I suppose you already removed the core from the platform clogging my cargo bay and have someone working on the programming." The captain looked sideways at the battle commander.

"I might. Would it go better for me if I did or did not take the initiative to improve our chances against the Malibor? I personally like the idea of using their own weapons against them."

Jaq shook her head. "*That's* not a leading question. I have no problem with anything that helps our chances without increasing our risk. How will we be able to test one of those monstrosities?"

"I think we can drop it into orbit around one of Farslor's two moons and fire it at the surface."

The captain drifted around to face the main screen and adjusted the view to show deep space. She produced a laser pointer and used it to circle a spot on the screen. "That's Septimus, where we're trying to go. What are we doing to get there?"

That was the hard question the crew of *Chrysalis* had to answer every day.

The captain continued. "Every single day, we have to weigh the risk against the reward. The scales of justice are harsh taskmasters. Will they weigh in our favor? How can we tip the scales?"

"Scales don't work in zero-gee." Alby rubbed his chin. The air handlers kicked on, which gave him a brief respite. After they shut down, he spoke. "But we know what does work, and that's the E-mags. The big guns. With each weapons platform, we add to our ability to defend ourselves and clear the sky of our enemies so we can complete our mission to return to Septimus."

"I know," the captain replied, keeping her eyes on the main screen. A warning flashed.

Chief Ping made the announcement. "Two ships inbound, a gunship and a much larger vessel. ETA six hours, maybe less. They are coming in hot, still accelerating."

"Can they see us?" Jaq asked. "It doesn't look like their projected course will intercept us."

Nav answered, "They are headed toward where we had the engagement with their gunship."

"They managed to report what they saw," the captain posited. The status of the ship's power filled a small inset on the screen. It showed seventy-nine percent. "Time to ninety-five percent?"

Alby looked at the engineering station, but it was empty. "Give me a minute." He pulled himself across the bridge, somersaulting when he arrived at the seat to throw himself into it. He tapped buttons while the captain stared at the main screen. "Three hours."

"Battle Commander, can we stay here for three hours without engaging? Will they see us and start dumping munitions our way?"

"We've been in low-power mode since *Chrysalis's* arrival to pick up the team and the weapons platform. It might take energizing the systems before they can home in on us. No active scans for three hours." He looked at the sensor chief for confirmation.

Chief Ping's face twisted, and his lip twitched. He contemplated not using the active systems for hours in the lead-up to combat.

The captain made the decision easy. "We can't take on those

ships without more power on hand. Make like a hole in space for the next three hours. Comm, contact the team on the surface and tell them to stand by. Slade, get me as much information about that second ship as you can passively gather.

"Alby, see if you can get that weapons platform programmed. It would be nice to leave a little present for the Malibor in our thruster wash."

Alby shook his head. "We might be able to reprogram it if we can use blocks of the Malibor code, but we'll never be able to replicate the power source in three hours. The weapons platform won't be ready."

"I hoped for a moment, only to have those hopes dashed by a comet tearing through the starfield of my mind." The captain briefly smiled. "Everyone get some rest. In three hours, I'll order battle stations, and we'll prepare to fight a ship that looks to be comparable to ours. Have we learned what we need to know to win this fight?"

"We'll see," Alby replied to the captain's rhetorical question. The battle commander flew across the command deck to hang above his position. He breathed deeply, as if the air were different at his station.

Tram Stamper, the offensive weapons officer, hovered nearby. "Back brief. What went well, and what do we need to do differently next time?"

Tram eased away from his station to grasp the rail Alby was holding. "All batteries fired and bracketed the enemy gunship. The missile killed it by working with the E-mags to channel it toward an optimal engagement envelope. We were able to maneuver away from the incoming gunship, but he didn't have as many batteries to bring to bear as we did."

"I don't expect we'll enjoy that advantage in the next engagement. What didn't go well?"

"Having to fire the missile and getting hit by rounds from

the gunship we never saw coming until the very last moment."

Alby made sure the defensive weapons operator, Gil Dizmar, was included in the conversation by motioning for him to join them. He was a couple meters away, watching intently from his station. He freed himself and floated to where the others were talking.

Alby chewed his lip as he tried to visualize the previous engagement to shape the next battle. "Those were misfires or something. If we don't see them coming, we have to assume they are not a threat. If they're low-speed, they don't have the power to penetrate our outer hull. Before you ask, Gil, I have no idea what the threshold is where we don't see the incoming projectiles but if they can't penetrate the hull, are they a threat? I doubt the Malibor were testing anything besides having a bad E-mag that didn't accelerate the rounds like it should have. Replay the maneuvers."

"Bringing it up."

They moved to the offensive weapons station and huddled around Tram's monitor. He sped up the computer replay that showed the moves and countermoves.

Alby asked, "What's the chance that the inbound ships have this info?"

"I think we'd be remiss if we assumed they didn't," Gil replied.

"My thoughts exactly. Seeing that now, with your offensive weapons hat on, what would you do differently if you're the Malibor?"

Tram pointed at the ships and the maneuvers. "With two ships, I'd catch us in a crossfire. They'll separate as they get closer. One ship? I'd maintain a standoff distance and lob volleys, hoping for a lucky shot. When he got too close, he died."

"Low risk, but also a lower chance to strike effectively. Are we going to get into a standoff where we wallow in gravity wells and toss salvo after salvo into the void?"

"How sturdy is that weapons platform?" Gil asked.

"It seemed like a framework with heavy steel wrapped around it. Not sure it was built with defense in mind besides those spikes and the electrical netting, but those were designed to keep people from doing exactly what we did—get on board and redirect it. What are you thinking?"

Gil waved his free hand. "Just looking for extra armor to strap on the front of the ship so we can show the lowest profile to the enemy at the lowest risk."

"The platform wouldn't do it, but I like what you're thinking. What about a small moon?"

"Strapped to the front?" Gil was confused.

"We use the moon to hide behind until a time of our choosing. What if we put a sensor on one of the platforms to make it look like we're somewhere we're not?"

The offensive and defensive weapons officers smiled. "Now you're talking."

"Even the odds a little bit by getting them to expend their ordnance at the wrong target. If we're going to do this, we better get to work."

Tram pointed at Alby. "You're the real engineer having spent most of your time in engineering. So, if anyone can figure it out, it's you. Sitting up here for the next three hours isn't going to get it done."

"Damn your logic!" The battle commander smiled. "Captain, permission to leave the bridge."

She waved. "Take care of it, Alby. If you can make two of them, that'd be even better. Use whatever bits and pieces you need from the weapons platform."

"I think I'll only need a little of the netting covering the outside to add to one of our old probes."

"Captain," the communications officer interrupted, "I have Commander Castle for you."

CHAPTER 11

After all the posturing, it comes down to putting rounds on target.

"We can't leave?" Crip was annoyed. The cascade of failures was going to ground them on Farslor for longer than they'd anticipated and far longer than was healthy. The Malibor weren't going to take it well. He'd have to talk with them again if he could.

The only thing he could think about was getting shot again. This time, it probably wouldn't be aimed at his chest.

"We're about to get attacked. You don't need to be flying a lander anywhere near that. One round would rip you in half."

"You could have started with that. Don't fly the flimsy lander into the middle of a space battle. At least we'll be one hundred percent before we fly. In case we have to return to the planet, we'll have enough fuel to do so."

"Don't launch until you hear from us, but be ready to go."

"We are going to have to patrol around the lander, so the natives don't get too close. That's higher-risk than we want. We could launch and hold at a safe location until we figure out whether you can come get us or not. If we launch the second we top off the tanks, we'll have more options."

"Stand by," the captain replied.

Max made sure the microphone wasn't active before he spoke. "I'd rather take my chances in space. If we go outside, we'll be taking a risk unless we kill them first. I hate to say it, but you have me liking that Malibor hunter when we're supposed to hate him."

"Do we have to? Hate them, I mean. They can be the enemy, but I don't want to let hate burn me up inside. I'd rather we be more antiseptic about it. Not kill unless we have to and only to save our own lives. These Malibor are no threat." Crip rubbed his hands together to keep them warm.

"They could damage the lander if we don't keep them back." Max didn't like any of the options. They were all bad.

"We'll put our people under the lander, prone and looking outboard but not out on patrol, where the Malibor have the advantage. Four on, four off, swap out hourly."

"I don't think we have any choice. I say we launch the second we can and wait for *Chrysalis* in orbit. Where do you think the space battle is going to take place?"

"Isn't that the question of the day? Will they tell us?" Crip didn't know why he thought that way, but he did, and that bothered him more than the question did. They'd always been on the same team, but here they were. The combat team was trapped on frigid Farslor.

"Of course. In the end, it's always been our decision. We're the ones stuck on a planet a billion kilometers from home. We can take off whenever we want, and there's nothing they can do about it."

Crip chuckled. "Maybe a hundred thousand kilometers, but you've made your point. Autonomy since the risk is ours. We can't lose the team. No matter what, not another person dies."

"I feel you, Crip. I hope the Malibor are reasonable about another delay."

The team was sprawled across the deck and seats. No one was sleeping.

"You know they'll be good with us hanging around their planet for a little bit longer. It's a cool place to be," Crip said. "If I want to trade my rifle, I can get myself a big ol' fur. I'll be warm. I'm not sure what the rest of you will do."

Danzig tossed a crumpled wrapper at him. "We'll take it from you."

"I can't believe you think I'd trade my rifle. I know there are many like it, but this one is mine!" He laughed maniacally, then stopped and looked at the soldiers one by one. "You guys. We'll do everything we can to get everyone home."

All eyes turned to the two stiff bodies covered by one thin sheet.

"We know, but we have to jag you. This trip has been less than optimal, but it's been enlightening. We'll get better. Our problem was that we thought we were good. We didn't know what we didn't know." Danzig said what they were all thinking. Their arrogance hadn't been the cause of the deaths, but they hadn't been as careful as they could have been.

"We need more technology. We need to see in the dark. We need to see where the enemy might be. We went out there blind." Crip was looking for answers to avoid putting their people in harm's way unnecessarily. The Borwyn had the technology, but it was in limited supply since high-tech equipment couldn't be replicated easily. Very little aboard *Chrysalis* was new, except for custom parts for the ion drives.

The chips, computer systems, and everything else had been salvaged and reused. The last three years had been spent testing the primary and backup systems to make sure everything worked like it was supposed to. They had few spares, and those were kept secure to use for emergency repairs only.

It would take a lot of explaining to get an infrared system attached to the landers.

Unless...

"We need to explore those ruins," Crip blurted.

"Hang on, crazy man. Where did that come from?"

"We need more technology. We don't have spare parts or anything we can use to cobble tech together, but I bet there's stuff we can use over there." Crip pointed in the direction of the village.

"Scavenger mission instead of reconnaissance." Max hung his head. "The captain said they have to fight a battle, and then we'll meet them. Are we going to launch when we can, which will be before daylight, or do we stay here and hope they don't call us for a while?

"That makes no sense since they'll call while we're way the hell over there and want us to take off immediately. No can do, Crip. We'll get bounced off the team if we go rogue."

"Then we'll ask." Crip worked his way to the comm and activated it. "Captain Hunter, this Commander Castle. Request approval for scavenger mission."

The speaker crackled, then Jaq replied, "What do you want to do and why?"

"We want to recover tech that will help us. We need infrared detection on the ground so we can avoid what happened the last time we left the ship. I believe both deaths would have been avoidable if we'd had the right equipment."

"Tech is running even with people when it comes to what we can't waste. More of it would be good, but I don't think there's any need. Alby brought an entire Malibor weapons platform aboard. We'll dismantle that thing and take every chip and every strand of wire within it. We might be able to give you what you want after the battle is joined and won."

"We're singing the same song, Jaq. I'd rather not go to the ruins, and it sounds like we don't have to. Less exposure. We are going to have to go back outside, but we'll stay within arm's length of the lander. A whole weapons platform? That's pretty bold."

"Bold actions for challenging times. Now is the time of pain. Now is the time when we learn if we deserve to be home on Septimus. Our survival depends on us winning not just this battle but every battle. We cannot lose any more people needlessly."

"I hear you loud and clear, Captain." Crip was happy he didn't have to return to the village.

He looked at the combat team. They were relatively happy, too. No one looked at the two bodies.

Crip stretched to his full height and spoke in a loud and clear voice. "We engaged the enemy, and we killed some of them. They gave us no choice. Peace first, as Septiman guides us, but when we can't have peace, then let there be war. The battle is joined! If we must fight, we will fight to win."

"Victory is ours!" the team shouted at him.

Max cracked the hatch to reveal the light of a false dawn. "I'll take three with me, and we'll assume the first watch. Pull your cold-weather hats down around your ears and prepare to be cold. Helmets overtop as an added layer." He pointed at the soldiers who would assume the first watch.

He pushed the hatch open the rest of the way and eased out. He stopped at the top of the ramp. He slowly turned his head from one side to the other, listening and watching for movement. The Malibor hunters could move without being seen or heard. He wasn't sure they were out there yet, not if they'd returned to their village the previous night.

Max continued to the ground and ducked to the left. The next man out hurried down the ramp and went right. The final two dispersed left and right. Barrington stopped two steps to the right of the ramp and took a knee, then settled to the ground, prone, aiming his pulse rifle toward the scrub.

"Barrington, aiming east, I think."

"Tremayne, aiming west," Max reported from the other side of the lander.

The last two soldiers reported cardinal directions. They had the ship covered from their positions next to the landing struts.

Crip closed the hatch and secured it, then faced the remaining three members of the team. "Get some rest. Except you, Larson. Bring up another movie. We've got an hour to kill."

"Of course. I always carry a pile of movies just in case the boss man wants entertainment."

"Tell me you're kidding."

"Well, as long as I don't have to reveal my secrets, but no. I'm not kidding. I have an entire library in my pocket, along with a complete collection of other tools I thought might come in handy if any of the software driving this thing zeroes out."

"You brought a backup of our flight programs. Larson, I like you best. Bring up the vid, and let's do our best not to freeze. One hour, then we relieve Sergeant Tremayne."

The hour passed in an instant since the team fell asleep the second the video started playing. The alarm Crip had set woke him out of a sound sleep and he hopped to his feet, hoping to clear the cobwebs from his brain. He shook the others to wake them, and they all lined up at the hatch.

Crip opened it. He knew that if he stood still for too long, it would make it worse, so he took that first step and then another. The cold bit his face, hardening his skin until it felt like it would shatter if he bumped into the ship.

In the early dawn, the breeze had died down. The scrub stood starkly foreboding as light danced across the stunted branches. Mist rose due to the warmth of the ground against the cool of the air. Crip worked his way around the lander to take a spot next to Max.

The sergeant had to work his jaw before he was able to speak clearly, and his words still came out rough. "I thought I saw movement." He motioned with the barrel of his weapon.

"Animal or man?"

"Movement is the best I can do. It's tough staring at the scrub for an hour, but there's no wind. If a branch or leaf moves, it's because someone moved it."

Crip shivered as the ground threatened to sap the warmth from his body. "Get back inside and try to warm up. Sub-team Castle has the watch."

Max stiffly got to his knees, then used the lander's strut to pull himself upright. "This gravity is getting me down."

"Is that a pun?" Crip smiled but closed his mouth when the cold hurt his teeth.

"A little. Trying to keep it light..." His words drifted off, and he pointed at a tendril of black smoke climbing skyward not more than fifty meters away.

"Keep your heads on a swivel and watch out! They're out there," Crip shouted. "Get down."

Max returned to the prone position, wide eyes darting across their field of view. He was looking for the perpetrator of the fire.

"Got smoke this side," Danzig reported.

"And this side," another soldier added.

"The tanks were at seventy-two percent when I came out here," Crip reported.

"We can't take off yet. We wouldn't be able to return to the planet if anything happened."

"I don't want to test that premise. We need another thirty minutes, but two hours would top us off."

Without the breeze, the oxygen processing station within the ship's nosecone droned faintly. It was a good system from the before-time, and it still worked. A secondary processor was located between the engines in case the primary failed, but the backup couldn't be run at the same time. The battery drain would be too great, reducing the effectiveness of both and risking system failure.

They'd been warned by Engineering.

"Maybe Larson can increase the processing power," Max suggested.

"I think we simply need to buy time. Watch the fire, let it warm us, and keep it away from the ship by clearing the weeds out to about ten meters. There seems to be a lot more smoke than fire."

"I see it too." Max pushed off the ground, kneeled, and called to the others under the lander, "Clear the scrub out of the area in front of you. Ten meters ought to do it. Leave nothing but dirt in a circle around the ship."

The soldiers crawled forward and hacked at the bushes with knives useful for hand-to-hand combat but not the best for hacking at weeds. They needed something more substantial but would have never thought to include a machete or axe in the lander's emergency supplies.

The fact that none of them had ever been on a planet had stymied their ability to contemplate emergency scenarios. No matter how far-fetched, they would have never come up with being burned out by the natives.

Maybe their training wasn't about planning for what they'd come across but being able to respond to any situation. Assess, evaluate, decide, and act.

"I know what we need to do," Crip said out the side of his mouth, moving to the next bush.

"Besides digging out this Septiman-awful growth?"

Crip half-smiled. This stuff was horrid. "Train to respond. We can't guess everything that might happen. We'd weigh the lander down with a kiloton of garbage. We wouldn't have any room for the people. Defeats the purpose of what we're trying to do. How would the lander have fixed itself if we weren't here to clear the vents?"

"Wouldn't an axe be nice right about now, though?" Max yanked on the recalcitrant growth before going back to hacking and sawing through its heavy stems with his ill-suited blade.

Crip chuckled while watching through the scrub. The Malibor were out there, and they were starting fires.

On the opposite side of the lander, someone fired their pulse rifle. Max whirled as fast as he could while prone.

"What'd you see?" he called.

"These roots are less belligerent after they've been blasted," Danzig shouted back. He fired again. "That'll teach you!"

"No using the rifles. We don't have enough power packs after yesterday's firefights," Max reminded them.

An arrow flew over the scrub and skipped off the top of Max's head.

Crip fired into the air. "Next one blows your chest apart!" He stood and tucked his chin into the top of his ballistic protection, holding his pulse rifle in one arm. He caught the movement and dodged as an arrow whizzed past where his face had just been to ricochet off the lander's hull.

The commander fired one-handedly into the scrub from where the arrow had come. He expected the hunter had already shifted position. "We had another delay because the ship is broken! These things are fragile. I know it makes us look like liars and scumbags, but we'll leave when the ship is fixed."

"You'll leave, or your ship will be consumed by the fires of our rage!" It was the hunter from the previous day, but he was out of their line of sight.

"Fire can't consume this ship. It's sturdier than that. You're risking the fire getting out of control. I've seen your village. Fire *will* destroy it."

"It's worth the risk to see you gone."

"It's not *worth the risk*. We will leave when we can and not before. Only a little while longer. Leave us be. We're not hurting you. We're not even leaving our ship. Why do you want to push us to the point where we have to kill you? You're making it a lot easier to fly down that gravity well to your destruction. We can't see you, but that doesn't matter. We'll destroy everything within a hundred meters of this ship, and that'll include you."

The Malibor hunter finally stood, but only his head and shoulders appeared above the scrub. His bow was nowhere to be seen.

Crip took two steps forward but remained within the cleared area. The smoke curled up behind the Malibor.

"Why are you on this side of the fire?" Crip wondered.

"I know the way out."

"I know there's more smoke than fire," the commander replied. The expected flames licking across the diminutive leaves on the heavy branches weren't enough fuel for the fire to spread quickly or burn too hot.

"Give it time." The Malibor waited as if he were expecting something.

Crip decided to make a bold move. He ejected the power pack from his pulse rifle and tucked it into a pouch on his vest while leaving the projectile load intact. He held the weapon out before him. "Trade. A rifle for your fur."

"Two rifles," the Malibor hunter countered.

"The negotiation was yesterday." Crip stopped a few meters short of the Malibor, looking down at him because the native was standing in one of the ditches that ran through the area.

He moved out of it to be on equal footing with the commander.

Crip tossed the rifle to the hunter, who caught it with his free hand. He strung his bow over his shoulder and examined the Borwyn weapon, then pointed it at Crip and pulled the trigger.

"It's broken. Just like your ship." He tossed the rifle back. "No deal."

Crip slapped the power pack into the rifle, pointed it skyward, and fired. "Not broken, just incomplete like our spaceship. Hear that sound?" He cocked an ear toward the lander. "It's the liquid oxygen reclamation equipment. It takes oxygen out of the air and liquefies it to mix as a propellant with hydrogen and other chemicals we have on board.

"We're short of what we need but close. We're going to wait until the tanks are at one hundred percent. Then we'll launch. Anything that's not burned up before we go will definitely be on our way out."

The commander mimicked a blast cloud coming out of the bottom of the ship with his hands, making the noise to go with it. He wasn't sure it translated appropriately since the Malibor looked singularly unimpressed.

The Malibor held out his hand and twice crooked his fingers. Crip ejected the power module and tossed the rifle to him.

"That thing, too."

"You tried to shoot me last time, so I can't give you the power module. You'll have to build your own like we did."

The Malibor slung the rifle as he'd seen the soldiers carrying theirs.

"I think there's your side of the bargain." Crip pointed at the fur.

"The deal is changed. For one of your rifles, we won't burn your ship. If you're not gone by midday, the deal is off. The flames will melt your ship, and you will all die."

"They won't melt the ship, and we're doing our best to leave. You have no reason to believe me but look at us. We're cold and miserable. This is not a place we want to call home or even come to for a visit."

"Where do you visit?" the Malibor asked. He leaned on the pulse rifle like it was a cane.

"What's your name?"

"They call me Gregor."

Is Gregor your name? Crip thought, but he didn't want to play games. The Malibor seemed ready to open up. They wanted to know what that power source was. Maybe Gregor knew.

"Gregor, as grim as it sounds, we don't go anywhere. The entirety of our existence is on one ship, the *Chrysalis*." He pointed straight up, even though he was sure the ship was no longer directly overhead. "We might go to the hydroponics bays to breathe deeply of oxygen and moisture-rich air. Maybe go to astrogation for an incredible view of the stars and planets in the Armanor system. This is the first time most of us have left the ship, even though we have taken shifts working in the mines on Krador's fourth moon during its orbital perigee when the working conditions weren't so harsh."

"Your words are strange, yet you speak them as if everyone should know their meaning." The Malibor sneered. "Everyone doesn't."

Crip had looked past the accent and the furs to talk to the Malibor hunter as an equal. He was, albeit technologically regressed. He didn't know space terminology since it didn't apply to him, but he undoubtedly knew all there was to know about the scrub, the plains, and the hills beyond, or enough to hunt for food and clothing. He had survived and would be as eloquent as Crip when he described things he had grown up with.

"The closest point between the planet Krador and Armanor, the star in the sky that brings warmth to Farslor. It may not be much, but it's more than what the distant planets get."

"Farslor. Is that what you call our planet? It is known to us as Homeworld."

"I understand." Crip fidgeted with his gear. Although the conversation was fascinating, he was freezing, and it was affecting his ability to think. Given the cold, the gravity, and the long days, Crip was a shell of his former self.

The Malibor waved. He knew the conversation was over. He laughed as he walked away, then ducked into the gully and disappeared.

CHAPTER 12

Septiman made Armanor so his people could bathe in its light.

Their passive sensor systems had zeroed in on the Malibor ships. The two flew in close formation on a direct line toward the previous engagement with the gunship. The chrono counted down while the power plant renewed the energy stores. They hit ninety-five percent right on time.

"Recommend we power the engines and move to the engagement point designated Devious Two," Captain Hunter offered.

"We haven't been spotted yet. We could churn toward one hundred percent. I'd be more comfortable with full power on hand," the thrust control officer replied.

"We're well within their engagement envelope. Sitting still makes us a big and juicy target, and without power, we won't be able to get away." The battle commander checked his systems again. "I concur with the captain's recommendation. Devious Two at full speed, jinking course."

Jaq listened to their viewpoints. Moving before they were spotted by the enemy was a critical factor in her decision. She tapped her controls to give her ship-wide communication. "Battle stations. All hands to battle stations. Department heads report status when green." She looked at the shepherd in the far reaches of the command deck. "What's the good word, Shepherd?"

She climbed into her seat while the Borwyn's spiritual leader spoke.

"Hallowed are the children of Septiman. Blessed be their return home." When he finished, he sat and belted in.

The crew mumbled an amen, and one muffled voice said, "Back at ya."

The others laughed. That had stopped the building tension.

The captain cleared her throat to keep from showing disrespect to the shepherd, a holdover from the days when the Borwyn had been deeply spiritual.

Those born and raised on the ship leaned more toward technology. They'd survived because of the work they did with their own hands. No star in the night sky guided them. No magic elixir of light and soil brought food out of the ground. Technology did those things, but no one was bold enough to swear off the shepherds and their mission. Down to only two, the shepherds calmed everyone.

That was why the captain wanted one on the bridge. She wanted to believe in a higher power because sometimes, the technology failed. In those instances, everyone became a believer.

The department heads reported in, changing their statuses from red to green. In less than two minutes, the board showed green. The crew was ready.

"Full speed ahead, vector one-five-one, star angle minus four zero."

The ship's ion drives immediately came online and slowly built forward momentum. This was when the ship was most vulnerable. It would take a minute or more to reach a full gee, but their acceleration would build more quickly after that. The slow start also helped them keep from being noticed unless the Malibor's sensors were more sensitive than the Borwyn's.

Or they just happened to be looking in *Chrysalis's* direction.

The captain compulsively checked the ship's status, noting that the energy meter had ticked up to ninety-six percent before dropping back to ninety-five after the engines kicked in. That made her smile, as did the rapid response of the crew. The systems were ready to perform. The ship was moving. The crew was softly communicating with others throughout the ship. The command deck was humming in a good way.

The first engagements had prepared them for this one.

The battle commander said, "If they keep sending ships onesy-twosy, we might be able to eliminate their whole fleet without breaking a sweat."

The crew shouted their support.

"We haven't even started this fight yet, so we can't presume we'll win. Of course we'll win because if we don't, we end our species, at least everyone we know who survived. There might be more on Septimus, but if we don't win, we can't free them.

"If we don't free them, they'll remain under Malibor control. If they survived, they will have had a rough life. We have to win. Let there be no doubt about that, and don't take it for granted."

"Sobering and wise words, Captain," Alby stated loudly enough for the bridge crew to hear. "Preparing to engage. Defensive weapons are active. Offensive weapons are idle. We'll bring them online after we arrive at Devious Two and launch the decoy."

The decoy. It had taken almost the full three hours they had waited to cobble together a system with a small power supply, a radar transmitter, and a communications link. It was set to physically deploy a net made from the copper wires taken off the surface of the weapons platform. Oriented properly, it would magnify the reflection from an active scanner to make it look much bigger than it was.

The point was to buy *Chrysalis* a few seconds to attack unimpeded by enemy fire so they could bring all their batteries to bear. They had twelve E-mag cannons and four anti-ship missile silos. It would be enough.

"Passing one gee," Ferdinand reported from the thrust control station.

"On course, vector one-five-one, star angle minus four zero," Navigation announced.

The captain trusted them both but checked the numbers on her screen to confirm. "Radiate systems, full power. Tell me what that big ship is, Chief."

"Sensors at max. Ten seconds." The Malibor ships weren't more than ten light seconds away. They were only two, but it would take time to radiate, return, and process the data.

"Begin evasive maneuvers," the captain ordered.

Nav had input a series of random course changes. Mary pressed the button, and the attitude control thrusters took over to change the ship's orientation while the main engines continued pushing them forward on the longitudinal axis. It would take a lucky guess to hit *Chrysalis* with a long-range railgun shot.

"Malibor ships are changing course. They are in pursuit and gaining."

Of course they would gain. They already had a full head of steam, but *Chrysalis* was building speed quickly on a trajectory away from the Malibor and beyond the planet's horizon to where the second moon was located. Devious Two was between the planet and the moon.

"We have a good angle on the enemy ships. E-mags, online and fire!" the battle commander ordered.

"E-mags coming online," Tram reported. "Firing swirl pattern one five with four batteries." The pattern started broadly, with the target plus point-two percent off bullseye, and reduced the diameter of the circle by a hundredth of a percent with each rotation. At long range, that left huge gaps in the pattern. It was more to keep the enemy off guard and prevent the Malibor from dictating the terms of the engagement.

"Bring us to course one-five-six, star angle minus two five."

Nav tapped the controls to change the course. The evasive maneuvers continued while the vessel shaped its trajectory to the new vector.

"Jaq," the battle commander stated, his voice barely perceptible above the ship's hum. "It's the same class as *Chrysalis*. I checked it twice. It's our sister ship *Butterfly*."

"Cease fire!" the captain shouted. "Give me a ship-to-ship channel."

"Borwyn command channel is active." They hadn't used that communications link and protocol in fifty years.

"*Butterfly*, this is *Chrysalis*. Command code seven-bar-seven, level four. Please confirm." It was one of the oldest communications protocols, and each captain and the ship's senior leaders had to memorize it. It confirmed that the Borwyn fleet was still active.

The command crew collectively held their breath as they waited for a reply.

"Time?" the captain asked to confirm that the signal had reached the ship.

"We should have received a response by now," the communications station replied.

"Send it again." The comm station recorded all communications, so they replayed the captain's message.

The comm crackled as the channel opened between the two ships.

Jaq tried to lean forward, but the maneuvers held steady at three gees, pinning her to her seat. She wanted to float free so she could think, but it wasn't to be. She'd have to keep her wits about her while the seat kept working to squeeze blood from her extremities to where it could best be used.

"Borwyn vessel. This is the Malibor cruiser *Hornet*."

Blood pounded in the captain's ears when the message came through, crushing her short-lived hope that the Borwyn left behind had survived.

The enemy voice continued. "You are to leave Malibor space immediately, or you will be destroyed."

Jaq contemplated her answer, then muted the channel from her control panel. "Stay the course, Mary. Ferd, hold steady on three gees. Battle Commander, recommendations."

"Resume firing. Continue to Devious Two. Execute the plan and destroy the ship called *Hornet*."

"I concur. Resume firing, four batteries only. Conserve power." The captain grunted her last orders as gee forces increased with the ship's acceleration toward Farslor. "Don't skip us off the atmosphere until we're ready to slow down."

Nav confirmed the request, although Mary knew what to do. She'd be double-checked until she re-earned the captain's trust.

"Reducing thrust," Ferd said. "Conserving power."

That made Jaq check the control dashboard. Ninety-one percent power reserves. Right on track.

She activated the command channel. "My apologies for the delay. Bring your ship to a complete stop, power down your weapons, and prepare to be boarded."

"Are we going to board that ship?" The battle commander would have looked at the second's empty position, but he couldn't see while he was embedded in his chair and transitioning through six gees. He spoke through clenched teeth.

Chrysalis was missing half its small contingent of soldiers. They couldn't board a ship of *Chrysalis's* size no matter how much they wanted to, even with a fully cooperative Malibor crew. "You're bluffing."

The captain closed the channel. Any further conversation with the Malibor would be fruitless. Also, they'd lose the connection as soon as they passed out of direct line of sight, which would happen at any moment.

"Of course I'm bluffing. I prefer to think of it as posturing. Force him to take unnecessary risks out of anger. It saddens me to see our sister ship wasn't destroyed as we assumed but survived because the Malibor recovered it. That means we need to finish the job the Malibor started."

The gee forces transitioned to eight before dropping back to seven. The crew was pressed hard into their seats. They rode out the maneuver, the fifth pass around the planet since their return.

That had not been the plan. This stop was only supposed to be temporary.

And they still had the combat team on the planet's surface.

"We need to recover the team as soon as they can get back to orbit. They need to hold for a little while longer, but they should prepare to launch."

"That's the instructions they have, Captain," Alby replied.

They both knew Crip Castle would launch as soon as they were ready. Repeating the order wouldn't change that. Fight on the surface or fight in space? On the surface, they had a chance.

Chrysalis continued around Farslor.

"Did they follow us?" Jaq asked.

Chief Ping replied, "If they didn't, they would have had to change their orientation and run at full power to achieve half our speed. We'll get to Devious Two well before them. They were on course to follow us. I assess that *Hornet* is following. The gunship disappeared in the cruiser's shadow. Its disposition is unknown."

"Understand. *Hornet* remains the primary target. The original weapons configuration of *Chrysalis* was eight E-mags and eight anti-ship missile tubes. Do they still have the same weapons?"

"Unknown," Slade Ping replied.

"Unknown," Alby added. "We have to assume they are as potent as *Chrysalis*."

"We must assume at least that capability. Twelve E-mags if they upgraded, and eight anti-ship missile tubes. Forward or bow approaches limit the number of weapons they can bring to bear, but I fear the missiles most. Our defensive systems can deal with two or three inbound missiles, but not eight if they flush all tubes simultaneously."

Gil Dizmar interjected from the defensive weapons console, "Maybe as many as four if they stagger their approach. The good news is that we're not outclassed. We're equally matched."

"*Chrysalis* is crewed by Borwyn who have trained for this day their whole lives!" the captain shouted. The gee forces of acceleration kept dropping as the ship rode its momentum around the planet. She didn't add, 'The battle is joined.'

They had joined it the second they'd arrived at Farslor, or maybe long before.

Win or die trying. They had two ships chasing them.

Right into a trap.

The captain released herself from her seat and floated free. "Everyone remain in your seats. I need to think."

She glanced from the main screen to the individual stations to the small panel in the captain's chair and back at the main screen. She mumbled to herself. "Drop, disappear, reappear, wait, fire, move, and fire again."

She kicked off a rail to shoot across the bridge to Alby's station. "We need to know where they are when we can't see them."

"They can't see us either. We could launch a lander while we still have momentum, so it continues around the moon. It'll see them but shouldn't hit their screens since it won't be what they are expecting, and it's not a threat."

"And losing it is better than losing the whole ship."

"A trade-off. They shouldn't shoot it. We can pick it up later."

The shepherd interrupted from the back of the bridge. "May the hammer of Septiman smite them!"

The captain looked at him. "I didn't know Septiman carried a hammer."

The shepherd dipped his head. "Septiman probably has one. We simply have not heard of it because peace first, but just because we have not heard of it, it doesn't mean he doesn't."

"Convoluted logic, but that's the spirit, Shepherd." She returned to the battle commander. "That means we'll have to slow down after launch, and the second moon has no atmosphere."

"The drain on our energy reserves is a higher cost than the loss of the lander, but both must be done. If we come out from behind the moon too early, we'll lose our advantage."

"I submit to you that the losses are the same," the captain replied. "Which means we need to do both. Prepare the lander to bounce a signal off so we can get a view of the Malibor." She turned to swim back to her station.

"Already done," Alby replied.

The captain stopped and spoke over her shoulder. "That was quick."

"It was always part of the plan." Alby winked, but the captain didn't see it.

"What else do you have hidden in your cargo pocket that you're not telling me about?" She pulled away from the battle commander's station.

"That would spoil the fun. Let's just say we're better than the Malibor because we have better people."

The captain eased into her chair but sat on the edge so she could look around. "Time to break orbit?"

The navigator responded, "Four minutes and thirty-eight seconds to Devious Two. Braking maneuver in one minute."

The captain worked her way into the gel and belted in, then checked the status board. Energy reserves were down to eighty-three percent. She hoped the atmospheric braking would do the trick before they needed to fire the engines on the far side of the second moon at full power to slow down fast.

The ship slammed into the upper atmosphere. Had the crew not been strapped in, they would have been thrown into whatever immovable object was in front of them. As it was, an explosion of air came from most of the crew at the violence of the impact. The ship jerked in bone-jarring increments over the course of the next thirty seconds before slipping away from Farslor's worst influence.

"Prepare to launch the decoy," the captain announced.

The crew watched the countdown clock on the screen, but Jaq kept track of each step on the tactical engagement plan.

"Offensive weapons coming online," Tram stated.

"Launch." Jaq gritted her teeth as the decoy was mechanically tossed out of the rearmost cargo bay. It would continue along the vector with whatever momentum it had from being thrown out on *Chrysalis's* course.

Thrusters pointed the nose of the ship at the outer edge of the second moon.

"One minute to pass into the moon's shadow," Mary reported. "Inverting the ship."

The thrusters turned the ship for an agonizing twenty seconds, aligning the aft end along the direction of travel to slow the forward momentum.

"Sensors, keep an eye out for the Malibor."

"Watching. Bouncing an active signal off the decoy."

"Which creates the impression that it's us." The captain nodded in approval of her crew's efforts to devise a strategy to surprise the enemy and get more shots on target than they'd managed on *Chrysalis*. Volume and accuracy of E-mag fire would make the difference.

A well-placed missile to finish *Hornet* off.

"Contact. It's the *Hornet*. Pinging him from the decoy."

Thrust Control made the next announcement. "Four, three, two, one. We are around the horizon. Ahead full, ion drives at maximum."

"Launch the lander," the battle commander ordered before the engines engaged.

On the captain's panel, the lander's launch registered while the engines ran up to full power. A small line on the main board followed its progress through space.

Once again, the crew was subjected to the gee forces of deceleration, but since they were facing backward, they were pushed into the gel of their seats, a kinder and gentler assault on their bodies than being restrained by the seats' straps.

The captain asked the hard question. "Did the Malibor see us?"

"Unknown," Chief Ping replied.

The braking maneuver continued for another twenty seconds to keep the ship from launching them out from behind the second moon.

The captain needed more information. "What's the decoy show?"

"Not yet registering. Last data showed *Hornet* coming around the planet. We lost contact with the decoy when we moved out of line of sight." The sensor chief didn't sound happy about it.

"E-mags at one hundred percent. Four missiles in the tubes. Outer doors are open." Alby was focused on one thing. When the shot came, he'd be ready. "Change the orientation of the ship, please. Nose-first."

"Roger," the navigator confirmed. She tapped the screen to bring the ship around.

"Anything?" the captain asked, leaning out of her chair to look at the battle commander and the sensor chief.

They didn't retort that they would share any information the instant they had it. Everyone was tense. Both shook their heads.

The captain leaned back and tried to control her breathing. Blood pounded in her ears. She stared at the main screen, willing it to report something she could use. It flashed with an update.

"CONTACT!" the sensor chief bellowed. "Coming around the moon right in front of us."

Hornet did not yet show on the main screen.

"All batteries fire mark one, orientation zero, pattern one." Tram's fingers flew across his controls. The ship hummed as the E-mags sent clouds of obdurium projectiles ahead of the ship. "Firing Missiles One and Two on a positive vertical approach. Three and Four on a negative vector. Launching now."

The electromagnetic launch system sent the missiles into space and clear of the hull before the engines kicked in, accelerating the missiles to fifty gees. Two raced in one direction, and the other two flew in the opposite direction. Then they all turned toward the projected course of the inbound Malibor ship.

The ship's E-mag launchers pounded in a staccato rhythm. Tram increased the rate of fire to maximum.

"The lander has been destroyed," Alby announced. The loss of the lander was trivial compared to *Hornet* guessing their maneuver and getting in front of them.

"Hard burn, vector zero, star angle nine zero. Now, now, *now!*" the captain shouted. The new course would take them ninety degrees away from their current course. The Malibor had guessed exactly where *Chrysalis* would be. She needed to change that in a hurry, or they'd run into a wall of E-mag projectiles the second they were visible to the enemy.

The ship's thrusters twisted the vessel, and the ion drives engaged at one hundred percent thrust.

Energy was down to seventy-one percent.

Seventy percent. More than they needed to survive the next few seconds.

"Maintaining fire from eight batteries," Tram reported. With the change in the ship's orientation, they had lost targeting for four E-mags. "Missiles flying true."

Hornet emerged from beyond the moon.

"Eat me!" Alby shouted.

The stream of projectiles had been placed perfectly. The Malibor ship shuddered under the first barrage. Lights winked within as power fluctuated until automatic rerouting routines kicked in. Defensive systems lit the void the instant *Hornet* detected inbound missiles.

An explosion signaled a keel impact.

The lights flickered again from the barrage. The ship flew through more of Pattern One's projectiles. Defensive weapons stopped firing for a second, then two. They resumed firing when the missiles were on terminal approach.

A second missile exploded fifty meters from the hull and washed the ship with superheated plasma and bits and pieces of the missile.

The last two raced through the gaps and simultaneously slammed into *Hornet*'s spine and keel, breaking each and threatening to tear the ship in half.

With an eruption of quickly extinguished flame, atmosphere vented into space, bringing with it anything loose from the interior sections. The explosions had shattered structural integrity and the airtight bulkheads.

Hornet lost power, and the engines went cold. They had old engines of the type the Borwyn had replaced with ion drives.

Old tech suffered greatly under catastrophic failure. Explosions made no sound in space. The only indication it had happened was that the rear of the ship tore away from the primary hull, blasted off. The bulk of the ship spun, throwing people and materiel out of the failed hull.

"Cease fire," Alby ordered softly. The eight batteries had poured accelerated projectiles into the hulk of the Malibor cruiser until he was sure it was dead. "Firing a magnetic beacon at the hulk in case we have time to recover some of that choice metal and any circuit boards that survived the conflagration."

"Roger. All ahead slow," the captain ordered. "Chief, find me that gunship."

CHAPTER 13

In combat, information is paramount.

"What are you going to say about the lost pulse rifle?" Max asked as the team strode up the ramp to the lander's hatch.

"The truth, my man. Traded it without a power cell to a Malibor so they wouldn't cause us any grief while we restored our LOX to get out of here. I don't know how the conversion motor would work if it was choked with smoke." Crip pulled his collar tightly around his neck. His helmet barely covered the tips of his ears, but it would have to do. He tucked his hands into his sleeves and hunched next to the landing strut.

"Are you staying out here?" Max took a step up the ramp.

"I just got out here. You know the Malibor are watching. Might as well give them something to see."

Max had been outside for over an hour. The cold was wearing on him. "Do you need company?"

"I'll be fine. Take everyone back inside and warm up."

Max offered his pulse rifle, but Crip shook his head and held his hands up.

"Naked before your enemies. You're a legend. I'll make sure

we don't forget your name. Shepherd will keep you in his prayers."

"Go on, you knucklehead. Pray for Gilmore and Andreeson. They went out the airlock without ever knowing they were being spaced." The Borwyn used that saying when someone died unexpectedly. All they knew was the ship and the death from the void of space that enveloped *Chrysalis's* hull.

"It's a better way to go. Old age isn't for people like you and me, Crip. Blaze of glory. I'll check in with *Chrysalis*. See if we still have a ship to return to."

"Don't even joke like that, Max. I don't want to live the rest of my life on this frozen rock. Let the Malibor suffer that fate."

"They *are* suffering. None of them looked like they had a good or easy life."

Crip jerked his chin at the partially opened hatch. Max took the hint and went inside, securing the ship from Farslor's cold.

Wisdom came from experience, and experience came from learning from one's mistakes. In the short time they'd been on Farslor, the commander had learned much. It had come at a high cost, like all the best lessons. Crip and the survivors on the combat team were wiser and hardened now. They'd finally seen death. They'd finally killed.

It hadn't been a blaze of glory, but he'd reconciled himself to it.

Already.

It took his smile away. Maybe it would come back when they were on the ship. Maybe it would return when he saw Taurus. Having someone to go home to had assumed new importance. He'd always thought it mattered, but after the trials on Farslor, it was the *only* thing that mattered. Getting home to their loved ones.

They still hadn't determined the power source, but they had learned something more valuable about the Malibor.

They were willing to talk.

The brush rustled beyond the cleared patch.

"Don't shoot me," Crip called. "Is that you, Gregor?"

The Malibor stood head and shoulders above the surrounding growth. He carried a fur in his hand as he nonchalantly walked toward Crip. The hunter didn't have to look around to know that the rest of the Borwyn were inside the ship. He'd been watching.

Gregor tossed the fur, and Crip caught it in two hands and wrapped it around his neck and shoulders. Despite the smell, it took the edge off the blistering cold, blocking the wind and holding in the warmth Crip's body generated.

"What do you want to talk about?" Crip asked.

"Why now? Why did you return?"

"To live. To see if more Borwyn are alive. We've been scraping out an existence at the outer edges of the system. Once the ship's drives were replaced, we were able to return. We're from Septimus. We only want to go home."

"This isn't Septimus."

Not a bad observation for a supposed caveman. He knew a great deal more than Crip had guessed. "It is not. It's Farslor, the next orbital pair away from Armanor. This was a Malibor colony. We wanted to see if someone was going to sneak up from behind us from here. We have our answer. No one is following us from here to Septimus."

"Are you sure?"

Crip laughed. "Pretty sure. You're not hiding any ships on the planet. Why would you when you couldn't keep active ships or weapons platforms in orbit? You're out of power."

"Maybe. We would never give up all our secrets."

Crip noticed that the pulse rifle was nowhere to be seen. "We wouldn't either."

The hatch cracked open. Gregor dove into the scrub and disappeared.

"One hundred percent," Max reported.

"Be there in a minute."

"Nice fur."

"For the low, low price of a pulse rifle, you too can be protected from the elements," Crip joked. He waved for Max to hold the hatch.

After the ship was sealed, Crip called to Gregor, but the Malibor didn't reappear. "We can go now. Get clear and cover your ears. One day, I hope to call you friend." Crip held his hand up in a quiet salute to the Malibor hunter. The commander returned to the ship, hurried inside, and retracted the short ramp.

The hatch closed and sealed.

"Buckle up. We're heading to orbit." Max was in the seat next to the bodies as if he were guarding them.

The others had stored their gear and piled into their seats.

Crip was last to get in and buckle up.

"Are we under remote control?" Crip asked.

Max clenched his lips until they turned white, then shook his head. "No contact with *Chrysalis*. We'll activate the beacon when we exit the atmosphere."

"Not our best plan, but the only choice we have," Crip replied. "Victory is ours."

The others mumbled their agreement. The autopilot took over and ran the engines up to maximum for liftoff and sustained ascent. The soldiers were pressed into their seats hard as the lander accelerated toward breakaway speed. That took five minutes and fifty percent of their liquid oxygen supply.

"I love this part!" Crip shouted over the roar of the main engines. They were driving the lander to eleven kilometers per second, enough speed to tear through the atmosphere and into deep space.

The trajectory took them on an equatorial orbit. Acceleration ended, and zero-gee took over. At that point, they were slaves to astrophysics. Crip accessed the comm panel. "*Chrysalis*, this is the combat team aboard Lander Zero One. Please confirm pick-up coordinates."

They heard only static, followed by silence.

"We'll keep trying," Crip told the team.

The friction of leaving orbit had helped heat the interior of the lander. With the engines cut off, the internal system burned the available LOX to maintain the life support systems. Crip unbelted and removed his fur, then floated to an overhead storage compartment, opened it, and tossed the fur inside. Everything else was cinched to the deck. The fur wouldn't hurt anything by not being strapped down.

Danzig spoke. "Is it just me, or does that thing stink?"

"It's an acquired taste, Danzig. Smells like a fresh breeze blowing the scrub of Farslor straight up your nostrils."

"A coolant leak would do the same thing," Danzig replied.

Crip floated close and clapped Danzig on the shoulder. "That's the spirit. For the record, it reeks of burned fertilizer. I traded a pulse rifle for it, so it's now my most *prized* possession."

"Your woman isn't going to let you have that in your quarters. She'll make you decide. Her or your fur."

"Is there a pun in there?" Crip countered. "And she's not my woman."

"You can say that again," Max interjected into the quips and banter.

The soldiers laughed heartily at the commander's expense.

Crip glanced from face to face. They were ecstatic about being off the planet and headed home, despite the problems they had faced and the ones still before them. They didn't know if *Chrysalis* would be able to pick them up. They barely had enough LOX to get back to the planet in one piece. They had plenty of hydrocarbon fuel for multiple trips as long as they could refill the LOX tanks. Liquid oxygen was the variable. The limiting consumable.

"Maybe the wisdom we gained was worth it," Crip muttered. A tighter team. Seasoned soldiers. He locked his boots to the deck and sidestepped around the circular cabin so he could shake everyone's hand and thank them for being on the team. When he reached Andreeson, he knelt and said a short prayer, then vowed to engrave his name on a panel in the team room. He did the same with Gilmore, resting his hand on the dead soldier's leg while he prayed.

He didn't know if either soldier would have an afterlife. No one knew for sure except for the dead, and they weren't talking.

"*Chrysalis*, this is Commander Castle. Please advise the recovery coordinates."

"Commander Castle, this is *Chrysalis*. Stay your course. We'll come to you."

The soldiers cheered, but Crip stopped them with a gesture. He blew out a breath, and his head dropped. He keyed the microphone. "Captain Rodrigo, great to hear your voice. We'll stay the course and look forward to pick-up."

"See you soon, Commander," the voice replied.

The combat team stared in disbelief.

"We could be in trouble," Max blurted.

The temperature seemed to drop precipitously. The combat team shivered as one.

"The last thing we're going to do is stay the course. Larson, switch us to manual."

Captain Hunter angled *Chrysalis* away from Farslor to put space between the planet and the ship. That would give the gunship less room to maneuver if it took advantage of the planet's gravity for either acceleration or deceleration.

"Battle Commander?" Jaq asked.

"Weapons are hot. All we need now is a target."

"Systems are active and radiating at one hundred percent," Chief Ping reported.

"I have something on passive," Dolly Norton said, holding her hands over her ears. "It's the Malibor replying to someone that they'll pick them up."

Jaq knew who they were talking to. The lander was in orbit. "Buckle up, people. All ahead full. Vector eight-five, star angle plus five."

Navigation and Thrust Control tapped their screens to bring the ship to its new heading and speed. The crew was once more pushed into the gel of their seats. The captain stared at the energy status.

Fifty-two percent.

There better not be any more ships inbound for a long while, she thought. The meter ticked down to fifty-one percent as the ion drives continued to fire. The ship drove away from the planet hard, giving it a better angle to see past the planet's shadow.

"One Malibor gunship, slowing." Chief Ping shared the image on the main screen. "No lander in sight."

"He's slowing, so the lander must be behind him. Can you get a shot?"

Tram replied. "I can angle it on the deep space side to make sure we don't hit the lander. Our people will be in a lower orbit."

"Fire at will, Tram."

"Firing six batteries, sustained fire of ten rounds per second.

Lobbing high to let gravity pull the projectiles toward the gunship."

Range to the target wasn't extreme, but it was long. Good sensors would pick up the incoming ordnance, and when they saw it, they'd start maneuvering erratically to foil the Borwyn's targeting systems.

"Gunship is turning toward the planet," the sensor chief announced.

"Taking away our angle, putting the lander into the line of fire. I recommend one missile," Alby stated.

The captain checked her status. They had nine more missiles in their inventory, but they had to fire four at the cruiser. They'd only started with fourteen. If they let the gunship turn, it could use the lander against them, either by killing it outright or to gain leverage by capturing it.

The lander was helpless.

"One missile, Alby. Approved."

"Launching from Tube One."

The missile arrowed into the void, accelerating at speeds only an unmanned craft could. It raced down the gravity well from deep space on a mild trajectory toward Farslor. The E-mag assault created a curtain behind which the missile traveled, but when it got closer to the gunship, it would be visible. Then it would have to survive the Malibor ship's defensive fire.

"Nav, take us toward the planet and give us a better firing angle." The captain didn't specify a vector, flying by the seat of her pants to create a firing solution that didn't drop the lander into the background.

Mary tapped the screen to pause the main engines and adjust the ship's orientation before re-engaging the drive to cement the ship on its new vector. With gravity's assistance, *Chrysalis* accelerated quickly.

"Incoming. Big miss." Chief Ping kept the command deck

crew informed by maintaining a running dialogue in addition to keeping the main board updated.

The salvo of E-mag rounds from the gunship headed toward deep space. They were going too fast for evasive maneuvers. They'd have to ride out the incoming.

"Eight batteries targetable. Match bearings. Steady. Fire." Alby stared at his screen unblinking, taking in every element and second of the engagement. "The missile is tracking true."

The main board showed the anti-ship missile crossing space quickly. Not as quickly as the rounds from the E-mags, but it evaded, unlike projectiles that counted on speed and momentum to make an impact. It undertook a series of evasive maneuvers, slowing the point at which it would go terminal, then accelerated with the remainder of its fuel to drive the penetrator through the hull before the warhead exploded.

"*Incoming*," Chief Ping shouted.

New streams of projectiles populated the main board. The gunship had once again guessed *Chrysalis's* new course.

"Evasive," the captain ordered calmly.

The ship jerked when the thrusters changed its orientation. The main engines drove the ship forward. *Chrysalis* slid toward the upper atmosphere.

"Bring us up, Ferd, Mary."

"Ion drives are at all ahead full, one hundred percent of capacity."

"We are aligned on new course one-three-five," Mary stated.

The ship was being pulled sideways. If it hit the atmosphere at that orientation and speed, it would be destroyed.

"Engineering, give me more power! Bec, work it."

"We're at one hundred percent," his disembodied voice shot back. "Try firing the E-mags at the planet. All of them."

"Make it happen, Tram."

The batteries swung off target and pointed at the planet.

"Max rate." The offensive weapons officer rapidly tapped his screen.

It wasn't much, but it was the nudge the ship needed. The ship bucked and screamed when it slammed into the upper atmosphere, then slowly dragged itself onto the new course. The buffeting continued for a solid thirty seconds before *Chrysalis* cleared the atmosphere.

The status board blinked, and red lights appeared. Two, then a third, and finally a fourth.

Structural integrity at Frames Two Hundred Four and Five Thirty. An airtight bulkhead that wouldn't cycle, trapping crew in the compartment behind it.

Two crew injured, thrown from their seats when they were trying to head out for damage control.

The dreaded sound of a high-velocity penetrator hitting the hull rang throughout the ship, louder than any klaxon.

"Automated damage control foaming the penetration. Minor loss of atmosphere," the environmental control officer stated.

A second round hit, then a third.

The captain gritted her teeth while holding her breath, waiting for the explosion that would end them. Each impact could hit a critical system. They wouldn't know until the systems or personnel viewed the damage.

It was a big ship with a great deal of non-critical space.

"Bring those batteries to bear and fire!"

The hum of cycling E-mags vibrated through the command deck.

"Six batteries on target."

The cruiser groaned while it struggled to gain altitude in its fight to get away from the planet.

Thirty-four percent energy remaining.

"Missile on final approach. Defensive weapons are engaging. Missile has exploded five hundred meters short of the gunship."

The captain grumbled while running up and down the status board, looking for additional damage to *Chrysalis*. No other warning lights flashed.

The gunship assumed a ballistic trajectory and stopped firing. The explosive wash had damaged it.

"Bring us around. All batteries, destroy that ship, please."

Chrysalis changed orientation while it continued on its current trajectory.

"All batteries firing."

The ship sluggishly moved straight toward the gunship, following its line of fire.

The gunship was nothing more than a practice target. The first obdurium rounds that hit it cracked its spine, and the next ones split it in half.

"Slow us down, please. Standard atmospheric braking maneuver." The captain tapped her comm to make a ship-wide broadcast. "Victory is ours! All hands prepare for an atmospheric brake and the turbulence that comes with it. As soon as we return to zero-gee, damage control teams deploy.

"Find where those last two rounds hit us. Fill the holes. Get us back into shape while we're working to recover the lander with the combat team. Well done, people. We just took on a cruiser and gunship with a few scratches of the paint. That's three active Malibor ships destroyed."

"Septiman's hammer has struck a blow for all Borwyn," the shepherd droned from the back of the command deck.

Or a dedicated crew with the tools given us by our ancestors, the captain thought.

CHAPTER 14

Stay the course.

"I see the lander. On the board."

The sensor chief transferred the lander's position to the board, which was half-filled by the planet.

"What's he doing way over there?" The rhetorical question demanded no answer. The captain accessed an external comm channel. "Commander Castle, we have dealt with the Malibor. You may come aboard *Chrysalis* at your convenience."

"Good to hear your voice, Captain," Crip replied, his voice tinny. "We're a little low on LOX. Could you pick us up?"

"We're on course zero-seven-four, star angle zero. We'll need you to come to us. Nav will send you the coordinates for pick-up."

Mary transmitted coordinates on the far side of the braking maneuver, where they would come to a full stop.

"Roger. We'll make it, but we won't be able to launch Lander Zero One again unless it gets its tanks topped off by the ship."

"Consider it done," the battle commander interjected. "We

were able to stockpile one lander's worth of LOX. Find us and return home, Crip, Max, and the rest of your team."

"We have the coordinates. We'll make the necessary adjustments. Where'd you get the LOX from?"

"We'll cover that when you get back aboard. We have a lot of debriefing to do," the captain replied.

She closed the channel. She didn't want any more information transmitted in the open. The Malibor had tried to spoof them once.

The external view showed fireballs when sections of the gunship entered the atmosphere. Reentry wasn't kind to the descending debris cloud.

The rough response from the atmosphere was nothing like the previous impact. The ship bounced and jerked, thrusting the crew against their restraints. When the navigator brought the ship away from the planet, it was a gentle climb. She spun the ship and tweaked the drives to slow down until their velocity was zero.

"Medics, see to our injured crew. Get those damage control teams out there. Fix the ship and get it ready for our next engagement." The captain released her restraints and maneuvered around the bridge while the crew updated their systems by running diagnostics and adding reports from crew members throughout the ship.

She checked the ship's energy status. Twenty-nine percent. If another Malibor ship appeared... They were dead in space, not much more than a hazard to navigation. Little more than floating debris.

Jaq looked at Alby. "Take charge of the command deck. I'll be in Engineering, seeing if there's any way we can speed up the recharge process."

The captain left the command deck and pulled herself to the ship's central shaft, then got in without a second thought.

She maneuvered around others moving up and down the shaft. She maintained her blistering pace to reach Engineering as quickly as she could.

When she arrived, it seemed as if Bec was waiting for her. She clamped her boots to the deck to keep the wind from his rant from blowing her down the corridor.

"We can't charge them any faster. That's what you're here for, isn't it?"

"Why else would I be here besides to tell you that your people did great? The engines and the technical systems worked magnificently."

Bec threw his hands out and turned back and forth to take in the energy generation section and the ion drives. "We're trying to put the ship back together. You almost split us in half! Do you know how big that crack is at Frame Five Thirty? It's two meters long. Two. Meters."

"Since the ship is over a hundred meters wide at that point, I'll take that as a win."

"It's not a win. It's catastrophic!"

"Weld eyebolts on either side. Wrench it back together, then weld that crack. Strap it, then move to two-zero-four and do the same thing. Then decrease the recharge time. We're nothing more than a target right now. If we can't get the energy levels up, we'll die together, naysayers and visionaries alike."

"Which are you?"

"Chief, you sly space amoeba. You'll figure it out. Two meters? We got off light."

"Sometimes you befuddle me, and the rest of the time, I'm simply appalled."

"I'll take that as a compliment." She clapped the chief engineer on the shoulder. "I have confidence in you. Understand, we're nothing more than a big target as long as our power is below fifty percent."

He didn't dignify her statement with an answer, just pushed off to join one of his people on top of the reactor.

The captain wasn't sure she'd made the situation better or worse by talking to the chief engineer. Bec Draper was his own man. It might have helped. They'd talked about faster recharging often enough. He had to have ideas about how to do it.

She'd given him a greater sense of urgency, but they needed it. Power was survival.

They were on the far side of the planet, not far from the second moon but blind to anything coming from the direction of Septimus.

The captain wandered the corridors in zero-gee, bumping into damage control teams working on issues caused by the impact with Farslor's atmosphere. She made her way to Frame Five Thirty, Deck Two, where a major spar was critical to hull integrity and orientation.

If the hull wasn't straight, all the E-mags would need to be recalibrated. Then they'd have trouble keeping them calibrated on a crooked ship. Same for the speed. The ship would shake itself apart, trying to fly true. They'd gotten a small sample of that with the final full power run.

They'd suffered through the time of pain. Now was the time to heal. Now was the time to recover and reorient the Borwyn people toward their goal while accepting that they had to scavenge from the damaged and destroyed to rebuild that which could be rebuilt.

Missiles. Maybe there were some in *Hornet's* launch tubes that had survived the destruction of the cruiser. With only eight remaining, they couldn't take on the bulk of a fleet.

Jaq had to believe the Malibor had only sent scouts. Reconnaissance in force, not the bulk of their combat fleet. They might have abandoned Farslor, but that didn't mean they'd abandoned the war.

Unfortunately. The war might have continued apace.

The Borwyn had the element of surprise, and maybe that would continue if the latest casualties hadn't gotten off a distress message. They shouldn't have been able to from the dark side of Farslor.

The Malibor knew a Borwyn cruiser had returned, and when their ships had sallied out to see, they hadn't made it home. Let the Malibor ponder that. Another advantage for *Chrysalis* and her crew. After surprise came intimidation.

A veritable ghost ship. Let the stories commence.

They'd be dangerous again if they had the time to recharge.

The first step was to repair the most immediate damage, then recover the combat team. After the crew was on board and accounted for, they could return to the business at hand.

Returning to Septimus. The threshold had been crossed.

At Frame Five Thirty, the captain controlled her shock at what she saw. The two-meter crack was a lateral break that had split one of the main spars nearly in half. The steel was ten centimeters thick, yet it had cracked like poorly made pottery.

They had welded on eye bolts and were clamping hydraulic jacks to them. They stopped to greet the captain.

"Don't stop on my account. The best service you can perform is repairing that ugly scar. Our home deserves better than the likes of that." She pointed at it, distaste flavoring her words and expression.

"We're on it, Captain."

The two got back to jacking the two sides back together. One jack first, then the other, then back to the first. Ratcheting back and forth to get the metal to accede to their desires. The two parts of the spar snapped together with the sound of an E-mag firing. The three crew would have jumped, but they were all clamped to the deck.

"That was exhilarating," the captain said with a reserved smile.

The damage control team checked the fit and turned back, grinning.

"Just like it grew there. Step back a little. Sparks will fly."

The one with the welding torch gestured, and the captain backed away. The weld arced and delivered heat and melted metal along the tiny crack until the entire two meters had been addressed. They added the straps and alignment bars and tracked beads along the entirety of the repair, giving extra structure to the break.

"Fascinating." Jaq shook both crew's hands, then continued to the lander control room.

The remote pilot was twirling in the zero-gee. He waved.

"Looks like the lander is inbound. I'll take control in..." He checked his screen. "Ooh! Thirty seconds." He settled into his seat and toggled the joystick and other controls while they were still disconnected from the lander.

Commander Castle spoke into the small space. "It's all you, Benjy."

"I have the bubble." His panel lit up, and the screen showed the lander in orientation to the cruiser. He fired the engines briefly to slow the ship until it was nearly stationary. Benjy touched the attitude thrusters to move the lander at a centimeters-per-second pace to bring it into the launch tube.

The captain leaned against the bulkhead, anchoring her boots to watch the delicate procedure.

She had once been a remote lander operator when all they were using the landers for was asteroid mining. She still loved the precision.

Benjy brought the nosecone into the tube and hooked up

the tethers. After that, he stopped flying the ship and retracted the cables to pull it into the tube. Rollers kept it from bouncing off the walls and aligned it, but it had been oriented perfectly and didn't touch the sides. When it was locked to the docking ring, the remote pilot closed the entry door and pressurized the space.

He brushed off his hands, grinned, and powered down the system.

"Nicely done, Benjy." The captain headed for the access ladder, arriving before the soldiers made it out.

Commander Castle was the first one to the top of the egress tube. He pushed his gear before him, which was easy in zero-gee.

"Welcome home, Crip."

He nodded without smiling. "Everyone made it, but not everyone is alive," he started. "We can talk to them. Maybe Andreeson and Gilmore will be the last to die in this war."

The captain stepped carefully to her deputy, then gripped his arms and looked up into his face. "I doubt that. We faced *Butterfly*. She had survived, and the Malibor made her spaceworthy. We fought a replica of this ship and two gunships that both landed rounds on target."

Crip stared into the distance while the soldiers disembarked one by one. Danzig was the second-to-last one out. He pushed his gear in front of him while dragging Andreeson's body behind him.

Max was last with Gilmore.

The captain shook each of their hands, then placed her palm on the chests of the fallen one by one, saying a short prayer for each.

The combat team continued toward their team room, leaving Crip to talk to the captain privately. Max called for the medics the second he could access an internal comm.

"Where's your pulse rifle?" Jaq asked.

With everything else to talk about, that was the thing the captain had noticed.

"Funny thing, that. I traded it—without a power pack, mind you—to a Malibor for a fur and his promise not to start a wildfire that would burn the lander."

"Can they reverse-engineer it?"

"They were wearing hides and carrying bows and arrows. They lived in mud huts. I think there is zero chance that they can reverse-engineer a pulse rifle. It'll probably be a status symbol for Gregor, like a shaman's staff. Nothing more."

"What if we can't replace it?"

"I felt like I had no choice. The conversation with the Malibor was worth the permanent loss of one rifle."

"Turns out we might be able to replace it," Jaq said with a smile. "Alby recovered a full weapons platform. We have all the magnets and metal we need to fabricate a few things. Alby has a plan to get more, too."

"I missed a lot of the action. I'm sorry, Jaq. My place was at your side as your deputy."

The captain gave him a playful shove. "Your place is where I need you, which happened to be with that team on the planet. It couldn't have been easy."

"I could say the same for what you did up here. I'll admit it was traumatic. We killed a bunch of Malibor before we got everyone on both sides settled down. The team changed, no doubt about that."

"Two days into our return, and we've all changed. Harder? More focused? Better understanding of the magnitude of the challenge before us?"

Crip studied the captain's features. She hadn't slept much, judging by the dark circles under her eyes and the lines around her mouth. "All that and then some. It was violently cold down there. Everyone's envious of my big fur."

"That might be the most ridiculous thing I've ever heard."

Crip held up a finger. *Wait one.* He dove into the access tube and was gone for less than a minute. He returned with the fur.

The captain had to cover her nose. "Get that off my ship."

"It's how the Malibor smell."

"The violence wasn't from the cold. It was the assault on your senses. You better get your head checked. Right after you flush that thing out the airlock."

"No can do, Captain. This is my war trophy. It came at a great cost." He turned deadly serious. "A very great cost."

"Make the smell go away, and you can keep it. If that gets into the air handling system, I'll send *you* out the airlock *with* your trophy."

The captain looked toward the team room. She understood what Crip had implied. "Get yourself ASAP to the command deck. We have a great deal to talk about. Malibor tactics have changed, and we're behind the times."

"The Malibor defeated our forebears. Did we think it would be easy to defeat them this time around? Necessary, yes, but not easy."

The captain was taken aback. "No, not easy, but our ion drives give us an advantage. We can accelerate faster and maneuver better. They gave us the edge in our first engagements. Get to the bridge. We'll review our tactics when we have the command team together. Wait. No. Clean yourself up first. Get that stench away from me and whatever you do, don't bring it on the command deck."

CHAPTER 15

The focus of one's life will change over time, but never the desire to keep going.

Crip snorted, but deep sadness threatened to consume him. "I'm sorry we lost two of our people."

The captain leaned close. "This is the last time I'm going to talk about this. Speak with the shepherd. You don't have time to vacillate between being focused and wallowing in despair. You need to shake it off."

Crip looked the captain in the eye. "If it was that easy, I would have already done it. I'll stop for a moment with the shepherd, but I don't see how he can relate. He'll spout some nonsense from the good book. It will be tangentially related, and I'll nod and make believe it's insightful."

The captain turned away. For her entire life, she had been focused on the technical and tactical strategies that involved the Borwyn's return to Septimus. She wasn't ill-equipped for the deeper questions Crip Castle had brought up, but she needed time to internalize them.

If it was not derived from Septiman, where did the

Borwyn's higher purpose come from? What made them different from the Malibor? Maybe their embrace of peace made them more sensitive to loss? The shepherd and his teachings... sacrilegious. It was what they all thought, yet no one had said it aloud.

"We can talk privately. Maybe the shepherd doesn't have the answers, but we have to let him try, just like we have to let Sensors, Nav, and Thrust Control do their jobs. Everyone has a role to play in the overall health of this ship and our crew, who are the last remaining Borwyn as far as we know.

"The re-appearance of *Butterfly* crushed my soul. Marry that to the disappearance of the Malibor from Farslor, and the only conclusion I can draw is that the Malibor took over Septimus so thoroughly that they completed the genocide of our people.

"Maybe it's better if we believe Septiman is testing us than turn our backs on a higher purpose. I also doubt what I cannot see." The captain stared at the bulkhead beside her. She chuckled and looked around before whispering, "What else would the shepherd do if he wasn't ministering? Can you imagine him flying the ship?"

Through the trials of their return to the battlefield of a fifty-year-old war, the one constant was the absurdity of it all.

"Of anything you could have said to get my head in a better place, that was it. Thanks, Jaq." He gripped her shoulder in a moment of warmth. "I'm going to turn the temperature down in my quarters and strap my fur over my bed. I'll sleep like a baby."

"Remember what I said about that smell getting into the air-handling system."

"You're already used to it, and it's not so bad," Crip countered.

"It's the most revolting thing I've ever smelled, and I used to work the ship's sanitation and reclamation system. One of many sordid jobs that weren't as horrible as that *thing*."

"I love you too, Jaq." Crip winked.

The captain shook her head. "Be on the command deck in thirty minutes."

"Thirty. Great! I have time to stop by and see Taurus."

Jaq planted her palm in the middle of Crip's chest. He floated backward from the impact.

"If you want to have any chance with her, you won't. There's some womanly advice you didn't ask for but you're getting, regardless."

Crip whistled. "Sounds like someone's jealous. I never thought you would be pining over your deputy. I guess there could be stranger things, like the shepherd flying *Chrysalis*."

He pushed off and sailed down the corridor, dragging his fur over the captain's body as he passed.

She grimaced and brushed her nose. Jaq noticed that he was headed toward his quarters, not the thruster control engineering station. She accessed the internal comm. "Chief Ping, anything suggesting more Malibor ships are on their way?"

"Nothing inside Farslor's shadow," he replied. "The decoy isn't beyond the horizon to give us a clear view of Septimus.

Jaq had thirty minutes to check the damage on the forward hull spar and how the repairs were going before she needed to be back on the command deck. It was on the way, and with a favorable tailwind, she could make it in less than ten minutes.

A tailwind only the air-handling system could provide. She'd take a shortcut not available to most of the crew.

She worked her way toward an access hatch that abutted the main elevator shaft and went through, closing it behind her. The wind pulled her hair toward the bow, so she eased into the flow and let it carry her. She dragged her hands along the smooth sides of the shaft to slow her down.

The air was the cleanest on the ship since it had just gone through the filters on its way to being dispersed. A tube on the other side of the main longitudinal shaft carried CO_2-heavy air away and returned it for processing, removing contaminants and scrubbing the carbon dioxide until the oxygen was back at twenty percent.

Frame numbers showed on her way past. She took it easy. She was rarely alone, so she reveled in the brief periods between engagements with the crew. She had to always be "on." She could never let her guard down, but everyone needed to feel that it was okay to let theirs down with her as Crip had just done.

Everyone had someone to go to except the captain. It was the burden of command, even though all Borwyn were on a first-name basis. The crew wasn't just the crew; they were all family and friends. They'd grown up together, but like cancer, if a tumor was allowed to fester, it would infect the whole body. She couldn't let people see her as anything but confident. She needed them to get past their doubts and inhibitions.

For the greater good of *Chrysalis*. For the survival of the Borwyn.

Even if Septiman didn't exist, they still needed to believe since the greater purpose would drive and succor them when nothing else was left.

She realized her answers while she was alone in an air-handling tube. "For the greater good of Septiman, may the Borwyn realize your vision of a united people since it's our vision, too."

Jaq dragged her boots down the inside of the shaft, in addition to her hands, to slow down by Frame Two Hundred. At the next hatch, she climbed out.

"Hey, there you are!" someone shouted.

The captain waved and smiled, but the owner of the voice was looking down the corridor.

"I have it." A young child hurried up and handed a heavy spool of welding wire to a crew member working on the cracked spar.

The captain stepped closer to the group, her magnetic boots clumping on the deck. She kneeled to intercept the youngster. "Thanks for carrying that for us."

"Doesn't weigh anything," the child replied.

The benefits of zero-gee.

This crew didn't have hydraulic jacks.

"Hold up." Jaq gestured for them to turn off the welding equipment.

The team complied, and the welder raised her goggles.

"The aft team is finished with the jacks. That's the best way to pull this together and weld it after the gap is eliminated. I'll have them sent up."

"We've been struggling with this," a team member admitted.

Jaq pointed at spots above and below the crack. "Weld eyebolts here and here. You can connect the jacks, then crank the two halves back into place. It was great to see."

"Maybe they could come here and do it?" the welder asked.

The captain wanted to agree, but everyone needed to get better at what they did. Jaq shook her head. "I'll call them and have them come, but I'll need you to do the work under their guidance. It won't be as easy, quick, or efficient, but it's for the best. Next time, you might have to take care of it yourselves."

The welder looked disappointed and set the torch aside. "I'm not very good at this."

"I am!" the child declared.

Three sets of eyeballs went to the youngster. "Let me show you."

"We need those eyebolts welded on," the captain offered helpfully. "I have a call to make."

The training began, but not the team training the youngster. The boy secured his boots to the bulkhead, then crooked a finger at the grinder. When it was in his small hands, he cleaned the spot to the bare metal. He pushed the grinder away and motioned for the eyebolt and the welding torch.

With a pad to hold the bolt, he settled it into place, eyed it, adjusted it, and then with one small hand driving the welder, tacked the eyebolt into place. He removed his heat-resistant pad to check it, then turned to the damage control team for confirmation.

"Looks good," they told him in unison.

He attacked the eyebolt with both hands on the welding torch and the eyebolt centered in the middle of his wide stance —another benefit of zero-gee. He stood on the wall, and the others stood on the deck, at ninety degrees to each other.

He demonstrated his sinuous flexibility as he twisted and contorted to give himself the best angle to deliver the bead. After less than a minute, he was finished. He held his hand out for the next eyebolt.

The captain had called the other team, and they were on their way.

"Where did you learn to do that?" Jaq asked.

"My dad is the welder on the other damage control team. He's the best on the ship."

The captain realized there were more reasons for her to smile than not when it came to the crew, the situation, and the Borwyn as a whole. If one had to fight for their survival, one might as well do it with the good people she was surrounded by.

"I think your father might have some competition. Get to it. Don't leave a whole lot for them to do when they get here. I'm sure they'll be pleasantly surprised. I need to get to the command deck, but I know these repairs are in good hands. Carry on."

The captain pulled herself horizontal and kicked off the bulkhead toward the central shaft. The command deck and, more importantly, her command team awaited.

Jaq moved slowly down the final corridor to the command deck. The droning of the air handler greeted her like an old friend. She first went to the sensor section.

Slade was ready for her. "Still nothing, Captain. You'll be the second to know."

"Why second?"

"We'll see it first since there is nothing more important than feeding you information. It's my reason for living."

Absurdity again. "I accept your deification as part of Septiman's greater plan for us all."

"*All hail Septiman!*" the shepherd shouted from the back of the bridge. With his eyes closed, he rocked gently.

"Carry on," the captain agreed as she returned to her seat. "Staff meeting in five minutes. A meeting to end all meetings that could go on for hours. So much talking. You will all be blessed to be a part of it."

Let them mull that over, she thought.

Tram leaned toward the battle commander. "She's kidding, isn't she? Please tell me she's kidding."

"I wish I could." Alby placed his hand over his heart and muttered a prayer.

CHAPTER 16

Fix the ship. Rally the crew. Get back into the fight.

The command crew assembled, faces dark with trepidation about what was to come. The captain had had her fun. She didn't need to torture those she trusted most.

"This will take five minutes." Their looks of relief made her laugh. "What, you don't like my meetings?"

Crip came to her defense. "We need to talk about what happened and how we can be better in the future, from the combat team to the tech recovery team. That is new, by the way. Also the coordination of the crew during combat. It all funnels through this space."

"Indeed, it does. How important was it for the combat team to have primary and secondary plans?"

"We had a primary plan for engagement, but nothing in case of a shipboard emergency and getting stuck on the planet. We were ill-equipped for the cold, even though we thought we were fine. Now I have my fur, and no one can take that away from me." He locked eyes with the captain and stared in an impromptu chicken-blink contest.

"What fur?" Alby asked. "I was trapped in a weapons platform. We need to carve up the one we have, then get ourselves another one. Sensors have coordinates on an additional three. Firepower! More firepower."

"I can do the battle commander's job," Tram joked.

"I'm not obsolete yet," Alby replied.

The captain blinked first, then looked from face to face. "We've always been spread thin. Here's what we're going to do. We'll hold a ship-wide memorial service for Andreeson, Gilmore, and Nanticoke. Then Alby will head to the cargo bay and continue the recycling of the Malibor's junk pile.

"Throw anything that's not useful into space, but the railguns, mesh, copper, and interior circuits? Get that stuff out of there, then clear the cargo bay for the next one we'll dismantle. Crip, prepare the combat team to board the hulk of the ship formerly known as *Butterfly*. We need to recover any surviving missiles or confirm that they were destroyed since they should fit in our tubes. We need any weapons and power systems that are intact. Slade, we need systems we can bounce sensor signals off. The decoy Alby put together worked well to give us a good view. I'm not sure why the spoof didn't work, except that the Malibor probably saw us with their naked eyes before we got into the moon's shadow. Questions?"

"I'm relegated to weapons research and development?" Alby asked, his head cocked in surprise.

"Yes. We need you there more than we need you as the battle commander. We need weapons to give us an advantage. Better and more, plus a remote capability like a weapons platform that we control."

"I'll take it. Good luck, Tram. You're it." Alby gave his replacement a thumbs-up.

The offensive weapons operator was surprised, even though it was inevitable that he would move into the billet.

"Train your replacement." The captain tipped her head to peer down her nose at the new battle commander, Tram Stamper.

"I already know who it should be. Taurus Lindman." He smiled broadly.

Crip shook his head. "You guys are not my friends."

The captain ignored the quips. "I'll need the combat team to focus on tech recovery. I see no value in sending you back to the planet."

"If that's the best use of us, so be it." Crip didn't just look disappointed; he *was* disappointed. He had hoped for another opportunity to talk to Gregor, but the captain was right.

"Septimus is our goal, but if we're to put the combat team on the ground on our home planet, the skies have to be clear of the enemy. Judging by how quickly three ships made it to Farslor, the Malibor have a healthy space presence. We're going to have to peel them off one by one and destroy them. To do that, we'll need a lot more missiles."

She didn't have to expound. Each Malibor ship had come to the end of its useful service life thanks to a Borwyn anti-ship missile. They only had eight left, and it was her belief that they'd run out of missiles long before they ran out of targets.

If only a Borwyn colony existed that they could use for resupply, but no such thing had survived from fifty years ago.

Could they build one?

Probably, but they didn't have enough people to staff it and work on building missiles and weapons while *Chrysalis* made hit-and-run attacks on the Malibor. Jaq didn't want to go into combat any more shorthanded than she had been in the previous battles. Everyone had a role to play.

Even young boys who knew how to weld. She shouldn't, but she was convinced she had to. The boy was going to be assigned to a damage control team. He had talent and desire, and the captain believed in those qualities. Everyone who could contribute did. She was surprised she hadn't heard about the lad, but it was a big ship. She had seen him and knew who he was, but nothing else about him.

That wasn't good for a so-called family. Had she dismissed the youth on the ship? If they hadn't told her about Dolly, the thirteen-year-old wouldn't have been working the sensors.

It made Jaq long for a time when children could be children and not hardworking members of the crew who were held to a performance standard like every crew member.

When they started working was irrelevant. There was only one ship. There was nowhere else for any of them to go.

The former battle commander broke her reverie. "Captain, I think we can do it." Alby leaned close to see if she was listening. "A construction platform using, say, the recovered remains of *Butterfly*."

What Alby was saying finally registered.

"How much work will that take?" Jaq asked.

"We don't know what shape the cruiser is in," Alby replied. "It might be relatively minor."

Jaq blew out a long breath. "You pounded it with everything we had. Have some faith in yourself, Alby. You killed it good and dead. I doubt there's much to recover, but I can hope we find something useful on board. I don't think we want to go down the road of splitting up our people. The next engagements will be worse for *Chrysalis*, which means we need everyone we have to keep us flying."

"You handled the first engagements with twenty fewer crew, lacking your engineers and soldiers. You can do it. *We* can do it."

"We had no reserve if we ran into real trouble." The captain shrugged. "A major hull breach. Loss of the drives or attitude thrusters. We lose one compartment's worth of people, and we're all going to die. I'm sorry, Albrecht, but I can't take that risk. We might have to at some point, but not yet. Wherever we go and whatever we do, we're going to do it together."

Alby slapped his thigh. "Then that's what we'll do. Thanks for listening, and even more, thanks for explaining. I know you're right, and I also know we will need weapons if we're going to prosecute this war to a conclusion that's favorable to us —as in, we don't die."

The captain scanned the command deck. The crew had drifted back to their positions. Most were going about the business of putting the ship back together for the next engagement. The sensor section was actively scanning widely, with occasional focused scans close to Farslor to see if a ship was sneaking around it.

Nothing showed. Space was clear except for two distant weapons platforms, dead in space without their power cores.

Chrysalis's energy reserves were up to forty percent, enough that the ship could maneuver. If the enemy appeared, the only tactic would be to run to deep space, if necessary, as undesirable as that was.

They had too much work to do right here in the shadow of the second moon. They had more farther out, where the beacon showed *Butterfly* on its ballistic trajectory along the orbital plane but away from the Armanor star, which meant farther from Septimus. Intercepting the right sections and slowing them down would be another engineering challenge, but when they had sufficient power to chase down the hulk, they would. Then the weapons platforms, when there was space available in the big cargo hold.

Which reminded the captain. "Shouldn't you be aft, stripping that Malibor platform?"

Alby threw his hands up in surrender and unlocked his

magnetic boots. "I was hoping for a bite to eat first. It's been a while."

"Wait one," Jaq said. "Comm, get me the ship." She locked herself to the deck. When the intercom crackled to life, she spoke. "All hands, let me get your attention. I want to pay my respects to those we lost in our first battles. Gilmore, Andreeson, and Nanticoke were our friends and our family. Know that they didn't die needlessly. Their sacrifice makes us better. Their names shall be remembered. Say them with me. Gilmore." She waited while the command crew repeated the name. "Andreeson. Nanticoke. Their names and their contributions will be forever etched in Borwyn lore. They will remain in our hearts. May Septiman welcome them into his home as friends."

She pointed at the shepherd, who continued the prayer.

"The will of Septiman is a mystery we will never solve. Know that to Him, it makes sense, and our brethren join Him in the wider universe to continue working for the greater good of all Borwyn. Amen."

The crew mumbled their amens and went back to work.

"Crip." The captain waved her second to her. "Start cycling the crew through chow and rest periods."

"What if the enemy appears?"

"Then we'll sound general quarters. Life has gotten real hard, real fast. We're all going to have to adjust."

Crip knew exactly what she meant. "I'll take care of it."

He moved to his station and climbed into his seat before scrolling through the department heads and checking repair progress. Two departments had started sending their people to the mess deck, even though it wasn't showing as active. The crew who worked there were still on damage control projects.

Jaq waved at him. "While you're at it, can you get the mess team back to the mess hall?"

"I didn't miss this," he admitted, but he went back to his

communications board and contacted the right people to arrange the breaks.

"Someone has to do it, and I'm the captain. I missed you, that's for sure." Jaq waggled her fingers at him.

He waved her away.

"Ten minutes before it's up. Chief cook is in place. Port and starboard watches set. We'll see the implementation over the next thirty minutes. May I recommend we move into the shadow of the second moon?"

Forty-two percent. "Nav and Thrust Control, calculate energy usage from a low power burn to get us to zero thrust station, keeping behind the second moon."

The captain floated free above her seat. She did a somersault while she waited.

"Three percent, Captain. We can get there in two hours, using mostly attitude thrusters. Max acceleration half a gee."

"Take us around the moon and park us somewhere we can recover and recharge." The captain activated the ship-wide comm. "All hands prepare for movement. Acceleration to reach half a gee. Collect up your tools and lock down your floaters."

The ship moved at a pace that barely affected the gee forces within the ship. They pulled the captain to the deck, but they wouldn't keep her there should she try to move. She waited as the force increased until she was steady at half a gee.

Being used to zero-gee, half a gee felt heavy. The captain walked across the command deck without using her magnetic clamps. "Crip, you have the command deck. Chief Ping, you are the eyes and ears of this ship. Don't let anyone sneak up on us. Work with Alby on extending our eyes and ears. I'm not willing to sacrifice another lander."

"We sacrificed a lander? Is that why we had extra LOX?" Crip finally realized what had happened.

"It kept us from dying an ugly death," the captain

explained. "Yes, we sacrificed one of our landers. We pumped the tanks dry before sending it out."

The deputy leaned against his seat. "Infrared. I'll add that to the needs. Combat team needs better eyes."

"Information will give us a continued edge, along with our ion drives. The Malibor can't match our speed. Make better decisions faster and react quicker with a more nimble and meteoric ship."

"Nimble and meteoric?" Crip laughed. "Someone's been reading too many of those old motivational books."

"You should try them." The captain waved over her shoulder on the way through the hatch. "I'll be in my quarters."

Jaq had a lot of thinking to do, and the war had just begun.

CHAPTER 17

Duty before self.

"One hundred percent," Crip announced to the command crew.

The captain had been hovering in the hatchway, but at their moment of triumph, she was nowhere to be seen. Crip laughed it off and returned to the task at hand, planning the intercept of the destroyed cruiser.

Mary offered, "Recommend course vector three-zero-four, star angle plus nine. Overtake speed of thirty kilometers per minute for two hours five minutes."

"That's the easy part. The hard part will be grappling that thing to slow it down, and we won't be sure how to do that until we see the ship." Crip glanced at the corridor and saw the captain talking to a crew member.

He moved out of his seat and used the rails to move to the hatch. He waited politely while the captain talked through solving an engineering problem. When the crew member's eyes lit up with understanding, they shook hands, and the captain returned to the command deck.

"Ready?" Jaq asked nonchalantly.

Crip pointed at the main screen. The three green digits told the story.

"That's nice to see. Let's see how long we can keep it above fifty percent." Jaq moved into her seat and informed the crew that the ship was going to move. The standard message to secure equipment before it became a projectile went out. They needed no more injuries.

That reminded the captain she needed to follow up with the people in the small medical facility. Three crew had been sedated to aid in their healing.

"Course three-zero-four, star angle plus nine, all ahead standard." She went to the hatch. "You have it, Crip. Heading to Medical. I'll be right back."

Crip had planned on meeting with the combat team to prep for *Butterfly's* exploration. He'd call the team room and join them there when the captain returned.

She waited in the corridor, surreptitiously watching her command crew work. They had a sense of purpose.

Jaq walked slowly under the half-gee pressure holding her to the deck. She accessed the elevator in the central shaft and headed up one deck to where the medical facilities were located. It was little more than a big closet with four bunk beds end to end in the middle so the two medics could work from both sides of a patient. The walls were lined with cabinets containing their meager medical supplies.

The things they needed most were bandages for cuts and ice for bruises. Antibiotics were in limited supply since bacterial infections had been eradicated by the previous generation. Viruses were also a thing of the past. The crew generally didn't get sick, but going dirt side had enlightened them as to the challenges they had to be prepared for.

But some had been injured, and those three were occupying

the four beds. Two had broken bones, and one was still unconscious after hitting her head.

"What's the prognosis?" the captain asked the lieutenant on duty.

The woman was from the sensor maintenance group. There was no doctor on board, no person whose sole duty was to look after the medical needs of the crew. Everyone performed double duty. Jaq decided it was time to give the shepherd an additional duty.

"We're letting the bones knit on these two for another forty-eight hours. Then we'll turn them loose with simple support braces. We've had our share of head injuries, but this one isn't responding to the usual treatments. She remains in a coma. We would like to be sure her brain isn't swelling, but our scanner is currently out of order. We'll need an engineering team up here as soon as someone is available."

"What can you do for her?" Jaq asked. The patient's complexion was a waxy gray but lacked the sheen of perspiration. "She looks like she's dying."

"I think we'll have to relieve the pressure on her brain, but we can only do that when we're not moving. There cannot be any disruptions since we have to cut a section of her skull away and let her brain swell. We'll keep it hydrated with a special fluid until it retreats into her head, and then we can reattach the section of her skull. She'll be heavily sedated throughout."

"That sounds horrific." The captain brushed a stray lock of hair out of the woman's face. "We should be stopped and at zero-gee in three to four hours. Plan the surgery for that time. Have your team assemble, and as soon as we're at a full stop, start the procedure."

The medic furrowed her brow while staring at the patient. "I've never done one. The last one was done by the oldsters. There's a video and instructions. I'd better watch it."

The captain lightly rested her fingers on the patient's head. The warmth belied the complexion. Her body was fighting, but it was losing. "I fear that if we do nothing, Annabelle will die. Is something better than nothing? I'd like to think so. Worse might mean she passes a little more quickly. I can live with that. You should, too, because doing *nothing* will kill her as surely as making a mistake while trying to do *something*."

"Maybe we can wait until the scanner gets fixed." The medic sounded hopeful.

"Once time is lost, you can never get it back. It's already been too long if you ask me, and that's not a dig or a condemnation of any sort. We can only do the best we can. Get your team together, and get ready to perform the surgery. The good news is that you only need to remove a section of the skull, not cut into the gray mass. We have the tools. You only need to use them."

"That's all? Why was I worried?" The medic tried to keep it light, but it wasn't working. Her hand shook. She examined it as if it were a detached limb. "I'll do my best."

"You know what needs to be done. Don't be afraid. Have a healthy respect for what you don't know while trying to fill the gaps during the time you have available. I'll send the shepherd down. He needs to learn this stuff so he can take a rotation in Medical."

"The shepherd?"

"He can look out for our health and well-being too. Is a spiritual guide that different from a physical one? I'm going to argue that it is not." The captain nodded once and stepped toward the door, then hesitated. "I hope he doesn't faint at the sight of blood."

She walked out slowly and headed for her quarters. They were on the same level as the command deck, attached to what used to be the ready room. Separate and private meetings were a thing of the past, however. The staff met in their workspaces, and the former meeting room had been turned into a couple's quarters. It would have been for her deputy, one Crip Castle, but he wasn't half of a couple, so he shared the quarters with Albrecht Risor, who had also put the ship and its mission before a relationship.

Everyone had to share except the captain.

Outside her quarters, she ran into Sergeant Tremayne. "Coming to see Crip?"

"I am since he's trapped up here while the captain is roaming unsupervised." He raised an eyebrow to see if his volley had made an impact. It wasn't his first and wouldn't be his last.

The captain laughed. "'Gallivanting' is the term I would have used." She turned serious. "Good luck with the wreckage. We're not sure it's worth going over, but it was a clean split along the hull, from what I saw. There might be nothing to salvage, or there might be a lot. You and your team will have to figure that out."

"We will. We're adding an extra layer of armor to our spacesuits. I think it will be a razor maze over there, and we don't want any breaches."

"No breaches for the combat team. That'd be something to see." She tipped her chin and entered her quarters, leaving the sergeant to figure out what she'd just said.

Jaq sat at her desk and leaned back. Her computer screen replicated the dashboard on the captain's chair. The energy store drifted down, as it did during any use of the engines, but barely. It showed at ninety-nine percent. At low levels of usage, power generation matched output. They'd never been able to generate huge amounts of power, but they had figured out how to store it efficiently. Had they not done so, they wouldn't have been able to operate.

That was something else Jaq wanted to see. The old *Chrysalis* had no power storage since the reactors had a greater amount of fissile material available, so it could be run a lot hotter. Maybe they'd be able to recover some from *Butterfly*.

The captain had been blessed with hope based on an abundance of vision, but she'd started seeing even more possibilities, thanks to Alby's recovery of the weapons platform. Everything they came across had potential. She'd been fixated on destroying the Malibor when she should have looked at how the Borwyn could use every bit of processed metal and technology against their enemy.

We didn't need to come fully armed to fight every battle, she realized. *We only needed to come with the attitude that we'll take what we need and use it to take more.*

Did that make them scavengers? Did it matter? It did make them efficient. Conquerors took from the conquered like the Malibor had done with *Butterfly*. They'd renamed it *Hornet* and flown it into a battle against the people who'd built it.

Lessons taught by the enemy. "It doesn't make us the same as them."

She would keep making that point to herself as long as she could defend it. They had to defeat the Malibor to reclaim Septimus, and she was willing to do what it took. She activated the comm on her desk to call the command deck. "Crip and Max, can you meet me in my quarters, please?"

Twenty seconds later, they showed up. That was another benefit of her quarters being next to the command deck. Crip knocked once and opened the door.

Jaq waved them in. "You talked to the Malibor," she started. "Did they seem interested in peace?"

"They seemed curious, although we've been the demons in their children's bedtime stories their whole lives. I think the reality of who we are surprised them. We had superior firepower, and although we killed a bunch of them, we didn't kill them all. I think they recognized that we tried to talk to them," Crip explained.

Max added, "They seemed to have their own issues. The hunters from one village were indifferent to us killing hunters from another village. They live in a harsh environment. We gave a different view to their survival-focused existence."

"Our lives are survival-focused," the captain replied.

"Their lives are focused on their next meal and not freezing to death in their sleep. That's what I saw. They've learned to live in their domain, but they are not masters of it."

Crip looked at Max. The sergeant hadn't been fully supportive of his first efforts at talking to the Malibor, but he'd come around. They hadn't wanted to antagonize the locals. They had no technology and were dangerous, but they were no threat to *Chrysalis*. Once they were managed, they were little threat to the combat team.

"The Malibor abandoned their own people. Maybe they thought they were dead." Jaq steepled her fingers before her as she ran through the scenarios in her mind.

"Someone bombed them. Are we sure it wasn't us?" Crip asked.

"I'd like to say it wasn't, but *Chrysalis* lost contact with the fleet when it was sent spinning toward deep space. It wasn't this ship; that we *can* be sure of. *Chrysalis* didn't have the capacity to deliver nukes to the planet's surface."

"Maybe with a lander?" Max suggested.

The captain pointed down. "We had all six intact. It wasn't one of ours."

Max nodded. "I feel like an idiot."

Jaq waved the statement away. "It wasn't us, but was it other Borwyn? Since we are the only Borwyn we know about, we can say categorically that we didn't do it and don't know who did.

"Also, that was fifty years ago. We didn't wantonly raze their villages this time. I want to win this war, but I'm not going to make war on people who are just going about their lives. As you said, just trying to survive."

Crip and Max looked at each other.

"How did you feel when you blew that gunship out of the sky?" Max asked.

"What do you mean? Relief. It stopped them from shooting at us. What else would I feel?"

"Nothing. On the planet, seeing them as you put a projectile through their body is a little harder. Never mind. It was an errant thought."

"It wasn't." Jaq studied the two men before her. She could empathize that their experience had been different and far more personal, but she couldn't completely understand. The gunship had tried to spoof the lander, and the only Malibor the captain had seen had tried to kill her. She had no problem destroying their ships.

"Maybe there are different Malibor. Like you said about the villages, some might not care what happens to the others. What if the Malibor have descended into factions that are fighting each other?"

"Interesting premise," Crip mused. "How do we find out without getting ourselves killed?"

"Disable them so bad that they have no choice. Leave the hulks of their dead ships where they can find them. Instill fear while showing compassion."

Crip chuckled. "We shall terrorize you into appreciating how peaceful we are!"

Max laughed until he gasped. After he caught his breath, he added, "That didn't work so great on Farslor. Crip went to talk with them unarmed."

"After you hit them hard enough for them to know what you were capable of."

The men nodded.

"That was all I wanted. Your experience on Farslor is the best we have. Your insight is important. Before we returned, we had time. Now, everything is happening so quickly. Time used to be our friend. Now, it is most assuredly not. I won't hold you up any longer. Send the shepherd to me if you'd be so kind."

They excused themselves and left.

Jaq stared at her screen. The dashboard showed all systems green, which meant the structural repairs had been completed. The time suggested they'd gotten done early. She wondered if their new young welder had been responsible for hurrying things along.

Everyone contributed to the greater good, like the shepherd.

He knocked gently. She had to shout that the door was open before he'd enter.

He sat on the small bench against the wall.

"What do you think about dual-hatting as a medic?"

"No shepherd has ever had another job besides being the spiritual guide of the Borwyn. I don't think we should change that."

"I don't think we have any choice. Since we've returned, this crew has lost three dead and has one critical and two injured. How much longer can we go on without everyone pulling double duty?"

"But I'm the shepherd."

"And a fine one at that. Get yourself to Medical and work with Vantraub. She's going to have to cut Annabelle's head open, and she's going to need your help."

The shepherd swallowed heavily and turned pale.

"You better get down there. Annabelle's already prepping. The second we're motionless, she'll start the procedure. We don't have any extra hands because we're sending the combat team to the wreckage of the *Butterfly*, and then we'll send anyone who can suit up to dismantle it. By then, Annabelle will have either lived or died. She's in your hands."

"She's in Septiman's hands," the shepherd countered.

"May Septiman work through you and Vantraub to save Annabelle. His hands have become your hands." The captain knew how the game was played.

"I shall endeavor to follow Septiman's will...and yours."

"Better hurry. I'm told there's a lot to learn."

"Learning the spirit has taken me a lifetime. Learning the body? It appears I have a few hours." The shepherd stood, frowning at the change in his future.

He had never thought of himself as lazy, but he admitted that he didn't work nearly as hard physically as the rest of the crew. That was about to change.

"More like two hours, but this challenge is one we're all taking. Our world is different now, especially if we're to win this war without losing our souls." Her mind returned to the conversation with her deputy and the combat team leader.

"We can never lose our souls, no matter the physical cost. May Septiman grant you His wisdom."

The captain smiled, close-lipped. The shepherd opened the door and stopped. He looked over his shoulder, but he didn't say anything. After a few moments, he walked out and gently closed the door behind him.

Jaq ran through her status screens. Satisfied that everyone was doing what needed to be done, she returned to the bridge. It wasn't that she didn't trust her crew, but they'd be diligent about their problems to the exclusion of asking for help. As with the shepherd, the captain could shift people to the greatest need.

Nothing else needed to be done except to turn Crip loose to prepare to work with the hulk of the former Borwyn ship drifting through space.

Max was still on the command deck, huddled with the

former battle commander at the weapons console. They were pointing at the screen by his seat.

"New strategy. We're going to scavenge everything we can to help us win this fight. Go on, you two. Help us to help ourselves."

"Consider it done, Jaq." Crip climbed out of his seat and pumped his fist. "The battle is joined!"

"Victory!" the captain shouted.

The crew reacted as they'd been raised, with cheers and waving arms.

The captain was serious. After the initial shock of the attacks, she'd started to have doubts, but after contemplating a different way, she'd realized that their chances of winning increased greatly with additional firepower and supporting platforms. Draw the enemy into traps. Overwhelm them with E-mags and missiles. Separate them and kill their ships one by one.

"Sensors?"

Chief Ping wasn't there, but Dolly Norton was. "Nothing on the scopes, passive or active."

"Let's stop shining like a beacon. Focused beam active on the target only. Let's not give the Malibor extra ways to see us. Even if one of their ships shows up around Farslor, we're nowhere near there. We're nothing more than debris floating in space."

"Fifteen minutes to the braking maneuver," Thrust Control announced.

"Debris that's in control of its own destiny," Jaq clarified. "Tram, you've got it. I need to talk with Engineering. I'll be back."

Tram waved. He was getting used to being the permanent fixture on the command deck, and he still had a lot to learn about defensive weapon systems. He'd been focused on offensive weapons for too long. "Defensive weapons on standby in case the Malibor left us a present."

Jaq gave him the thumbs-up as she hurried off the bridge. They'd soon lose their half-gee of acceleration to a negative gee force that lifted them off the deck. It would be harder to maneuver around the ship after it changed orientation.

She used the elevator to get to the stern, which was where the engines and power plant were located. She rushed in and found Bec Draper.

"No," he said firmly and hammered a fist into his hand for emphasis.

"I wish I could be more like you," Jaq replied. "Annoy people for no reason, although I'm sure I've asked for plenty of things that put your teeth on edge. However, that's not why I'm here. We're going to need to slow down a pile of space junk that's as big as *Chrysalis*, as I'm sure you're aware. That's all. I want you to be ready to figure out the cabling we'll need, in addition to the energy output to pull that thing to a dead stop so we can take everything we want off it. Couldn't you use replacement circuits from *Chrysalis's* sister ship?"

He threw his head back and snorted. "Are they still compatible? The Malibor probably replaced everything with their trash. Fool's errand, Captain."

Jaq smiled pleasantly. "Crip will coordinate with you. Figure it out since we're going to board that wreckage. We need what they have, even the bits and pieces that weren't destroyed."

"I'm going, too," Bec blurted. "And why slow down? We can match its speed, and then it'll be like we're both dead in space."

"What if it's spinning?" Jaq countered.

He waved his hand dismissively. "Temp thrusters. We have a couple in storage. Now go away. I'm still working on the power problem."

"How's that going?" The captain took a half-step toward the

hatch. She wanted to return to the bridge before they changed the ship's orientation.

"See? I knew you'd get in my business. I have nothing for you. I'm too busy figuring out everyone else's problems."

"Doing a fine job of it, too. Keep on carrying on, Bec. You are the lynchpin for *Chrysalis's* success."

"Don't you forget it. Maybe tell Crip, too."

The captain jogged down the corridor to the elevator that would take her back to the command deck. Match speed with the non-spinning hulk. That would work.

She would have gone to Medical to inform them of the change in plan, but a steady speed would provide the same stability as a full stop. It would have to work since doing nothing would be fatal.

CHAPTER 18

Stay out of the firing line – it can be deadly.

Crip and Max inspected the spacesuits the team planned on using. The extra ballistic material had been cobbled together from their combat suits. It would have to be changed back before they conducted another land-based operation. They only had so much to work with. Each mission was tailored to its anticipated needs.

It was the best they could do, just like the landing on Farslor. With each active mission, they'd learn more and get better.

The comm buzzed.

"Captain's calling," Danzig said. He was leaning against a locker.

"You rang?" Crip replied. He was next to the comm unit.

"Just a quick heads-up. Bec said he's going with you."

"No. There's no way." Crip leaned close to the microphone to make sure he was clear.

"Way. I'll let you get back to it." Jaq signed off before he could argue.

"This is going to be miserable," Max muttered. "That guy is impossible to work with."

Crip stared at the comm as if the short conversation had not been real. "Sounded like we have no choice. Who would know better what's going on with a busted-up ship than Bec Draper? Let me handle him. You keep the team focused on the broader mission."

"I'll hold you to that," Max replied. "Keep him out of my face, and by Septiman's good graces, don't let him boss us around."

Crip smirked and prepared to leave when the call came that the ship was in the final slowdown to match the speed of the wreck. "Prepare to deploy. Move to Cargo Bay Four. We might not have to deal with Bec after all."

Max gestured for his team to suit up, another exercise in which they were well-practiced. It took two minutes for the team to get into their suits and start moving toward the cargo bay, which was on the same level as the team room.

Max and Crip brought up the rear.

"Do you think the thruster pod plan will work?" Max asked.

"I suspect it will. As long as we put them in the right place..." Crip let the thought drift off. He knew they needed Bec. He just didn't want the chief engineer deployed with them.

They reached the cargo bay to find Bec Draper there with two thruster units.

"Boys!" He waved at them. He didn't have his helmet on since he was talking to two unsuited assistants. His boots were clamped to the deck. The combat team walked on the ceiling, upside-down in relation to the deck since that was where the reverse thrust put the half-gee.

The two thrusters were strapped to the deck. Mobility packs lined one bulkhead of the cargo bay. Most importantly, the combat team had attached ribbons of tools to each suit. From powered units to manual, they had everything they needed to salvage hardware from the ship.

With a final adjustment from *Chrysalis's* attitude thrusters, the cruiser stopped decelerating. The two assistant engineers hurried from the bay, swimming through the air with the ease of those who'd lived half their lives in zero-gee.

After the bay was secured, Bec put on his helmet and gave a thumbs-up. The team responded one by one until they were all accounted for. One hundred percent were self-contained. Crip did the honors of recovering the atmosphere into a tank secured within the bulkhead. When the inside pressure had equalized with the outside, they opened the cargo bay door.

Before them were the remnants of a twin of their ship. It slowly rotated end over end as a single hulk, split laterally in the rear by the engineering section and separated longitudinally along the spine. A debris cloud floated around the ship. In the forward section, the lights were on.

Bec watched it while mumbling to himself. When he was satisfied with what they needed to do, he gestured at Crip. "Bring those." He pointed at the two thrusters, then busied himself with climbing into a mobility pack.

Max looked at Crip and pointed at the thrusters. The commander replied, "I got them. Give me Danzig. We'll take care of it. Get your people into the rear section first. See what kind of engine hardware they have. We could use fissile material, along with all the control interfaces."

"Don't go into Engineering without me," Bec interrupted.

"Go into that forward section and see why the lights are on." Crip adjusted. He wasn't going to play Bec's game of having people wait for his next good idea.

"I'm going to need people," Bec stated, confirming Crip's impression.

"You'll get what you need when we can spare the people. Can you tell us why those lights are on?"

"A battery is still functioning." He flipped his hand as if the answer were obvious and Crip was intentionally being annoying.

"We'll check it out, just in case. A functioning battery. You could use that, couldn't you? And maybe some replacement light fixtures?"

"You're confusing me with the maintenance team. Spares are their business." Bec tossed his hands up. "Are you coming?"

Crip took a deep breath, deactivated his magnetic clamps, and pushed off to fly to the bulkhead. He helped himself into a mobility pack and ran it through a quick service test. When he was ready, he found Danzig beside him, ready to go. The soldier punched him in the arm. Crip couldn't help but appreciate the support.

"You're the man, Danzig. Let's stop that thing from spinning until it pukes."

"Nice analogy, Crip. Everyone hates that!" He glanced at the increasingly impatient chief engineer. Bec had moved to the edge of the cargo bay and was flexing his legs as if he were getting ready to jump.

The thruster tie-downs' buckles released with a single latch. Crip popped his and pulled one thruster to his chest to limit its effect on the rig's balance when he flew into space.

Danzig followed Crip's lead, and they waddled to the edge of the cargo bay using their magnetic boots. Once there, Bec counted down on his fingers. When he reached one, he eased into space, activating his jets when he was clear of *Chrysalis*. He accelerated toward one end of the tumbling hulk.

Danzig and Crip followed, but both had problems flying straight. Each slowed to recover and adjusted course repeatedly while Bec increased the gap between them. The engineer rotated and slowed, then caught one end of the big ship. It spun past, leaving Crip and Danzig behind.

Crip activated his comm. "Stop here. We'll wait for it to come around. Bec, we can't maneuver very well lugging these thrusters and their attachment assemblies."

"I'll mark the attachment points while you laze about."

"Bec, I swear I'm going to punch you in the face so hard when we get back to the ship."

A separate channel crackled to life. "That's you handling him, huh?" Max laughed.

"It's the best I got, Max. Watch those sharp edges and take care. There's more going on with this ship than we think."

"We'll take care. Keep your wits about you, and maybe you'll survive your afternoon stroll with the Becenstein." Max closed the channel.

Up close, the cruiser was massive. The spin made it more intimidating. The fact that they were also traveling toward deep space was irrelevant since everyone's momentum carried them in the same direction as if they weren't moving. It would only matter if they ran into something.

Crip looked ahead and saw nothing obstructing their line of travel.

The section of the ship with internal lights slowly rotated by. The commander could see nothing exceptional within. Max and his team had landed and were working their way toward the impact point where the missile had split the ship open. Once inside, if there was power, they could raise and lower bulkheads to move through the ship.

Crip wished he was doing that instead of the more important work of stopping the spin. Not that he considered it beneath him, but he wanted to be at the front of the fun stuff. He chuckled to himself. When he'd taken the position as the captain's deputy, he'd known it would come with perquisites as well as sacrifices. He was out here, ready to board *Butterfly*, the first Borwyn on her decks in fifty years. He was doing engineering work, though.

The best, or the worst, of both worlds.

The aft end of the ship approached. Crip and Danzig touched their mobility thrusters and accelerated slightly, then harder to get in front of the upper section of the ship. They shut down their thrusters and oriented their feet toward the hull coming at them. Their forward speed was a little less than the angular speed of this section of the ship.

Crip and Danzig touched down in silence. Bec waved them to him with exaggerated arm movements. They cradled their thruster load and clumped in deliberate magnetically attached steps until they reached the chief engineer.

"One there and one there." He pointed at spots that were painted white.

Crip went one way and Danzig the other. Bec joined the commander and watched him fumble the attachment, which he hadn't looked at in the cargo bay.

"Give it to me."

"That was my first choice," Crip replied. He wanted to slam it into the chief engineer, but they were in space, and he didn't want to rip his suit or send him spinning away. He held out the thruster for Bec to take. "Why are you so mean?"

"I'm not. I'm intolerant of incompetence. There's a difference." Bec quickly attached the thruster and adjusted it using a small tethered device he produced from a thigh pocket.

"If you ask a human to breathe in space, he won't be able to, but organisms can survive in the void. Does that mean the human is incompetent?"

"If he was trying to live an organism's life, then yes. We're on *Chrysalis* together. You'd think the technical health of the ship and how it works would be important to every last crew member, even the babies."

"When people do their jobs, certain things can be less important so we can focus our pea brains on what we have the capacity for." Crip's mood was growing fouler by the moment. He had little patience for the chief engineer's antics.

"Exactly. Like I said, incompetent." He walked toward Danzig, who had his thruster attached and waiting. "See?" Bec pointed.

"I watched you install yours," the soldier replied.

Crip and Bec had been talking on the team channel. "It's amazing how people can become less incompetent when they're shown what needs to be done."

Bec grunted an answer while making a final adjustment, then stepped back. Crip and Danzig put the chief engineer between them and the thrusters. Bec accessed his wrist computer and tapped buttons to activate both thrusters.

Chrysalis hovered nearby as the stationary point to judge the rotation. It slowed quickly. Bec adjusted the energy flow, and when he was satisfied, he shut it down. The *Butterfly* had achieved equilibrium with *Chrysalis* but started going the other way. Bec flipped the thrusters, touched them to stop the reverse motion, and shut them down once more.

Butterfly was aligned in parallel with *Chrysalis*.

"Let's see what this baby has to offer!" Crip broadcast. He headed for the nearest hull breach, but a hand caught his arm.

"Engineering." Bec pointed forty-five degrees from Crip's direction of travel. Fissile material from the reactor was the second-highest priority. The highest was anti-ship missiles. Had any survived?

Crip didn't want to, but he had promised. "Danzig, check the missile tubes. I'll go with Mister Abrasive."

"I'll ignore that," Bec said.

"I hope you don't. Take it to heart because you're a grinding wheel to our clear windows."

The chief engineer used his mobility pack to cover the distance quickly. Crip found it easier to fly without carrying the thruster. He kept up with Bec, and they landed together. They surveyed the damage to find the best way into the section, but the bad news was that the split cut through the engineering space. The power plant was nowhere to be seen.

They pulled themselves over the ledge and followed a pipe toward the ship's central longitudinal axis to orient themselves with the engine room and power production area. Crip marveled at the size and complexity of the ship's internals. He'd never contemplated them from this perspective. He knew what systems did what but wasn't particular about how those systems integrated with each other.

Now, he could see it all in the greatest of detail.

"Impressive," he said. "There's going to be a great deal we can salvage from this ship. Good job figuring that out, Alby."

"Any idiot would have known this ship contained materials we could use." Bec's condescension was more pronounced than usual.

"Aha! You were initially against it. You idiot!" Crip chuckled as they walked down a radial support beam leading from the double outer hull to the central axis.

The comm crackled, and Max spoke quickly. "We're taking fire."

CHAPTER 19

If something doesn't look dead, it's not. If it does look dead, it still might not be.

A laser lanced from the cracked-open hatch.

"Get back!" Max pulled a soldier away from the opening.

Barrington clutched at his sleeve as he tried to close the tear in his suit.

Max and Barrington remained around the corner of an adjoining corridor. The hull breach was behind them, open to space. The atmosphere within was long gone, but the space where the laser had come from had power and was sealed against vaccum.

Max had tried to penetrate the interior and had released an emergency bulkhead. As soon as it started moving aside, they were surprised. Max removed tape from his kit and wrapped it around Barrington's arm to seal the breach.

The combat team didn't have weapons.

"Did you see them?" Max asked.

The soldier growled and snarled into his helmet. "I can't

believe they got me. Yeah, I saw someone in a suit, but just a flash. It wasn't an automated system."

Max ducked his head around the corner and pulled back before anyone could draw a bead on him. The bulkhead was closed.

"The Malibor are making me angry," Max admitted. He opened the team channel. "I want to know we have all hands. Sound off."

One by one, each gave their name, followed by their percentage of combat capability in the order they'd joined the team. The soldier with the tear in his suit claimed one hundred percent.

When Max was certain he hadn't lost anyone, he reported on the wide broadcast channel. "*Chrysalis*, this is Sergeant Tremayne. We have Malibor still alive and blockaded in the forward section of the ship in an area that includes the command deck. Please advise."

"Stand by," the captain replied. She needed to mull over the unfortunate turn of events. "Recommendations?"

She put it in Crip's and Max's hands.

"If I may," Crip began, "let me talk this out. We can do nothing, and eventually, they'll die. But doing nothing takes time, and at some point, other Malibor are going to show up looking for the ships they sent to investigate us. They'll figure out what happened and come after us. We could try to burn them out, but we'll have to return to the ship. Or we could try to parlay with them. Start a conversation."

"Where would we put prisoners?" The captain snorted. She wasn't loving the idea.

"We can figure that out if we take any. I'm confident this ship has stuff we need and a lot of stuff we can use. It would be better if we didn't accidentally blow anything up. Danzig, what did you find in the missile tubes?"

"Still trying to get one of the outer hatches open. Doesn't look like it's been opened in a while. Cutting away. I'll report when I have access."

"That tells me we need to get inside this ship," Crip continued. "We need our weapons so we can negotiate from a position of strength. They are probably on minimal life support, however many of them there are. They'll be desperate, and the fact that they've made it this long means they want to live. With what they know and what's on board this ship, we'll be light-years ahead of where we are now."

"I don't think we have any options at all. I'll send Alby and his recovery team with your weapons. Remain in place. Once you have firepower, attempt to make contact. Alby will join Bec and start dismantling that ship. With the engineers and the combat team over there, we're out of suits and mobility packs. After Alby deploys, there will be no other assistance."

"Understand, Captain. We'll contain the threat and then continue our survey."

"I'd like to add something," Bec interrupted. He continued before anyone could tell him no. "Crip is right. We need access to the space the Malibor occupy, and we need it to remain intact. What I see is that this ship has possibly been in cold storage for a long time. Original technology is in place and functional."

"Alby will bring the engineers and your weapons. Be on the lookout for him. You have your orders."

Jaq waited in case there was something else. The teams working on *Butterfly* were the focus of effort for *Chrysalis* and her crew.

"We'll take care of it," Crip promised. He closed the broadcast channel and accessed the team channel. "On my way, Max. Let's get the most out of the combat team while we wait for our pulse rifles."

"I'm here at Frame Two Seventy-five. Larson has accessed the central shaft. Where are you exactly, Larson?"

"Frame Two Hundred, and you're right. I'm in the central shaft. A fireball must have run through here. Most cabling is melted, but only the protective covering. The metal within is intact. We'll get kilometers of high-capacity fiber if we want it. Heavy haulers, mainly. The lighter stuff branches off the main trunks, and I'm sure we'll get as much of that as we want, too."

"Circuits, control interfaces, junctions, relays, inverters?" Bec asked. "Cabling isn't our challenge. Circuit boards and chips are."

"I know, but how much of that stuff is in the central shaft?"

Bec was ready with an answer. "Then leave the central shaft and go where that material is located."

"Like the area where the Malibor are holed up?" Crip answered. "That's what we're trying to do. Haven't you been listening?"

"Only superficially. I've found reactor fuel. The original reactor is gone. It's somewhere in space, blasted out when this section came apart, but the rest is surprisingly intact, including the engines."

Crip moved slowly toward the damaged section of the ship where Max was. He finally stopped trying to walk and used his mobility pack to steer him away from the hull and through clear space. "Those engines are the old ones. We don't use that tech anymore."

"True, but the control interfaces are almost all the same."

Crip understood. He wanted to argue with Bec and put him in his place, but they were working toward the same goal—to make *Chrysalis* better through quicker repairs and upgrades to older but intact systems versus using the cobbled-together workarounds currently on board the Borwyn cruiser.

"Alby and the team of engineers are on their way. It'll be great to have stores of spare parts. I haven't ever seen that."

"Neither have I, Crip," Bec replied almost warmly. "Don't blow up the ship before we can get the equipment I need off of it."

Crip laughed. He had almost been suckered into thinking the chief engineer was decent. "We'll do our best, Bec, but no guarantees. Good job finding toxic stuff."

"Radioactivity isn't toxic if you're properly shielded."

"Are you?" Crip replied. The suits had a thin layer of interlocking lead plates, but over the years, they had weakened. They hadn't tested the equipment since there was nothing they could do if it was compromised.

Bec didn't answer. In his mind, Crip could see the engineer moving away from his new find. Crip accessed the channel to the ship. "Make sure you bring extra power packs for the rifles and radioactive containment blankets. Bec found fissile material."

Lead blankets were easy to move in zero-gee. Under acceleration, not so much.

Crip had made his point. He put it behind him since entrenched Malibor were in front of him. He needed to get them out of there without compromising the integrity of the surviving section of *Butterfly*.

It was a tall order. Crip inverted to slow down and stopped where the combat team had accessed the section in which the lights were on.

"I guess we got their attention," Max said when Crip arrived.

Crip unhooked the mobility pack and strapped it to an outcrop of metal at the entry point.

"No kidding. Barrington! How are you doing?"

"I guess it could have been worse. They missed me while

still hitting me if you know what I mean." The soldier flexed his taped arm to show the temporary repair.

"How do we make contact?" Max asked.

"Send a portable comm through the gap and hope they don't blow it up?" Crip suggested. "They can't hear us unless they're in atmosphere."

"Those pesky sound waves. I have to point out that there's one drawback to your plan." Max stabbed a gloved finger at the bulkhead. "They're shooting at us."

"How about a big sign that says, 'Don't shoot?'" the commander joked. "Although, how did they know we weren't Malibor?"

"Different suits? Maybe they've been trying to contact us, and since we didn't reply, they knew we weren't on their side."

Crip opened a channel to the ship. "Have there been any emanations from this ship? We think the Malibor might have sent a distress signal or tried to contact us somehow. Even if they haven't, can you try to contact them? We'd like to open a dialogue."

"We will review our broad-spectrum recordings," Chief Ping replied. "Stand by."

Max looked at Crip. "How long do you think we'll need to stand by?"

Crip shrugged. "I don't seem to have anything else to do. How about you?"

"Nope." Max studied the bulkhead. "We could storm it if we hit them hard the second that bulkhead opens. Spray inside. Rush in. Open the next and keep going."

"Do you think they're all in suits?" Crip eased into the corridor and maneuvered to the bulkhead. He flattened himself against it so that if they cracked it open, they wouldn't see him.

"What are you doing? It's not like we can cover you unless

we use harsh language the Malibor can't hear." Max stayed back and kept Barrington with him.

"We've detected no emissions from the hulk," the sensor chief reported.

Crip studied the emergency bulkhead. It was identical to the one at the same frame on *Chrysalis*. This deck and the two above had power, so three decks on one side of the ship. It was a significant amount of space.

"Can we access these spaces from a different direction?" It was a rhetorical question. Every crew member of *Chrysalis* knew the ship inside and out, and there were multiple access points vertically as well as horizontally.

"Do we want to?" Max countered. "What about air handling and environmental control? If we cut those, they'll have to surrender."

"Just have to find where the primary trunk is and, most importantly, what is powering this section. The power plant is gone." Crip waved indiscriminately at the gap in the hull that led to open space.

The bulkhead started to ease open. Max threw a piece of metal debris and dodged out of the way. The metal clanged off the emergency bulkhead.

The barrel of a laser pistol poked out of the opening beyond the edge of the frame. Crip swiped his hand past and tried to grab it. The wielder lost his grip and the weapon spun away, but two hands followed it out. Crip clamped one boot to the deck and kicked with the other, catching the suited individual in the midsection. The body recoiled, but being magnetically attached, the person rocked back and forth.

Crip kicked the suit once more, but the individual inside fought past his boot, and a second individual popped out through the opening. Crip removed his multi-tool in one quick motion and leaned away from the pair of Malibor coming for him.

He reoriented himself, flashed the knife, stabbed, and stopped millimeters from the Malibor's suit. He held up his other hand in a gesture he hoped the Malibor would understand as "cease fire."

The individual froze. If Crip slashed, the suit would depressurize, and death would follow. The second individual angled around the first. Crip hugged the bulkhead to keep the first Malibor between him and the newcomer. The first didn't struggle against the knife. The risk was too great, which showed Crip that he wanted to live.

A movement beyond the two caught his eye. Max and Barrington rushed to his aid. Max jumped, caught the free-floating laser pistol, and continued until he bounced off the side bulkhead. He activated his magnetic clamps to keep from flying into the middle of the standoff, then touched the laser's trigger and fired into the bulkhead above Crip's head, where they all would see it.

The second Malibor stopped and raised his hands, Barrington caught an arm and held it. The five stood that way until Crip secured the blade and put his multi-tool away.

The respite gave the Borwyn time to notice the differences in the spacesuits. The Malibor's suits were gray and red, and the Borwyn's suits were white. The environmental pack was integrated with the back and waist of the Borwyn's suits, but the Malibor's was a big, boxy contraption worn like a backpack with a separate pair of hoses attached to the suit near the wearer's neck.

Crip dug out his emergency comm and turned it on. He offered it to the first Malibor and motioned for him to return inside. It was difficult to see through the mirrored visor, so they could barely make out that the Malibor was talking. They had private communications channels, like the Borwyn.

It made sense.

The first Malibor took the device. Both tried to return through the opening, but Barrington held the second tightly. He was keeping a hostage.

Max pulled himself across the ceiling to point the laser pistol around the corner into the opening. He looked beyond. It was a short section of corridor with another emergency bulkhead in place. No other Malibor were inside.

They were using this section as an airlock. Crip pushed the first toward the opening. Once inside, the Malibor faced the three Borwyn and their hostage while the bulkhead closed.

Then they waited.

They could only guess how long it would take for the ad hoc airlock to pressurize and the Malibor to return inside.

CHAPTER 20

Space was never intended for habitation, but here we are anyway, letting it impose its will on us.

Jaq watched the parade of individuals leave the ship to go to the hulk, but she had something else on her mind. Her people were doing their jobs, watching for the enemy, ready to move the ship and defend it. That left her as the only one without an immediate task.

"Tram, you have the conn. Don't scratch the paint."

She hurried to the central shaft and up one deck, then quickly pulled herself to the medical facility. The two crew with broken limbs were in the corridor. The doors to Medical were closed and sealed.

"Are they operating?" Jaq asked. She knew they were but wanted to hear it out loud.

A patient nodded. "It looked grim. The instrument tray was filled with tools you'd find in Engineering, not in the med space. The cutter finished whining about five minutes ago. That put my teeth on edge."

Jaq nodded. "I can imagine."

"What's going on? No one seems to have the time to tell us." A broken limb didn't mean their minds weren't alert.

"I like that you want to stay engaged. We'll have you back to work soon. Right now, we're working to recover as much technology as we can from *Chrysalis's* sister ship *Butterfly*. We have survey teams over there now."

"Captain to the command deck," Tram announced over the ship-wide comm.

Jaq furrowed her brow in worry and hurried to the nearest wall-mounted comm. "Captain here. What's up?"

Tram spoke quickly. "The combat team has re-engaged the Malibor and given them an emergency comm."

"Of course they did. I'm on my way." Jaq touched each of the patients to reassure them, then headed toward the shaft. She returned to the bridge in less than thirty seconds. "Report."

"No casualties." Tram gave her the answer she was hoping to hear.

Given the recent combat, personnel was foremost in her mind. They couldn't afford more losses, even though she knew they would incur them with continued fighting.

"Crip made contact and wants to open a line of communication," the captain muttered. "That's the best course of action, but I still have no idea where we'd put prisoners."

Thrust Control eased out of his seat. "Lander Bay Two is empty. We could probably get the materials we need to refit that into a living space from *Butterfly*. That ship gives us a lot more options than we'd otherwise have."

That was why the captain had agreed to salvage it, but she hadn't expected to find living Malibor. Still, the intelligence coup of finding individuals to interrogate and computer systems to exploit was too much of an opportunity to pass up.

"Lander Bay Two it is." The captain went to the comm. "Get me Crip, please."

The comm crackled to life. "Commander, how are you holding up?"

"We have a hostage. The second Malibor returned inside. It's been ten minutes. Why is it taking him so long to key the microphone?"

"They're probably discussing their options just like we are. We can put any prisoners in Lander Bay Two. It's got a single access and has a decent amount of room, assuming there aren't too many survivors. Any estimate on numbers?"

"No idea," Crip replied. "All I can say is at least two. It is a fairly big space, so I suspect there are more, but until he talks to us or we go in rifles hot, we won't know. We'll have one prisoner, that's for certain."

"You take the conversation, Crip. You're the only one who's talked with a Malibor in the past fifty years. That little bit of insight could give you an edge. Do us proud."

"My negotiating position is that if the Malibor tell us everything they know and give us everything we want, we'll let them live."

"I hope you can do better than that," Jaq said with a snort and cough. "We'll listen in, and good luck. Jaq out."

"Malibor!" the communications officer said with a hint of awe.

"They are the enemy until they prove otherwise, and they haven't proven that they aren't. Keep that in mind," the captain replied in a motherly voice. "Also remember that we've won every battle since we returned, but we're not letting that go to our heads. It should serve to knock the Malibor off their pedestal. They might have won a battle fifty years ago, but they have not won the war. Also, they weren't fighting us. They were fighting those who taught us to be better."

The captain pointed at the main screen and the floating hulk that still had life.

"This has taken us farther away from Septimus when we're trying to go home, but sometimes, the best route is not the most direct. This is a minor but necessary delay. Septimus, we're coming to liberate our people."

The captain wasn't sure anyone was alive, but like their faith in Septiman, they needed to believe there were survivors on their home planet. They were alone, but they didn't need to feel alone. They would find the truth soon. The Malibor hiding in the ship on the screen would know.

She wanted to know, but only if the answer was yes, Borwyn still lived on Septimus.

"Bring me that Malibor," she told the screen.

"Comm channel is closed, Captain," the communications officer said. "Would you like me to open it?"

"No, that's okay. I was talking to myself. I want to know what that Malibor knows. What have we missed in the past fifty years?"

The comm officer nearly came out of her seat. "Emergency channel is active!"

"Borwyn scum," the voice started.

The captain snorted. *Didn't miss that.*

"Give us a ship by which we can leave, or we will destroy you."

The captain closed her eyes and waited for Crip to answer. She wanted to fire a full broadside of E-mags into the surviving hull section, but her people were there, as well as the equipment they wanted. She smoldered while during the interlude.

Crip replied, "You have limited power and limited resources. The best you can do is blow yourselves up. How about we stop the posturing and have an adult conversation?"

"We will destroy you." The Malibor's vigor was fading.

"I'm Commander Crip Castle. You can call me Crip. Who do I have the pleasure of addressing?"

"I'm Captain Delong'sa. The honorific 'sa is added when we have a confirmed kill of a Borwyn. What do you think about that?"

"I think you're in a tough position, and if you want your people to survive, you need our help. We blew you out of the sky, along with three gunships. No Malibor are coming to help you. Since we're here, we offer our assistance, but you have to stop with the doom and gloom routine. It's tiresome."

The captain gestured madly at the screen. "Tell 'em how it is, Crip!"

———

The commander eased away from the bulkhead and motioned for Barrington to bring the prisoner with them. They moved into the corridor around the corner while Max waited with the laser pistol.

"I'm not sure how much power this thing has left," Max said. "It's kind of weak. I can't wait to get my pulse rifle."

Crip replied on their direct link, "If negotiations keep going as they are, you could get a chance to use it. Might want to rally the team and prepare to go hot on an entry and space-clearing action."

The team had trained for that among many options. They had staged realistic training in space-clearing aboard a ship, specifically the *Chrysalis*, whereas practice for landing on Farslor had been nonexistent.

The Malibor spoke again. "We want a ship."

No threats. It was progress.

"We don't have any extra ships. All we have is *Chrysalis*. I'm not sure you can see outside, but there she is. During the fight where *Hornet* was damaged, you might have seen us right before you suffered a catastrophic reactor failure. *Hornet* is a very old ship, after all."

Crip gave the Malibor an out, a way to lose without admitting defeat.

"Weapons are here," Max reported over the team channel.

Crip shut the extra channels down. He needed to focus on the Malibor.

"What do you want with us?" Finally, the Malibor admitted his predicament.

Crip replied, "We have a space on our ship where you can temporarily quarter until we can put you down with your people. We also wanted to take a look at your ship. See how it survived the past fifty years when we were sure it had been destroyed. Can you tell us what happened and how the ship was saved?"

"This has always been a Malibor ship. Where did you steal your ship?"

Crip wanted to rub his head to alleviate the rapidly increasing throbbing within his temples, but his spacesuit precluded that relief.

"We seem to have different perspectives about what happened fifty years ago. It doesn't matter. What's important is the here and now. Do you have enough spacesuits for your survivors?"

"We do not."

"We can shuttle your people to *Chrysalis*, bringing the suits back for reuse until your people are all on board. We will feed you, keep you warm, and provide a place to rest."

"You'll torture us! That's what Borwyn do."

"It's not what Borwyn do. You have no reason to trust me, but I did send your person back inside with a comm instead of killing him."

"But you didn't send both. We're still missing one person."

"You attacked us, so until we can trust you, we needed to reduce the odds. We figured you were limited on spacesuits. If you can't come into space, we remain safe. Your man had to see that we aren't carrying weapons, so who's the aggressor, Captain Delong'sa?"

"You killed my ship."

"You had a reactor failure, nothing more," Crip lied. "How many people do you have?"

"Seven. Eight with Lieutenant Delong, who is your prisoner."

"A relation, perhaps? No harm will come to her as long as she doesn't try to hurt us. We're not out for vengeance. The war was fifty years ago."

"Then what do you want?"

"Same as you—to go home."

"My home is the station orbiting Malpace, the moon of Septimus, the home of the Malibor race."

It hurt Crip to hear the Malibor call Septimus their home. The crew was listening to the captain's words, and he felt the weight of them bearing down. *Home to the Malibor.*

Fifty years earlier, they'd had a different home. "Your home used to be Sairvor and Fristen." From Crip's short time on Farslor, the twin planet occupying the same orbit as Fristen, the conditions had been cold and harsh. Why wouldn't they move to a developed planet that was warmer and more welcoming? But what had happened to Sairvor?

"That was the ancient times. Now, we are from Septimus." The captain seemed content to deliver this news. He knew more than he was sharing and was guarding his words, shaping them to stab the Borwyn.

Fristen was the Malibors' real homeworld. It had been developed like Septimus, or that was what the Borwyn had thought. The land masses were different, with less habitable space and more water that froze with great regularity. The Malibor had moved to Sairvor, but they had been restless on that planet despite its congenial climate.

Sairvor wouldn't be so bad as an alternative to fighting the Malibor entrenched on Septimus.

Crip got angry with himself for how easily he had shifted from going home to the idea that Sairvor would be good enough. He was ashamed of himself but glad he hadn't shared his thoughts with anyone.

He never wanted to say that out loud.

CHAPTER 21

Vacuum is the test we all fail.

"Was *Hornet* the flagship of your fleet?" Crip asked to get back in the right mindset. They were going to Septimus, and they had a space station to deal with on top of the Malibor considering the planet their home.

"Why would I tell you that?"

"Because I lulled you into a false sense of security since I'm such a nice guy." Crip made light of the question. The Borwyn could find out from the ship's computers if they could get them intact. Something as simple as sensor logs would paint a robust picture of the forces arrayed around Septimus and between Septimus and Farslor. "What made you come to Farslor?"

"We noticed an object arriving at Farslor from deep space. We had to check it out. Surprise, surprise. Borwyn! Where did *you* come from?"

"We had a broken ship. It took us a long time and an entire generation to fix it, but we're back and a little more lethal than when we left, as you noticed. We aren't out for blood. We only want to go home, but we are more than capable of defending ourselves." By reiterating his point, Crip hoped to appeal to the Malibor at the most basic level.

"Fine. Turn your ship over to us, and we will take you to Septimus."

Crip thought he heard the captain grinding his teeth.

"You know that won't work for us, but I applaud your attempt. With your help, maybe we can end this war before too many more Malibor lose their lives. You have eight crew remaining out of two hundred and fifty? No more people need to die. You can be responsible for changing the trajectory of these misplaced hostilities."

"We aren't the hostile ones. Borwyn attacked us."

"If the Borwyn attacked you, why are you living on Septimus?"

"Because it's our home, and the Borwyn tried to take it from us. Are you okay? Have you hit your head too many times?" The captain was now friendlier, although his grasp of history was far removed from what the Borwyn understood.

"You need a big dose of truth with a capital T," Crip answered. "If that's what you've been told, you've been lied to your whole life. You were the captain of a Borwyn ship. You never wondered why it was different than other ships in the Malibor fleet?" He guessed it was only one of its type because the Borwyn had only built two cruisers that size.

Every other ship had been smaller due to resource limitations. The Borwyn had been restricted in how many metric tons of finished shipping they could produce each year during the lull between the passes.

The passes were the nearest point between the two planets. Only happened once every four years. And offset by two years was the pass near Fristen. The rest of the time was known as the lull. It would work against the Malibor and their old drives but not the Borwyn.

With the varied orbits, every four years, Fristen and Septimus were close, minimizing the amount of fuel needed to move a fleet from one planet to the other. In one passing year, the Malibor attacked after a lull of three years, during which both sides had rebuilt and rearmed.

In the fourth year, it would start afresh. The Borwyn's new ion drive obviated the need for proximity. They could travel anywhere with minimal impact on their overall fuel supply.

Fifty years. This was the passing year for Farslor. If they had come from the far side of the orbit around Armanor, the Malibor wouldn't have been able to react as quickly, if at all.

"It is unique because it is a test design, but once we repelled the Borwyn assault on our planet, we had no need to build more *Hornet*-class ships."

"Because you couldn't, but we deviate from the main purpose of this conversation. If you want to live, you'll need to move to *Chrysalis*. Otherwise, you'll run out of air and food, and you'll die. How's the temperature in there? Probably not too warm."

"It's cold, and we're losing air. We're at eighteen percent oxygen with no ability to scrub the CO_2. You have us in a place where a delay will indeed kill us. We only have two suits. One now."

"Why are you telling me this?"

"You have all the time in the galaxy, and we have none. I am out of options if I want to save those of us who remain."

The capitulation had come too suddenly unless his crew was leaning on the captain to end the standoff. Not everyone was willing to give their life in a fruitless endeavor.

"Your bridge crew? The only ones who were protected well

enough to survive the catastrophic damage to your ship. Prepare to transfer them. Send out the individual in the suit. We'll take him and your daughter to our ship and return with those two suits and one more. We'll shuttle the last six in two trips. You'll need to hang on."

"I never said she was my daughter." The Malibor captain paused. "I wish there was a way where we could face off against each other in a proper battle and fight to the death."

The captain couldn't help himself. He continued to seek a route that was no longer available to him. He had lost the straight-up fight, but he wanted to go out with honor. The next best result was that he would save the lives of some of his crew.

"You still have your honor, Captain. Let's start transferring people. Otherwise, all our efforts will be for naught. And thank you for talking with us. There's no need to keep the fires of hatred burning." Crip closed the emergency channel and opened the team channel.

"I'll need three soldiers to escort the prisoners and three soldiers to prepare to breach the space. Two levels up, there should be an access point directly above since this is supposed to be the same configuration as *Chrysalis*."

Max repeated the order, assigning names to each task. "I'll go with the first group back to *Chrysalis* and return with the Malibor spacesuits. We can't loan them one of the combat team's suits since we have gear in the pockets, plus ours our up-armored with the little bit of extra we've added for protection."

"Then they'll have to deal with two at a time. Danzig, are you through the missile hatch yet?"

"It's been two minutes since the last time you asked," Danzig replied, which wasn't an answer but was.

"It's been closer to twenty minutes. Keep grinding. Those missiles are pri one."

"Pri one. I feel like I'm an army of one. Any way I can get an extra set of hands and maybe a plasma cutter?"

"If you hang out with Bec near the fissile material, you can grow an extra set of hands and help yourself. Or we can ask Alby to give us a hand. He's big into weapons."

"I heard that," Alby said, stepping on a retort from Bec. "You're right. I'll send a couple engineers your way, and they'll be hauling a torch. We'll be able to look inside soon. We'll pop all the hatches. Maybe we'll get lucky."

"We've already been lucky, so anything we find is an added bonus. Thanks, Alby. Crip out."

Crip opened a direct link with Max. "Take care, Max. That captain, Delong'sa, rolled over far too easy. There was posturing, then complete surrender."

"I think he gave in because you showed no interest in doing anything quickly. They have to be running out of air and power, and the heat is long gone. They're barely holding on."

"You're probably right. It won't hurt to double-check them before we haul them to *Chrysalis* and stuff them in the lander bay."

Max handed Crip a pulse rifle. The commander gripped it tightly while checking its status, then slung it, attaching it to the shoulder of his suit with two magnetic fasteners. It could easily be pulled free, but the sling kept it from flying away.

Ten minutes after the bulkhead closed, it opened again to reveal a suited form within. The Malibor stepped out, and Crip waved him toward the connecting corridor in which he waited with Barrington. The soldier still had a tight grip on Lieutenant Delong's arms. The rest of the combat team, minus Danzig and Larson, filled the open space beyond the corridor, pulse rifles at the ready and mobility packs in place. Crip waited beside the hatch.

The new prisoner walked slowly toward the corridor without glancing sideways. He moved like an automaton.

"Something's not right," Crip said on the team channel.

"Watch out!" Barrington shouted. "She blew up."

"What are you talking about?" Max asked, turning his whole body to look at Barrington and his prisoner. An expanding red cloud drifted past the soldier as two halves of a space suit spun in opposite directions.

"She blew up. She must have been wearing a bomb or something." Barrington's voice shook with horror. "She just...*exploded.*"

"Check your suit for leaks." Max's wrist computer verified that his suit was uncompromised. Barrington's showed that it was fine. Concussion wasn't effective in the vacuum of space, but if she had been carrying projectiles, they would have been deadly. "I don't think she intended to blow up out here."

Max turned back to the individual in the suit perambulating toward him with a mechanical stride, magnetically connected boots maintaining a regular pace.

Crip leaned toward the opening to look inside when suited fingers gripped the side of the bulkhead. Before he could shout a warning, two individuals shot out of the opening and flew down the corridor in the zero-gee past the walking dead.

The commander raised his rifle, but the team was beyond the two. He dared not fire. He grabbed the bulkhead and yanked himself around it to get out of the line of fire.

He slammed into two more suited individuals inside and snap-fired a low shot into one's leg. The Malibor recoiled, then reached for his leg to staunch the flow of blood and air.

The second Malibor grabbed for the pulse rifle, but it was tightly slung on Crip's shoulder. They wrestled, each trying to get control of the rifle. Crip clamped one of his magnetic boots to the deck and one to the bulkhead. The wide stance stymied the Malibor, who had both hands on the pulse rifle.

Crip removed his multi-tool, bared the knife, and slashed the arms of the suited individual before him. The fight ended as quickly as it had started. The leg wound had proven fatal, and the second Malibor lost his grip on the pulse rifle when he convulsed from lack of air and being exposed to space. He tried to tamp down the cuts on his suit, to no avail. Crip slashed the exposed middle of the man's suit to be certain.

He was angry at the Malibor captain's outright lies. He had been honest with Delong'sa, if that was who he'd been talking to. How would the captain ever have killed a Borwyn? Delong'sa. What a rube. The man had blown up Lieutenant Delong, whoever she was. He was a monster.

"Call me Castle'sa," he muttered, posturing even though there was a fight outside the makeshift airlock. He took one step toward the bulkhead and stopped to watch it trundle closed.

"Max, how you doing out there?"

"Two unarmed Malibor against the whole combat team? They didn't last two seconds. And we caught it and deactivated the robot suit. We might be able to use it. Where are you?"

"The bulkhead door closed, and the air is cycling. Either more want to come out and play, or they're hoping to trap me inside. In either case, I have a pulse rifle, and they don't. I also have two dead bodies to use as shields. They probably won't like that, but then again, they started this. I have no sympathy for them. I'll try to cycle the airlock after I'm through so you can join me. I'd prefer not to do this alone, but we have to play the cards we're dealt."

"Stay frosty, Crip. I don't want to be responsible for hauling your dead body back to the ship." Max had descended to the apex of military camaraderie with the darkest of humor. A blood fog had expanded, frozen, and now pelted the inside of the corridor in which he stood, along with a cloud that had since disappeared into the void beyond. Part of a body was caught on the ragged edge of an exposed spur.

"Despite our desire to capture the stuff inside intact, liberal use of the pulse rifle is called for since I don't want to be that dead body. I'll keep my channel open. Gotta run, which means I have to stand here and be ready to shoot bad guys."

CHAPTER 22

"To the stars and beyond" is a rallying cry for those who are nurtured by their home planet, not those who have lived their lives in space.

The captain fumed, not at her deputy but at the Malibor. She had started to believe they could be reasoned with, but now she was going to paint them all with the same brush, limiting her options going forward.

In every engagement, she would assume the Malibor would try to kill them, even if they clearly lost the battle.

"Kill them if you have to, Crip. Don't take any risks because you think they might be willing to talk. *They've already shown that they won't.*" Her voice had increased in volume, and she delivered the final piece as a crescendo.

"Channel is *not* open," the communication officer said in a quiet voice. "Commander Castle did not receive your message."

The captain waved her hand and sighed. "He knows everything I said. I was venting because the Malibor made me angry. That's okay. We'll clean them out of that Borwyn ship and take our equipment back.

"We've had enough of their duplicity. May Septiman guide Crip to victory. We tried peace first. The Malibor slapped our faces, and they'll pay for that with their lives. Tram, target an E-mag broadside on that section of the ship, but hold fire until our people are clear."

"Are you recalling our people?" Tram asked.

"Not yet, but if we do, I'll want to hit the section that still has power with direct strikes to kill those within while doing as little damage as possible."

Tram understood the order. He was the backup in case the Malibor killed Commander Castle. Retribution would be quick and without mercy.

"I'm happy to put that firing package together. If we need it, it'll be ready." He looked at his new offensive weapons officer, Lieutenant Taurus Lindman. "Are you okay? You understand that we probably won't need it, but it's great practice. Crip will take them out. He's very good."

Taurus nodded. "I'm okay," she replied, but she had a dark cloud hanging over her features. She targeted six E-mag cannons at the starboard side. She'd had to review what the obdurium projectiles would pass through when they pierced the hull and what was on the far side of the affected spaces to limit collateral damage, as well as damage to primary systems that might be recoverable.

Taurus focused on her screen, manipulating three-dimensional models to develop optimal firing angles. She then programmed each cannon, running through the calculations and instructions like a pro.

"I guess that confirms you were the best choice for this position. Who would have thought sensor systems had such a crossover with offensive weapons? Besides me, that is." Tram smiled at the wisdom of his choice. He was now in the position he wanted, so he didn't need to work the captain. Tram was happy to see Taurus take to the position.

"Do not shoot my deputy, Lieutenant," the captain cautioned.

Taurus raised her eyebrows. "I have a vested interest in not shooting him as well."

The captain mumbled, "It's about time. Come on, Crip. I need you to come home. It's been three years since the last wedding. I'm itching to hold another one."

Air filled the space and pressurized, then the internal bulkhead ground to the side. The hideous screech of metal on metal vibrated his helmet and reverberated through his boots. He crouched, holding a body in front of him. It was light in the corridor beyond the opening, but there was no one there.

Crip waited until the bulkhead opened all the way to make sure no one was hiding behind it as he'd done. It was clear. He didn't want to, but he pushed the body before him, staying behind it. One magnetic boot step followed another until he was inside the Malibor-controlled space. The command deck was straight ahead. To the left was the captain's cabin, or that was where it was on *Chrysalis*.

The commander was torn. He could continue forward, but they could come from behind him if he didn't clear the spaces as he went.

The body was stiff, which meant the temperature equaled that of deep space. Anyone inside without a suit and environmental controls would be suffering greatly. Crip ripped open the door to the captain's quarters. It came away easily. He dipped his head to look inside and ducked back out. He didn't see anything big enough to be a person bundled against the cold or in a spacesuit.

He continued past the door that led to the captain's briefing room. That space was quarters on *Chrysalis*. Crip checked the room, keeping the body in front of him while he held it up with his pulse rifle barrel. He could fire from a covered position, which was only possible because of zero-gee.

Another empty room. Next stop was the command deck. The hatch was cracked and he edged it open, pulling back when he saw people inside. They were heavily bundled in blankets, so he could barely see their eyes. They didn't have their hands where he could see them.

"I don't appreciate the subterfuge. The people you sent against us are all dead, and their deaths are on you," Crip announced, using his suit's small external speaker.

Someone spoke. Crip heard it on the emergency comm channel. "That's not the only card we can play."

The tone was ominous. Self-destruction was the only ploy left to them. Bomb and destroy. Deny the Borwyn anything useful.

Crip could stop it right there if he killed the four people who had been waiting for him. He ducked back and glanced around to make sure no one was coming in from his six, then moved through the hatch and closed it. He shoved the body toward the one standing closest to the captain's chair.

Crip kneeled and aimed down the barrel. Shooting while wearing a spacesuit wasn't very precise, but at this range, he wouldn't miss with more than one or two shots. There were four people, and he had at least twenty shots before he'd need to change the power pack. Maybe seventeen since he'd already fired a few times.

The Malibor awkwardly caught the body but didn't take their hands out from within the blankets.

He saw a movement from the one he had guessed was the captain. A hand placed a microphone closer to his mouth. Crip relaxed.

"Using a prisoner as a shield is not very civilized."

"First day at war, Captain Delong'sa? Like taking names based on killing an enemy is better. We have suits and will stick to the terms I gave you. We'll give you food and shelter until we can put you down with your own kind. I don't want to kill you."

"I'm afraid we will not let you kill us," the captain replied. He pulled the blanket away from his face. His grin was sinister.

Crip fired his pulse rifle one time. The round ripped through the center of the man's chest, flinging him back. Blood volcanoed from the impact crater, and much of what was inside splattered out of the exit wound. The captain would have floated free, but his magnetic boots held his lifeless body in place. Gore floated in a cloud toward the main screen.

A second Malibor moved to the side. Crip fired again, clipping an arm, but the velocity of the round tore the arm off. Blood spurted from the brachial artery, adding to the gore and chaos on the command deck.

"Freeze!" Crip shouted. "Put your hands up or you die."

One of the two pulled her blanket away from her mouth so she could puke. It was nothing more than bile that floated as an ugly yellow string. Crip kept his rifled trained on the other while the first pulled her blanket back into place over her face. He gestured for her to get her hands up with the rifle's barrel.

He had credibility and their full attention. They stayed where they were with their arms twisted in blanket rolls over their heads.

"Max, are you there? You should be able to cycle that bulkhead and come inside. I'm on the command deck. I have two dead and two potential prisoners unless they get cute. Then I'll have four dead. It looks like the captain was telling the truth about eight people total, but they had four suits. The others are bundled in blankets and still freezing."

"There's no way to cycle the airlock from out here," Max replied.

"Let me shepherd these two. I'll be back." Crip switched to his external speaker. "Listen up, you two. We're going to go cycle the airlock so the rest of my team can get in here. If you do anything funny, you die. There's zero sense in trying to be a martyr at this point since no one will know you ever existed. You were here. You saw. We lived up to our word. I do not want to kill you, but being willing to and wanting to are wholly different. Now, play nice!" Crip had had enough. He moved closer to the prisoners and motioned with his weapon's barrel, almost pushing them toward the hatch.

One of them spoke in a muffled voice.

Crip couldn't decipher the words. "What are you saying? You have to use the comm device inside your captain's blanket."

The woman shook her head. The other individual remained stoic. Crip guessed it was a man. If someone tried to be a hero, it wouldn't be the puker. It would be the person who kept his movements to a minimum.

Crip took one step back, then another. That put him next to the captain's body, but it also took him closer to the captain's chair. The screen was active, with lights blinking. They had done something, and it was in action. Crip wanted to look but couldn't take his eyes off the two in front of him.

"No!" Crip shouted as loud as his small speaker could. "We're leaving the command deck. Come on. Into the corridor with both of you."

The man took one more step, and Crip fired into the captain's body. The sound of the pulse rifle in the enclosed space shook their eardrums and pierced their brains. The man wheeled too quickly.

Crip pulled the trigger. The pulse rifle barked, and the Malibor took the shot in the face. It ended him in the ugliest way. Crip turned his attention to the woman. The blankets covering her face shook as she sobbed. Crip slung his rifle since he could manhandle the single prisoner. He moved behind her and took her in both hands, then lifted to carry her before him. She was wrapped so tightly in the blankets that she could barely move, let alone reach behind her to cause Crip trouble.

He used his foot to open the hatch and headed into the corridor. She was little more than a rag doll. When they reached the bulkhead, there was no panel or way to cycle the airlock.

"How do we open this thing?"

He held his head close to the opening in the blankets.

Finally, the shouted words made sense. "Command deck."

Crip wondered if the others were trying to cycle the airlock, but they were no better than fanatics, still married to a fifty-year-old misunderstanding that the Borwyn were the aggressors. One had blown himself up. He couldn't trust anything they said. With their last breaths, they'd tried to kill Borwyn. Crip had personally killed many of the Malibor, so he was reinforcing their preconceived notions.

Despite his best efforts to the contrary.

Would the enemy always be the enemy?

If they were taught to be, their beliefs would perpetuate.

Crip kept a tight grip. "Where is the console to control the bulkheads and airlock?" he shouted into his helmet. The small speaker did the best it could. He repeated himself, pressing his helmet against the mass of blankets.

The woman was shaking. Whether from fear or the cold, he couldn't tell, but she wasn't a threat to him.

An elbow pressed against the blankets in a generic point.

Crip studied the console. It was based on icons, not written language. He couldn't decipher them. He had to trust that she wouldn't blow up the command deck.

"Max, do we have an extra suit?"

"No extra suit. The bulkhead door hasn't opened yet. Are you working on that?"

"Still working on it, but we're going to need a suit for the last crew member who is alive, and we need it soon."

"Belay my last!" Max said with a note of triumph. "They sent a robot out in a suit. We didn't have to shoot it, only plant it against a wall. We'll remove the robot and bring the suit with us. We don't have any robots on *Chrysalis,* so we'll set it aside to take back to the ship for study. We might learn something."

"I'll let her know. And bring Larson. We might need his expertise with this technological madness." Crip changed back to the speaker and spoke loudly, enunciating each word. "We have an extra undamaged suit. Open the bulkhead and let our people in. We'll bring the suit to give you some heat and air. Do you understand?"

Crip pressed his helmet against her blankets. His suit's lights finally caught long eyelashes covered with frost above bloodshot crystal-blue eyes. She blinked and nodded. Crip moved her close to the terminal she'd indicated with her elbow. Slender fingers snaked out from near her waist and tapped an icon on the screen. The hand quickly returned within the fold for what warmth was there.

The icon, which had been green, now blinked red. Five minutes later, it changed to solid red. The fingers snaked out to tap another icon, and it changed from green to red without flashing.

"Bulkhead is opening," Max reported.

Crip held the Malibor tightly as if his suit would help her stay warm. He could feel her shivering. He eased around the command deck, still holding his prisoner. The captain's console drew his eye since it had icons flashing, although the other stations had none. Crip couldn't decipher them. He saw numbers, but nothing was counting down.

He had been convinced that the captain was going to blow up the closed areas rather than let them fall into Borwyn hands. But how? Overload?

"Where is the power source for this section of the ship?" Crip asked, leaning close to the Malibor.

Her eyes rolled up, and she went limp. She stopped shaking.

"Hypothermia. You need to hurry to the command deck if we want this one alive, Max. And we do."

"Inside door is opening. Be there in ten seconds."

True to his word, Max hit the hatch frame to the command deck in the time he'd guessed and caught it with one hand to slow down since he'd foregone his magnetic boots to take advantage of zero-gee. The extra suit was draped over his arm and was almost as big as him.

They opened the suit and unwrapped the blankets from around the now-unconscious woman.

"Holy Septiman," Max said when he saw her.

She looked nothing like the Borwyn and nothing like the Malibor either. Her hair was jet-black, almost blue, and her features were lighter. Her skin was pale and almost translucent. She was lean as if she hadn't gotten enough food.

They quickly worked her into the suit and secured it by activating the systems.

An error code flashed on the wrist control.

"No idea," Crip said before Max asked.

They checked the suit and the backpack.

"It's not heating up," Max said after removing his glove to check the feed. "That's why they put a robot in it."

"Stay here." Crip vaulted over the consoles, inverted to kick off the ceiling, and propelled himself through the floating frozen gore to the front of the command deck and the other body in the suit. The arms were slashed, but he only needed the backpack, and the quick connectors for the hoses made it easy to detach. He kicked off the front screen to return to Max and the woman.

They changed out backpacks and fired up the blood-spattered one.

The sleeve interface showed green lights. Crip released his glove to check that the suit was warming by using his bare hand. Air was flowing. Her breath came in shallow, ragged gasps, fogging the inside of the helmet's shield.

"She's alive. We need to get her back to the ship and into treatment."

"Take her," Max told him. "We'll do the dirty work here."

Crip wanted to agree, but he was a far better engineer than Max. "You need to take her. I'll work with the systems here. There are a lot of unanswered questions."

"As you wish, Castle'sa." Max chuckled. "I'll get her to the docs. Then we'll see what she knows."

"Be quick about it," Crip blurted.

"Okay, Mister Smitten Man. Malibor. Tried to kill you. Taurus is waiting for you on the bridge." Max carried her under his arm as if she were a plank. "Get a grip on yourself."

"She's the only one who can tell us what we don't know," Crip countered. "Go on. She hates us all at the core of her being. We should never doubt that, no matter how much she bats those eyelashes."

"Those *are* something, aren't they?" Max replied, continuing toward the airlock.

Once inside, Crip hit the icon on the control panel, then showed Larson which ones did what. "Cycling through the screens. I'll be back." He turned to Max. "And yes, they are the most magnificent eyes I've ever seen. Make sure she's under guard at all times."

"Of course. I'll turn her over to the captain. She's the best one to manage our prisoner," Max agreed.

When the airlock showed red, Crip opened the outer emergency bulkhead.

"Larson," Crip started, "find where this power is coming from. *Chrysalis* doesn't have anything like it. We want it if they've modified their systems to add a backup using a smaller power station like Alby found on the weapons platform. At least, he found where it was supposed to go."

"I need to trace these lines." Without waiting for approval, Larson started pulling up floor panels, under which the wiring for the command deck was located. "These guys have no class and no sense of style. Would you look at this?"

Crip would have ignored him, but Larson gestured at the crawl space beneath the command deck.

Crip leaned over the console. A spaghetti farm of the worst order was wedged into the space below, with too many splices to count and wire color changes at each repaired connection.

"That's pretty bad," Crip agreed. "Find us that power source. I'm going to check if anyone else is floating around in here."

The commander moved into the corridor and took a moment to bring his pulse rifle around to the front. He had no desire to use it, but the Malibor had been raised to be hostile toward Borwyn, even if their enemies were there to save lives.

Maybe they'd been told that Borwyn ate Malibor babies for breakfast to keep the hatred alive. "This fight isn't just about our technology defeating their technology. We can beat them, but can we stop them from fighting?" he asked himself.

The question would continue to haunt him.

CHAPTER 23

Peace will be achieved when the fear of dying overtakes the fear of failure.

The corridors were empty, but the rooms were not. Many Malibor had died in them. Though the space had power, most were blue, as if a lack of oxygen had killed them. Then they'd frozen. It must have taken the Malibor crew too long to get the system even partially functional, and they hadn't been able to add heat, even in a limited way.

"We have a lot of bodies in here," Crip reported. "And they didn't die from our weapons. Their deaths were slow and painful."

The captain came on the channel. "We never expected to find live Malibor. It was a miracle they survived as long as they did. However, they tried to kill us, but we killed them first. Find us what we need to help *Chrysalis*, Commander Castle. And I don't know what's up with this woman's eyelashes, but I can't wait to see for myself."

"I'm pretty sure that was on the point-to-point channel with

Sergeant Tremayne. Maybe we weren't. I stand humbled before Septiman. The battle is joined!" Crip rambled.

"Find us what we need, Crip. Jaq out."

The channel crackled to silence. Crip double-checked his communication system. He'd been on broadcast the whole time he'd believed he was switching back and forth.

He wondered if he would ever live it down. He thought he heard Max laughing, but all the channels were closed. It was only in his mind, even though he probably *was* laughing.

Crip carefully opened the team channel. "Larson, any progress?"

"Slowly working my way toward the bulkhead. This is a mess, but I'll figure it out."

Crip continued until he reached a vestibule. There was a head in that gap on *Chrysalis*. In this space, a one-meter by two-meter device hummed. It didn't look like a CO_2 scrubber. "Skip down the corridor to the head on the port side. I think I found what we're looking for."

Larson didn't respond, just clumped into the corridor before releasing his boots and pulling himself along the rails to the far end of the corridor where Crip waited.

"Oh, yeah. Talk to me, baby," Larson purred.

Crip stepped back to give the tech wizard room to work.

"What do we want to do with it?" Larson asked.

"Shut it down, unhook it from the grid, and take it to *Chrysalis*."

"We'll lose power throughout this section." Larson continued to study the device.

"We're going to have to take it down at some point. We need it powered down so we can dismantle the bridge equipment and take it all home with us. Then we can depressurize this whole section to make it easier to get in and out."

Larson stepped back and crossed his arms.

"That doesn't appear to be a turning-off pose." Crip stared at the soldier.

"It's a mini reactor," Larson said. "We have to stop the reaction, but that's not something we want to do manually since there's no manual controls on this thing. There has to be a control system, probably on the command deck."

"Which means we need a battery backup to keep the system active while the reactor is shutting down?" Crip guessed.

Larson tapped his face shield with one finger.

"Bec, we need you near the command deck. We're going to depressurize the entire space first. Hop on over here and be ready to enter when we open the bulkhead."

"I've been waiting for this call," Bec replied. "Where else will I be summoned on this monstrosity whilst cocooned inside a spacesuit that keeps the outside from getting in?"

Crip wanted to hold the moral high ground when dealing with the chief engineer, but it wasn't always easy. "Wherever we need your expertise and insight, Bec. You'll just have to live with constantly coming to our rescue. Our unending praise will have to be sufficient to keep you going."

A call came over a point-to-point channel. Crip triple-checked that it was only him and Max talking.

"He's on his way," Max said. "I'm almost to the ship. I'll give you an update on the mystery woman when I have it. I don't want her to die."

"I don't want her to die either, or anyone else. I've had my fill, although it does get easier."

"That's an ominous proclamation, Crip. Gotta go. Heading into the airlock now, but the medics are still working on Annabelle. It might be a little bit before the Malibor gets seen. At least we can warm her up and give her some fluids. Max out."

Crip closed all his communications channels. He'd get a

notification if someone tried to contact him. He hesitated. Standard procedure was to stay in contact. Crip reopened the team channel but didn't speak.

The command deck had the majority of the hardware they wanted from this section, although the small reactor held promise, if for nothing other than to power a weapons platform to provide additional firepower for *Chrysalis*.

Crip returned to the command deck and the panel that controlled the airlock. He had to guess that a third button below the other two vented the space, and it had to be pressed multiple times. Warnings appeared. Crip read them to the best of his ability. He assumed they were doom and gloom, but he couldn't get past them as they kept circling back. He leaned on the interior bulkhead door button until it flashed red, then let up. Warnings flashed across the screen.

"Don't make me blow you up!" Crip shouted at the screen. The air outside his suit whistled, and he was pulled toward the open hatch. "That's more like it. Command deck space is venting atmosphere to equalize with the great outdoors. I'm opening all the bulkhead doors I can access."

Crip went from screen to screen, looking for bulkhead icons. Lights flashed red on all screens, warning of the decompression. The emergency bulkheads automatically released after the interior equalized with space.

"Come and get it," Crip announced. He stopped when he noticed a sensor screen and climbed into the seat behind it. The gel seat was nearly frozen solid, so he perched on the edge, then scrolled through the screens to find historical information.

He reached a view showing a ghost ship in orbit around Farslor. Unclear images. The gunship in deep orbit sent to learn more. The gunship and *Hornet* on their way. In their wake, they left a fleet.

Crip's breath caught when he saw the numbers. He tapped

the screen with his finger to keep track while he counted. Gunships and small cruisers. Too many gunships. Too many cruisers. All were in orbit around Septimus and the moon the Malibor called Malpace. A long time ago, it had been called Alarrees.

Bec flew down the corridor past the command deck. He didn't acknowledge Crip's wave.

"Butter nugget," Crip mumbled, continuing to take in the Malibor's complement of space frames. Spaceships were arrayed around Septimus, ready to deploy when they received the call. To Crip's eye, the Malibor fleet looked formidable and ready to fly.

"We can take it down without battery backup. There's a panel right here. Did you remove it?" Bec sounded like he was berating Larson.

Crip hurried into the corridor and down to the left. A moment later, the lights went out, but the commander's suit's lights revealed the way ahead.

He found Bec wrenching on a connection at the base of the power plant. Larson held up his hands on his way by.

"Bec, a heads-up would have been nice."

"Why? We want the power plant. In two minutes, we'll have the power plant. This is something we might be able to replicate. I can't wait to tear it down for a good look."

"That's exactly what I meant. Carry on, wayward son."

"You are hard to work with," Bec muttered while continuing to free the connections holding the small reactor in place.

"My apologies, sewer sludge."

"Crip," the captain interjected. "A word, please."

"Yes, master of all things space, air, and land."

A private channel beeped, and Crip answered. "He's such a throbbing purple…"

"I know," the captain interrupted the tirade, "but you need to work with him. We need him, and what's with the names?"

"There's power in names." Crip's adrenaline waned. "I had to kill those people."

"I know, Crip. I heard the whole interaction. Is that what this is about?"

"It's about Bec being hard to work with and my tolerance being at zero."

"Come on back to the ship, Crip. Let Alby and Bec handle it. Lots of engineers waiting to head over if they only had a suit. Max will also return to *Butterfly*, but it's time for you to come home. We have a war to plan now that we have more information. Did you find the Malibor order of battle?"

"I was trying to study it when Bec cut the power. I'm not sure what it would take to bring it back up. It's in the system somewhere, but I had it right in front of me!"

"The power plant is free," Bec announced. "Moving it to the collection point."

"Complete disregard for what anyone else is doing," Crip finished.

"What'd you see?" the captain wondered.

"Twenty or thirty gunships. Eight or ten light cruisers. Nothing as big as us." Crip was crushed. They would face more than thirty ships. Their goal had gone from believable to unachievable in the course of two minutes.

"We'll figure it out," the captain assured him. "As long as we're not in a hurry, we'll be fine. Just need to tackle them one or two at a time. Did we find any missiles on that ship?"

"Don't know yet, Jaq. We'll have that answer soon enough. The good news is that on the screen, *Hornet* and that gunship were already well toward Farslor. The next closest ships were in orbit around Septimus."

"Focus on the here and now. The way ahead will present itself when the time comes. Return to the ship. That's an order."

"On my way, Jaq." Crip didn't want to argue when there was no reason to. The captain was right. His presence was counterproductive. The gore floating around the bridge reminded him of the earlier chaos. It had cost plenty, but they'd learned what they wanted to know, even though it wasn't what they wanted to hear.

Crip took one last look at the command deck before working his way through the open bulkheads and into the corridor that was open to space. His mobility pack was where he'd left it. He strapped it on, and his comm crackled. Bec was calling.

"Since you're going and I'm stuck here on the captain's orders, take my power plant."

"Say what?" Crip peered around the corner and was almost face-rammed by a big piece of gear coming toward him. He slipped in front of it to catch it and held it while he stretched out his legs to absorb the impact when he hit the bulkhead.

An idea flashed into his head. He activated his jets and slowed down before he crashed into the bulkhead at the turn of the corridor, then adjusted to push the small reactor into space. Bec had headed back into *Hornet*.

"Take it all, Bec. Get us everything there is to get."

The chief engineer didn't reply.

Crip pushed off toward open space. He touched his jet pack and accelerated toward *Chrysalis* with their second-greatest acquisition.

The first was the Malibor prisoner—if they could keep her alive.

CHAPTER 24

People are the only reason we're doing what we're attempting to do.

Jaq hung on to Tram's console. "Twenty to thirty gunships and a dozen light cruisers. Start thinking about how we can blast them out of the sky."

"We need more missiles," Tram replied without hesitation.

"Working on it." Jaq gave him the thumbs-up.

"Captain to Medical," someone announced.

Jaq didn't know if it came over the intercom or if the comm officer relayed the call. She didn't wait. She kicked off the nearest rail to jet into the corridor and continued to Medical without wasted effort. Vantraub and the shepherd were in the corridor, still wearing their blood-spattered smocks.

"What's the prognosis?" Jaq didn't want dissembling or vague pronouncements. She wanted ground truth.

"She's stable but in critical condition. She's sedated. Now we wait and see before we can reattach the front section of her skull. She won't recover consciousness until after we've put her back together, so to speak. We won't know if she'll survive. Only time will tell if we relieved the pressure in time or in the right way."

Jaq gripped both their shoulders. "Thank you. There's nothing else to say."

The shepherd spoke. "She's in recovery now. Annabelle is being carried by Septiman's hands under our medic's steady direction." He nodded and pointed down the corridor. "I'll be in my quarters recovering."

"Not yet, Shepherd. We have a hypothermia victim on her way in. Crip was able to capture one Malibor, but she's in bad shape. This could be an intelligence coup if we can save her."

"Saving souls is what we do," the shepherd proclaimed. "Whether now or in the afterlife."

Vantraub snorted and shook her head.

"Now would be better. Max will bring her up, and, needless to say, keep her under guard. They tried to kill us multiple times. I don't know her role in it, but until we find out, we have to assume she'll sabotage the ship if given a chance."

"Of course." Vantraub looked down. "I've never seen a Malibor."

"Very few of us have."

"I will pray for her soul to know peace," the shepherd offered.

The captain nodded congenially.

Max appeared, pushing an individual wrapped in a pile of Borwyn blankets from when they transferred her out of the suit on the lower deck. She was smaller than the sergeant, even with the blankets making her look bulky. He held her in one arm while he pulled himself down the corridor. He clamped his boots to the deck and held out his charge for the medical team to take control.

"We'll need to warm her up," Vantraub stated. "The physical therapy room, please." She clumped away.

Max held the Malibor close and hurried after the medic. She opened the door of the room next to the small clinic. It was tiny, only big enough for one person, and had pulleys connected to the walls for exercises of all the major muscle groups as well as most of the minor ones.

She pointed at the bench in the middle of the room while she kneeled to unfold the brackets under it that would brace a person working with resistance weights. After getting the Malibor on the bench and squeezed tightly between racks lining the wall, Vantraub turned up the heat in the room to that of a person's body, nearly thirty-seven degrees Celsius.

Max peeled back the top of his coverall to reveal his bare chest. He was already sweating.

"Help me get these off her." Vantraub unwrapped the blankets one at a time, leaving only the last one. She saw that the woman was wearing a coverall similar to those the Borwyn wore.

She removed the final blanket when the room's temperature reached a blistering level. Vantraub checked the Malibor's pupils, then her body temperature. The woman violently shivered.

"What's happening?" Max demanded.

"That's a good thing. She's coming back through the levels of hypothermia. Shivering is a good sign. It's the body's attempt to burn calories to keep her warm. The next phase is the body shutting down blood flow to the limbs and focusing on the core. Her limbs might not have been in jeopardy for long." Vantraub checked her toes and fingers. She didn't see the black of frostbite, but the digits were ghostly pale since the blood flow had been interrupted. "Rub her legs and arms. Get that blood flowing again. I'll get a dextrose/water mix directly into her veins."

"I'd go with kava, but that's just me," Max quipped. He vigorously rubbed the Malibor's limbs from mid-thigh to ankle, then switched legs and did it again. He kept going back and forth while Vantraub excused herself to get the IV solution.

The captain entered and started fanning herself. She studied the small figure, then took the woman's face in her hands. "I see what you mean," Jaq said. "Not a Malibor. She doesn't look like the pictures we have."

"That's what I thought. She doesn't look like either Malibor or Borwyn."

"Is there another race?" Jaq threw her head back and gaped at the ceiling. "That would explain some things while opening a cargo hold full of new questions. Who is our enemy?"

"History suggests uniting to fight a common enemy. If they joined forces with someone else, that could explain how they defeated us so soundly in the last battle over Septimus." Max had studied the past battles, and some things had never made sense to him. Instant dominance wasn't natural. It took time to develop an advantage, like the fifty years it had taken the Borwyn to create the ion drive.

Max kept rubbing the young woman until the medic returned.

Vantraub started an IV and hooked the self-pumping bag to the wall. "She's all yours. Make yourself comfortable." Vantraub clapped Max on his bare shoulder, then pulled her wet hand away and frowned at it. "You might want to keep yourself hydrated."

There was a water spigot on the wall. Max took the advice to heart and helped himself to a long drink, shooting the water into the zero-gee air and catching it in his mouth.

"What are your secrets?" he asked. "Who are you, and where do you come from?"

The woman couldn't answer. Not yet.

"I'll leave you to it." Jaq stepped out before she sweated through her clothes. In the corridor, the captain looked at the closed door of the physical therapy room.

"Let me know if she recovers consciousness. I have questions for her." Jaq held Vantraub's gaze. "Get yourself cleaned up and get something to eat. I doubt she'll be conscious anytime soon."

The medic nodded.

The shepherd floated behind her, looking hopeful.

"You're on watch until Vantraub gets back." The captain shook his hand, something usually not done with the shepherd. Greeting him was generally more ritualistic. Not this time. It was a simple thank you for taking on the extra duties.

Jaq returned to the command deck. "Call up your reliefs. Time for you guys to take a break. You've been too long on shift."

"I'll stay if you don't mind," Tram offered. "I'm in the middle of something."

The others made their calls. The captain casually cruised across the space and settled in next to her new battle commander. "What are you doing that can't wait?"

"I'm working on a new configuration to add twelve E-mag cannons to the bottom of the ship. With extra metal from *Butterfly*, we can add an entire deck of nothing but firepower."

"Twenty-four batteries? That would lead to some broadsides." The captain couldn't deny the advantage it would give them, but Tram hadn't been out of the chair since they'd first engaged the Malibor. "Don't burn out. I'll give you two hours, and then you'll be on mandatory downtime for four. Understand?"

"Clear as the night sky," Tram replied, returning to his computer screen.

Crip floated slowly across the command deck, grabbed a rail at the last second, and stopped by the captain's seat. "It's good to be back."

"Get something to eat, and then we'll talk."

Crip produced a nutrient bar from his pocket and started eating it.

"I don't know what I can tell you. You're at the pointy end of the missile. You hit the target first, and it's not always going to be pretty," Jaq said softly so as not to disturb the others getting ready for their reliefs.

Crip smiled but couldn't force himself to laugh. "I guess that's one way to put it."

"We're going to have to kill them unless they're quicker about surrendering. This group's willingness to sacrifice themselves when they had no hope concerns me. It's not like Farslor, where you had the advantage in technology. This is going to be a slog."

"Your pep talk sucks." Crip poked the captain's shoulder, then gazed at the main screen. It showed the damaged ship, *Chrysalis's* twin.

"You get a special one. That's the harsh reality of our existence, and we're learning that it's only getting harder with each engagement. Every battle is going to be to the death unless we keep beating them so badly that they get a clue."

Butterfly's hulk occupied the most real estate on the main screen. Lights flashed from space suits and plasma torches. Otherwise, the ship was without power. Bec had disconnected their jury-rigged supply, and Crip had brought it back to *Chrysalis*.

"Commander Castle and Sergeant Tremayne, Danzig here.

I hope you didn't forget about me. I would like to report that we have four missiles in tubes. Alby is on it."

Crip motioned that he wanted to reply. The captain nodded her approval.

"Noted. Took you long enough," Crip joked.

The captain scowled at her deputy.

"No respect, but you're right," Danzig replied. "There was no way I was cutting my way inside. It took a plasma torch to convince the outer door to show us the prize within."

The captain cut in, "That's the best news I've heard all day. Thanks, Danzig."

"Just a lonely soldier out here doing a lonely job with two of my best engineer friends and their toys."

The captain smiled, but he couldn't see that over the comm. "Good work, you guys. Take care while getting my missiles out of that ship and bringing them home. We'll cuddle them and caress them and put them to work for us. We'll give them a purpose for the greater good."

Crip winced.

"Too much?" she whispered.

He nodded vigorously.

"Keep on it. Captain out." Jaq closed the channel. She had never let her attention waver from her deputy. "Changes the dynamic in our favor, at least for the time being."

"Then we'll find something else. It's easy to get down and just as easy to see the upside."

"Embrace the feeling of the upside, Crip. We need all the hope we can wrap our arms around. Four missiles and a small reactor give me a lot of hope. And maybe twelve more E-mag cannons? Things are definitely looking up. Did you know we found a new welder? He's incredible."

"We can always use good welders. That requires an artist's touch and a soldier's diligence."

Jaq glanced at the screen, then Crip. She never got to enjoy the pleasure of exclusively focusing on one thing. "A kid. Thirteen. Son of our best welder. Did anyone know this kid had been watching his dad?"

"Third generation now working the ship." Crip furtively looked at the sensor section where Dolly worked. She was tiny within the confines of the gel seat.

"Ownership," Jaq replied. "This is their only home."

"I know this is my only home, but I also recognize it's a ship of war." Crip took a deep breath and slowly exhaled.

"Built to protect Septimus from the Malibor. It saved a few of our forebears, and now we're back. Well, almost back. The Malibor have been busy trying to make Septimus their own. Have they?"

"That's the big question. I'd like to think we still have people on the surface fighting them. They could not have landed enough troops or bred enough over the past fifty years to occupy all of Septimus. *There's no way.*"

Crip laughed. "Upside. I see it now. In the absence of information, we'll fill the blanks with what we want to believe as opposed to the worst thing imaginable."

"Now you're getting it." Even though they'd kept their voices low for privacy's sake, Jaq moved closer. "I need you with me, leading the crew to a better place. I also want you to make peace with Bec."

"If I make peace with him, I'll be the only one on the crew. People will think something is up." Crip spoke in his best skeptical voice. He preferred to avoid the chief engineer. "Can't you put Alby in charge of keeping the peace?"

"Something is up—our morale. And no, I'm not putting Alby in charge of you doing your job. That's *my* job. We all win together. The battle is joined, Commander Castle."

"Victory..." Crip didn't finish the rest of it. He knew his role on the ship, but he'd been up close and personal with the Malibor more than anyone else. On the planet, they could be reasoned with. In space?

Those Malibor were different. Jaded.

Crip conceded, "To defeat them, we have to show no mercy. They cannot get the benefit of the doubt since they'll use that to kill us. They tried to coerce the lander using subterfuge, and then they were willing to blow themselves up to stab us. Two different ships, one state of mind. We're the good guys, but we're going to have to act like the bad guys if we're to defeat them."

He paused. "I shot those people. I had a pulse rifle, while they didn't have anything but a button on a computer that I thought would activate a bomb. Because they weren't keen to freeze when I told them to. I'm still trying to get my head wrapped around it. I don't want to be the bad guy, Jaq."

"We're not. *You're* not. Our goal hasn't changed. We're going home. Our tactics will adjust as we learn more about the Malibor, but they're still the enemy. Their ancestors drove ours from our home, and now they are claiming it as their own. That doesn't work for me. It doesn't work for the Borwyn. Are we condemned to live our lives on a single spaceship because of one battle fifty years ago?"

"We are the starship lost," Crip replied when the realization came to him. "The Malibor still don't know who we are. They haven't broadcast that they recognize us. Most actions have taken place in Farslor's comm shadow. *Hornet*, aka *Butterfly*, was surprised. I don't know how much longer we'll maintain our advantage, but I think we'll have it for the next engagement, too."

"What did you see on their radar scans of friendly territory?"

Jaq's forehead was nearly touching Crip's as they floated

above the captain's chair. The intensity of her gaze helped him focus.

"I saw that they are concentrated around Septimus and her moon. Just because they have numbers doesn't mean they have quality. Let me work with Tram to come up with an attack plan. We can draw them out, or we can attempt a hit and run by taking out their supply base."

"Where is the supply base? The space station orbiting Alarrees, or Malpace, as the Malibor are calling it?"

"There are families on board. The captain said he was from there."

Jaq scoffed. "Is that the same captain who surrendered but didn't?"

Crip snorted. "I have to reevaluate everything he said and trust what I see, not what I've heard. I'm too trusting, it seems."

"That's fine when dealing with Borwyn, but not so much when Malibor are involved."

Crip grasped the captain's arm. "Thank you, Jaq. I'm glad you're the captain, but I'm still not sure I can make peace with Bec. He's a jerk and not even a lovable one. But there *is* someone else I need to make peace with. Can I have a couple hours off before bending Tram's ear?"

"Yes, and I'll chase Tram out of here, too. Take six hours to sleep. See you after that."

Crip smiled and waved while backstroking across the command deck. When he caught Taurus' eye, he gestured with his head. She winked and returned to her changeover brief.

He rolled over and eased into the corridor, catching the rail to stop his momentum. He waited there until Lieutenant Lindman appeared. She didn't bother with the rail, choosing to grab Crip's uniform and pull herself close. Then she wrapped her arms around his waist.

"Okay," she said simply.

"I like where this is going." Crip cocked his head. "Where *is* this going?"

"Alby is still on *Butterfly* and will be there for a while longer," she stated matter-of-factly.

Alby was Crip's roommate. Privacy was a rare thing on *Chrysalis*.

"We only have six hours," Crip countered. "Is that enough time?"

CHAPTER 25

When up isn't necessarily up, you must be in space.

Max took another long drink but sweated faster than he could refill his reservoir.

The prisoner's eyes fluttered, and she groaned. She left her mouth open and gasped for air as if she were claustrophobic. That was not a good fear for a person who lived on spaceships, even big ones like the *Chrysalis* class. Or maybe it was a panic attack.

Her eyes shot wide and she jerked upright, wincing at the quick movement when the restraining belt caught at her waist. Max held his hands up, hoping to calm her. She covered her head with both hands as if he were going to hit her.

"I'm not going to hit you. By Septiman's good graces, I couldn't contemplate such a thing." Max activated his boots to lock him to the deck.

She slowly pulled her hands away from her face, then her eyes darted from one wall to the other. "Are you going to torture me?" she asked in a small voice. The IV dangled from her arm.

She looked at that too, her crystal-blue eyes widening with each new revelation.

"What?" Max followed her line of sight. "No! Those are weights. This is a physical therapy room for rehabbing people who have been injured. We used it to warm you up after you suffered from hypothermia."

She finally saw Max and registered that he was half-undressed. She covered her face and turned away.

"What? No, nothing like that. I didn't have hypothermia, but I had to stay in here with you, and it's hot as the engine room on a full-power burn." He pulled his uniform up, unsavory as it was, to cover his sweaty chest and zipped it shut.

"I'm sorry about my appearance. We're Borwyn, and we don't do anything to people under our protection. We don't torture or anything like that. We can't turn you loose since your people tried to kill us multiple times in many different ways. I hope you understand, but your time with us won't be painful."

She relaxed, then her shoulders slumped. "I'm tired," she admitted. "Did anyone else make it off *Hornet*?"

"No. The fighting was more intense than we wanted. You're the only survivor." Max leaned against the bulkhead.

When she stared at the deck, he looked at the environmental control panel and reduced the temperature five degrees to something a little more tolerable. She was still staring at her feet when he looked back.

"How old are you?" Max asked.

"Why do you ask?"

Max shrugged. "I guess it doesn't matter. The commander's offer stands. We'll drop you off at the nearest Malibor outpost that doesn't shoot at us."

She harrumphed. "I doubt you'll find one of those. The Borwyn are evil and the enemy of all Malibor."

"Are you sure of that?"

"You destroyed our ship and left us to die until you showed up and killed the survivors, so yeah, I'm pretty sure."

Max frowned. "Maybe that's right from your perspective." He stayed at the far end of the bench and crouched so he wasn't looming over the prisoner. "*Hornet* used to be called *Butterfly*, and it's the sister ship of this one, *Chrysalis*. Both were built by the Borwyn during the last war over fifty years ago.

"*Chrysalis* was nearly destroyed back then but was saved by an innovative crew. The ship was spinning out of control on a trajectory that almost sent us out of the system. It took us all this time to rebuild the ship while also making an engineering breakthrough with the ion drive, a system that's more efficient than the old drives like the ones you had on *Hornet*. We're trying to get back home to Septimus, but the Malibor presence is making us reconsider how to do that."

"You didn't expect us to be on our home planet?" She shivered.

Max picked up a blanket and draped it around her shoulders.

"We didn't expect the Malibor to take over our home planet." Max avoided saying "you" so as not to personalize the issue.

"It's *our* home planet."

"About that. It's not. Fristen was your original home planet. Then the race of people known as the Malibor moved to Sairvor. I guess in the past fifty years, the Malibor claimed Septimus. Why do you think there are so many Borwyn on Septimus?" Max took a stab that his people were still there.

"They live like wild animals outside the cities. They aren't much of a threat to us, but it's important to only go to cleared and secured areas to enjoy nature."

Max had a hard time containing his excitement at the revelation. "Would you like to talk with our captain? She wants to talk with you, but she'll wait until you're ready. Just let me know."

"I'd like to rest. Is there somewhere more normal?" She patted the bench beside her and blinked quickly.

That froze Max as readily as if he'd run into a door. When he was finally able to speak, he asked, "You look different from other Malibor. Are there a lot of people like you?"

It was like he'd hit her with a hammer. Tears welled in her eyes and ran down her cheeks. Max didn't know what to do, so he sat there until she stopped crying.

"My mom is a Borwyn. I'll never be able to live it down."

The sergeant smiled. "A child of both worlds. I don't need to hear any more. We don't care about stuff like who your parents were. Being part Malibor doesn't make you bad. Being bad is what makes you bad."

She returned to staring at the deck. Max stood and felt along the bulkhead until he found the comm. He tapped it to bring up a channel to the command deck. "Captain Hunter, Sergeant Tremayne. Our guest is awake."

"On my way," came the immediate response.

"Once the captain gets here, we'll find quarters that will be suitable for you. I think you'll like our captain. She's nice."

"She? Your captain's a woman?"

"Presently. We've had both. Does it matter?"

"I guess not. It's different, that's all."

"We don't have very many people. Everyone works the same jobs. Everyone fights the same fight. It's the only way we can survive."

"I understand." She didn't sound as if she did, but she didn't need to understand to answer the captain's questions.

Max had to remind himself that she was a prisoner and their enemy.

It was better that they thought of her as an antagonist, in conflict but not at war.

Max shook his head as if trying to clear the cobwebs. The Malibor cowered.

"What's your name?"

"Deena. Deena Vanderpohl."

"Nice to meet you Deena, Deena Vanderpohl. I'm Max, Max Tremayne."

"Max Max." She smiled furtively like she didn't want him to see.

The door opened, and the two looked at the captain, who hovered in the corridor. The shepherd was behind her.

"Wait out here," the captain told him.

"She needs to find her way to Septiman sooner rather than later," the shepherd intoned.

"Of course, but it's going to be later rather than sooner." Jaq backed into the space and closed the door in his face.

Max shook his head.

The captain studied the woman in their charge. "How old are you?" Jaq asked.

"Max Max asked that, too."

The captain turned a harsh gaze upon Sergeant Tremayne before returning her attention to the Malibor.

Max introduced her. "Meet our guest, Deena Vanderpohl. She's half-Malibor, half-Borwyn. She says the Borwyn on Septimus only live outside the cities."

The captain's relief was visible. She too had experienced doubts. The older generation's vision of returning to free their people had not been mistaken. The efforts to fix the ship had not been in vain.

"Half-Borwyn. That's interesting."

"My father told me when I turned eighteen since I didn't

look like my brother and sisters. My mother was killed by her people after I was born." She spat at the deck, but nothing came out. "Savages."

Max's instant thought was "collaborator." He had to turn away since he knew his expression belied his empathy for the young woman from Septimus, a place he could only dream about.

"That's a hard story." The captain hooked the edge of the bench with her toe and pulled herself toward the deck. She activated her magnetic clamps. "It had to be hard growing up, but that's behind you. You joined the space fleet at eighteen, and you've served for a year or two?"

"Just one. How did you know?"

Jaq shrugged, denying Max the opportunity to learn how she knew. "What did you want to get from your service?"

"Off Septimus," she replied simply.

The captain had wanted to interrogate the prisoner, but she too was captured by the innocence of youth. "You made it off Septimus onto the biggest ship of the Malibor fleet. Did you get what you hoped for? Peace of mind, maybe?"

The young woman shook her head. "Nothing changed except the gravity and the air. Max said you built the *Hornet*. Is that true?"

"The Borwyn built the *Butterfly*, which the Malibor turned into the *Hornet*."

"Your air handling system drones so loudly you can't hear yourself think."

Jaq burst out laughing. "Then you'll feel right at home here since we have a couple legacy systems that do the same thing. Everyone stops talking when they kick in and resumes their conversations when they shut down. We've learned to live with it, but we've been on this ship our whole lives."

The young woman's eyes widened and she nodded, but she didn't say anything else. Deena punctuated her silence with a long yawn.

"You're our prisoner," Jaq stated abruptly. "But that doesn't mean you're in prison. It only means that you're on *Chrysalis* without a job until such time as we can find a place to drop you off."

Max interjected, "I was going to work with Crip to find a place for her and an escort." He turned to Deena. "Are you going to try and sabotage our ship or hurt any of our crew?"

"What? No."

"What was your job on board *Hornet*?"

"Kitchen help."

Max studied her features as if that would reveal if she was lying. He couldn't tell.

"Perfect. I hope you don't mind working in our kitchen. All our cleaning systems are automated. The majority of the work revolves around the hydroponics bays and the creation of balanced protein and nutritional meals."

Deena's eyes drifted back in her head. She jerked as she caught herself falling asleep.

"Quarters? I'll get a hold of Crip."

"No," the captain replied quickly. "He's...let's say occupied. Take her to the mess hall. I think Chef has an extra bunk. Take care of it, Max."

"What's Crip doing? We should probably get in the rotation to head back to the ship to assist with recovery operations."

"In due time. Give him his time off. You should probably clean up. You smell like an old sock that was found in the black water recovery tank."

"That cuts me deep, Captain. I was doing Septiman's work in here, making sure no harm came to our guest."

"Then you better put on your armor to protect her from out there."

"No one on the crew is going to give her any problems. I'll make sure of it."

The captain mouthed, "Shepherd."

"Oh. There's him. I'll deal with him, too. We can't have him giving Deena grief." Max touched her shoulder. "Who do you pray to?"

"No one."

"That answer probably won't send the shepherd into convulsions."

Max removed the intravenous drip and applied a small bandage after a single drop of blood escaped. He motioned toward the door. The captain released her boots and opened it, then pulled herself through and crashed face-first into the waiting shepherd. Their limbs tangled, much to his dismay.

Max released the belt holding Deena to the bench. She floated free and missed her grab for the rail. Max scooped her up with his arm and held her on one hip as he skipped out the door and past the shepherd. She hugged his neck, but not tight enough to cut off his air. He liked it.

They hit the shaft, and he rotated his body to orient toward the aft section. With one hand, he expertly pulled them down two levels, then caught the alignment ring and flipped through the opening on the level with the mess deck.

He slowed as they approached the open doors and guided Deena's hand to the rail. "Can you make it from here?" Max asked.

"Where are you going?" Fear lit her eyes.

His voice caught in his throat. "Nowhere. I'll be right beside you, but I didn't want the crew's first impression of you to be of me. We're all equals here. I'll introduce you. Try to relax."

"I'm tired, Max."

"I know. The medic said fatigue is one of the after-effects. She doesn't think you'll have any other lingering issues. You weren't on ice for too long."

"It was far too long," she countered.

"I imagine minutes became hours."

Her hair flowed away from her head, making her look like she was wearing a fan. It was typical when those with hair didn't tie it up. Max had extremely short hair, so he never had to think about it.

"Can you tie your hair up?"

"I used to have a hair tie. That must have gotten caught up in the blankets." She shivered. "The blankets. It was so cold."

"Let's go say hi and grab a bite before we get you settled. Food will warm you up. Something we call 'hot wet,' a brothy soup."

They entered the mess deck side by side. Only six crew were there, eating from the usual squeeze tubes operated by a manual plunger.

"Hey, everyone. This is Deena. She'll be joining us for a while."

They waved but didn't say anything.

"They're at the end of their shifts. They'll be asleep in five minutes. There!" He pointed behind the counter. "Chef!"

An older woman moved out from the back area, clumping heavily with each step. "Captain says you're getting a roommate. Meet Deena."

Chef crossed her arms. "Never seen you before." She looked at Max. "Why me?"

"She's trained in the kitchen. Well, it was a Malibor galley aboard *Chrysalis's* sister ship."

Chef studied Deena's features. "You don't look Malibor."

The young woman turned to Max for help.

"In due time, Chef. She's our guest, and I ask that you treat her nicely."

"I'll do my best, but you know how I run the mess deck. No quarter for slackers! No time for roughhousing. No joy in foolishness."

Deena snickered, earning herself a steely-eyed glare. "You sound just like the cook on *Hornet*. Exactly. Are you sure you don't have a Malibor twin?"

Chef's body flowed forward while her boots remained fixed to the deck. "I like this one, although there's not enough meat on her bones to make a decent stock, let alone a full stew. Take her to my quarters. The second cubicle is clear."

The crew slept on bunks, but they were inside cubes to accommodate the residents no matter which direction gee forces pushed them in.

"Serving the soup or being in the soup?" Deena asked in a whisper.

"If you don't know the answer to that, Chef is not exactly like the Malibor cook. As long as you aren't sure, you'll get along great with her. Why do you think the second bed in her quarters is empty?"

"You are incorrigible." She took his hand as they sailed across the dining area and into the corridor. "Your people are nice, but I think you're doing it on my account to lull me into a false sense of security, so I'll tell you everything I know."

"We want to know what you know, but we don't have the energy to use subterfuge to get there. Our people are nice. You're finding that out. I wish your captain had spent more time talking with Crip and less time trying to kill any Borwyn within shouting distance."

"I wish he hadn't done that too. More of my people would have survived."

"All eight would have. For now, let's get you settled.

Tomorrow is going to be a big day." Max had no idea what the next day would bring, but he expected it to be great. Since they'd won the battle with *Hornet*, everything had gone their way. Max thought it was a good sign.

CHAPTER 26

The stars might disappear, but never the Borwyn's desire to go home.

"These missiles are one step above a rectal rocket," Bec complained while Alby carefully directed their extraction. Four had been in the launch tubes, and four more had been in the loading gantry. Eight missiles in total.

"Even if they aren't optimal, that gives us more punch. It doubles our delivery yield," the captain replied.

"If the Malibor accidentally fly into them. I'm not sure they'll even fly."

"Have a little faith," Alby interjected. "You need some shepherd time to restore your belief in the greater glory of our mission."

"A proper shipyard with modern facilities would give me much greater confidence and even brighten my day." Bec sounded upbeat.

"Too bad we don't have one of those, but we were talking last year about a staging facility. Maybe that was just a few days ago. Whatever. Could we build one from *Butterfly's* wreckage?

If the missiles are unstable, they can be reworked by a team there without any risk to *Chrysalis*." The captain cocked her head, waiting expectantly for Bec's reply.

"Yes, that would be the best case."

Bec should have seen it coming. Being positive about something had been his downfall.

"Great. I'll need you to oversee the transformation of that hulk into a floating resupply, rearmament, and research and development station. We don't need to strip it *now*, but we do need to. That's a big ship. There's a lot to work with."

"*Hang on!*" Bec shouted his objection.

"This isn't a decision I make lightly." The captain raised her hand to forestall more objections. "It means splitting our crew. Sending fifteen to twenty of our people to our new station, along with equipment that we can't spare, all in the hope that we'll have a place to return to. It isn't speeding toward deep space. We'll have years before it travels too far to be of use. First order of business, put that power plant back and restore power, including heat in the livable section."

"There are bodies in there!" Bec's voice was shrill.

The captain felt sorry for whoever would be left behind with him. She didn't want to reply since the answer was obvious, but sometimes Bec disappeared on a tangent, and the obvious was no longer right in front of him. "Move the bodies before you turn the heat on."

"You big baby," Alby added. "I'll do it. Bec is going to have a meltdown if you put him on that station. I think it'll be a great challenge, and from a strategic perspective, I believe it's a critical addition. I'll ask you to capture a few gunships we can study. If we could add a remote piloting component, we could build a fleet. *Chrysalis* with two or three gunships? The Malibor would never know what hit them. And think about it. Gunships were constrained on maneuverability by a living crew. With remote piloting, they could accelerate and maneuver at twenty gees or more."

"No guarantees, but we'll try. Thanks for volunteering, Alby. I knew you were the better man."

"Hang on." Bec tolerated snide comments except when they hit too close to home.

Jaq envisioned the engineer's eye twitching and berated herself for the jab, especially after her request that Crip make peace with him.

"You know it's for the best, Bec. We need you here to keep *Chrysalis* running at full speed, especially after each battle. Who else will help us pick up the pieces?"

"I'm not sure I like either option."

The comm was silent as the three parties contemplated their fates.

First to renew the conversation was the captain, but it was one-way since she'd made her decision. She finalized the order. "You're in charge, Alby. Pick no more than fifteen people. A general specialist, a welder/maintenance specialist, suit repair, and ten engineering types. I have final approval on all personnel. Submit your list to me.

"Bec, you'll have to deal with who moves over to the platform. I'll get Crip on the transfer of supplies. Two months of food and water for fifteen people, plus one lander fueled at one hundred percent. If need be, you can transfer all personnel to the planet and then get back, keeping in mind that the locals are hostile and the conditions are harsh.

"You better take personal defense weapons, too. And Bec, get that power plant back to where it was and turn the heat and lights on before Alby moves in."

"That means I have to move the bodies out. What do you want me to do with them?" Alby asked.

"Put them in a section of the ship that isn't completely open to space. Keep them on ice and secured. I don't need dead bodies floating around, not if we're ever to sue for peace. I think it will strengthen our hand if we can prove we showed respect for the Malibor dead."

"I'll take care of it. Thanks for this opportunity, Jaq. I won't let you down." Alby closed the channel. He had to consolidate the list of the personnel he would need.

Jaq wanted the list to contain only volunteers, but Bec didn't want any of his best people to go. "I'd like to recommend people I don't want on that platform." The engineer wasn't kidding.

The captain found it humorous. "Alby will take volunteers, and you and I both know some of your best people are going to be in that group. That means you might want to re-evaluate your leadership style."

"I think people should refrain from projecting their ignorance onto me."

Jaq considered his words. "I think you need to rethink your definition of ignorance. Having someone disagree with you doesn't mean they don't know what they're talking about. Sometimes, it's a matter of perspective."

"Most of the time, people can't do math or handle basic logic."

"We'll see who volunteers. Maybe I'll be surprised." The captain spoke in her most calming voice. "I'll make the final decision on who goes."

Bec was agitated, which didn't take much. "How can I run the ship without my people?"

"You'll figure it out. I have to go now. You know, to run the ship." She signed off before he could reply and chuckled softly. He got under everyone's skin, but he was the reason they had the ion drive. He was why they'd made it this far. His genius had given them a chance.

Yet they still argued with him.

"Why can't you be a genius *and* easy to get along with?" Jaq mumbled, although she admitted that she'd rather have the former without the latter than vice versa.

She had to run the ship. That meant monitoring what was going on to make sure it was ready for combat at the earliest possible moment and ready to continue the war for as long as necessary.

The power reserve was at ninety-nine percent. The systems were running full, managing the transfer of materials from the hulk to *Chrysalis*, but the power plant was keeping up since the engines weren't driving the ship around.

The ion drives were power hogs but worth it.

Alby would keep the missiles with him to rework as he could until they were minimally viable as Borwyn offensive weapons, as well as anything else they recovered from the wreckage and could put to use against the Malibor. His job could prove critical, and the transfer of the lander gave them an out if *Chrysalis* never returned from a foray into enemy territory.

"Alby," the captain commed.

He answered quickly.

"Once you have the power on, pull up the sensor screen and confirm what Crip saw. Dissect it and give me exact information, then dig deeper. We need the information if we're to devise a plan to defeat them.

"How do we confront them on our terms? We have to minimize our exposure. If the Malibor bring half those ships against us simultaneously, we'll be destroyed. Even a quarter of them. We can't take on ten ships."

"We cannot. After the power plant is installed and operational, my first priority is reestablishing the sensor log and taking a good look. We haven't dismantled the command systems since there were more pressing concerns about obtaining materials that were far easier to access. Bec can get the heat on while I fire up the command deck."

"Be kind to Bec, please." The captain wasn't talking to only Alby. She was trying to convince herself, too.

"I'll do my best. I expect I'll have most of his people, and even if I don't like the guy, I don't want to set him up to fail. I've sent a note to the engineering department asking for volunteers. I did not sweeten the pot at all. I made sure they know that conditions will be austere, with lots of time in suits and all of it in zero-gee."

"With the thrusters attached, you might be able to impart some spin and give yourselves the feeling of a little gravity."

"Then it would be harder to move the heavy stuff around. I think we'll keep it at zero-gee. There will be detriments to the body, but we'll set up the usual workout facility and program."

The captain signed off. Alby was well into the planning and execution of the support platform's operation. That pleased the captain more than the details. It was far easier to do her job when those supporting the ship took their roles seriously and performed their jobs well.

Crip reappeared, looking both haggard and refreshed. Taurus was with him. She went to her position, and he went to his.

"I thought I told you to take the full six hours."

Crip smiled weakly. "It's been most of that."

Jaq checked the time. She wasn't sure about her internal clock, given the buzz of activity surrounding the recovery of *Butterfly*. She hadn't thought six hours had passed. Maybe two.

"Couldn't sleep," he explained. "I'll catch up next time."

Taurus looked as ruffled as Crip, but she kept her head down and focused on her work. The captain eased over to talk to Tram.

"No missiles until later, but eight are better than nothing. Just knowing we can resupply is comforting," Jaq started. "What's the status of the weapons platform's E-mags?"

"We've pulled off four. The problem is with the targeting. We can't make heads or tails of the Malibor system. We want to slave them to our current cannons, creating a double-barreled barrage from each system. It's not optimal, but it multiplies our firepower, if only over the short term, since there's also the reloading system. We'll have to reload the platform's guns manually." Tram shrugged to indicate he was sorry.

He and his team were doing all they could with the limited assets available. Most of the crew was engaged in efforts that weren't their primary duties, and they had attacked their tasks with the greatest of zeal. Like Danzig using a small cutter to get through a missile tube's outer door. He would have stuck with it as long as it took since the missiles were important to the ship.

What was important to the ship was important to the lives of its crew. To stay alive, they had to win the fight against the Malibor.

The crew trusted the captain more than ever. They'd finally rejoined the war. They had no allies and no support, and every battle was more critical than the last, yet they had hope that they'd return to Septimus and find the Borwyn left behind. Borwyn who had survived in conditions that might have been even harsher than those the crew of *Chrysalis* had survived.

"Captain." Crip motioned for Jaq to join him and pointed at his screen. The final oldster had been found in her rack. She'd died somewhere in the past day. "The trials of high-gee maneuvers on her aging body."

"Full honors when we get underway. A short high-speed run directly at Armanor, and we'll launch her toward the star. It'll take her a year to become stardust, but her life force will be returned to the universe."

"I'll take care of it." Crip stared at the screen.

The end of a generation. They'd thought they were ready for it, but the actual moment in time when the baton passed wasn't something they could insulate themselves against.

"Mark this moment as a time for remembrance. May Septiman carry her soul for them both to watch over us and protect us." Jaq let go of the rail and drifted. Weightlessness allowed a person to free themselves from the pull of the universe. Although they were used to operating in zero-gee, it remained a source of freedom and the inner connection for a contemplative and meditative state.

No external stimulation until the air handler kicked in and droned on. After it finished, Jaq opened her eyes. The command crew was engaged with their individual tasks, diligently working on getting the ship ready for the next deployment.

With an acrobatic somersault and precise kick-off, Jaq returned to her second's station. "It's nice having you back," she told Crip. He was the person she most liked to bounce ideas off. "You saw the sensor screen. Is it that bad?"

CHAPTER 27

May Septiman's star guide you to paradise.

Crip leaned back to let the gel in his chair nearly consume him as he thought about shaping the conversation to best deliver the information the captain needed.

"I can't tell you which ones were idle and which had full crews. What we saw with the Malibors' *Hornet* was that the crew wasn't up to speed. Sure, they guessed our maneuver around the moon, but probably because they saw us, but they didn't capitalize on it. They were young, like Deena, from what I saw of the bodies.

"I'm not sure the Malibor were serious about the war continuing. They have a military, but they aren't top-notch. They have a lot of ships, but they might be in poor repair or in cold storage, like the one we took out in orbit over Farslor.

"Look at the missiles we've recovered. We can't even use them since they're not good. Maybe that's why the Malibor didn't fire them at us. I'm just thinking out loud."

"That's what I need." Jaq nodded her approval. "When is their command deck going to be online?"

"Did the power source make it back? I have to say that bringing it to *Chrysalis* was a huge pain in my backside. Disconnecting it prematurely resulted in extra work and duplicated effort. I hope Bec learns from this."

The captain snorted but kept her reply soft. "What do you think he's going to learn?"

"That we're stupid and shouldn't tell him what to do?" Crip guessed.

"Not that harsh, but that we should know what we want before we give the orders."

"You're probably right, but I don't think I'm wrong. When Bec gets it reinstalled, hopefully we'll see what we need to see and get the data behind it. I'd like to know what their operational fleet consists of and where are they. What are they going to bring against us? Until we know, planning will be nothing more than a guessing game."

Jaq faced the screen. Twenty members of her crew were on board *Butterfly*, working diligently. That led to another problem. "If we put fifteen on that ship to turn it into a resupply station, that leaves us with five suits."

"We can repair the Malibor suits, or a few of them. A couple suffered catastrophic damage, like the one that was blown in half. I'll bring them aboard. That will give us another three or four operational suits."

"We'll need every one we can get." Jaq pushed off and drifted to the next rail. She held onto it while she studied the main screen. The view hadn't changed for two days. She maneuvered across the command deck and hovered over Dolly Norton's position.

The young sensor operator looked up and smiled.

"Anything?" Jaq asked.

"I've refined the parameters of the passive search to better pick up the engines of a Malibor gunship."

Jaq was pleasantly surprised. "I look forward to seeing them sooner and better. With a well-planned series of E-mag barrages, we can forestall much of the maneuvering and posturing. This would give us an edge."

The sensor operator beamed. "That's my job."

"Tell her about the ghost," Chief Ping suggested.

"I've been watching a ghost. I'm not sure if it's debris or something else, like a powered-down weapons platform."

"If it's a platform, we want to recover it. Could it be a ship? Another gunship on ice?"

"Unknown. To learn that, we'll need to radiate the active systems. Do you want me to do that?"

Jaq leaned over Dolly's shoulder to see her screen. "Has it moved?"

"Hard to tell. Possibly a bit. Could be from a stellar wind or gravitational pull." Dolly stared at the image on the screen, which refused to answer her questions.

"Crip, what do you think?"

"Accessing the feed," he replied from his position. After a few seconds, he made his recommendation. "We have to take a closer look. Let's secure the ship for movement and send the crew to battle stations."

Jaq moved to her second's side. "What are you seeing that I'm not?"

"Call it a hunch. I got the impression that *Hornet* wasn't alone, above and beyond the gunship we saw with it. What if it had another ship in tow or attached to it that it released before they ambushed us on the near side of the moon?"

"Then it would be right where it is, watching like a sensor buoy. As long as it stays there, it can't report back to Septimus."

The moon had passed between *Chrysalis* and the planet a couple times since they'd joined *Hornet* on its slow journey toward the far reaches of the system. It wouldn't be long before they were out of the planet's shadow, but the sensor ghost would remain within Farslor's gravity well. The ghost would stay in the shadow indefinitely with its current positioning.

"Isn't that an unnatural orbit?" Crip pressed. "That was the first thing that struck me. It's there but shouldn't be. It should either be orbiting faster in a lower orbit or geostationary. In either case, it would have circled the planet, and more times or fewer times is immaterial. I think we need to send a clear message that we're not to be spied upon."

Jaq turned to the sensor team. "Good job, you guys." She returned to her seat. "Tell our crew on *Butterfly* to hunker down. We'll be back as soon as we address this anomaly. Sound general quarters."

The alarm klaxon rang throughout the ship before they could warn the crew on *Hornet*.

The captain drew a line across her throat. "Secure the alarm, please." Silence returned to *Chrysalis*. "Comm, give me a channel with our people."

The communications officer signaled when the channel was open.

"We've discovered an anomaly that might be an enemy ship, and we need to check it out. You're doing critical work on *Hornet*, so stay the course. Bec will reestablish an environmentally controlled area within the ship, including heat, that you can recover to and recharge your suits or decompress. Maybe he will get the toilets operational as well. In any case, help each other until we get back." The captain twirled her finger above her head. "Maintain general quarters."

The command deck crew scrambled to get into their seats and prepare their systems. Thrust Control brought the engines online. Nav charted a course. Sensors used low-power mode to scan the immediate vicinity for debris that might interfere with the ship's route away from the wreckage.

"Clear on vector one-eight-zero," Slade reported.

Mary tapped in the course and waited for Ferd to add power.

The captain eased into her seat, watching the status lights turn green for each department. Engineering was the first to change. She accessed her direct line to the engine room. "Well done, people. You were first to green."

"It's not a source of pride, Captain. We only have four people down here when we should have twelve, and they're all right here. Power is up, engines are idling and will respond to Helm. The battle is joined."

"Victory will be ours," Jaq replied and closed the link. She adjusted the main screen's display to show the sensor ghost. It was nothing more than a tiny blip, even magnified.

When the ship's status showed green across the board, the captain gave the order. "Get us underway, please. All ahead slow."

Attitude thrusters adjusted the heading while the main engines powered up to drive them at half a gee of acceleration. Compressing into the seats was uncomfortable for the first few seconds after two days of zero-gee.

The ship nosed away from the wreckage and accelerated toward the distant blip.

"Vector one-eight-one, star angle zero, please," the captain ordered. "Slade, when the planet fully blocks our signal, activate sensors. Light that blip up."

The sensor chief tapped, stopped, mumbled to himself, and tapped some more. "Time to sensor sweep, forty-seven seconds. Nav, please verify."

Mary checked her numbers. "Time to optimal scan location, one minute three seconds."

"Son of a meteor!" Slade scowled and hammered his screen

with greater vigor. "Now fifty-two seconds. Concur." He tried to relax as the ship powered ahead.

The captain had to throw a wrench into the gears. "Accelerate to one gee."

The engines delivered the requested power, and the ship responded smoothly.

A glance at the power reserve showed ninety-eight percent.

Slow is smooth, and smooth is fast, the captain told herself.

"Offensive Weapons, prepare for a precision attack. If this is a living ship, take out her engines. Crip, if this ship is dead, prepare to tether it and tow it back to our resupply station."

Crip grunted in discontent. "Not sure how successful we'll be since we have no operational spacesuits on board. Maybe we can attempt a connection to the ship's airlock."

"We'll work it out, depending on status. I think that ship's filled with a living crew, and it's watching us. They're going to run when we paint them with our active scans."

Slade counted down. "Three, two, one."

The sensor operators focused on their screens without blinking. The systems energized and started to radiate. Data would come in shortly.

"Offensive weapons active," the captain ordered, bypassing Tram as the battle commander. She considered it a learning moment for him.

"Bringing the systems online," Taurus confirmed.

"On screen," Slade reported.

The consolidated radar images built a three-dimensional representation of what they saw.

It was similar to a Malibor gunship but different. Sleeker. Smaller.

"Bracket that ship with projectiles but do not hit it." The captain tried to lean forward, but *Chrysalis* continued its one-gee acceleration. "All ahead slow."

The gee force eased when the engines throttled back. *Slow is smooth.*

"Firing," Tram confirmed after Taurus recommended the firing angles for the forward E-mag batteries.

The screen showed the actual course and projected course for the obdurium projectiles. The double-barreled batteries were not yet operational, which limited the ship to ten projectiles per E-mag per second. Four cannons fired, followed by four more, forming a barrier in front of the ship but leaving an escape route that would bring it closer to *Chrysalis*.

"Give me an open channel." The captain was finally able to lean forward so she could see her crew.

The communications officer confirmed the command, and the channel opened.

"Unidentified vessel. Stand to and prepare to be boarded by order of Captain Jaq Hunter of the Borwyn cruiser *Chrysalis*."

"What if they don't have an airlock?" Crip whispered.

"Then we'll jettison our weapons platform and bring them into the cargo bay."

Crip cleared his throat but didn't reply.

"I'd much rather have an intact ship than a pile of scrap," the captain explained.

The small ship didn't move.

"Are we sure it's alive?" Crip wondered.

The captain was beginning to have her doubts. "How long until we have to slow down?"

Mary replied, "Forty minutes to a full burn and forty-five minutes to intercept."

"We have that long to figure it out." The captain scratched her face and contemplated the geometry of the engagement. The three-dimensional model on the screen continued to refine itself and expand. "Overlay a Malibor weapons platform."

A minute later, Slade delivered on the request. The ship was smaller in all aspects.

"Are there any weapons on that ship?"

"None that I can see," Slade replied. "There is power, a low-energy output. That ship is not in cold storage. I say again, that ship has power."

"Get Deena up here," the captain ordered.

Crip activated his direct comm link to Sergeant Max Tremayne and delivered the news. "Max said to give him five minutes."

"What do you think of our Malibor *guest*?" The captain didn't take her eyes off the main screen. "You can remove the platform overlay."

The second image disappeared.

"I think she could be a wealth of information if we can convince her that the Borwyn are the good guys. But she was raised Malibor, and that will continue to pollute her thinking," Crip replied.

"We were raised to believe the Malibor were the enemy and had the single goal of eradicating the Borwyn from existence. It appears that we weren't wrong." Jaq crossed her arms and tried to relax.

"From the Malibors' perspective, they weren't wrong either. A Borwyn ship appears after fifty years and destroys every Malibor ship it runs across."

"It's a sticky situation. If we announce our return and try to play nice, they'll come after us with everything they have. We'll lose the element of surprise, which has been our most effective weapon so far."

"And our ion drives and our missiles. We've been preparing to fight this war our whole lives, but they have not. Their technology has not advanced. They're stagnant." Crip monitored the systems while Jaq contemplated the strategies of the war and the tactics of each engagement.

A red light flashed. The medical team.

"Vantraub, Commander Castle here. Report."

"The patient died. The acceleration was too much for her injury," the engineer-turned-medic explained in a tired voice. The medic had missed her last sleep cycle because of the surgery. She'd been up for too long.

Crip sighed. "You did everything you could. Secure Annabelle. She'll get the same treatment as Crewman Ellis, the last of the previous generation."

"I hadn't heard. That news is unsettling. We've always had someone of the last generation on board."

"It's up to us to carry on. Return to Engineering. They could use your hands. Let the shepherd tend to the broken flock."

The captain turned to look at the empty seat at the rear of the command deck where the shepherd should have been. She should have sent him to Medical a long time ago, but the previous generation's faith had carried them when nothing else could. They credited Septiman with their survival when Jaq chalked it up to good engineers working with a well-built ship.

The crew settled into waiting while the target ship taunted them through its inaction.

Deena appeared with her arm draped over Max's shoulder as he helped her walk.

The captain climbed out of her seat. "You were raised on Septimus and should be better under gee forces."

"It's been a while," Deena replied. She blinked and rubbed at her eyes. "I'm sorry. I'm tired beyond being tired."

"That's an aftereffect of hypothermia, added to the strain of the last couple days. Maybe you can help us out. Do you recognize that ship on the screen?"

"Harmless," she replied after a glance. "Can I go back to my quarters now?"

"In a moment. What do you mean 'harmless?' Isn't that a Malibor ship?"

"No. We don't know what it is. It appears on occasion and disappears as quickly as it arrives. We have taken to paying it no mind."

The captain and Crip studied the young woman's features. Neither saw subterfuge. She believed what she had said.

"Max, take her back to her quarters. Let her get some rest. Thank you, Deena. We won't bother you again. Well, not for a while, anyway." The captain tried to deliver a matronly smile.

Deena tipped her chin in response, and with Max's help, they departed.

When they were gone, the captain asked, "Are you thinking what I'm thinking?"

Crip shook his head. "I don't know what to think, but that sounds like a scout vessel. Small, quick, and unthreatening. If the Malibor have grown accustomed to seeing it and it's a scout, what's it doing with the information it gathers?"

"There are holes in my theory, but that's what I'm thinking too," the captain replied. "This is a Borwyn ship. A survivor. Where is *their* base?"

"We look just like *Hornet*, their enemy, and we're bearing down on them." Crip gave the captain the view she needed without it being advice.

"Invert and slow the ship. Maintain all ahead slow." They would fly forward, aft end first. The captain jumped back into her seat before they performed the maneuver and held on while attitude thrusters rotated the ship and the engines fired to slow their forward momentum. "Open the old Borwyn command channel."

"Stand by," the communications officer requested. She

failed to hide her frantic search for the right frequency. After a few frenzied moments, she found it and brought it up. She proudly reported, "Channel is open."

"Borwyn scout ship, this is *Chrysalis*. Please respond."

The comm crackled, but they received no other response.

"Borwyn scout ship, this is *Chrysalis*. May Septiman's star guide you to paradise." The old code required a saying from the book of Septiman as a challenge and response. The captain wasn't sure what the response was supposed to be. She was happy she'd remembered the challenge.

The comm crackled once more, then the static cleared. "May paradise bring us peace. *Chrysalis*, we have waited a long time to hear your voice."

CHAPTER 28

In the void, there is vacuum, and sometimes, there's life.

"Airlock linkup is confirmed," Crip stated.

Jaq, Crip, and Max waited for the airlock to cycle. Crip and Max carried their pulse rifles and wore body armor in case of duplicity.

Jaq stood behind them. "Pressure has equalized."

The outer hatch opened, then the inner hatch with access to *Chrysalis*. A tall and much older man stood inside. He wore an old-style jumpsuit. Behind him, two younger men watched.

"I'm Captain Brad Yelchin of the Scout Vessel *Starstrider*. You are young." He looked from face to face.

"We're second-generation Borwyn. Born and raised on this ship," Jaq explained. "I'm Captain Jaq Hunter. Please, join us. I doubt there's room on your ship for us to join you."

"That's the truth." Yelchin's easy smile was surrounded by a neatly trimmed grizzled beard. The other two were clean-shaven. "We're a long-range scout ship on patrol between Septimus and Farslor. We noted *Hornet* hurrying to Farslor and followed to see what it was up to. Then it was destroyed. Its twin appears and hunts down the gunship, which also gets itself killed. This was of great interest to us, but as we've seen before, it could simply have been yet another Malibor civil war."

Jaq closed her eyes to think about what she'd just heard. "I expect that's why they haven't advanced militarily. However, we're one ship, and they have many. With your information, I think we'll be able to develop a strategy to defeat them."

The captain clicked his tongue and cocked his head. "I'm not sure we want to stir them up or give them a focus, so they bring all their forces to bear on a single target. As long as we're not fighting them, they fight among themselves. I'd encourage you not to restart the war. Do you have any of the previous generation on board? Maybe I can talk with them."

The captain raised one eyebrow. "The last passed away. It's just us. Our mission, as given to us by our forebears, was to return to Septimus and free our people from the Malibor."

"Even though their ships are not as advanced as this one, they have too many, and you'll die in the attempt. You'll not serve the Borwyn by doing that. You'll be defying Septiman."

"We'll not be defying Septiman by freeing our people on his planet. Why are you like this?"

Yelchin was taken aback. "Because we've been here for the past fifty years while you've been gallivanting around the galaxy. We've kept the faith."

Jaq looked away, but her magnetic boots kept her attached to the deck. Her movements would have sent her spinning like her head. Here were Borwyn, but she was starting to doubt if they were allies after only two minutes.

"Let's talk in our mess hall. We can show you how we survived all these years. *Survive*. That's the word we use, not 'gallivant.' Don't be so hasty to judge us, Captain, or we'll put you back on your scout ship. I would like to think we have a great deal of common ground to explore."

The captain took in the two men who glared at him. "You can call off your attack dogs."

"I am remiss," Jaq replied smoothly. "My deputy Commander Crip Castle and our combat team leader Sergeant Max Tremayne."

They both nodded at their names and rotated their pulse rifles to the slung position.

"I like the Malibor more than him," the sergeant blurted.

"That's enough, Max. Tend to your duties. We'll take it from here."

Max backed away a few steps, then released his boots and launched down the corridor.

"What's your date of rank, Captain?" Yelchin asked.

Jaq held up her hand. "We're not playing that game, Brad. Call me Jaq. Call him Crip. Max is Max. We're a family and friends here who believe Septimus is our home and we're returning to it, but we're going to be smart about it.

"We don't need to win the battle but lose the war if no one is able to set foot on the planet, even if we have to pass the responsibility to the next generation. Understand that I don't care if you're from the previous generation. You have no authority on this ship except what I give you. Are we clear?"

The captain rarely had to show her edge and never had to pull rank. She was the captain. She looked out for the crew, and they respected her for it. She gave them guidance.

Crip smiled with newfound respect. He didn't like the scout ship's captain either.

Brad realized the fragility of his position and held his hands up in surrender. "Crystal-clear, Jaq. We've been doing things one way all this time while you've been doing them another. Please forgive my foibles. Of course we want to return to

Septimus after defeating the Malibor. We also don't want to die in the attempt. On this, we are in full agreement."

"Wait until you see what we have to offer before you judge. With our ion drive, we are faster and more maneuverable than anything the Malibor have."

"Ion drive. I look forward to learning more." He gestured behind him. "These are my boys, Hammer and Anvil."

Crip clenched his teeth to keep from laughing, although he didn't understand why he found the square-jawed young men's names so amusing. "How are you doing?"

Hammer and Anvil nodded, close-lipped. Hammer raised his hand as if to ask for permission to speak.

Crip tipped his chin.

"What does your combat team do?"

"In the last week, we went to the planet and engaged the Malibor who still live there. We also boarded the wreck of the *Hornet* and cleared the spaces of the Malibor who had managed to survive the battle. We were only able to secure one prisoner since the others seemed more than willing to die for their cause."

"You engaged the Malibor?" Hammer glanced at his brother as the group clumped down the corridor.

"Those on the planet's surface have degenerated to using bows and arrows. They seem to have been abandoned. Those remaining on *Hornet* had one laser pistol, which was no match for our pulse rifles. One also blew herself up rather than get captured. That was a bit disconcerting."

The trio stopped. Jaq and Crip kept going for two more steps before they realized the others weren't with them.

"Brad?" Jaq smiled pleasantly.

Her patience was wearing thin, but she wanted the information they had rather than trying to get it from Deena. The prisoner was loyal to the Malibor, although the captain didn't consider her a direct threat. She doubted the young woman would sabotage the ship, thereby killing herself along with everyone else. Jaq didn't think Deena had the required knowledge to create a catastrophic explosion aboard *Chrysalis*.

"You've engaged the Malibor twice in person?" Captain Yelchin sounded skeptical.

"And three times ship to ship," Jaq clarified.

"We've never survived an in-person engagement. That's why we have avoided them for decades. And ship to ship combat? That is beyond our capability. You've already surmised that our scout ship is unarmed. Stealth and speed are our secrets to surviving."

"With your ability to see what we cannot, I think we could deliver a potent punch, but only if we can separate the Malibor ships. We don't want to fight more than two or three at a time."

"I can't envision what that looks like. We had to abandon our desire to build warships because we simply did not have the ability."

"Where is your base?"

The captain was hesitant to answer her question.

"Still don't believe we're Borwyn?" Crip asked.

"It's hard to trust someone I don't personally know. There aren't very many of us."

"Now you know how we feel. The good news is that there are Borwyn survivors on Septimus. Turns out, our Malibor prisoner is half-Borwyn."

Brad snarled, "Collaborators! May Septiman curse their souls."

"I'm not sure they were willing collaborators, if you get my drift. Our prisoner says her Borwyn mother was killed shortly after Deena was born. I'm sure the situation on Septimus is complex.

"The Malibor fear for their safety outside the cities, which tells me that our people are fighting the good fight, even if they're doing it with bows and arrows like the Malibor on Farslor. Where is your base, and can it handle a ship like *Chrysalis*?"

He hesitated but quickly capitulated. "We're on Rondovan, Sairvor's moon. There is a narrow passage to an interior base. We've been expanding it since the war, but it's way too small for this big beast, and with the cruiser in orbit, the Malibor would spot us. You can go nowhere near Rondovan."

"It's good enough for us to know that Borwyn are there, especially those who survived the war. What kind of Malibor presence is there around Sairvor?"

"A cruiser and two gunships. They have a small mining facility on the planet's surface, but they've mostly abandoned the planet and moved to Septimus."

The next step in her strategic plan came to mind. "What if we cleared those ships out and freed Sairvor? That could become our new base of operations. The Malibor will come, but they won't know about the moon base.

"If they bring a sizeable force, we can run past them and hit their station orbiting Malpace. We'll have them jumping back and forth. Isolate and destroy. We will kill all their ships, then liberate our people."

Brad Yelchin smiled. "I like that your energy and your enthusiasm are tempered by reality. Maybe there *is* hope for the Borwyn besides waiting for the Malibor to kill each other in one of their short civil wars."

Jaq pointed in a direction that made no sense for the conversation or where they were headed. "So much opportunity. We need to get back to *Butterfly* and download everything Malibor-related. Maybe we can play them off against each other. Then there will be that many fewer we'll have to kill. When we first got here, what did I say? We need the intel!"

"Looks like we have as much as we can use." Crip punched Jaq's shoulder. She swayed from the soft blow.

Jaq led the group to the mess deck. They had to squeeze in between the crew, who gave up space to the captain, her deputy, and the newcomers. They watched suspiciously until the captain decided she needed to end all rumors. She moved to the comm on the bulkhead and dialed the ship-wide intercom.

"Attention all hands. This is the captain. We have multiple guests on board *Chrysalis*. First is Deena Vanderpohl, formerly of the Malibor fleet. She does not have freedom of movement throughout the ship, but I ask that you extend her all courtesies. She is as much a victim of circumstances as we all are. She's also half-Borwyn, which begs a great number of questions. Those will get answered in due time.

"Also, we have three Borwyn on board, Captain Brad Yelchin and his two sons, Hammer and Anvil. They fly a scout ship watching over the Malibor fleet. They are operating out of a secret base, but we won't share its location.

"We shall be returning to our people who are currently stripping *Butterfly* for the parts we need. At that time, we'll decide our next steps, but I have an idea that will get us closer to a free Septimus and the liberation of the Borwyn who remain alive on the planet's surface.

"We have received a great deal of positive news since we arrived, and I think we deserve to celebrate. Soon, good people of *Chrysalis*. Jaq Hunter out."

The captain trudged between the tables rather than risk upsetting anyone's lunch by pulling herself over their heads.

"Do you tell your crew everything?" Brad wondered.

"Everything that matters, yes. In an information void, people fill it with the worst thing they can imagine. I'd rather not let them devolve into quivering masses of negative energy."

Brad guffawed with the greatest of gusto, drawing looks

from every person who was getting something to eat. His boys chuckled at their father's laughter.

"I'll grab something for us to eat and drink." Crip unbelted from the seat and headed for the galley. Chef was filling the zero-gee food containers with vegetables, proteins, fruits, and drinks.

"I need meals for five. Better make it seven since those are some big boys. Obviously, they're feeding them differently than what we have."

Chef bundled the containers with a single strap Crip could carry one-handed. He flew through the room, staying close to the deck until he reached the group. He distributed the food by touching each serving to the table in front of the recipient. Small magnets grabbed the metal strips in the bags.

Crip described the food and how it was grown. After a few tastes, the three Borwyn guests inhaled the bags and briefly argued over the extras, then split them.

Brad Yelchin didn't pull any punches. "Ours tastes like it came right out of my ass and onto my plate. Yours tastes like real food. Is there any way we could get a little extra to take with us when we go?"

"We'll see if we have any extra supplies. Our hydroponics bays support our needs, but unfortunately, they're not big enough for extras. We have recently lost four people, which will reduce our consumption rate accordingly." The captain dipped her head and glowered at the table. "I hate that I think about things that way."

"It's the captain's trial. You have to so others don't. I get you, Jaq, and what you're going through. I got to bring my boys on the scout ship, but that's because my wife died from a lethal dose of radiation when she was repairing an external exhaust nozzle.

"She knew she was getting fried, but she stayed out there. I had these two inside with me. Three of us made it back." He stared at the wall while his eyes glistened, then blinked the tears away.

"Where were we? How to defeat the Malibor by attacking them at Sairvor."

CHAPTER 29

It's not confidence that matters but the appearance of confidence.

"That's what I'm thinking. If we can get your sensor logs and orders of battle for the Malibor fleet transferred to our sensor team, they'll get it into our system so we can start tearing it apart. Strategize. I'm glad we ran across your ship. It's time for the Borwyn to reclaim what is ours."

Crip gathered the empty food packs and took them to the scullery. Jaq led the way out amidst cheers from those still eating.

Brad waved.

"The battle is joined, eh, Captain?" Jaq asked.

"I haven't heard that phrase in fifty years," Brad admitted. "It would have led to our demise. However, it's nice to add it back into our lexicon, as long as we can ensure that our ships and base are not compromised as part of the retaking of Sairvor."

"As the first step in the ultimate liberation of Septimus," Jaq clarified.

"Maybe the second or third step." Crip smiled. "We've already fired the first shots and reduced the number of ships in the Malibor fleet."

"And you've taken out their flagship. *Hornet* was the ultimate prize in their victory over us. They didn't even build it."

"They're telling their people they did. They think it's a Malibor design."

"Where did you hear that?" Yelchin had decades of information to rely on.

"From Deena, our prisoner-slash-guest. She was adamant that the ship was Malibor from start to finish."

"The Malibor propaganda machine." Brad hammered a fist into his hand. "You can't trust anything a Malibor says because most of the time, they don't know what the truth is."

The wheels turned in Jaq's mind as she moved from the mess deck to the command deck. She didn't know if her companions kept talking. She could only hear her own thoughts. So much information to process.

So little time.

"Crip, can we return to our people with the scout ship attached to the airlock?"

Crip shook his head. "No. The ship will be ripped off, even at minimal acceleration."

Jaq looked at Captain Yelchin, and he smiled. "You want us to return to our ship." It was a statement, not a question.

Jaq replied, "However many crew it takes to fly the ship. We'll reconnect at *Butterfly*, our temporary resupply station."

Captain Yelchin stopped and raised his hand to hold his boys up. "We'll follow you. If we can return to our ship, that would be best. Once there, we'll transfer the sensor data."

The captain nodded and gestured for Crip to escort them to *Starstrider*. She shook hands with Brad. "You look far too young to be one of the oldsters."

"We've found nutrition inside the moon that interrupts cellular decay. The only problem is that it tastes horrible. But given your return, I'm glad I'm here to see it. Until next time, Captain. I have to admit the pleasure was all mine." He rotated her hand to kiss the back of it.

Jaq stared at the wet lip prints he'd left behind. Brad, Hammer, and Anvil stepped away. Crip had released his boots and was pulling himself down the corridor using the rail. He waited for the other Borwyn to catch up, then they disappeared into the central shaft on their way to the airlock.

"What the sulfur sweat was that?" Jaq mumbled, continuing to stare at her hand. She diverted to her quarters to take a shower. When she returned to the command deck, she'd bring the team together to brainstorm around the sensor data.

She also wanted to warm up the E-mags. If *Starstrider* tried to run for it, she'd blow it out of the sky. They knew too much about her ship and her people to let them disappear. That knowledge would be enough to sway the balance of the new war in the Malibor's favor.

Jaq didn't know why she didn't completely trust her fellow Borwyn, even though she was convinced that was what they were. She wasn't convinced that they were on her side and would follow her lead. Should they attempt subterfuge, it would be to their detriment.

Being ready for betrayal wasn't the same as expecting it, however. She had to protect *Chrysalis* and its crew at all costs. She had to think terrible things that they did not. She had to deal with the loss of crew members and still keep the ship operating.

The captaincy was something very few people could handle. From a firm hand to empathy, she had to be all things to all people. The greatest friend or the worst enemy. Captain

Brad Yelchin didn't want to find out the hard way what she was willing to do.

After cleaning up, she used the free flight of zero-gee to get to the bridge in mere seconds and eased inside to a buzz of activity. On the main screen, a great deal of data was displayed: weapons platforms, gunships in cold storage, and the active Malibor fleet.

"This stuff is incredible!" Chief Ping exclaimed. "If we had flown around the system radiating at max power, I'm not sure we would have gotten all this. It's years' worth of information."

"Looks like our fellow Borwyn came through. Tram, dig in and find their weaknesses." The captain hooked an arm around the rail above her seat to angle herself in. She settled into the gel and informed the ship that they were getting underway. "Taurus. Warm up the E-mags."

"Captain?" the offensive weapons officer wondered.

"In case we need to shoot something. There's a remote possibility." Jaq decided not to explain further. She let the team assume the crew from *Starstrider* had told her about a secret enemy.

Taurus responded by bringing the E-mag cannons online. It didn't take long for them to warm up.

Crip hadn't made it back yet, but the captain's system showed that the airlock was clear. "Slade, track that ship, please."

"On screen." The sensor chief shifted the external view to an inset on the main screen.

The scout ship rotated and sped clear. The captain leaned forward and watched intently. *Starstrider* slowed and came about after it was clear of *Chrysalis's* maneuvering envelope.

"Take us to *Butterfly*, please, and our people we left behind."

Nav tapped in the course while Thruster Control changed

the attitude of the ship. The main engines engaged, and the ship accelerated.

Energy storage had climbed to one hundred percent during the conversation with Captain Yelchin. It almost immediately fell to ninety-nine percent, with the main engines propelling the ship forward.

"One gee, please," the captain requested.

Thrust Control increased the ion drives' output.

"Fifty minutes at one gee before beginning our slow-down process."

The captain released the belt and climbed out of her seat. She moved around the bridge without the aid of her magnetic boots. "Get some exercise, people. You heard the pilots. We have fifty minutes to strengthen those muscles."

Jaq checked the board. The scout ship was mirroring their movements. "Taurus, maintain the E-mags in an active status for another fifteen minutes, then power them down."

Crip strolled through the hatch onto the bridge. "I prefer one gee," he remarked casually. "It feels natural."

Taurus threw a wadded-up towel at him, but it fell short.

He scooped it off the deck and brought it back to her, handing it across her workstation. "Why are the weapons powered up?"

"Captain's orders."

Crip nodded and walked across the command deck. He raised his eyebrow when he reached the captain, but she didn't share her reasoning.

"Captain?" he pressed.

She put her finger to her lips and continued watching the main screen. The inset of the scout ship showed it traveling behind and to one side of the cruiser, matching course and speed.

"Concur," Crip stated softly.

"We have the sensor data. Go through it with Tram. Get Alby's input too, if you can get a few minutes of his time. Find the weaknesses and develop a plan of attack. Minimize our risk while maximizing damage to the Malibor fleet."

Crip crossed his arms and stood with his legs braced as if he were riding a sailing ship on a raging sea. "As soon as they realize we've come to make war on them, they'll begin professionalizing and modernizing their fleet."

"That's why we need to formulate a plan that pits the Malibor against themselves. If they fight each other, that saves us a lot of energy and weapons. We can keep those missiles for real emergencies."

"We can build more missiles. We have the plans, and the Borwyn on Rondovan have the ability to build scout ships. They can make missiles for us."

Crip and the captain stood side by side, watching the main screen. There was no blip in the distance showing where the remains of the *Butterfly* floated on a ballistic trajectory heading away from Farslor. An icon showed its location directly ahead.

"If we can get our new Borwyn allies raw materials from recovered scrap like weapons platforms and heavily damaged former-Borwyn cruisers..." Crip completed her thought but left the final words dangling.

The captain glanced at Crip but didn't continue the conversation. It was all speculation until they had a solid plan.

"I'll be in my quarters," she said. Jaq needed private time to evaluate Yelchin's information. Her shower didn't clear her mind of his departure. She didn't have a role for them, although there had to be something they could bring to the battle. Maybe delivery of a weapon.

She was missing something.

Jaq hoped time alone would bring light into the darkness that was preventing her from seeing the strategic picture. It wasn't overwhelming. She had been looking for all there was to see when it came to the Malibor fleet. Now that she had the information, it wasn't an extreme departure from what she'd considered her worst-case scenario.

It wasn't bad. Maybe those were the prickles in the back of her mind—disbelief that *Chrysalis* and her crew would be able to accomplish what they'd set out to do. At one point it had been an ideal, but now, after multiple battles, it was a reality. They were fighting the Malibor and winning.

She had never shared her doubts with anyone, not even Crip. She still wouldn't. Not until after it was all over, and then it wouldn't matter. Jaq needed to remain the bulwark of confidence.

She jogged along the corridor, passing crew doing the same thing as they hurried from one space to another, exercising their muscles along the way. After ten precious minutes, the captain returned to her quarters and sat, slightly winded.

Getting old, she thought, though she knew that wasn't the case. Especially if Captain Yelchin, who was easily seventy years old, could look the same age as she was—barely forty. *But it tastes like garbage.*

She chuckled. What was a long life worth?

A lot, if you lived long enough to see your people return home. That was worth the sacrifice. Jaq had never asked if Brad had set foot on Septimus. With the last of the oldsters having passed on, Deena, their new addition, was the only person on board *Chrysalis* who had been to Septimus. She'd lived on the planet nearly her whole life.

Jaq wanted to know more. She wanted to taste the air and feel the sunshine on her face through an atmosphere that turned cerulean blue under Armanor's light.

She duplicated the ship's main screen on the smaller screen at her desk. She had to magnify the sectors of space to get a fuller picture. She thought she saw the same ship in multiple locations since each carried a unique identifier.

That put her mind at ease. After the duplicates were removed, she could develop a correct order of battle, then attrit them one by one or two by two.

She smiled. Their future was bright indeed.

CHAPTER 30

To win a war, last one to commit their reserves wins.

The captain went from one station to the next, verifying that each crew member knew the first steps of the multi-phase plan. It was complex yet simple. The first step would be the hardest... until the second.

Alby Risor stood beside Brad Yelchin. *Starstrider's* captain towered over the new commander of the ERS, the expeditionary resupply station.

"The two missiles have been transferred. I can't guarantee they'll work how you want." Alby lifted his hands and shrugged as if that would relieve him of the responsibility for his role in a future battle that he would not be a part of. Not personally, but his role would show what was possible.

"They need to work. Keep tinkering with the programming if you need to. You can send us software patches, and we'll upload them before deployment. I have full confidence in you." Jaq gave him the thumbs-up.

He returned a weak smile. He still had six missiles on the remnants of the cruiser but no way to test them.

"I'll be on my way, then. I want to arrive at our base well before you if possible." Brad pulled himself toward the corridor and spoke over his shoulder. "I haven't seen what this ship is capable of, have I?"

"Not even a little bit," Jaq replied. "Get into position and rally your people. The Borwyn have come out of their cocoon and are ready to deliver a great deal of pain to the Malibor for what they did in the war and, more importantly, for what they're still doing.

"They're teaching their people to hate Borwyn just because we are Borwyn. It's genocidal. We could probably live on Septimus together, but no. The Malibor won't have that, not if our interactions with them so far are any indicator. So they force us to fight. That will be their downfall."

Brad Yelchin waved and headed off the bridge. His boys were waiting in the corridor, and as he flew past, they joined him.

"Transfer of foodstuffs and supplemental oxygen generator is complete," Crip reported. "Our supplies are less than fifty percent of normal. We need that restock from the Borwyn outpost."

"Better increase the supply of salt and peppercorns," Jaq warned. "Brad didn't paint a rosy picture about the taste, although the health effects can't be denied. I look forward to meeting more of our fellow survivors."

Jaq braced one leg on a rail and leaned against the captain's chair. The others remained in place using their magnetic boots.

Jaq gestured at Alby. "You better return to the ERS."

He blew out a long breath and turned away.

The austere conditions on board *Butterfly's* remains held little for them besides long hours of hard work in zero-gee with minimal heat. It would be cold and uncomfortable, and a demanding schedule faced the small team.

"Bec is on board *Chrysalis*," Crip told Jaq. "He wants to talk with you."

The captain closed her eyes and refrained from making a sharp reply. "I better go see him before we get underway. Crip, get the ship ready to fly."

The departments would gather their people to account for them. They would end up in their seats, safely ensconced in the gel packs.

The energy status was one hundred percent. Jaq loved seeing the green bar sporting triple digits.

She eased away from her chair and went across the command deck, down the corridor, and into the central shaft. She flew past other crew who were hurrying to their workstations. Jaq waved at them all. Everyone needed to be at his or her best until they set foot on Septimus. There wouldn't be a second chance.

Jaq didn't know why she had no trepidation about an impromptu meeting with her chief engineer. What was the worst thing he could say? She slowed, then kicked off the opposite wall to propel herself down the short corridor to the power plant area.

Bec was waiting for her.

"I quit!" he announced as loudly as he could.

That was the worst thing he could say.

"You don't have the luxury of quitting," she replied evenly. She had very little time to deal with his intransigence.

"I'm going to do nothing until you respect my decision to quit."

"*You*? Do *nothing*? That's not how you're wired. Talk to Captain Jaq. Where did this come from? Then let's work together to resolve your issue so you can get back to work with a clear mind. But first, thank you for keeping our power in the high nineties for the past two days. You are the engineer that all engineers aspire to be."

"Your platitudes won't work." He crossed his arms. His boots were clamped to the deck in the middle of the entry to Engineering. No one could get out. No one could get in.

"You're looking very fit and well," Jaq continued.

He covered his ears. "You can stop now. I'm not listening."

Jaq pointed at him and made a heart with her hands.

He kept one boot clamped to the deck and tapped the other at a high rate of speed. Jaq waited for him to make the next move. She would give him two minutes to make his point, or she'd return to the command deck.

"Don't you want to hear what the problem is?"

"Of course. What's the problem, Bec?"

"Plug in a power plant and turn on the heat. That shows you have no respect for my abilities. I was working on supplementary power for *Chrysalis*, yet another task you gave me without regard to my regular workload. What are you going to do about that?"

"It wasn't just 'plug it in and turn it on.' How many Malibor died because they couldn't get the heat on? I figured if all the Malibor on *Butterfly* couldn't do it, that left only one person from our side who could. Was my reasoning incorrect?"

"The Malibor were stupid." Bec's lips twitched, but he refused to smile.

"Them not seeing the genius of your solution doesn't mean they were stupid." Jaq gripped his arm. "It was the most complex problem plaguing us at the time. Why wouldn't I want the best person we have working on it? I'm not seeing the problem besides your ability to quickly resolve what a whole crew could not. That further solidifies your role as the go-to engineer. You are A-Number One."

"I don't feel like A-Number One. I feel like a single janitor tasked with cleaning the black water system with a hand brush."

"You shouldn't." That was the best she could do. She had no desire to delve into what would change his perceptions of being a janitor. "How is the energy generation problem progressing?"

"See?" He stabbed a finger so hard that he twisted sideways, his boot struggling to keep him rooted to the deck.

"I see." Jaq frowned. "Nothing. If that's all you have, I need to get back upstairs. We're going to move soon and make a high-speed run to Sairvor. I plan to run it up to seven gees for twenty minutes, then hold three gees for another hour. One gee for an hour, then ride the ballistic express until we need to slow down. That will take a few days, so we can recharge the banks."

"Is that all you want?" Bec scoffed and waved dismissively. "I will toss myself out an airlock if you give me sewage-scrubbing duty again."

"You won't because no one will appreciate your genius after you're gone. The only thing they'll remember is that you were a throbbing member and left systems no one could fix. If you know someone who can fix things as quickly as you, point them at me. I'll put them on it.

"Until then, train your replacement. I won't deal with threats. You are not suicidal. Your ego is too vast to off yourself, so don't. I won't ever have you scrub the black water system. Not when we have perfectly good mechanical pigs to send through the pipes."

"What happens when those break?" He jammed his fists into his hips and swelled to his full height.

"Then you'll deal with them. Until then, we're not going to worry about it. There's a lot of stuff on this ship that will break before our wastewater system. Don't forget where we're going. There's a cruiser and probably two gunships waiting for us. We have eight total missiles remaining. We have an additional four

E-mags slaved to two batteries, and that's it. We're hard-pressed, Bec. We need you. The ship needs you."

The chief engineer chewed the inside of his cheek as he contemplated his next move. "Next time, I really *will* quit."

"I have no doubt, Bec. Glad we had this talk. Systems are running five by five. Make sure your people keep them that way."

Jaq checked the corridor behind her, then pushed off the deck and backstroked toward the central shaft, waving as she went.

That wasn't so bad, she thought. Bec made a face and tried to storm away but lost his footing and floated into the air, arms and legs flailing to get traction.

The captain had to turn around to keep from laughing openly. Even geniuses had their limitations, although she was happy that his work stoppage had only lasted a couple minutes.

She headed up the shaft and down the corridor to the bridge.

The team was doing what they were supposed to, even though their ability to work was limited while *Chrysalis* was waiting to get underway. Crip was knee-deep in the details of their plan, but he was going through each individually at his position. Jaq felt compelled to interrupt him.

"What's your assessment of our chances?" She raised one eyebrow as if she were challenging him on his feedback.

He nodded without looking up. "One hundred percent."

"I don't know what that means." Jaq waited for clarification.

"Me neither. There are going to be a thousand actions and reactions. We want them to react more to us than we do to them," Crip explained. "Business as usual. We have the edge since we still have the element of surprise on our side, especially since we started near Septimus, but we're shooting all the way across the system to Sairvor. We'll split their forces. They need to chase us, but they'll never catch us."

Crip checked his screen, and Jaq peered over his shoulder.

"All departments are green. Cargo bay doors are closed. Comm, confirm that Commander Risor is on his way back to the ERS."

Jaq drifted across the command deck, taking her time while waiting for the confirmation.

"Commander Risor is clear."

Jaq slipped into her seat and settled into the gel. "Ferdinand, are you ready to take us out? Mary?"

"Nav is ready," Mary confirmed.

"Thrust Control at your command." Ferd waved his arm but kept his eyes on his screens.

"Course two-one-four, star angle zero. Accelerate to three gees and hold for ten minutes to confirm ship and crew stability, then accelerate to seven gees for twenty minutes before dropping back to three gees for the next hour. Evaluate ETA, and we'll adjust as needed."

"At that rate of acceleration, we will overtake *Starstrider* in twenty minutes," Thrust Control reported.

"They'll pass us after two and a half hours since they'll accelerate at three gees for the entire time and keep accelerating. We'll both be traveling at over a million kilometers per hour at that point. It'll make short work of the trip to Sairvor."

Every person on the command deck could do the math in their heads. That was critical for movement in space, coupled with energy management. Every action had a reaction. Every acceleration required deceleration.

"Sairvor awaits, and with it, a Malibor cruiser and two gunships."

CHAPTER 31

What cost war?

"Receiving advanced sensor feed from *Starstrider*," Chief Ping reported. He consolidated the input from multiple systems and timeframes and transferred a single image to the main screen.

"One cruiser, three gunships, and seven weapons platforms. One gunship is in cold storage, and the operational status of the weapons platforms is unknown," the captain read from the data.

"If the platforms are hot, that could lead to a real bad day," Crip suggested. "But if we take them out with long-range fire, we lose the element of surprise."

The captain was floating above her chair. "Query *Starstrider*. Which way are the weapons platforms oriented?"

They had not started the reverse thrust to slow the ship, so it was still traveling at well over a million kilometers an hour. They were going to maximize braking with a long-term seven-gee burn.

They'd recovered most of their energy reserves and were currently at ninety-seven percent. Thrust Control estimated twenty-five percent usage during the maneuver, dropping the ship into the low seventies.

In the captain's mind, evasive maneuvers and maximum weapons usage would burn another fifty percent. They'd be a drifting hulk for at least two hours after an extended engagement if they wanted to do anything besides run life support and repair systems.

Was that an acceptable trade-off? The captain wrestled with the problem. First and foremost, she had to survive the battle. Everything was secondary after that. Jaq planned for success and what to do after the battle to make sure the ship was ready for the next engagement while ensuring the crew was focused on the first fight.

It was more of what made Jaq Hunter the captain that she was. She didn't bother her crew with things that weren't important at the moment. When the time came when they mattered, she'd change their perspective.

Until then, they'd focus.

"*Starstrider* says they are facing away from the planet. They cannot confirm any power signatures."

"It looks to me like they have seven platforms when they should have a dozen or more. What about a polar approach, then dipping below their targeting systems? We can kill the ones in our way by shooting them from below."

Crip grabbed the rail next to the captain. "Nav, what kind of maneuver would we have to conduct to get below the platforms?"

"Woof!" Mary exclaimed and got to work.

Jaq and Crip made faces at each other, but they waited patiently for the answer.

"Slingshot around the moon?" Mary requested.

"No. We'll steer clear of the moon. It'll be a straight approach." At Captain Yelchin's request, Jaq had agreed to stay away from the moon and the secret Borwyn base. Plus, they didn't need the extra speed, even though they could use the cover a lunar approach provided. It would block the view of some of the sensor systems, but enough wouldn't be affected, so it wasn't worth the additional energy usage.

"Anywhere from six- to nineteen-percent drain. Depends on how much speed we've bled off and the angle of approach. The shallower the angle, the easier to maneuver away without increasing engine output. With too much speed, we'll blow past the platforms. If we haven't destroyed them at that point, we might have some issues. There are a lot of variables, Captain," Ferd explained.

Jaq checked three different courses, steep to shallow and high-speed to low-speed approaches.

"Can you hit two weapons platforms while coming up out of the upper atmosphere? There could be some turbulence," the captain asked the offensive weapons officer.

Taurus looked at Tram Stamper for the answer.

"We'll get them. You put us in between your two target platforms, and we will bring eight cannons to bear on each. We'll do them nasty." Taurus nodded to add emphasis.

"Is that good?" Jaq asked, unsure of his meaning.

"We'll destroy the targets, Captain," Tram confirmed.

Crip gave Taurus a thumbs-up.

The captain made her decision. "Nav, descent to the pole will be thirty degrees, a shallow dive. Use the atmosphere to slow to five thousand kilometers per hour for the upward leg. Bring us up between Platforms Four and Five as designated. Prepare for aggressive braking maneuver in three minutes."

Aggressive. "Seven gees for sixty-six minutes will slow us to twenty-five thousand kilometers per hour. Atmospheric braking will slow us to five thousand."

Jaq accessed the ship-wide intercom. "All hands. We're

going to begin an hour-long seven-gee braking maneuver. You'll be in your seats. Breathe and relax. When we come out of it, we'll hit the turbulence of Sairvor's upper atmosphere to further slow the ship.

"The instant we achieve our desired speed of five thousand kilometers per hour, we're going to light up the sky with a cyclic E-mag barrage to clear our maneuver area of two weapons platforms. After all that, the real fight will begin. We have one Malibor cruiser and either two or three Malibor gunships that require servicing.

"I won't go into how important it is for us to win this fight, but know that we're not in it alone. Not anymore. Borwyn with their own space fleet are with us. Borwyn also live on Septimus. Those people are counting on us, the flagship of the Borwyn fleet, to carry the day and bring victory.

"Now is the time of pain. Now is the time when we liberate any Borwyn on Sairvor as a critical step on our way to Septimus. All hands, prepare for high gees. The battle is joined."

"Victory is ours!" Crip shouted to lead the response.

"May Septiman guide the hands of His children in this holy quest," the shepherd droned from the rear of the command deck.

"Shouldn't you be in Medical, ready to receive anyone who gets injured?" Jaq wondered.

"Septiman shall see to our needs."

"Of course. And you will, too, from Medical. You have less than two minutes to get down there!" The captain gestured for him to go.

He grumbled more than any other crew member would get away with, but he made his way into the corridor and flew toward the central shaft.

"Thirty seconds," Thrust Control announced.

"Secure the hatches and airtight doors throughout the ship."

Crip handled that personally. With a few taps on his screen, he ensured that the bulkheads were sealed, a step they had not taken during the previous engagements. Part of their learning process was to improve with each effort. The automated systems would have taken over in case of catastrophic failure, but seconds were critical.

Focus. That was Jaq's beacon for the crew to follow.

"Inversion complete," Thrust Control announced.

They couldn't feel the subtleties of the maneuver since they were ensconced in their seats. Ferdinand counted down until the engines engaged. The effect was immediate and severe.

Their bodies were compressed incrementally from one through to seven gees, which they had felt before. Jaq gritted her teeth and grunted with the effort of tightening her muscles.

The first few minutes were easy, but as time dragged on, the constant compression took its toll. Their recent high-speed maneuvers had taken the surprise out of the effort but not the duration.

The air handler kicked on and off, drowning out the sound of the crew's labored breathing. Jaq was tiring. She had the self-discipline and drive to power through her fatigue and expected her crew to do the same. Adrenaline would start pumping more than it already was.

Jaq struggled to activate the comm, though she was using the eye control interface. She kept blinking against her eyes closing. The outer edges of her vision had darkened, and unconsciousness called to her. She tried to rock to get her body more engaged, but the gel held her tightly.

The intercom crackled to life. "All hands, this is the captain. We've made it through two-thirds of our maneuver. Only twenty minutes remain. I know it gets harder and harder but bear with us.

"When we hit Sairvor's atmosphere, the real work starts.

That's when we open the outer doors, align the cannons, match bearings, and shoot. We have plenty of targets, which works in our favor. No matter which way we fire, we'll hit something. Stay focused. Put the ordnance on target, then look for another target until there are no more. Twenty minutes until the work begins. Hunter out."

She had done her best not to grunt the words but speak them normally, although high gees and the human body had a strained relationship at the best of times. Next time, she'd record the message in the peace of zero-gee and play it to make sure the crew could hear her words, and, most importantly, understand her message.

Focus.

Keep the crew operating as efficiently as they had since they'd left their mooring site far beyond the asteroid belt after they'd determined the ship was ready because the ion drives had been tested and had proven sound.

The war. The Malibor were still fighting, but not like the Borwyn, who wasted no effort. Every engagement was to improve the odds of a strategic victory. Despite the pressure on Jaq's body, she had a moment of exceptional clarity.

They were on the right journey. Her doubts disappeared, and the spatial mechanics of the upcoming engagement criss-crossed her mind. Iterations of the battle played in her head, each subtly different from the one before it.

Passive scans showed little in the way of data, but the live feed from *Starstrider* kept the captain informed.

One gunship had fired its engines and was slowly moving to a higher orbit. The cruiser and second gunship were still static, although Jaq wasn't counting on them to remain that way. Their approach to the planet's northern pole wasn't giving the Malibor cause for alarm.

Maybe they thought *Chrysalis* was a meteor that would

crash harmlessly into the ice. Jaq didn't care what they thought, only that their reactions were muted.

"One minute to target velocity of twenty-five thousand kilometers per hour. Inverting after engine shutdown. Prepare for turbulence," Ferd announced.

The captain informed the crew. "All hands. Well done and well met for surviving the longest high-gee burn we've ever attempted. That ends momentarily, and then we'll skip across the upper atmosphere to come at the equatorial weapons platforms from below. That will give us clear space to engage the Malibor. Primary target is the cruiser. Stand by for turbulence. Be ready to do your jobs no matter what is happening around you. Borwyn! The battle is joined."

The engines cut out, and attitude thrusters spun the ship until the nose pointed at the planet.

"All ahead standard," Jaq ordered. They needed to arc into the upper atmosphere, not hit it dead-on. "Vector one-four-one, star angle minus thirty."

Mary adjusted the ship's heading. *Chrysalis's* engines re-engaged, but not at the previous torrid pace.

Energy reserve was seventy-four percent and dropping.

It would have to be enough.

The bucking started almost immediately. They'd come out of the seven-gee burn with no room to spare. The atmosphere was unforgiving, protecting the planet from intruders and harsh rays from Armanor as well as ships that flew among the stars. *Chrysalis* bounced into the upper atmosphere.

"Bring all weapons online." The captain spoke softly, but the battle commander heard her.

"Weapons are energizing," Tram reported. "Defensive weapons, check. Offensive weapons warming up. Twenty seconds." The time counted down. "Four missiles in the tubes and hot. Sixteen E-mags ready for targeting information. Cooling systems are at maximum."

The E-mags would heat up quickly, given the combination of atmospheric friction and the expected high rate of fire, even afterward when the ship flew into the icy darkness of space.

The ship bounced so hard that a crunch reverberated directly into the crew's skulls. They were weightless for a second before wedging back into their seats.

"Nearly out," Mary shouted.

"Prepare to fire." The captain gritted her teeth against the intensity of the turbulence.

Sensor systems updated the instant they cleared the atmospheric blackout.

Slade was the first to see it. "Contacts are on the move!"

CHAPTER 32

The stars will guide us as surely as they will lead us astray.

"Firing port and starboard batteries, max rate," Taurus called. "Bracketing."

The first rounds went wide, distorted by the Sairvor's gravity more than Tram and Taurus accounted for, but the new offensive weapons officer adjusted after only two seconds. The obdurium rounds arced high before angling slightly toward their targets.

"Vector zero-eight-seven, star angle plus forty-one." The captain studied her screen. She'd input the course. It gave her a better firing angle on an intercept course with the Malibor cruiser.

Chrysalis quickly rose away from the planet. The low orbits of the weapons platforms gave the accelerating ship little time.

In the void of space, the E-mags' cyclic fire vibrated softly throughout the ship.

"Doesn't sound right," the captain called to the battle commander.

"That's the Malibor guns," Tram explained. "Weapons are five by five."

"Well done integrating the extra E-mags, Tram," Jaq replied.

"Platform Four is destroyed," Taurus announced.

The green line showing the flow of E-mag rounds into Platform Five told the command crew it would soon follow. They passed beyond the orbits of the now-dead platforms.

"All systems active." The sensor section needed direct information. Relay from *Starstrider* was no longer sufficient. The element of surprise was behind them.

"Retargeting." Tram transferred the new projectiles' pathways onto the main screen.

The cruiser angled away from them, and one gunship headed toward them. Sensors picked up the stream of projectiles coming their way.

"Evasive!" Jaq stared at the screen as the ship jerked sideways and the attitude thrusters kicked it off-course. The main engines continued moving it forward. Main thrust was always applied from stern to bow, but the ship's direction was controlled more by momentum than the new energy trying to drive it in a different direction. *Chrysalis* had bled off twenty thousand kilometers per hour of speed. It now struggled to gain speed and direction.

They had to accelerate. "Increase to five gees."

The twist in space helped the ship avoid the first stream of projectiles, but the second came in a spiral, much like the Borwyn's targeting.

The sounds of metal shredding shook their souls, and the ship reverberated under the impacts.

"Damage?" Jaq looked at Crip for answers.

Everyone was doing what they needed to do for the health of the ship.

"Integrity failure at Frames One Seventy-four, One Seventy-six, and One Eighty. Emergency foam deployed, and damage contained. No injuries. Water system for Decks Three through Seven is out."

"Septiman smiles on us." The captain kept her voice even. "Put rounds on target."

"Dialing it in," Taurus replied.

Projectiles continued to stream out of *Chrysalis*.

"Missiles inbound," the defensive weapons officer, Gil Dizmar, reported as Slade identified the new tracks.

"Fire missiles two by two. Target fore and aft," Jaq directed. "Vector zero-eight-four, star angle plus twenty-seven. All ahead full, three gees."

"Programming now," Taurus replied, tapping furiously despite the gee forces pressing on her. She kept her elbows tight to her ribs, and her wrists did most of the work.

Nav adjusted the course, and Thrust Control put the ship on it. Forward acceleration slowed to three gees, still substantial but not a brutal assault on their bodies.

A green line on the main screen tracked the latest barrage of obdurium projectiles until the line intersected the first gunship. It briefly flashed yellow, then changed to red. No one had to announce the first casualty in the Battle for Sairvor. Other things demanded the crew's attention.

"Take those missiles out, please. Crip, what did we learn about the ones recovered from *Butterfly*? Any terminal approach adjustments we can use to get in front of them?"

"Their terminal is like ours. The missile burns the rest of its fuel to accelerate to a maximum speed at or near impact. Their flight profiles aren't as sophisticated, allowing for course changes of one per second but no more."

"You heard him, Gil. Kill those missiles." Jaq wanted to

roam the bridge so she could think, but that wasn't going to happen.

Her thoughts raced. The second gunship was nowhere to be seen. The cruiser was still running from them, which was a scenario she hadn't contemplated.

Chrysalis's E-Mag batteries could fire projectiles that were much faster than the cruiser.

"Flush the mags," the captain growled.

A strange *ka-thunk* sounded through the hull, silencing the command deck. The crew listened intently for the next indicator of a system failing. Cascade failures were too common and always bad.

"Two of the Malibor E-mags are down," Taurus reported evenly. That broke the tension. Extra cannons were a bonus while they lasted, but nothing they couldn't live without. "System is sluggish."

That was bad news. The extra cannons slaved to one targeting system had overworked it in some way. That meant they'd lost four barrels, not two.

"Keep firing," Jaq called. "Vector zero-eight-three, star angle plus twenty-six. Accelerate to seven gees for one minute."

"Kicking it in the butt!" Ferdinand shouted.

Energy read sixty-six percent. Jaq's lips twitched.

"Missiles are clear of the tubes. Designated One and Two, outbound." Taurus' voice rang over the other noise on the bridge.

The ship accelerated as the air handling system kicked in. Combined with the rapid increase in gee force, the fan's drone gave the impression that the engines were working doubly hard. The fan finally shut down, and the ship continued to drive its crew into their seats.

A minute later, the engines drew back.

"One gee steady on the bow," Jaq confirmed. "Slade, find me that other gunship."

Jaq's eyes darted around the screen to no avail. Inbound missiles. Inbound projectiles. Outbound streams and missiles. Defensive systems lighting up. The board was a visual cacophony memorializing the engagement. They'd study it later, but for now, it was just a kaleidoscope of colors.

Taurus continued her emotionless reporting of the offensive weapons systems. "Three and Four are outbound."

The captain appreciated that it helped set the mood.

"Crip, what's the status of our prisoner?" Jaq asked.

"What?" Crip was caught off-guard. "Max is with her, I think. I don't know. We're in the middle of something that's got my attention. My apologies for my shortcomings." He didn't sound apologetic as he returned to monitoring the ship's status. Except for the three impacts from the gunship's E-mag, *Chrysalis* had sustained no damage.

"E-mag hits confirmed on the aft section of the enemy cruiser," Slade reported. "Damage unknown."

"Second gunship is coming around the planet at fifty thousand KPH," Dolly stated.

A new icon appeared on the screen, flashing to draw their attention.

"Maintain course and acceleration."

The *Chrysalis* had just passed forty thousand kilometers per hour. At one gee of acceleration, they'd pick up two thousand KPH every minute.

The math was clear. It would take too long before they could outrun the second gunship.

The first two Malibor missiles had evaded the Borwyn cruiser's limited long-range defenses, but as they approached knife-fighting range, the ship's short-range defensive systems lit up, sending waves of missile-penetrating projectiles into the void.

Like a cloud of death, it shielded the ship from the inbound missiles that were closing together.

Gil tapped his screen like a madman or maybe a virtuoso. The systems cycled back and forth to create an impenetrable shield through which the missile would fly and be shredded, its heart ripped out before it could land its deadly payload.

A bright flash filled the screen. Jaq suspected it was the destruction of a missile. An instant later, it sounded like their ship had been hit by a million projectiles in unison as if it had flown through a micro-asteroid field.

"Both missiles are destroyed. Damage assessment is ongoing."

"Passive Arrays Fourteen and Fifteen are down," Dolly announced in a small voice.

"Chain Gun Bank One is down," Gil added. "Bank Two is up but fixed on the swivel. It's not moving."

"We better hope the next missile comes down the same approach vector." Tram didn't have a better answer.

"What would it take to fix it?" Jaq asked.

"Engineers and maintenance people outside in space suits," Tram replied.

Crip added, "We currently have two cobbled-together Malibor suits we could use in a pinch, but I would prefer not to."

"Then we better use our attitude thrusters to help us target incoming."

The main screen showed two more missiles inbound, along with the four outbound missiles.

Taurus fired a full broadside across a wide front to bracket the inbound gunship before redirecting the operational E-mags to fire at the cruiser. Jaq watched the timing carefully to make sure the Borwyn missiles wouldn't have to fly through friendly projectiles to get to the Malibor cruiser.

"Tram, we need better firing solutions." The captain growled because the engagement was stretching out, which gave the advantage to the Malibor. *Chrysalis* had been hit once. They didn't need more damage to repair.

Maybe it was time to disengage. Take out the gunship and let the cruiser run.

"Seven-gee runs of thirty seconds each. Bump our speed to three-quarters of a million per hour. Offset angles of three to five degrees to stymy their railgun targeting while getting us closer. We have the advantage in firepower."

"That we do. Nav, vector zero-eight-two, star angle plus twenty-four, seven gees for one minute." Jaq activated the ship-wide comm. "High-gee maneuvers coming. Remain in your seats."

Max had been caught outside Chef's quarters when the first maneuvers began. He had to hurry inside and climb into Chef's sleeping cube below the one in which Deena was trying to recover.

After the long burn, followed by the rough ride through the atmosphere, he'd thought there was a respite and had made to leave.

The captain's announcement told him he needed to stay put.

"Don't you have a job you need to do?" Deena asked. Bloodshot eyes and crow's feet suggested she was nowhere near recovered from the hypothermia. The high-gee maneuvers weren't helping her get the rest she needed.

"Looks like we're both stuck here," Max replied. "I'm on a damage control team, but we won't go into action until after the battle is over unless there's a catastrophic emergency the automated systems can't handle."

"Is that what those thunks were earlier? They sounded horrific, like right before *Hornet* exploded."

"I think we were hit by railgun rounds from one of your ships."

"Good for them." She tried to sound upbeat, but it carried an acerbic edge. She mumbled an apology.

"It's okay. We're both along for the ride on this one."

"You're killing my people," Deena whispered.

The gee forces increased until they were wedged into their respective cubicles.

"They shot us too," Max ground out. "How do we get your people to talk to us?"

Deena wouldn't or couldn't answer. The sergeant focused on controlling his breathing to help him weather the physical strain. He was in good shape, one of the fittest on the ship. He recovered from high gees quicker than most, which made him an ideal addition to a damage control team.

After a minute, the acceleration subsided to three gees. Max forced his way out of the cubicle to check on Deena. He thought he heard her breath coming in raspy waves.

She was pale and shivering.

"I'm so cold," she murmured.

Max fought his way upward against the pressure and climbed into the tight space with her. She tried to push him away but went limp. Max pulled her close, making sure he wasn't on her arm or hand for when the gee forces increased with the next minute's acceleration.

With her head cradled on his arm, he massaged enough gel under his head to support him. The pressure increased as the ship accelerated. He held on tight to keep her warm while digging deep into his psyche to understand why he had stayed.

She should have been locked into Chef's quarters while he went on his merry way.

But he'd taken a personal interest.

She hated him for being Borwyn. She hated all of them. *Good*, she had said about the railgun impacts, but she didn't want to die. Cheering the death of that which you depend upon for your survival made no sense.

Yet that was the logic she had employed.

He stared at her as she remained unconscious. Max found her fascinating. That was going to get him in trouble if he couldn't articulate why.

CHAPTER 33

The pain of battle comes in the aftermath when there's time to think about one's failures.

"Time to impact on One and Two, thirty seconds."

Chrysalis was gaining on the Malibor cruiser.

"Incoming!" Dolly shouted, her voice urgent. "Weapons platform, zero-eight-four off the bow, relative angle minus one."

"A flank shot," Crip muttered.

"Vector zero-seven-nine, star angle zero. Roll the ship and take out that weapons platform," the captain ordered.

"Terminal. Splash One." Taurus sounded like she had been wounded. The first missile had been destroyed at the distant edge of its engagement envelope. Any damage from the explosion would have been minimal. "Splash Two."

Two missiles fired, and two missiles wasted. The captain ground her teeth.

Mary plugged in the coordinates, and Ferd fired the attitude thrusters, then re-engaged the main engines and fired them at one hundred percent. The ship lumbered through the changed course, and the incoming projectiles changed from red to a harmless green. Green was good for the Borwyn. Projectiles on track to hit a Malibor vessel were green, changing to red if they weren't going to hit.

Chrysalis's defensive systems banged away, creating a din much louder than the E-mags that stood off the hull. The defensive systems were integral to the surface of the ship, and they were cycling through ammunition as intended, throwing mass quantities of hot metal into the paths of the incoming missiles.

The second pair of Malibor missiles came in fast, accelerating toward the midship sections. *Chrysalis* rotated off-axis, bringing the damaged defensive systems to bear. They fired anew, rejoining the fight to protect the ship.

Inbound and outbound. Danger was danger.

"Roll our final four missiles into the tubes." The captain hadn't made the decision lightly. With the crossfire from the weapons platforms and the gunship flying an erratic course to avoid the E-mag barrage headed its way, *Chrysalis* might receive more incoming than it could handle.

"The Malibor cruiser is changing orientation." Slade sounded like he was on the deck, his voice projecting into the overhead.

"On screen." The captain wanted to see what her sensor chief was saying. Was the orientation a new threat or not? As it was, they'd forced *Chrysalis* to react. The Malibor were driving the engagement. Jaq needed to force them onto the defensive. "Let's see what you're trying to do."

"Broadside," Crip said.

The ship had turned sideways to *Chrysalis* but continued on its original course.

"Vector one-three-five, star angle minus five. Get us turned, please," Jaq said in a far more patient voice than she felt.

The ship was still sliding through its last course change, and the forward thrust had not yet overtaken the existing momentum. Attitude thrusters fired. The course the captain had given was opposite the direction the Malibor cruiser was facing.

Turning the tide. They would have to come after *Chrysalis* if they wanted to shape the engagement.

Jaq Hunter was off to pick the low-hanging fruit. "Kill that gunship and those weapons platforms. Launch the decoys."

The E-mags stopped firing for a moment. The defensive systems had cycled down after destroying the four inbound missiles. The silence created a sound all its own, a hum of activity that was there but couldn't be heard, yet the crew listened.

Until the E-mags re-engaged and the batteries sent a hailstorm of rounds downrange.

Incoming trails turned green with the newest erratic maneuver while the last salvo fired toward the cruiser was mixed red and green. To change course, the cruiser had slowed. The cannons' last spiral patterns had it right in the middle of their target area.

The last two missiles lagged far behind the much faster E-mag salvos, which were traveling at one-tenth the speed of light.

The green trails followed the E-mag trails until they finished with a flash. The red trails continued beyond the cruiser.

The ship continued traveling sideways, its engines struggling to drag it away from its previous course.

"What happened?" Jaq wondered. "Could the cruiser have been lucky enough that we didn't hit anything important?"

"Active scans show a small amount of debris in the ship's wake," Slade reported. "Nothing more. Engines are hot and running at an estimated one hundred percent."

The last two Borwyn missiles adopted evasive maneuvers on their final approach. Their active radars had caught the ship trying to turn and adjusted, albeit incrementally. Defensive fire flooded into the void. The Borwyn and the Malibor used the technique learned in the last war.

The crew suffered through the change in orientation and the engine surge to send the ship down the new course. The E-mags raged into the void. A second *ka-thunk* signaled that the second pair of added Malibor railguns had run empty and were down.

"Targeting system on the cannons appears to be unaffected," Taurus reported, answering the inevitable question.

The ship vibrated while the engines fought the previous momentum. The shaking increased as harmonic vibration took over.

"Cut the engines!" Jaq roared before the ship shook apart around her. She flowed against her restraints since anything not fixed in place continued forward while the ship stopped accelerating and assumed a ballistic trajectory on a hybrid of its last two courses.

"Engage the engines, all ahead slow." Jaq stared at the main screen.

The last two maneuvers had been so erratic that the Malibor railguns had fired in the wrong direction. Those salvos were cutting through space far behind *Chrysalis's* current location.

"All ahead slow," Ferd confirmed. He tweaked the ship's orientation and engaged the engines.

The surge pushed them into their seats at a mild one gee. Jaq released her restraints, something no one else was allowed to do since they needed to be ready for a change in course or speed.

The captain had to be the captain. She wanted to float around the bridge, thinking and talking, if only with herself.

"Why is that gunship not dead yet?" she asked, letting the sting of her words drive a flurry of activity.

Green lines traced the last barrage.

"Soon," Tram promised.

The gunship attempted to evade the incoming ordnance by turning to dive toward Sairvor, but the E-mag projectiles were too fast for it. It had used the planet's gravity well to slingshot it faster than it was able to recover. It had changed orientation but couldn't change its momentum. The only thing it had managed to accomplish was to take its guns off the target line.

The lack of incoming from the gunship gave *Chrysalis* a short respite. Four more missiles lumbered toward the Borwyn from the enemy cruiser.

"Status of our decoys?" Jaq requested.

Crip was watching them intently since that had been his implementation of the captain's idea. "Continuing on a ballistic trajectory toward the cruiser. They are on track and under our control."

A low-power communications beacon linked the two Malibor missiles with *Chrysalis*. The intent was to activate them when the ship came close, well within the engagement envelope. The drawback was that space was vast. Predicting where the cruiser would be was challenging at the best of times. Close would have to do.

The missiles had big engines with solid fuel that would wait until it activated. Once fired, there was no coming back. The fuel would burn until it was gone.

If the missiles didn't hit their target and weren't damaged, they could be inverted and engines fired to slow them enough to be recovered for refurbishment. It wouldn't be easy, but it was better than starting from scratch.

Assuming the Borwyn had control of the space after the battle.

"Scratch our final two missiles," Tram reported. "Malibor defensive fire destroyed them five kilometers from the ship. No damage."

"We hit them with the E-mags and they streamed debris, but it wasn't enough. One more salvo at the gunship, then turn all cannons on the cruiser," Jaq had put them in a precarious position. Now she was trying to extricate them.

"We can't maintain a cyclic rate of fire, Captain," Tram replied. "We need to dial them back to a sustained rate of five rounds per second until they cool. Then we can tick it up to ten rounds."

Jaq's facial muscles twitched at the limitations of the offensive weapons. She had hoped they would be dialed in on only the cruiser at that point in the battle, but it was taking too long, and the enemy ships were forcing her across too great a swath of space.

Energy was at forty-eight percent and dropping quickly.

The E-mags hummed with a final salvo before being retargeted. When they came to life once more, it was with a lower-pitched staccato. Each pulse could be heard versus the hum of the faster rate of fire.

The green tracks of the second-to-last E-mag salvo tracked toward the gunship, then the icon flashed from green to yellow. It stayed that way despite the crew willing it to turn red.

Slade reported, "Gunship has lost power."

The final salvo headed toward it. With no ability to maneuver, the first rounds would sail through the previously projected course, but the next would stitch a line from stem to stern. Jaq knew the end was imminent unless the crew got the power back on in the next ten seconds. If any Malibor on board were still alive.

Those seconds passed slowly as she stared at the main screen.

The icon flashed red, then disappeared. The remnants of the ship were headed toward the atmosphere, where they'd burn up on entry.

"Brace for impact!" Dolly shouted.

The captain grabbed the nearest rail with both hands and wrapped her leg around it, not questioning her passive sensor operator. She held on and waited.

"What did you…" Slade didn't finish his question.

The roar was like nothing they'd ever experienced. The impacts shook *Chrysalis* and her crew, deafening them with the pounding of metal on metal and the screeches of failure and penetration. A round plunged through the side wall of the command deck and pierced a status monitor, then sailed across the captain's chair and between the battle commander and the offensive weapons officer before ripping through the other side wall. Taurus screamed.

Atmosphere briefly vented before the automatic systems sealed the hull breaches fifty meters away.

Tram groaned after the projectile cracked the sound barrier less than a meter from his head.

Blood trickled down the side of the captain's head. The boom had burst her eardrum. She struggled to hang on to the rail, face contorted with the pain of her injury. "Damage report," she managed to say.

Crip accessed the systems screens, looking for failures. Red lights blinked, but one stood out.

"Ion drive is down."

The captain struggled to access her comm screen. She gave up. "Get me Bec," she told the comm officer.

"Engineering is active."

"Bec, can you fix it?" Jaq asked. She floated into the air with the return of zero-gees.

"Of course I can fix it. I designed it."

"I don't have time for your idea of foreplay. *When* will you have it fixed?"

He was slow to answer. "It's a flow regulator. A projectile

plunged right through it. We'll need to replace it in its entirety or fix the internals, which may be more expeditious. Give me time to look at it, and don't call back. I'll let you know when I know." The link went dead.

Crip continued, "We have impacted systems throughout the ship, everything from Environmental Control to Hydroponics. How did we not see this coming?"

Slade replied, "The missile explosion damaged our active systems. We thought they were working, but they weren't. That left us blind on a single vector. It was a lucky shot, Captain."

"That lucky shot might not have killed us, but it didn't do us any favors. The next shots will assuredly spell our demise if we don't get out of here. Deploy the damage control teams. Priority to Propulsion, then to Environmental Control." The captain wiped the blood off her neck. She couldn't hear in one ear, but the other was picking up the slack.

"Three dead, six injured. Injured are remaining at their posts." Crip continued down the flashing red icons, waiting for the damage control teams to report the status of repairs.

"Now we face the real battle. Who can fix their ship the fastest?" Jaq pulled herself toward the hatch. "I'll be checking the damage. Crip, you have the command deck. If I'm not back before we can move, get us underway."

CHAPTER 34

Fire! By Septiman's holy grace, fire!

Max squeezed out of the cubicle. He felt like garbage. Given the railgun projectile that passed through the space and the thunder from its passing, his head throbbed, and he was barely able to think.

"Don't go," Deena mumbled, wincing through the pain.

"Nothing like work to make you feel better. Come with me."

She grunted but lifted her head to look at him through severely bloodshot eyes. "Seriously?"

"Yes. We have to go. They're calling all damage control parties to their stations. Judging by that," he pointed at the holes in the deck and overhead, "and that we're not under power, the ship's in trouble. We save it, or we die. Come on. This isn't a request."

"I'm your prisoner." Deena tried to pull herself toward the opening but failed when weakness seized her.

Max helped her out of the bunk.

"What better way to watch you than by keeping you with

me? An extra set of hands will help. I'm sure we need all the help we can get."

When Deena was floating free, Max put on his boots. She worked to get hers on. Max just watched. He wanted to help but was still skeptical.

She smiled weakly. "Are you afraid of me?"

He laughed, which made his head hurt. After the pain subsided, he answered her. "I don't want to get kicked in the face if you're feeling feisty. No, I'm not afraid of you. I respect you. There's a difference."

He opened the door and she swam into the corridor, grabbing the frame at the last instant to keep from slamming into a crew member who was flying past.

"This way." Max turned toward his damage control station near Environmental Control amidships. He couldn't hear the air-handling system. He couldn't hear any mechanical noises. "We're in big trouble. We better hurry."

The energy reserves dropped to forty-four percent without the main engines running. Crip activated the ship-wide intercom since he wasn't sure where the captain was. He was happy to see it come online. "All hands, we're bleeding energy somewhere. Find the leak and fix it. That is your number one priority."

Crip's comm buzzed.

"Any idea where to start?" the captain asked.

"Not the slightest. Power is draining and fast. Just ticked over to forty-three percent. I'm sending the command team on a scavenger hunt. No one's any good up here without power."

"Do it." Jaq clicked off.

"Slade, you and Tram stay. Everyone else, report to your

damage control section and get to work finding that power leak. It'll probably be a main cable that's been split and is arcing into the ship." Crip pushed out of his seat. "Let's go, people."

He shoved hard on the rail to be the first out. The rest pushed out after him. When they hit the central shaft, some went up, and others went down. Crip stayed in the shaft to check the primary cables. He went down toward the engines first.

The captain popped out of a corridor two decks down.

"Same idea?" Crip glanced her way before peering between plunging piping and air shafts to find the shielded power cables. He figured there would be black scorch marks showing where the armor surrounding the cable had been breached.

The lights flickered and went out, but the red emergency lighting came on quickly. The captain pulled herself to the nearest deck access and disappeared. Her voice echoed into the silence when she asked for an update.

Bec had made a command decision to cut the power before they lost it all. It had been the right call, but now they were blind and deaf in addition to being immobile.

The very definition of a sitting target.

The captain returned to the central shaft and mirrored Crip's movements on the opposite side. Primary and secondary systems ran up and down the shaft, each protected differently. All were separated from the others as a redundancy for the survival of the ship.

Yet there was a power loss somewhere within. Automatic systems should have overridden the short and shunted the power, but given the damage from the numerous railgun strikes, the backup and safety systems had been affected.

The captain hurried but had to be thorough. One minute became three became five as she and her second worked their way down the shaft.

Crip stopped a deck up and started unscrewing an access panel.

"Crip?" She launched toward him, hit the wall beside him, and seized a rail.

"What do you see in there?" He turned off his penlight.

She looked at him skeptically before sticking her head into the opening. "Light. Could be sparks. I'm going in."

"We have to get the right equipment. I'll call."

"No time, Crip. Light says it's still live and bleeding energy. We have to stop it right now, or we die the second that cruiser draws a bead on us. I'm surprised we're not already dead. We're on borrowed time. Give me a push." Jaq worked her shoulders inside the narrow vent with her arms in front of her.

With one hand gripping the rail, Crip put his free hand on the bottom of the captain's boots and pushed until he'd shoved her into the access. She worked her way inside.

"What are you doing in here?" she asked.

Crip couldn't see anything. Even the light was blocked.

A young voice answered, "Welding it closed. This is busted bad."

Crip didn't recognize the voice, but the captain did.

"You need an insulator between the armor and the cabling."

It was the young welder who had been recruited to work on damage control. The thirteen-year-old.

"I don't have anything," the welder replied. "Wait, I'll use my shirt. It's sweaty, so it shouldn't catch fire when I weld it in."

Crip had to interpolate the faint sounds of the young man removing his shirt to stuff it into a gap before he finished his welds and sealed the power breach.

The captain inched backward. Crip grabbed her boots with both hands and braced his feet on the shaft wall to pull her out. When she came free, they both floated to the other side.

"Yell when you're finished," the captain called. She eased toward the nearest access.

A minute passed before the boy declared victory. "Done!"

The captain bolted out of the shaft. Ten seconds later, the power came on.

Crip waited for the welder, but he never came. "Are you all right in there?"

"I'm using the far access. There's more room. Gotta go. More stuff needs to be welded back together. Whatever hit us, it was bad!"

"You can say that again," Crip mumbled while reattaching the small hatch. He returned straightaway to the command deck.

"Slade, what's the status of the enemy ships?"

"Gunships One and Two are destroyed. The cruiser is maintaining a steady distance from us, circling his previous position. It's like he has a bad attitude thruster keeping him from flying straight."

Crip pursed his lips as he studied the screen. "Could it be that simple?"

"We still have four missiles headed our way," Tram reminded the commander. "I've recalled Gil. He's got work to do. Belay that. The missiles have stopped their burn and assumed ballistic trajectories. We'll only be in danger if we remain here."

"Thirty-nine percent." Crip wasn't pleased with what he read on the display. The energy was stable, and they were no longer burning through it. They wouldn't until they fired their weapons, and if they had to maneuver, the ship would shut them down the instant they hit twenty-five percent, forcing them to stand down until the power recovered.

Twenty-five percent was the hard deck. Below that, only life support systems would operate. It was a safety margin built into the ship for survivability.

It would also be the death of them if they were still engaged.

"We need the override changed to ten percent. Who can program that?" Crip wondered.

Tram and Slade replied with one voice, "Bec."

"I'll be in Engineering. Recall the captain to the bridge, along with the rest of the command crew." Crip disappeared down the corridor.

"Bec, we need you to change the safety margin. Do it now, please." Crip blocked the chief engineer from moving away. He was elbows-deep in the internals of the damaged ion drive, and he ducked his head back inside the housing.

"Busy fixing stuff. No desire to break that which is intended for our safety. *SAFETY!*" he yelled from within. It had to be louder for him than Crip.

"We *were* safe all the way to our deaths at the hands of the enemy. Then we sat idle, not moving when we could have. We need *power,* and we need *engines.*"

"What do you think I'm doing?" Bec pulled out of his baby, the ship's advanced propulsion system. "If I don't fix the drive, changing the power limit means nothing. The engines have to be repaired, and they have to be repaired *first*! That's non-negotiable. Leave me alone."

"I thought the problem was with a relay." Crip looked at the outside of the housing. It hadn't been penetrated.

"I have people fixing that. With the opportunity, I thought I'd tune the drive to meet the captain's requirements for increased energy output. One way to tackle that was to reduce the engine's draw. Make more power or use what we have more efficiently. I'm improving that efficiency."

"Bec, you're killing me. We need the engines running inefficiently now rather than efficiently later. Like, *right now!*"

"Can't. My people are still repairing the relay."

A call came for the chief engineer. Crip stepped back.

"What?" Bec asked brusquely. "Okay."

He closed the channel and crawled back into the housing.

"Bec. We need the engines running." A thought came to the commander. "Was that a call to tell you the relay is fixed?"

"It was. I have one final tweak, and then I'll bring the engines online."

Crip threw his head back and, with his mouth open, silently screamed into the void. "Please, Septiman, see us through these trials so I can shove Bec out an airlock headfirst without a spacesuit. For a few seconds, we'll watch him gasp and freeze. May his pain bring us joy."

Bec climbed out and refitted the housing cover. "What are you mumbling about?"

"I'm extolling your virtues and worshipping your genius on the altar of envy."

"That could be the smartest thing you've said this week. Maybe even this year."

Bec put the housing on without a scrape or a clank. He clipped it into place, another of his design elements for rapid maintenance. He took one magnetic-booted step to his panel and tapped the screen.

"Wish us luck," Crip grumbled.

"There's no luck involved." Bec stared at Crip as he tapped the screen without looking. A low hum started, then disappeared to be replaced, not by a sound but by a sensation. Ions were actively slamming into the drive plate to push the ship forward.

Crip accessed the nearest comm unit, the one Bec had just used to talk to his people. "Engines are online, Jaq."

"Roger. We're out of here," she told him. The ship-wide intercom crackled to life. "All hands, prepare for movement. We're going to accelerate at one-point-five gees so you can keep working damage control. Fix the ship as best you can. We're going to head around the planet. We need time to recover, and then we're going after that cruiser. We'll be back, and the Malibor will be sorry they didn't run sooner."

The overhead clicked off.

"One and a half gees? How am I supposed to work like this?" Bec complained.

Crip clapped him on the shoulder. "The same as the rest of us, my man. Grit your teeth and just do it." He clumped toward the central shaft. He wasn't finished with the ship tour. He had to support the crew as they fought to repair the ship. He wanted to thank the young welder for his work in stopping the power drain. The captain would fight the ship. The second would work to keep crew morale high.

He would do that despite the three deaths, one of which had been Taurus' former workmate at the thrust control engineering station. Had Taurus been there, she would have died, too. Crip felt guilty that Taurus was still alive because of her promotion.

Was she the best person for the job?

Undoubtedly. She'd taken to it with minimal training. Going from thruster management to weapons was a leap, but she had trained in different sections. Alby and Tram had known.

He had to put her out of his mind while he worked with the crew and the ship. Their rapid liaison on the break had cemented their relationship. Next off-period after the battle, when they were safe once more, he'd explore what that meant for their way ahead with Taurus.

For now, he could smile at the memory while reminding the crew that they were doing what they'd set out to do.

Wrest Septimus from the Malibor while disappearing behind the planet below to foil the four missiles headed their way.

CHAPTER 35

The stars care not for the machinations of man.

"Incoming contact from *Starstrider*," the comm officer said.

"We thought we lost you," Captain Brad Yelchin began. "The cruiser was damaged but is finally moving toward you."

The captain looked at Slade for confirmation. Despite the heavier-than-normal gee forces, Jaq was walking around the command deck rather than remain in her chair.

He nodded and pointed at the main screen. She followed his finger to the icon for the enemy cruiser. It wasn't moving quickly, and it wasn't firing.

"Increase speed?" Ferd asked.

The captain shook her head. "Maintain course and speed. He might think we're crippled even though we're shooting at him. Taurus, dial it back. Two cannons at five rounds per second. Cycle through the batteries to give them all a rest. We'll deliver a full barrage when he gets closer. Your target coordinates are to channel them through the area where the decoys are."

Jaq waved at the screen. "Slade, put those on the board."

The two Malibor missiles appeared as ship icons moving at a slow speed in the general direction of the Malibor ship. Their engines had not yet fired, and the missiles continued on a trajectory toward the Malibor at the same speed *Chrysalis* had been moving when the missiles were dropped from the cargo bay.

"Brad, are you able to drive those missiles?"

"We have been unable to establish an uplink, Jaq. Sorry."

"We'll see if we can control them from here. Stand by," Jaq replied.

"Working it," Slade reported. Sensors had the active systems to create a technical handshake. The remote-control link would be lost in the noise of the active scans if they could establish it. "It's not responding."

"Are you trying both missiles?"

"Cycling between the first and second." Slade changed tactics. "Tentative handshake with the number two missile."

The captain waited. *Chrysalis* accelerated in an arc around the planet. She could save power with a slingshot maneuver and come at the cruiser at a much higher rate of speed. She didn't have enough power to do much else. The readout had ticked down to thirty-seven percent.

The engines were spinning up, and the E-mags were banging away. It all took power.

"Back it down to one gee acceleration," the captain ordered. "What does that mean, 'tentative handshake?'"

Slade replied, "It means we can talk to it, but it's not responding to our orders. It looks like some of the software has been corrupted by lousy Malibor circuitry. I'm attempting to reload the program through the handshake pipe. This will take a while."

"Will it take longer than we have?" The captain had plunged into a foul mood. She didn't have the missiles to waste, not even bad ones, and there were two of them languishing in space. "Belay that. Just keep doing what you're doing."

She appreciated the return to standard gravity. She stretched until her back cracked.

"You okay?" Tram wondered.

"It was that loud, huh?"

"Probably heard you in the engine room." He chuckled and went back to work.

The E-mags kept pounding, but the streams showed red on the main screen. There was little chance of hitting the ship, but more importantly, there was zero chance of hitting the two missiles.

"When will we pick up planetary gravity?" Jaq asked.

Mary tapped her screen. "Sphere of influence in thirteen minutes at this acceleration."

Thirteen minutes to fix the ship before the crew would have to return to their chairs. The ship would accelerate quickly under the influence of the planet's gravity.

Jaq returned to her station and brought up the status screen. She was relieved to find that half the flashing red icons had returned to green. A quarter were yellow, and the final quarter were still red. She went down the list. Thrust Engineering had been destroyed. It would remain red. If the thrusters went down, they'd have to work on them from elsewhere.

There were redundancies, but they were neither convenient nor efficient. Repairs would take double or triple the time.

Jaq hoped they wouldn't need them until the station could be resurrected, probably with parts from *Butterfly*.

Odd that she was thinking beyond a battle that was still underway. The operational pause allowed her to gather her thoughts. The enemy was out there, and they were headed her way. Would they fall victim to the slingshot maneuver by following or by trying to intercept? Either choice would put them at *Chrysalis's* mercy. Speed was paramount in space.

Thirty-six percent.

"Captain?" It was Brad. He was still on the channel.

"Almost forgot you were there." She *had* forgotten.

"New contact," he said softly as if he were trying to lessen the blow. "A gunship passing through the moon's shadow. We don't know if he knows you're here. He seems to have no sense of urgency."

"On the board," Slade called.

"Nav, bring us around. Arc off the atmosphere and back the way we came. Head straight for the new contact. Cease fire on the cruiser. Prepare to fire on the new contact."

The E-mag noise stopped, and banging from down the corridor reached them. Damage control was attempting a percussive repair.

Jaq activated the ship-wide intercom. "All hands, battle stations. A third Malibor gunship wants to say 'hi,' so we're off to meet him. We'll be bouncing off the atmosphere sooner than we'd planned. Get yourselves buckled in. It's going to be a bumpy ride. Crip, return to the command deck."

The captain settled into her seat and did her best not to stare at the energy gauge and its countdown to catastrophic shutdown.

"For your approval," Mary asked. The proposed course appeared on the main screen.

"Approved." It was what the captain had envisioned.

Another yellow turned green, and a flashing red turned yellow. The energy gauge ticked down to thirty-five percent. The breath caught in the captain's throat. It would take another five percent to engage the gunship. If the battle was short and *Chrysalis* wasn't further damaged, they'd have five percent to re-engage the cruiser.

They'd have to launch their final four missiles. Probably waste them since the enemy's defensive systems were the only things working. Their offensive weapons appeared to be out, but then why were they accelerating toward an engagement with *Chrysalis*?

"It's a trap. All hands brace for impact. Head straight for the planet!" The captain's voice carried the urgency she felt.

No one had any idea what had spooked her. Not Slade. Not Tram, and not Crip, who ran the last few steps onto the bridge and dove into his seat.

The alarm klaxon echoed down the corridor. The hum of the ship's engines increased as Thrust Control urged the ship to maximum speed.

An impact shook the ship, then another. A hull breach briefly registered before being extinguished.

"Both hits on the cargo bay with the weapons platform. Minimal damage."

"Get us below those active platforms."

"Sensors are damaged," Slade reported. "We need time to repair them, or we will continue to be half-blind."

The captain hadn't asked why the platforms hadn't been seen. She knew the sensors were damaged, and she also knew they'd been running blind for ten agonizing minutes. Maybe it had been longer. She didn't know. The only gauge that mattered showed her the remaining energy.

It ticked inexorably down, and their demise waited at the bottom. It was like they kept starting the battle anew, being worn down more each time until they wouldn't be able to rise again.

The ship bucked and shook against the steep descent while Mary and Ferd fought to get the nose up and the ship climbing out of the dive before they went too deep into the upper atmosphere.

Crip grunted his report. "We're beneath the platforms' engagement zone."

Chrysalis vibrated with the change in orientation and hit the extreme upper atmosphere sideways. It jerked so hard that it seemed like the ship would come apart. Jaq flinched and winced with each creak and groan from the struts and spars that held the ship together.

The descent slowed as if there were buoyed on a cushion of air, the atmosphere refusing to let the big ship in. *Chrysalis* accelerated bit by bit along the edge of space, keeping the planet centered below.

The E-mags hammered at the weapons platforms above them. From this angle, they were easy targets. Taurus had already destroyed two. The next three were easy, opening a huge swath of the sky to *Chrysalis*.

If only they could take advantage of it.

They had had to descend too steeply. Instead of using the planet's gravity to slingshot around it, they'd used their power to fight it. However, the ion drives had answered and pulled the ship away before any real damage had been done.

The bad news showed on the power gauge as it ticked down to thirty-one percent. The ship was still using a significant amount of power.

"I'm doing the best I can," Jaq whispered to the ship. She would have pleaded with Septiman for a break, but she didn't believe He would listen to her whining. They still had fight in them for a little longer. "Prepare to fire."

"Target is locked."

"Fire."

Taurus mashed the fire button before she verbally acknowledged the command. The gunship was close, and less than three seconds passed from when she pressed fire until the stream rammed into the ship. The gunship didn't have a chance.

"Cease fire. Target the cruiser."

"Incoming," Slade announced. "And upload is complete."

"Evasive maneuver. Vector two-nine-four, star angle minus eighteen, two gees." Jaq couldn't afford to be more aggressive with the acceleration. "Match vectors, Firing Pattern One Baseline, all guns shoot. Sustained rate of ten rounds per second."

"Firing."

The air-handling system kicked in to cover the sound of the E-mags engaging. Slade said something and Crip replied, but the captain couldn't hear either of them.

The Malibor cruiser continued to accelerate. Its icon overtook and passed the two missiles floating in space. The ship was firing its railguns, at least ten batteries, filling the void with deadly projectiles.

Jaq didn't want to find out how much more *Chrysalis* could take.

"Captain?" Slade sounded insistent. "Should I fire the missile at them?"

"Fire!" Crip shouted, almost coming out of his seat.

The captain fought the two gees to lean out and look at her deputy.

"We have a shot right up the bell housing of the cruiser's exhaust pipes. It's a beautiful angle."

Jaq gave him the thumbs-up. "I didn't hear. Thanks, Crip. Good call."

The spiral pattern of the E-mags kept the Malibor cruiser from gyrating to avoid the incoming missile.

"Put the enemy in a dilemma. Give them two simultaneous threats." Jaq glanced at the screen. The Malibor railgun fire was doing the same to them. They had nowhere to go.

"Accelerate to nine gees. Get us out of that engagement envelope!"

The ion drives responded flawlessly, driving the crew deep

into their seats. They grunted and gasped against the pressure as the ship clawed its way through empty space, racing to escape the incoming projectiles.

Twenty-seven. Twenty-six. The ship continued to accelerate. The E-mags cycled to the max rate of fire in one final effort to contain the enemy cruiser.

Twenty-five percent. Jaq closed her eyes, expecting the ship to shut down, but it continued to press her deep into the gel of her seat.

She opened her eyes to a flash on the main screen. The Malibor missile had hit home on the enemy cruiser. Big and unsophisticated, it had done what the Borwyn missiles could not—hit its target.

The icon changed to yellow but not to red. The enemy cruiser stopped firing and accelerating. It was hurt and badly.

Jaq couldn't issue an order. She squinted at her panel for the eye control to direct Ferd to slow the ship to three gees the instant they were clear of the incoming projectiles. The instant the leading edge would pass behind them.

She couldn't send the order before the ship eased back to three gees, then two, and finally to a single gee of acceleration.

The energy gauge showed twenty-three percent and was yellow, not red.

"Kill that ship!" Jaq surged out of her seat and stabbed a finger at the screen.

The E-mags pounded away, focused on the ballistic target, leading it, knowing that it wouldn't change course. A long stream from multiple batteries tore into the cruiser and the thousands of obdurium projectiles shredded it, showing how frail an armored warship ship could be.

The icon turned red, flashed three times, and disappeared.

"Space is clear. *Starstrider* reports no weapons platforms in range." Slade climbed out of his seat to wipe the sweat from his face.

"Now they tell us," Jaq muttered. She accessed the ship-wide intercom. "All hands, stand down from battle stations. Crew rest is ordered for A shift. Everyone else to damage control stations."

The entire command team eased out of their seats to take deeper breaths and be free from the restraints that had held them throughout the engagement. The captain went to her helm team first.

"You two saved the ship. You kept us out of the worst of it." She shook Mary's hand, then Ferdinand's. "Put us in a lunar orbit, then go get some sleep."

The two returned to their seats to change the ship's course at all ahead standard to deliver it into orbit around the moon within which the Borwyn had a base. Jaq was sure she'd need help with parts and supplies. Anything they could provide would be welcome.

The captain closed on her deputy. "Twenty-three percent, and we didn't shut down."

"I asked Bec to override it and let us go to ten percent before shutdown. He argued to make a point, but he did what needed to be done. I shouldn't be so hard on him."

"Would he have done it if he didn't respect you or appreciate your justification? Keep doing what you're doing."

"I like how you think, Jaq. I really didn't want to change. I think I like fighting with him."

"Don't admit that." Jaq shook his hand. "Maybe you can find our wayward combat team leader and our prisoner. I'd still like to talk with her."

Crip acknowledged the order and headed off the bridge. He caught the rail and spun toward the weapons stations.

Taurus intercepted him, and they spoke with their noses almost touching.

"See you later?"

"I'll be in our quarters unless you get there first." She rested her finger on his lips before pushing him toward the hatch.

The captain had been watching. Crip shrugged but wore a smile that split his face.

"What took you idiots so long?" Jaq asked.

Taurus shook her head and returned to her station to prepare a final report on ammunition usage and required repairs.

Crip was two decks toward Engineering, where Max's damage control station was located. An air-handler panel had been removed, but the insides had been rewired, and the pump was in operation. There were patches where a railgun projectile had gone through it, missing the brushless fan but ripping through the wiring and the casing. The repairs were complete, and the tools had been secured in the kit that was magnetically attached to the deck.

Floating beside it were Max and Deena.

Kissing.

Her arms wrapped over his shoulders and clasped behind his neck. He held her around the waist.

Crip cleared his throat.

Twice.

Max broke free, wearing a sheepish expression. "Sorry. Nothing like damage control to light the fires, if you know what I mean."

Deena looked down, then buried her face in his neck.

Crip stared. "No. I really don't." He did. "You made the repairs?"

"Done and operational. Deena was a big help. Small hands for getting at the wiring."

Crip chewed the inside of his cheek. "Go get some rest."

Max eased Deena away from him, and they put the panel in place and screwed it down. They walked hand in hand, magnetic boots clumping toward the central shaft.

"I have no idea what to do about this," Crip called after them.

"Nothing," Max replied over his shoulder.

"*How to Win the Enemy to Your Side* by Max Tremayne," Crip said to himself. He continued down the corridor, noting the numerous repairs completed by the damage control teams. The battle had been won from the inside of the ship, not the outside.

It would take a while before *Chrysalis* was back to its former glory, but with the Sairvor Borwyn's help, maybe it wouldn't take so long.

CHAPTER 36

Sometimes the moon shines the brightest when it's in the hands of friends.

The crew relaxed in and around their stations. The command deck buzzed with low conversations.

"We have two ships making sure nothing is sneaking up on us. The Malibor are nowhere to be found." Brad sounded sure of himself.

Jaq wanted him to keep the scouts in space to let them know days before a Malibor ship arrived.

"Scrub three more gunships and one cruiser," Jaq added.

Tram had consolidated the Malibor order of battle based on the information the Sairvor Borwyn had gathered over the past fifty years and was keeping count.

The Malibor had started with twelve cruisers and thirty-one gunships. They were down to nine cruisers and twenty-five gunships.

That should have brought some solace to Captain Jaq Hunter, except she was down to four Borwyn anti-ship missiles. She needed more. A lot more. However, her three top advisors had developed a plan, and the first part of it—liberating Sairvor—was underway.

Thanks to *Chrysalis*, the Borwyn owned the skies above the planet, with the minor exception of two functioning weapons platforms.

They had a plan to take those out, too. A scout ship would transport a team of engineers to board them and power them down, or better, put them under Borwyn control.

Jaq had put Bec in charge of the effort, much to his over-vocalized chagrin. The scout could come from the planet side, where the approach was safe from the platforms' weapons. Using what Alby and his team had learned, the engineers could safely disengage the platform.

Bec wouldn't go on the mission if he didn't think the plan would work.

The final two weapons platforms would have materials they could use if the crew wanted to dismantle them, or they could provide additional defensive firepower to protect Rondovan, the moon with the secret Borwyn base.

"Are you going to show us your base?" Jaq asked.

Captain Yelchin quipped, "You showed me yours, so I guess I can show you mine." He chuckled at his jibe, the sign of a person who spends too much time alone.

Hammer and Anvil waited near the bulkhead at the back of the command deck. When the shepherd entered, they moved away.

"I don't bite, lads. Come here and accept Septiman's blessing." He held up his hands, but the young men remained where they were.

"We never had any shepherds with us after the fall, and we may have lost our way."

"When's the best time to find your way to Septiman?" the shepherd droned.

They didn't answer. "Twenty years ago, but the next best time is right now. Come, pray with me."

"Dad?" Hammer eased toward the hatch and escape.

"Come on, boys. There's no time like the present to learn about the religion that used to be the foundation of Borwyn culture. I have to warn you, Shepherd. We counted on Septiman to save our people, and He did not. We were abandoned in our time of greatest need."

The shepherd lost his perpetual smile. "Borwyn society was finding it easy not to have Septiman in their lives. Our demise was a test. You've seen that we've passed the test, but we will continue our trials. We failed Him. The pain in our lives is of our making."

"I'd like to think it's of the Malibor's making," Brad replied nonchalantly. "But if we can throw a few kind words toward the stars, who am I to stand in your way?"

"Septiman's way, not mine."

"Shepherd, I fear we'll remain at odds on this issue, but you have a job to do, as do I. One prayer, then we'll be on our way. We have a lander to lead into Rondovan and a celebration to prepare!"

Yelchin and his boys huddled with the shepherd.

"May Septiman guide us on a path of virtue to deliver our people into His good graces."

"Amen, brother!" Brad clapped the shepherd on the back. "We're off. We'll wait for your lander."

"Sacrilegious non-believing blasphemers!" the shepherd blurted at the backs of the three large men.

They continued off the bridge and down the corridor.

"You're not going to win them over like that, Shepherd," Jaq cautioned. "You have your work cut out for you. Join us, and we'll deliver you into the middle of the unsuspecting Borwyn colony."

"You make me sound like a virus," the shepherd replied.

The captain tipped her head back to look down her nose at the shepherd. She started to say something to him but thought better of it. "Crip, you're with me, and Taurus, Tram, Slade, Dolly. Let's bring a couple engineers. And Max, but not Deena. She's still Malibor, and we can't show her the Rondovan base. Let's bring Zoola to talk to them about hydroponics. We should be able to share a few seedlings to get them started on growing stuff that doesn't taste like...how did Brad put it? Like it fell out of his ass?"

Crip nodded. "It wasn't a compelling visual. I'll rally the troops and meet you at Lander Three."

The captain scanned the command crew. All eyes were on her. "Everyone will get their chance to visit Rondovan, but not all at once. You deserve it. You've earned it."

"Maybe we can recruit a few sailors to come to space with us. We're down seven crew. Eight if we include Crewman Ellis."

"That's a lot of empty beds," Jaq continued softly. She dropped her head for a moment of reflection before turning her attention back to the matter at hand. "Prepare the group to deploy to Rondovan."

"Aye-aye, Captain." Crip caught Jaq's arm as she brushed by on her way to the corridor. "I'm glad you're in charge. We wouldn't have survived without you."

Jaq smiled and replied, "Or that thirteen-year-old welder. Or Bec. Or any of our people. No one is indispensable and everyone is critical. We all work in the best interests of the ship and for the Borwyn on Septimus. We're coming, my friends. In due time, the Malibor will tremble in fear at the sight of *Chrysalis*. The battle is joined."

"Victory is ours," Crip replied.

"Victory will be ours when the Malibor run from us, screaming in terror."

To be continued in Starship Lost Book #2: **The Return!**

The Borwyn's fate could not be contained in this single volume. Please leave a review on this book because all those stars look great and help others decide if they'll enjoy this book as much as you have. I appreciate the feedback and support. Reviews buoy my spirits and stoke the fires of creativity.

Don't stop now! Keep turning the pages as I talk about my thoughts on this book and the overall project called *Starship Lost*.

You can always join my newsletter—https://craigmartelle.com or follow me on Amazon https://www.amazon.com/Craig-Martelle/e/B01AQVF3ZY/, so you are informed when the next book comes out. You won't be disappointed.

THANK YOU FOR READING STARSHIP LOST

We hope you enjoyed it as much as we enjoyed bringing it to you. We just wanted to take a moment to encourage you to review the book. Follow this link: **Starship Lost** to be directed to the book's Amazon product page to leave your review.

Every review helps further the author's reach and, ultimately, helps them continue writing fantastic books for us all to enjoy.

You can also join our non-spam mailing list by visiting www.subscribepage.com/AethonReadersGroup and never miss out on future releases. You'll also receive three full books completely Free as our thanks to you.

Facebook | Instagram | Twitter | Website

Want to discuss our books with other readers and even the

authors? Join our Discord server today and be a part of the Aethon community.

ALSO IN THE SERIES

Starship Lost
The Return
Primacy
Engagement
Devolution
Delivery
Arrival

Looking for more great Science Fiction?

"This stellar near-future tale masterfully fuses SF thrills with an enthralling mystery." —Kirkus Review

A lowly construction worker on the Moon is Earth's only chance... Nick Morrison always wanted to be an astronaut. When a startup company recruits him to build a lunar launch system at the Moon's south pole, Nick gladly leaves behind his troubled life on Earth—but Nick doesn't know that the company is in financial and legal trouble. Deprived of support from Earth, the team on the Moon must figure out how to survive on their own. Worse yet, there's another base at the lunar south pole, run by a ruthless contractor who has big plans for the Moon... and for Earth. Nick's team just so happen to be in the way. **Join them in their mission to stop the conquest of the Moon and Earth in this new Science Fiction Survival Thriller from Nebula Award Nominated author Rhett C. Bruno and NYT bestselling author Felix R. Savage. It's perfect for fans of The Martian, Artemis, and For all Mankind.**

Get The Eighth Continent now!

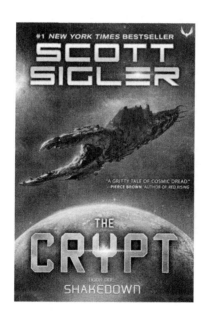

The only way out is to die... Few know the warship's actual name. Fewer still know what it really is. And almost no one knows of its unique ability, an ability that could tilt the balance of power if not outright win the war. But everyone has heard the rumors. Rumors about the worst place the Planetary Union Fleet can send you. Rumors of a ship with an eighty percent crew mortality rate. In these hushed, fearful whispers, the ship does have a name. People call it "the Crypt," because those aboard are as good as dead. The PUV *James Keeling* can do something no other vessel in existence can do — slip into another dimension, travel undetected, then re-emerge onto our plane and surprise enemy targets. But the thing that makes the *Crypt* unique also makes it a nightmare for those onboard; interdimensional travel causes hallucinations, violent behavior, and psychotic breakdowns. *Keeling* could be the Union's greatest weapon, a game-changing asset that can defeat the bloodthirsty zealots of the Purist Nation, the Union's mortal enemy. If, that is, the brass can find the right crew. But with those dark rumors traveling at lightspeed throughout Fleet, sailors with connections, with favors to call in, or those with careers on the rise pull any string they can to avoid being assigned to the *Crypt*. The brightest and best shield themselves from this top-secret craft, yet the brass *must* send it out on critical missions. As the war drags on and casualties pile up, Fleet crews the ship by assigning the worst of the worst. If you are convicted of assault, fraud, cowardice, theft, rape, murder — or you cross the wrong Admiral — you may find yourself aboard the *Crypt*. Most are given a choice: serve a two-year stint on the Keeling and have your record expunged, or be executed for your crimes. Welcome to the PUV *James Keeling*, where the only way out... is to die.

Get Shakedown Now!

STARSHIP LOST 357

For all our Sci-Fi books, visit our website.

AUTHOR NOTES - CRAIG MARTELLE

Written January 2023

I can't thank you enough for reading this story to the very end! I hope you liked it as much as I did.

Acceleration calculator because math is important in hard

science fiction. Even though this is in the future far, far away, it's still humanity. Advancements have been realized and lost, putting us right back where we are, which means no handwavium.

https://www.omnicalculator.com/physics/acceleration

Research: how many planets can a star system support? Theoretically, the answer is forty-two in an engineered star system. https://www.iflscience.com/this-is-the-maximum-number-of-planets-you-can-have-in-a-solar-system-like-ours-41537

Then there's the tutorial on particle beams. https://www.youtube.com/watch?v=GojYJcoqvOU

Astrophysics is crazy, and there's a lot of information out there.

I wrote the majority of this book while traveling in December and January. That was six weeks on the road. Lots of words on airplanes and in the early mornings in hotel rooms from Hawaii to Fiji to Adelaide to Sydney, then back to Adelaide in South Australia. I finished this book before I began my journey home. I'll be writing the eighteenth book in my *Judge, Jury, & Executioner* series from Adelaide to Auckland to Fiji to Hawaii and finish it when I get back home to Fairbanks, Alaska.

Why did I travel at such length and at such extreme expense? My son married into Adelaide. That's where they live and where they're raising their two children. To see my grandkids, I have to go down under. Because of my heart, I don't do long-haul flights well, so I puddle-jump my way from Alaska to Adelaide. The longest flight is a little over six hours from Seattle to Honolulu. After that, each long and direct flight was less than six hours. Direct flights tend not to lose luggage, like when I traveled to Dublin this past summer. Three flights and my bag was lost for ten days before it finally rejoined me in Madrid, Spain, thanks to the superhuman efforts of Sian Phillips in Dublin to hunt down the bag in the massive lost-luggage warehouse, which was comparable to where the US government hid the Lost Ark.

So there we are. Traveling long and hard to see family. It also helped me to avoid six weeks of frigid temperatures in Fairbanks. In any case, that was the winter of 2022-2023. This book won't publish for a while, so by the time you read it, I'll be on a new adventure, and I'll also have books 2, 3, and 4 of Starship Lost written:). I hope you enjoy the story.

Peace, fellow humans.

If you liked this story, you might like some of my other books. You can join my mailing list by dropping by my website craigmartelle.com, or if you have any comments, shoot me a note at craig@craigmartelle.com. I am always happy to hear from people who've read my work. I try to answer every email I receive.

If you liked the story, please write a short review for me on Amazon. I greatly appreciate any kind words; even one or two sentences go a long way. The number of reviews an ebook receives greatly improves how well it does on Amazon.

Amazon—www.amazon.com/author/craigmartelle
Facebook—www.facebook.com/authorcraigmartelle
BookBub—https://www.bookbub.com/authors/craig-martelle
My web page—https://craigmartelle.com
Thank you for joining me on this incredible journey.

OTHER SERIES BY CRAIG MARTELLE

 # - available in audio, too

Battleship Leviathan (#)– a military sci-fi spectacle published by Aethon Books

Terry Henry Walton Chronicles (#) (co-written with Michael Anderle)—a post-apocalyptic paranormal adventure

Gateway to the Universe (#) (co-written with Justin Sloan & Michael Anderle)—this book transitions the characters from the Terry Henry Walton Chronicles to The Bad Company

The Bad Company (#) (co-written with Michael Anderle)—a military science fiction space opera

Judge, Jury, & Executioner (#)—a space opera adventure legal thriller

Shadow Vanguard—a Tom Dublin space adventure series

Superdreadnought (#)—an AI military space opera

Metal Legion (#)—a military space opera

The Free Trader (#)—a young adult science fiction action-adventure

Cygnus Space Opera (#)—a young adult space opera (set in the Free Trader universe)

Darklanding (#) (co-written with Scott Moon)—a space western

Mystically Engineered (co-written with Valerie Emerson)—mystics, dragons, & spaceships

Metamorphosis Alpha—stories from the world's first science fiction RPG
The Expanding Universe—science fiction anthologies

Krimson Empire (co-written with Julia Huni)—a galactic race for justice

Zenophobia (#) (co-written with Brad Torgersen)—a space archaeological adventure

Glory (co-written with Ira Heinichen)—hard-hitting military sci-fi

OTHER SERIES BY CRAIG MARTELLE

Black Heart of the Dragon God (co-written with Jean Rabe)—a sword & sorcery novel

End Times Alaska (#)—a post-apocalyptic survivalist adventure published by Permuted Press

Nightwalker (a Frank Roderus series)—A post-apocalyptic western adventure

End Days (#) (co-written with E.E. Isherwood)—a post-apocalyptic adventure

Successful Indie Author (#)—a non-fiction series to help self-published authors

Monster Case Files (co-written with Kathryn Hearst)—A Warner twins mystery adventure

Rick Banik (#)—Spy & terrorism action-adventure

Ian Bragg Thrillers (#)—a hitman with a conscience

Not Enough (co-written with Eden Wolfe)—A coming-of-age contemporary fantasy

<u>Published exclusively by Craig Martelle, Inc</u>
The Dragon's Call by Angelique Anderson & Craig A. Price, Jr.—an epic fantasy quest

A Couples Travels—a non-fiction travel series

Love-Haight Case Files by Jean Rabe & Donald J.

Bingle—the dead/undead have rights, too, a supernatural legal thriller

Mischief Maker by Bruce Nesmith—the creator of Elder Scrolls V: Skyrim brings you Loki in the modern day, staying true to Norse Mythology (not a superhero version)

Mark of the Assassins by Landri Johnson—a coming-of-age fantasy.
For a complete list of Craig's books, stop by his website—
https://craigmartelle.com

Printed in Great Britain
by Amazon